I0742482

QUANTUM
CONSEQUENCES

Obeah's Three Laws of Change

A culture will resist change but once a shift occurs, change will escalate into chaos unless it's acted upon by an external force.

The force acting on a culture must be capable of generating emotions of fear or greed (or both) that are equal to any sense of comfort or peace the majority feel or change won't occur.

For every cultural change, positive or negative, there is an equal and opposite backlash of cultural behavior.

QUANTUM CONSEQUENCES

BY

MARIAN BLUE

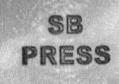

SB
PRESS

ISBN 13: 978-1-7321287-3-6 (paperback)
ISBN 10: 10: 1-7321287-3-1 (paperback)
ISBN: 978-1-7321287-6-7   (eBook)

Library of Congress Control Number: 2018913663

Disclaimer:
This is a work of fiction. The story and the central characters represent the author's imagination; any similarities are coincidental. Real individuals who are referenced in the context of the fictional story are well-known but their characters may be fictionalized to suit the story. Every effort has been made to be accurate for quotes attributed to real people. The setting represents recognizable locales, but changes have been made within the fictional context. Agencies and organizations have also been fictionalized. Environmental conditions facing world populations, however, are all too real.

Cover: Original painting by Dean Gibson
          Photo of original (sans words) can be seen at sunbreakpress.com

Interior layout and design by Blue & Ude Writers Services

Printed on acid free paper in the United States

Published by Sunbreak Press
PO Box 145
Clinton, WA 98236 USA
www.Sunbreakpress.com

Text set in Garamond

For my brother
Dean Gibson
who has made all the difference

ACKNOWLEDGEMENTS

This book couldn't have come into existence without the support of friends and family who read (sometimes multiple times), patiently commented on, and made suggestions about various manuscript permutations:

Dr. Lucas Tarr, a patient and detail-oriented physicist consultant, not only read an early draft but then continued to guide and mentor me through scientific conundrums. The voice of reason and logic that appears in the book comes from his continued correspondence for over a year about not only science but also about plot and contemporary technology. This book would be staggering under a load of my misconceptions without his patient help. Any remaining goofs are my own.

A special thanks to Wayne Ude who helped me improve characters, readability, spelling, and punctuation by reading various versions of the book. When not reading, he patiently endured my endless prattle about the book's development.

Cynthia Trenshaw provided comments, editing, and suggestions on an early draft. She also provided much-needed encouragement about finishing and publishing the book. Her gentle nature helped inspire concepts of kindness and compassion.

A special thanks to Lois Olsen, an outstanding sister-in-law and retired range conservationist and ecologist for the Forest Service, who read and commented on an early draft, giving me faith in the book's science. In particular, her enthusiasm for the book gave me confidence about references to climate change.

A special thank you to my brother and artist, Dean Gibson. He not only provided the painting for the cover, he also provided me with a foundation for writing about the joy and benefits of having a brother. A full color copy of his painting without book title and byline appears on the Sunbreak Press Web page.

Thank you to all the wonderful science fiction writers who have schooled me through their writing and also through their classes and workshops. From one of my earliest workshops, the Clarion Writing Workshop in 1982, through many university and private writing workshops, other writers have long been my mentors. To those members of our wonderful Norfolk, VA writing workshop in the 1990s, I'm especially indebted.

Thank you, too, to all the readers and family who have supported me and my writing, from newspapers to magazines to books, over the decades. Without all of you, none of my writing would have purpose.

CHAPTER ONE

Friday, June 29, 2029

Vala jacked her pod into one of the few slots available at the Pike's Place Market floating lot and clambered out. The weekend before the Fourth of July had all of Seattle jammed, including parking lots, not with individual pods, such as Vala Glen's, so much as extra renta-chairs, carts, and scootbots. Even the glide-walks were jammed with people, hopeful tourists or holiday-crazed locals.

The Fourth of July baffled Vala. Why would people celebrate massed together instead of escaping the cityscape to what was left of forest retreats? Or, since much of the forest was on fire, even beaches, dirty and jumbled as many were with remnants of the original Seattle beach properties...she switched her thought flow. She kept answering her own questions with descriptions. Why bother trying to go somewhere else when everywhere was the same? But, really? Why mass together like carp in a shrinking lake?

Vala started maneuvering through the hoards, easier for her since she could easily see over everyone's head and her size thirteen shoes made space for themselves. She parted a crowd like a tug plowing through fishing boats. As usual, individuals glanced her way, then turned to stare, their eyes glazed like a fish that had just been thrown down on a rock. Her thin runner's body dressed in stretchy and bright-colored running clothes was incongruous with her Eurasian features: high cheekbones, long and slightly up-turned eyes, and dark, straight hair. Mostly, it was her 6'7" height that grabbed the attention.

In turn, Vala tried not to stare at people who sported the latest glowing neon tats, especially those on bald pates or those that were animated so color ran down their necks, appearing and disappearing beneath scanty clothing. Most of them reeked of chemical fragrances that, in her opinion, were worse than the daily smoky haze. The latest implants plugged into body scent choices, so the smells could almost be seen like the old cartoons that had wavering lines trailing a skunk.

Fewer people were wearing masks today, either because of the slightly clearer air or because their nanobots were working effectively. Vala had adapted somewhat and rarely wore a mask. She wasn't about to inject AI into her system.

A logjam of people blocked Vala where the tunnels to the old market levels began. Large sheets of glass had been installed to keep the rising seawater out. The aquarium, flooded out a few years before, was now called wild although many of the parading fish were AI. Not able to tell the difference, people oohed and aahed at the wonders of nature in the murky waters below the floating parking lots, built to rise, engineers claimed, with the seawater.

Vala edged around the crowd and went up rather than down to the tunnels, so the crowd thinned. What was left of the food stands were on what had been the roof over the original market, and little else was here to draw people.

As the crowd thinned, Vala breathed easier although she still yearned to be hiding out either in her university lab or House. She cursed herself again for running out of live food: fresh veggies and eggs. The Market was one of only two places left in downtown Seattle that sold live food, most of it raised by Floaters who managed to produce enough to bring to the market from window boxes or small patches of dirt around their boxes. Some even still had shroud-boxes, a plot of earth to call their own, especially if they were located near drowned town, the flooded areas west of First Avenue.

Few if any Floaters had implants; they, like Vala, preferred not to be so easily tracked. Interestingly, many of them were very tall and lean as well, so Vala felt less conspicuous among them.

Live-food had faded out because of environmental factors: fewer pollinators, less irrigation water available, and severe storms. Besides, people had bought into food fads, the latest of which were Fab-Meals, test-tube created specialties like Muufri for milk and yeast-based egg whites blended and dried. Here in the city, the Floaters used hand pollination and individual plant production, so produce was both expensive and difficult to find.

Vala just wanted to get in the market, find live-food staples for her and Serein, her Rhodesian Ridgeback dog, and get out. Her Alki home wasn't far away, but in these crowds she might as well be in another country.

With the Fourth of July on a Wednesday, people were going to be blasting zilph, that cacaphonous mix of synthesizer minor keys and disaster sound effects to enhance booming fireworks for seven days straight. Her heart ached for the wild animals, what few were left, as well as the domestic pets. It would be like living in a war zone for them. Never mind the pollution after.

Vala had campaigned to end the fiasco for years, but she'd given up. If people still thought of themselves as patriotic after the 2028 election debacle when more than a third of all voters were disqualified or purged from the system because of failure to demonstrate an approved address, their delusions were made of more solid stuff than she could penetrate. Of course, the goal had been to eliminate the non-conformists, such as the floaters, the travelers and even those, like Vala, who still owned property. Independence. What a joke.

Even in the market, Vala felt the air pressure pounding at her from people yelling, boat horns blaring, ever-present zilph blaring its minor and off-key chords, and various explosions from firecrackers. She was grateful she'd left Serein at home. He brought great comfort to her, but he shouldn't have to endure this.

Vala quickly found some fresh eggs, carrots, spinach, and summer squash. Just as her hand closed over some cool, deep green and lacy kale, she was suddenly aware of a tonal shift in her ears. The pressure shifted as well. It was as if the market had been replaced by a meadow, a meadow alive with bird song and surrounded by large trees with a breeze whispering through them.

Then she saw a wavering figure, a man, in the meadow. He lifted a hand, palm out, just as she was overcome by dizziness, a swirling collage of green, bird song, coolness within tree shadows and, maybe, distant surf. Perhaps she made a sound. Perhaps she grabbed at the boxes of produce. She didn't know. She was nowhere and she was everywhere ... that man? palm out? what did he want?

Then, "Dear! Dear! Are you all right?" Then, in a lower voice, "Perhaps we'd better call the medicart."

That roused Vala's panic, sudden fear, sharp and metallic, at the back of her tongue, and she muttered, "No, no, no ... I'm fine. Let me up." She'd had enough of med-eval, suspicions, sanity questions. And more disappointments.

She got to her feet, somehow, while pushing well-meaning helpers' hands and arms out of the way. They were all floaters, wanting to help but like most of those not linked, not wanting to draw attention to themselves. But still they were trying to help this odd woman out. Vala pulled herself up to her full 6'7", knowing that her size alone intimidated people into backing off, while muttering "no, no, thank you" over and over.

They let her go, and she negotiated her way down to the stair-glide that led to the floating parking slots. As she reached her pod, she dropped into the driver seat and tried to relax. She would have to go back or she and Serein would have a hungry few days. She didn't even have any fab-meals on hand. She cursed herself again. She'd known the holiday was coming! Of course, Aunt Char would be willing to shop, but Vala hated to ask her. Vala would have to go back into the market. Besides, she'd left her bags there, too.

Then she started as someone cleared his throat beside her. She jerked her head around and looked directly into a pair of eyes that sparkled with—what? Amusement? His eyes, glittering with green and brown flecks kaleidoscoping into almost hypnotic patterns, were mesmerizing. Perhaps she was still dizzy.

He smiled. "I know you think you're okay and you want to be left alone, but I don't think you should drive yourself anywhere."

She found she couldn't look away from his eye contact; she felt comforted just by his presence. His hands, rather small, were both on the window frame, and she covered one with her hand, grateful for the connection she felt.

"Thank you" she finally said. "This isn't new for me. I'll just sit here for a while, and I'll calm down. I'll be fine. I can always use driverless mode if I must."

He smiled, and Vala felt as though she could tell this person anything and that she'd be safe in doing so. Aunt Char was the only other person for whom she'd ever felt such affinity; in fact, she had raised Vala.

Abruptly, a buzzing tension stopped her thoughts. Being trusting had proven dangerous to her in the past. Was he hypnotizing her? She needed Serein here to give her guidance.

"Look," he said. "My Name is Eric Kine. I'm not wishing to intrude, but I noticed that you left a cloth carrier with some eggs and some vegetables in it. I assume the kale on the floor was to be added. I can go in and get your groceries while you sit here and compose yourself, and then I'll bring them out. You'll wait for that, yes?"

She nodded. Why was she agreeing? She shouldn't ask a stranger to do her shopping for her. But she needed the food. And she was loath to return to the market.

"Is there anything else you need?" His head tilted slightly to one side. He looked like a friendly and gentle puppy. His reddish short hair looked as though it had never encountered a comb. He looked anything but frightening.

She shook her head, thinking of all she'd really need to get her through the week. "I was about finished. But–"

"No 'buts.' Just promise me you'll wait. I can't use many more groceries myself, so I'll get them all at the same time."

She nodded again, feeling like an idiot. "Let me give you money–" Floaters took only cash; none of them were linked.

"You can pay me back when I bring the groceries," he said. "If you don't, I'll manage to eat them myself. This is where I buy my live-food, too." He smiled again and turned to walk away.

Again, Vala felt surprise jolt through her. She'd thought he was kneeling by her pod, and she expected him to stand and walk, but he simply turned and left. The man was barely four feet tall. For some reason that increased her sense of disorientation. Why should someone's height disorient *her;* after all, *everyone* looked short to her.

She controlled her breathing, regarded the lenticular cloud hanging over Mount Rainier, barely visible through Seattle orange smog, which was getting worse every day as the summer wildfires ravished the peninsula. Today, though, the sky was bluer than usual, and the sun warmed her, helping her shake off the chills that followed this sort of spell. She brought Serein to mind, and she could feel his calming influence even at this distance. Irisations had formed along the edges of the lenticular cloud; the brilliant red, yellow, and blue gave Vala a focus for her thoughts, and the noise and smell of modern Seattle faded. She eased herself back into the idea of a *normal* day. Everything was fine, she told herself. Gradually, she merged with the lightwaves, and the colors began to sharpen, clarify–

A stab of fear intruded, a throbbing tsunami drowning her calm. This was the third time in the past ten days that this sort of event had occurred; usually she could go months. Of course, she'd always been odd, a fact repeatedly emphasized by her mother, but this current streak of episodes, especially with that shimmering figure of a man, had begun to interfere with her ability to focus in her lab. She'd always been able to focus, enter her work deeply. When others thought she was "out of it," she, herself, knew where her thoughts had been and she was usually able to surface with solutions to whatever problem she'd been analyzing. Analyze. That's what she needed now.

"Come on, Vala, get a grip," she told herself. She'd always been able to crawl back to reality and keep a focus that had allowed her to finish her PhD in physics by the age of 19 with a secondary environmental biology PhD by 21, just eight years ago. Indeed, everything was, according to everyone, going her way. Again, except her mother. Glen women didn't work in labs.

She inhaled deeply, exhaled slowly, went back to the lenticular cloud, the atmosphere itself. Finally, she let go of all the tension and the fear. Then she became aware of a presence. She glanced out the side window and saw Eric Kine, with a renta-cart, standing quietly by the passenger door, unmoving, silent. She popped the passenger door. "I'm sorry. I didn't see you. I just was, well…"

"You were calming and orienting yourself, focusing, which is just what you should have been doing." He quickly unloaded three bags into the area behind the seat.

"That's a nice space back there," he said.

"Yes. Normally I have my dog with me, but I didn't know

if I'd have room with the groceries." She was still stunned at his awareness of the personal room she needed, how he'd just quietly–patiently–waited for her to come around. No knocking on the window or yelling. How had he known?

He handed her a Floater's hand-written receipt. "I took the liberty of adding just a few other vegetables that just looked too good to ignore. If you don't want them, I'll take them."

"No, that's wonderful. There's no such thing as a bad vegetable. Thank you so much," she said as she reached for the receipt, read the total, and then pulled three twenties and two tens out of her wallet.

"No problem," he said. "I owe you a buck."

"No, no. That's okay. I'm very grateful, really."

"Are you sure you're ready to drive? I'd be happy to follow you to make sure you get there okay."

"No. As I say, I've been through this before."

He held a card–a real printed card and not an implant transfer–out to her. He didn't have an implant, she noticed. "If you ever need to talk–about anything–feel free to call."

She took the card and started to smile, but that quickly faded as she read

Dr. Eric Fergus Kine	901 Boren Avenue
Psychologist, Counselor	Seattle, WA
425-312—129-3333	EFKine.md

A Brain-Crank! Scheisse! Tension stabbed at the base of her skull and that sharp taste of fear hit again. What was he, an ambulance chaser? All he had to do was see her get dizzy, and he knew she was unzipped?

"Thank you," she said quickly and shakily as she ordered her pod to start. "I've got to go." She let the card flutter out the window and in driverless mode, Pegasus, as she'd named her pod, swooshed out of its slot and toward home.

She looked in the rearview window. He stood there, mouth open and one hand raised, almost like the man in the meadow–perhaps to get her attention? She ordered top speed.

By the time she'd crossed West Seattle Bridge, she'd stopped shaking, and she switched from driverless mode. She'd soon be in her own space at New Alki Point. Going against the movement to use government credits to stay in government-owned boxes, supposedly a way to avoid financial loss from effects of climate change, Vala had chosen to buy out property being sold cheaply as the old Alki Point flooded out beneath rising seas. It was the only way she felt she'd survive living in the city where she had to be to study, predict, and provide solutions to the congestion and pollution, including the growing radiation issues since 2026. The results of her work currently bordered all highways as living filters, made of various bacteria and plant growth, helping to absorb and convert CO_2 before it could become part of the atmosphere. More was needed.

She'd purchased all the land around Schmitz Preserve Park for little money because much of the housing along the shore had already flooded out. By buying off petty officials, she'd obtained permission to build House on a knob of rocky land below the park. Her garden now had direct access to the water and a view out into the Sound. Even though some of that property below her wasn't regularly flooded, the more powerful remnants of typhoons frequented the area and had devastated buildings there.

The park embraced the back of her place. She'd allowed the foliage to grow naturally, quickly turning the area into a jungle except trails she ran regularly. The plants consisted mostly of those that utilized wind and other forms of pollination. Vala had been experimenting with AI pollinators and different pollinator-attracting plants to help with growth.

At Aunt Char's insistence, her garden area, overlooking the beach, was sculpted and comfortable with various tables and lounging chairs, most of which were never used as she rarely had visitors other than Aunt Char and a host of animals that sought refuge in her mini-wilderness. She loved her garden; nestled within the mini-forest, the air was cooler and fresher, and even air transport and other city noise was diminished. This was her place to get away from people and problems.

At her driveway, the gate opened automatically as House recognized her pod. Creating House with AI was one of the concessions she'd made to contemporary technology—other than work, of course. She needed to be able to link House with the University of Washington, or U-dud as students called it, for her work. The current drive to link all computers and data into one system simply made everything more vulnerable to cyber-disaster or terrorism in her opinion.

She pulled up the drive to the garage entrance. The door opened automatically, and she pulled the pod into the garage slot for recharging. Vala sat for a moment, breathing deeply with relief at being back in her comfort zone, a place where she'd never had an episode.

Yet away from here, even at work at the University, such episodes were too frequent these days. Sometimes she felt like she was slipping out of the world completely. She might wind up in an institution again. The thought made her tense, then she heard Serein's huffs, not really barks, at the door to House. The door swung open at his insistence. If he'd thrown his 100 pound and three feet high massive body against the door, it would probably give way, but he'd learned to use the door handle. Vala smiled as she felt his concern at her shakiness. She stilled his voice with thought and a promise that she'd be with him all of the coming days. She'd learned years ago to not say she communicated with Serein and with other animals. Being crazy required walking a fine line, except with Aunt Char.

As she carried her bags inside, she felt a reluctant wave of gratitude for Eric Kine's help in making sure she had some groceries. His act had been kind. But then she wondered again if he was some sort of vulture, zeroing in on the defenseless. Human misery was high; in fact, it was popular, and the *human services* to mitigate that misery were increasing. It was one job that AI didn't handle well, and all sorts of unethical practices had evolved. Someone such as herself, a lumbering giant lying prone on the ground while clutching kale would attract vultures. She smiled. It probably took chutzpa for someone who was about four feet tall to approach such a giant.

Inside, Serein barely let Vala put groceries on the counter before he was demanding she join him outside for a game of catch. Vala spent a good fifteen minutes playing with him as consolation for having been left for an hour. He usually accompanied her everywhere, and his feelings were hurt, but playing catch for a bit relaxed both of them. Serein was doing his job.

As Vala was putting away the groceries, she found that she'd purchased, in addition to what she'd already selected, some heirloom tomatoes, spinach, peppers, broccoli, beets with greens, baby radishes, swiss chard, asparagus, cabbage, and one package of bean sprouts. There was even a package of goat cheese, a rare find, and a container of goat milk. He managed to buy everything she herself would have bought. She smiled. How long had Eric been gone? There was also a small bouquet of flowers. She double-checked the receipt, found they weren't included, and immediately felt uncomfortable again. Was he just hitting her up? Not looking for a client?

After putting away the groceries, Vala made a cup of tea and stood by the large kitchen windows looking out over the rambling gardens, and then the more distant Puget Sound, sparking light off the mini-white caps. No matter how stressed the environment was, the beauty remained. She heard a low rumble from Serein, noted he was staring in the direction of the birdbath. A coyote was sitting there eyeing one of the birds.

Not here, Serein was saying, and Vala added her own *no*. The coyote complied, walked over to the shade of a bush and curled up to sleep in safety.

Then something shimmered, again by the bird bath. A bird rose from the feeder and blinked out of sight. Vala closed her eyes, shook her head. Not again, not here at home, she prayed while carefully setting her mug of tea on the table. She looked back at the feeder. The shimmer was still there but then… someone? A person? Standing near the bird bath, looking right at her. The man, his palm facing out just as it had at the market, was looking at her.

Serein sat calmly, but his tail wagged. Vala sensed acceptance. The person must be there or Serein wouldn't respond, but his response signaled that there was no threat. Eric? Was he stalking her? But no, this man was nothing like Eric.

What she thought she saw was a very tall, at least as tall as Vala, and slim man, dressed in brown trousers and an open, loose-weave green shirt. He had a longish face, high cheekbones and thin, highly-arched eyebrows that matched the color of his dark brown hair that seemed long compared to today's skinhead look. His eyes were very wide and very dark, but Vala couldn't make out a color.

His body type was very like Vala's herself; was she just projecting a self-image?

He seemed to be gesturing for her to come out and join him, but she couldn't galvanize herself into action. He couldn't be there, yet Serein's tail continued to wag slowly in his reserved greeting for a safe stranger.

Vala closed her eyes again, focused on mind-clearing as she had learned with one of her therapists to try to keep a grip on reality. When she opened her eyes again, House was buzzing the gate alarm, and the hypothetical man was gone from the garden or from her mind or from wherever. She glanced at Serein; he'd lost interest and was checking out his empty food bowl. He never expressed concern about House's notifications.

"Who is it?" she asked House.

"Aunt Char."

"Well, let her in!" She kept telling House to automatically let Aunt Char in any time she arrived, but House kept resetting the programming to forbid entry. AI had not been all that had been promised, especially when one of the typhoon remnants or powerful thunderstorms that now plagued Seattle arrived. Nonetheless, she tried again. "House, you must always allow Aunt Char access."

"Understood."

Vala snorted; she always got the same answer from House.

Vala wasn't surprised by the visit; Aunt Char always had a sense for when Vala needed someone, and she'd probably been on the way before Vala had left the market. Vala regarded her as Mother, but Aunt Char wouldn't let her call her that.

"Dear," she would always say gently, "your mother loves you. She's just not good at expressing her emotions. She is your mother, not I."

Vala had always let that slide. Her mother had never had trouble letting Vala know she was a disappointment, a graceless giant that made stiletto heels a joke; to add insult, her Eurasian features hinted at an ancestry that was, at best, murky. Vala's father had been gentle and kind, but he had died when Vala was 16, and she had just retreated deeper into science, looking for answers to life and death.

Except for Aunt Char–she'd never retreated from Aunt Char.

Aunt Char met Vala in the kitchen and scooped her into a hug, something that always jammed the top of her ginger-blonde head into Vala's armpit. A scent of ginger made Vala smile. Aunt Char always smelled the same but never wore any scent; she simply was ginger.

"I've been worried about you today. I tried to call earlier, but your phone was off again. Really, dear, you must quit turning off your phone or get an implant or something. So what's wrong?"

"Sorry," Vala said. "I should have called you to tell you that I'm okay. I just had an episode at the market, but I'm home, and everything is fine. Mostly."

"Tell me over tea," Aunt Char said, followed by, "House, some oolong tea with milk."

Nothing.

Vala sighed. "House, always respond to Aunt Char."

"Oolong tea," said House as the drink dispenser hummed.

Vala reheated her own tea, and they went out into the airy garden to sit. Rhododendrons, pink, surrounded the area near the fountain where the lounging chairs were. The native rhododendrons were surviving the lack of pollinators by taking advantage of their large flowers to attract anything passing by, including birds, moths, and even small mammals. Vala's AI insects flitted, too, from flower to flower. The coyote looked up briefly as they approached but, upon receiving Vala's assurance, went back to sleep. Serein ignored the coyote after sniffing her briefly.

"Oh, what's that beautiful bird, Vala?" Aunt Char asked as she settled into the lounging chair.

Vala looked where Aunt Char was pointing and smiled. "That's a cedar waxwing. Aren't they startling? Unfortunately, with all the fires and human building, the habitat's vanishing; also, berries are few without pollinators. Seeing a cedar waxwing is a treat."

After a few moments, Vala filled Aunt Char in on the details of her day, including Eric and what she thought of as her hallucination of the man in the garden.

Char frowned, leaned forward, her bright blue eyes intense, and asked, "Are you sure the man in the garden wasn't this Eric person? Could he be stalking you?"

Vala laughed. "No, it wasn't he. There was a height difference of at least three feet, for one thing. I think what I saw was just a lingering effect of the morning tension."

Char leaned back again, set her cup down after another sip of tea. "You've been having more of these episodes lately. Should you go in to see Dr. DeVilbiss?" She spoke softly, rather like someone might to a frightened bunny, Vala thought.

Vala shook her head. "No." She reached out and patted Char's hand. "Don't worry. If I sense that I'm losing control, I'll contact him. I think that it's that time of year, summer, when I'm more sensitive to everything around me. The heat's intensity–you know, it was 103 degrees again today–smothers me, and this oppressive smoke, ash, and orange sun from all the fires combine with the crowds and noise of tourists for the Fourth and the usual city pressure...well, anyway, you know I would prefer to simply live in some remote place of quiet and solitude. However, I wouldn't be able to do my work, and I think it's important. I may go to Monument Valley again this Fall though."

Char sighed, sipped some tea. "Well, I trust your judgement, Vala. On the other hand, if you suspect that someone really is intruding on your property, you call the police immediately. That's not something you can control by being tall. As you know, women are victims of choice. And those horrible shootings last week at the Space Needle..."

Vala shook her head. "You know I avoid crowds. And I never run until late at night when it's quiet."

Char sighed. "Well, you know I worry about you running at night, too."

"I know. I always carry the Shocker-Block you gave me."

Char nodded, drank the last of her tea and stood. "I've got to go back to work. The university has some dignitaries coming in from Europe, and I've got to make sure everything is properly organized for their reception. Apparently, some idiot set up a theme that had pink plates for women and blue for men. He said he thought it would be fun to be retro. I was speechless!"

Vala laughed. "Aunt Char, you're never speechless. Thank you for coming over. I feel better. You've always been my ballast. Since Dad died, I'd have floundered without you."

"You are my pleasure in life, dear. Paul and I always wanted children, but you are my only one." She smiled, gave her a hug. "Now you call me if you have any more episodes, and I'll come over and give your House a lecture about making proper tea."

Vala smiled. "No mask today?"

Char shook her head. "The air isn't too bad today, and I'm using a driverless right to the door."

After Char left, Vala purposefully went to the window and looked out at the garden. Nothing. Undisturbed beauty, rare in the cityscape. Without being asked, Serein came and stood beside her and, together, they decided to go outside for a short walk to the water before dinner. *Later tonight,* she promised Serein, *we'll take a run.*

CHAPTER TWO

For as long as he could remember, which seemed like back in his crib, Eric Kine had known—felt in his bones—his life's purpose: he was born to help, support, and guide his sister, Sarah.

But he had no sister.

The Sarah that was to be had died before he was born two years later to Deborah and Kevin Kine; yet, that woman in the market today had renewed his conviction that he had to take care of his sister. His thoughts circled around again: but he had no sister.

He turned a page on the photo album he had out on his kitchen table and took a sip of ale as he studied the pictures of his parents on their wedding day, June 12, 1998. His mother's wedding dress, trimmed in scarlet just a shade darker than her hair, brought her to life out of the picture. Dad, in spite of the grin and the red tie to match his bride's dress trim, looked like little more than a minion.

He'd had great parents—for a while. Eric often wondered at their buried heartache from having a daughter die in childbirth and then having a son born with such an obvious defect: a little person or, as he was called constantly from the time he'd started school: midget, shrimp, stump, nano-brain, defect-o, and pocket-puppy.

Oddly and despite the invective, Eric never had felt defective, something he could attribute to his parents, although they themselves had been killed in a car wreck when he was seven. To them, he'd always been as normal and natural as smiles. However, they'd never understood his obsession over a dead sister, someone he'd never known; he, himself, didn't understand, but he couldn't shake it. His parents had tried to console him and had adopted a puppy for him when he was four to give him comfort, but he yearned for his sister.

Of course, Eric wasn't surprised, even at seven, when no one wanted to adopt him after his parents' deaths. They'd had no other family, so he'd dealt with foster homes and irregular schooling as well as the loss of his dog, Fergus. Fortunately, his large trust fund had helped him have necessities and also enabled him to dedicate himself to learning how to take care of others as he was convinced he was supposed to have done with his sister. His intelligence never dimmed: he finished high school at 16 and finished his MD at 24. He'd become a successful counselor and now had his own office just three years after getting his degree. Yet the loss of his sister continued to ache, shifting around in his body and mind like some phantom wound. Every time he heard her name, Sarah, he'd snap to attention. Although he knew that she'd died–he had the paperwork–he never stopped looking for her.

He closed the photo album–there were no pictures, of course, of his sister–and stared out the French window of his 40th floor box on 901 Fifth Avenue. Across Elliott Bay, a fog was building toward Alki. His own reflection in the glass morphed, became a wavering portrait of the tall woman–very tall woman, he reminded himself–at the market. He'd felt compelled to find her, talk to her, explain that he could help–

Yet, who needed help? He'd also seen another image that day, almost a ghost-like figure, briefly, across the market, just before the woman had collapsed. What was that about? Something had charged the air, too, like a sudden pressure change in an aircraft. At the same time, he'd felt a jolt, like standing too close to a lightning flash, striking between himself and the woman. And, of course, he was obsessed with his dead sister. Sure, he could help her.

He abruptly sat down again at the table, drank some more ale and wondered, *What would I say to a patient who had expressed these thoughts?*

You're being obsessive again, he answered his own question. He needed to drop the idea of a sister and instead figure out what these thoughts and visions stood for, what they really signified. Then he needed to fulfill his needs with accessible reality. Then he needed to replace unacceptable compulsions with healthy activity. That was what he'd say as a counselor.

As he finished his list, he felt another physical jolt, like a muscular twitch throughout his body, as a conviction hit him: that woman today was his sister. His missing sister. No, his dead sister. The impossible had become possible in his life. Forget the counseling. He *knew* her. He picked up his scalpel and a walnut and began randomly carving, shaping the shell.

Accept that, Eric, he told himself as he scraped away at the walnut. *Not everything is rational.*

Okay, he told himself, *if I accept that, the next step is to figure out how that's possible. Why did he know that he could not only help her as a stranger, but that also she was his sister who had died in childbirth, who had been cremated, whose ashes reposed in a nearby crematorium with his parents?*

He resorted to another mental list.

He *knew* she needed help. Every movement of her body, the way her amber eyes looked terrified like a trapped wild animal, said that she needed some guidance. He'd known, even, what groceries she'd want. Of course, he usually knew exactly what people felt and wanted, another non-rational component in his life.

He returned to the window, still carving without looking at his efforts. Keeping his hands busy. The cityscape sparked and wavered in the ever-present smog, smoke, and light fog that ghosted around Puget Sound. He fingered the slip of paper in his shirt pocket. He'd written down her pod license number, make and color. Was that inappropriate? Was he drifting into stalking thoughts? How could he find her?

Why did he think—no, *know*—she was his sister? As that question circled around again, it remained unanswerable.

She'd connected with him before he'd given her his card. She'd known him, hadn't she?

He'd seen a phone sticking out of her Pod charger, but she, like Eric, didn't have an implant, so he couldn't figure out a connection that way. Certainly, she'd made it clear that she wanted no more to do with him after she'd seen his card. She'd suddenly been frightened of him. Why?

He tried to comfort himself with the idea that she could call him. She knew who he was. He should leave her alone. That's what he'd tell a patient. He set the walnut and knife down with a sharp *click* on the table. The walnut resembled a laughing Buddha. That was a good message. He never knew what his unfocused carving would produce, but it was usually something he needed. Now he needed to quit taking himself so seriously and work with what he knew to be true: his sister was dead.

With that thought, he went into his bedroom to end the day. Patients had been scheduled all day starting at 5:00 in the morning. Tomorrow would be easier. He'd taken a break for the Fourth. He didn't want to be out in the noise and crowds.

He activated the steam shower to help with relaxing. As he was finishing off with the cold rain shower rinse, he felt an awareness, a presence. Peering through the foggy glass, he was suddenly convinced he could see someone just outside the shower. He wiped his hand on the glass. Not someone—more like a holograph, a faint holograph, of a very tall man. It was the same figure as at the market! Eric turned off the unit and opened the door.

Nothing.

But something. Someone? "Well, that's interesting," he muttered. Was someone trying to send him a message? He'd had images appear to him before, but he'd known who they were. He'd never told anyone of such visits—or even of his apparent ability to *know* what people were thinking or feeling. People already considered him peculiar. But this was new. Was his mind creating this image to communicate?

He shook his head. He definitely needed to relax and sleep. This was happening for a reason but he couldn't resolve anything now. He spent an hour in peaceful meditation, calming his rambling thoughts, and then went to sleep.

On Saturday morning, after a night of dreams about his sister and the stranger at the market, he told himself that one way to overcome a minor obsession was to act, bring the matter to a clear resolution. Obviously, she wasn't his sister.

He called a friend, Steve Brilling, CEO of Puget Investigations, specializing in trial investigations and high-level background checks for many businesses. Such investigation was essential before anyone could be hired for an organization that had government contracts, even if remote. Steve, a former foster-buddy of his, had always been a supporter of Eric's unexpected side trips from the mundane.

"Hey, Steve," Eric said, "I need some help."

"Eric? Eric, it's six in the morning. I don't get up until eight."

"So don't get up. I can talk to people lying down. That's what I do for a living."

Steve began to chuckle. "You win. Sermonize me."

"I'd like to have an individual checked out, under the radar. All I have is a license number and make of pod."

"That's all I need."

"She doesn't have an implant," Eric added.

"That's okay. Her pod does although she may not know that. One way or another, everyone is traceable."

After passing along the information, Eric made a conscious commitment to wipe his thoughts clean of both the woman and also the niggling guilt for pursuing information about someone who obviously didn't want his attention. He forced himself to focus on his activities as they erupted during the day. He had no scheduled appointments for the rest of the week, but holidays were always busy as slightly unstable and usually marginal people were put under added pressure, even for an artificially psyched-up holiday like the Fourth. Besides, Steve would put someone discreet and thorough on the job and would get back to Eric when he had something solid; Eric could let go. Probably.

Steve, Wyatt, and Eric: Crew of Serenity—outsiders, outcasts, brothers forever—as they'd labeled themselves when they were three misfit teens in the era of superheroes and video games. They had avoided being connected, having android selves, immersing themselves in the video world. They took on the streets, finding abuse of people or animals and reporting that abuse. They managed to bring down two dog-fighting rings; several child abusers, including some in the foster program; and a foster-care financial fraud scheme. They also took on bullies at their school. They shared everything. Eric had even shared his belief that he'd had one mission for being born and that he'd somehow lost the ability to meet that mission. Steve had never doubted but just nodded and said, "Maybe something else will clarify itself. The mission just hasn't found you yet."

Steve and Wyatt were probably responsible for Eric surviving public school. Of course, that had been in the early part of the century, before the public education system collapsed. From what he heard from his patients, however, the various private and charter schools were no better although more expensive.

In return for Steve and Wyatt's friendship and protection, Eric had been able to help them significantly by manipulating his trust fund monies, buying products to fit their needs.

For the first part of the day, his resolve to forget about his quest to learn more about Market Woman, as he had dubbed her, held steady while he fielded distress calls from patients and went to his office to meet two frantic individuals. But each time he was alone, he worried. He was invading someone else's privacy. On the other hand, the woman need never know, and Eric needed to know, needed to understand what had happened to him. He didn't even know why he'd written down that license number. He knew only that he'd had no choice.

His third unscheduled patient, Dakota, stooped as always to enter Eric's office then silently sat in the chair by Eric's desk. Dakota detested the couch, which was short for his seven feet. Dakota's tension filled the room as solidly as he himself did. His call had sounded near panic. "I'm desperate to get home," Dakota said. "It's beyond my reach, Eric. You know that, yes?"

Eric shook his head. "No, Dakota. Where is your home?"

Dakota sighed, then held out a closed fist.

Eric automatically extended his right hand, palm up, to receive whatever it was.

Dakota grabbed Eric's hand and looked at it. He nodded, then dropped his own hand into his lap. "You're gentem, too," Dakota said. "I knew you were the one. You know what it is to be alone. You need to fix this."

Eric looked at him for a moment, shifting uncomfortably under the wave of disjointed thoughts overwhelming Dakota, and then said, "I don't know that word, *gentem*. Could you explain?"

Dakota's eyes narrowed. "But you do understand. Your

palm–" He stood abruptly. "You have much to do. We're counting on you. I want to go home." He turned and walked to the door.

"Dakota, wait!" Eric called. However, moving quickly, Dakota opened the door, stooped, and then was gone.

Eric stood by his desk. He wasn't in the habit of chasing his patients down the street. And it wasn't the first time a client had become agitated and left abruptly. But Dakota hadn't been agitated. He'd been–what? Almost relieved. But also urgent. Why would he think Eric could help him go home?

Eric looked down at the odd birthmark on his palm, the incomplete spiral, broken here and there. He'd been assured that it was "just a birthmark" many times. He'd never believed it. Although birthmarks did occur on the palm, he'd never heard of one like his. Sometimes, it seemed to have colors in it, but no one else had ever seen them. However, ever since the encounter in the market with his sister, it had been tingling, like a small electric tickle across his palm. That had never happened before. What had Dakota seen there? Obviously, his hand gesture had been a ploy to see Eric's palm but why?

The questions stirred his excitement, which rose and fell like waves along the coast as he'd think he was on the edge of discovery and then be convinced he was simply fooling himself again. Yet change charged the air.

The proverb, "Physician, heal thyself" came to mind as he remembered the ghost-like figure from the night before and earlier at the market. He shoved aside a slight fear that he was losing his grip on reality. Yet there was change, something coming, like the charge in the air before a storm moved in. The game was, as one of his childhood heroes used to say, "afoot." He began closing up his office while resisting the urge to call Steve.

CHAPTER THREE

Saturday afternoon, June 30, 2029

Cassidy lay very still with his eyes closed, trying to sort out whirling colors and sounds from his…what? Dream? Was he home? No, it didn't smell right. What was that smell?

Omelet!

He sat up abruptly, opened his eyes, and then abruptly lay down again as the room whirled around him.

When he could open his eyes again, he looked around at the heavy tapestries over the soft bed and again sniffed the sweet scent of drying herbs and cooking omelet. Obeah's! Of course. When he turned his head to his left, he saw Obeah Jacoby silhouetted against a window by the counter that served as a make-shift kitchen in the clinic.

Cassidy smiled. He was back! Then he frowned. He had failed again. He swung his legs out of bed, stood, then dropped back on the bed.

"You're hungry. Don't start analyzing or trying to dash about. Eat first." Obeah walked toward him and handed him a cup with a green liquid in it.

Cassidy drank about half of the fruity liquid. "At least it tastes good this time."

Obeah smiled. "I took your complaints to my lab kettle." He gave Cassidy a steadying arm over to the table, then put the omelet in front of him. Cassidy couldn't resist rapidly forking the hot, vegetable-filled meal into his mouth. When he finished, Obeah handed him a mug filled with more of the fruity liquid, then sat across from him.

"That was just right, Obeah. Thank you."

"Not much progress, eh?" Obeah clasped his hands in front of him and shook his head, a sure sign of a lecture coming. "You know, Cassidy, this may kill you before you can make connections, before your ideas can succeed. This time you've been struggling since before dawn to come back."

Cassidy studied Obeah's face. Baggy dark circles lay under his almost-obsidian eyes, and his cheeks were gaunt. His skin, normally a burnished oak color, had paled. "I fear this has been difficult for you, Obeah."

Obeah shrugged lightly. "Dying isn't the issue for me, but as I become weaker, my ability to help sustain your body lessens."

"I almost made progress." Cassidy finished off the drink and did, almost instantly, felt better. He managed to stand and walk to the counter to set the mug down. "I think they both at least saw me this time." He stared out the window at the deep green of forest and the streamers of sun that splintered through fir and cedar. Steller's jays were screaming, probably at a local owl. Cassidy sighed. "I couldn't quite manifest enough to speak or convey a message, and neither showed the slightest recognition or interest in linking. Something is wrong, something that is preventing communication." He turned to face Obeah. "Worse...Obeah, I don't think they're aware of each other."

Obeah shook his head, and his silver hair caught light from the window. "None of this—not since the creation of the Membrane and Beta Earth—has worked out as planned. 'O, what men dare do! What men may do! What men daily do, not knowing what they do!' Disharmony is ripping our lives apart."

Cassidy shrugged. "As Einstein said, however, 'Just because something doesn't do what you planned it to do doesn't mean it's useless.' We just need to figure out how to coordinate the technology and the natural forces we've utilized. We succeeded in creating this place. Now, we just need to know what to do next."

"I happen to know that Einstein also said, 'The human spirit must prevail over technology.' Of course, he didn't know about gentem as far as we know, but the message is valid. Our effort to build the Membrane may have taken us in the wrong direction from the start. It's opposed to unification, to everything that the gentem, in principle, espouse."

Cassidy shook his head stubbornly as he sat back at the table. He knew that Obeah had always believed that separation from humans failed both humans and gentem. But Cassidy had spent long hours studying texts and talking to both gentem and the few humans that lived with them, and he'd recently concluded that unification between the two humanoid groups was unlikely. However, that didn't mean he shouldn't continue trying to contact their children. They could prove him wrong. That had been the plan: the children were supposed to have answers. He had to keep an open mind.

Obeah muttered something, stood, and walked over to his shelves. He pulled a couple bottles down and walked to the counter, and began mixing ingredients in a kettle. With his back to Cassidy, he said, "You need to know that the council met last night. I had to tell them that your body is weakening. Added to that are issues with the Membrane surrounding Beta Earth. Leakage between the two Earths is increasing. Marina says that for some reason we're not growing increasingly separate as we should; it's as though the space is trying to reintegrate, reunify the two worlds." He turned around, his long tunic following the movement. "Cassidy, some wonder if your continued attempts to contact the children are part of the problem, are somehow drawing us back toward Alpha Earth. So far, the council is still split on what action to take, but we're going to have to make a decision soon."

"I wonder what we'd be like as a culture had we remained there." Cassidy rubbed his lower lip with his thumb and stared into space. "From what I've read, gentem were growing increasingly secretive and isolated. With the world populated everywhere with humans, we had no place to call our own. Marina thinks we were headed for extinction." He studied the wood grain of the table—swirling llight and dark, intricately woven, seemingly random, yet alive with purpose. Elegant and simple life.

Obeah remained silent.

"Well, I'll have to try again soon, so the Council doesn't do anything idiotic. I think–"

"No. You have to rest. Cassidy, if the children don't even

know each other, then what's the point? Jasmine is gone." Obeah's voice caught, and he cleared his throat before continuing.

"The portal isn't open, but leakage flows like wine at a Bacchanalia. We don't know why. Humans must be polluting more, not less. We may have to undo this weaving, this manipulation, and start again." Obeah cleared his throat again and fell silent.

"But not Alarick's suggestion," Cassidy said while hoping that Obeah would agree. "Genocide and war? How can we justify that? How do we, as gentem, survive denying that we are a force for life, not death?" Cassidy's legs twitched as he felt an urge to run out the door and escape the conversation, the fear, and the hopelessness.

Bottles clinked and the stirring spoon clattered against the kettle, keeping time to Obeah's words. "I hate the idea. On the other hand, the humans will never know what is happening to them, or at least how, and they can't take any action against us." He slapped the spoon onto the counter. "We have a responsibility to consider *all* life. Would you kill a bacteria that threatened all life?"

Cassidy went to the doorway and stared out. The clinic stood at the edge of their village located upland from old Sequim. Other cedar buildings, irregularly spaced, lined the path that led out to Cassidy's own lab in a small clearing. "That's rationalization, Obeah," he said without turning around. "No terrorism is justifiable. If we could just talk to some responsible humans. If we could somehow communicate the problems. Isn't that why we left our children there?"

"You're too young to remember but you *know* the history. Living in harmony with humans was tried for centuries! Since before that!" Obeah put a hand on Cassidy's shoulder, pulling him around, making direct eye contact. Obeah, at eight feet tall, topped Cassidy by a few inches. "Our science, our skills, our connections to natural forces, and our scientists were ignored. *Humans will ignore you!* Our individuals were persecuted, laughed at, and banned from any kind of freedom to speak and act. Nothing worked then, and it appears that nothing is working correctly now." He put both hands on Cassidy's shoulders, gripping firmly. "We're rapidly approaching that point where turning the damage around will be as impossible here as it apparently is there. We'll have two worlds that are poisoned and dying. Or two worlds that collide and end everything."

Cassidy ignored the reference to his young age, a refrain that was pulled out every time he disagreed with those over 50. "Obeah, I need your support." Cassidy rested his own hands on Obeah's elbows. "I can't stop now. You said our scientists were ignored before the separation. Don't help make that true *here*, not now when we have to use science, technology, and our innate skills and knowledge together. Obeah, you must listen!"

Obeah turned and went back to his kettle. "My wisdom lacks the energy of your youth."

"I want to talk to the Council," Cassidy said.

Obeah shrugged. "Of course, you do." He smiled. "I just hope that somehow a solution can be reached. There is powerful good in you. Wash your dishes, then let Tandra know you're back; she's been here giving you reiki every day and acupuncture as needed. Her reserves, too, are strained. Then we'll contact the Council."

Tandra was there before Cassidy finished washing his dishes. She must have already sensed her little brother's return. She strode in the door and scooped him into a hug, then looked up at him and said, "The area below your eyes looks green, as though you've been bruised, and you've lost a lot of weight. This is draining you."

He patted her on the head, something he'd enjoyed ever since growing beyond her 6'8". "You look tired, too. Miss me, Sis?"

"Not particularly." She snorted. "Was this last trip worth it?"

Cassidy shrugged. "Trying is always worth it, no? It's at least *doing* something."

"No," she snapped. "It isn't, so don't take on a gooey philosophical tone. Sometimes it just becomes stupid like that movie character Yoda you kept quoting as a kid."

"Well," Cassidy said, laughing, "let's see if we can get the Council to talk to us."

Cassidy and Tandra left for Cassidy's lab to make phone calls where they'd be out of Obeah's way. They walked through the woods and past the meadow where the obelisk, shimmering in the sunlight, stood. The confined plasma unit was meant to amplify the linked implants between the children and Cassidy and Tandra, creating a portal that would allow them to interact—now it stood as a reminder of failure: of communication, of linking, of the Membrane itself.

A part of Cassidy wanted to stay outside, enjoy the fresh, sweet air. A slight breeze ruffled the evergreens and brought in the scent of low tide. He felt as though he'd been caught up in this mystery of trying to contact the children for his entire life, but it had really been only 29 of his 50 years, starting back in 2000, the year Sarah was born and the plans for saving the world were first implemented. And first started going wrong.

As they approached the lab, Tandra visibly tensed, her shoulders rising and her breath catching. Cassidy knew the lab felt alien to her. Being inside a quantum computer felt distant from the natural world, but constructing the entire lab as a computer had proven invaluable to his work. Cassidy had the walls depict forests and a waterfall. The holographic images helped Tandra relax slightly.

After tracking down various members of the Council at their studios or farms, each agreed to meet with him the next day for the mid-day meal. "I can't say any of them sound enthusiastic," said Cassidy as he finished his last call.

Tandra laughed. "They think you've been wasting your time and energy on this long-term pursuit of those two children. Council members want to simply write it off as a good idea gone bad for, by the human calendar, thirty 'misbegotten years,' according to Alarick."

"But, Tandra, think of the human response to the portal if we can open it. If they see how much healthier the world is here after those thirty years..." Cassidy gave up as he saw the sour look on Tandra's face. "At the very least, maybe we could figure out why the Membrane leaks. That's got to be better than waging a secret war." Cassidy shook his head. "If we turn against our own better natures, we, like the humans, will be unable to connect with the forces that enabled us to create Beta Earth in the first place. We may annihilate ourselves and both Earths."

"That's your theory, Cassidy," Tandra argued. "If we save Earth through our actions, how can it separate us from the natural world?"

"Computer, notify Delara that the meeting is set," Cassidy said. He took a deep breath and made direct eye contact with Tandra. "Committing genocide isn't *saving* anything. That's human-based thinking!"

Tandra looked like she was going to throw something at Cassidy but then she often did.

"You know, Tandra, our own genetic biologists claim our culture's non-violent nature began when the gentem diverged from the humans with the Neanderthal and Denisovan split. Humans are wired to respond more to the monkey world. What we can see and feel, humans must measure by effects or with instruments. Can we fight our natures or fifty-thousand years of evolution?"

Tandra's eyes darkened and she shook her index finger at him. "Cassidy, I know who we as gentem are, but you're saying we can't adapt." She shook her head. "You're just a stubborn kid!" Then she laughed. "Well, whatever your ideas lack in common sense, you make up for in enthusiasm." She put a hand on his shoulder. "For what it's worth, I understand what you're saying. It's the first time I know of when our culture has considered this sort of warfare, so we don't know what will happen. Perhaps we're just afraid. We've always retreated, isolated ourselves, hidden our identity. That's not a solution any more, Cassidy. While we were doing that, many of us were killed, abused, marginalized. The gentem want to be honored for who they are."

Cassidy studied Tandra. "What happens to your state of being when you're angry?"

"I, like anyone, am out of sync. Conflicted. Then I work on regaining my place, my harmony."

"What if you couldn't harmonize? Not ever again? Suppose you lost your temper, killed someone and could never practice your healing work again, never reconnect with the natural forces, even the simple gravitational and magnetic forces?"

Tandra shook her head, opened her mouth, closed it, then turned and quietly went out the door.

Cassidy let her go. He knew the question frightened her. Tandra not being able to bring herself into harmony with Earth's forces was a frightening thought. Who would she be without that? Yet, she did struggle with her temper and her patience regularly; at times it was debilitating. Of course, she was still young, only a couple dozen years older than Cassidy, but the idea of always being in a state of turmoil would terrify her. It would terrify him although he thought of it in scientific terms: modifying the zero point energy of quantum fields.

Cassidy spent the evening working on the material he wanted to present to the Council. Every time he'd met with them, their attitude toward him could best be described as condescension. Cassidy ground his teeth at the memory. Most of them, he knew, regarded him as little more than a child. Counted in human years, he wasn't yet fifty, so he'd been only 20, a mere child, when the Membrane had been created; that wasn't much to try to counter the millennia of persecution gentem had experienced from humans or the personal experience of individuals who'd known nothing but human oppression for five times Cassidy's lifespan. But he *knew* what he was doing! How could he convince them?

By the time of the next mid-day meal, Cassidy felt ready. He ignored the semi-circle of impassive faces and began strongly. Yet, within a few minutes of opening his mouth, he heard a pleading tone in his voice and paused to regain his confidence and study his notes. When he began again, he sounded more forceful.

"For this next trip, I'll follow the same method of travel as before, but this time, I'll focus on creating a digital message on one of their devices. I've not tried this before, but since I'm traveling on photon waves, I should be able to manipulate their technology. I'll use the photonics–" he broke off as he saw their expressions… most of them didn't want the details of science. "Simply, I'll interact with the computer to create a file that they will notice, read and understand. I'll copy the same message over and over in multiple places using multiple formats. It's like an infinite S-O-S."

Marina Lorca, who represented the technology community and was Cassidy's former mentor, shook her head. "I see problems, Cassidy. Although you don't need to give the Council all the science, we're ignorant about the current systems they have. It's been decades since we created the Membrane, and I'm sure the humans have changed technology, as have we.

"Second, I've talked to Obeah. He says that this conversion, or melding with light requires putting your body, in effect, in a death-like state, while your brain enters a meditative, dhyana-like state that is very near death, that then rides light, apparently, to *leak* through the Membrane as do the pollution and toxins. Obeah says you risk your life–not just your mortal life but your spiritual LifeForce–every time you do this. You may truly kill your consciousness or dissolve it. In effect, you're conducting experiments based on unproven theory. That's not logical process. Explain to me why you are willing to die to connect with these children."

Cassidy took a deep breath. Marina was probably one of the most intelligent individuals he'd ever known. She was his teacher of intuitive calculus and physics as well as standard technology, but he knew she thought humans were radically inferior. He would have to be clear the first time through his explanation.

He fought down feelings of intimidation and began again. "I don't feel I can NOT do it. We have to find a solution that is nonviolent to other creatures, whether human or Lumbricina. Everything we are as gentem is tied to LifeForce; everything you've taught me, Marina, about our intuitive physics tells me that who we are as a species means maintaining our connection with the LifeForce. To destroy any life, even to save life, is antithetical to the very concept of creation, to the notion of us as members within the LifeForce, not gods. Even the technology you know so well and teach here is tied to bio-sources. If we break those ties, what comes next?"

He paused, then stood to relieve the twitches in his legs. He had to move around! He paced back and forth across the room by the door while wishing he could just go out and run. He took a deep breath, then shrugged.

"I don't claim to know what the solution is, but I know an alternative to killing exists because an alternative to violence *always* exists. You once told me, Marina, that limited alternatives only symbolized limited thinking, and you quoted a journalist, Dorothy Thompson, as saying, 'Peace is not the absence of conflict but the presence of creative alternatives for responding to conflict– alternatives to passive or aggressive responses, alternatives to violence.' I never forgot that. None of us should." He stopped pacing, sat down again.

Devin, one of Cassidy's friends and a member of Cassidy's informal peace group spoke up. "The children were always part of the plan. Everything we've done has been predicated on their involvement. It seems to me that to give up on that contact is to tacitly agree on giving up. Forever. We'll never know the final solution or what we could have done. Even if it has taken longer than expected, even if it has taken unexpected turns, we're not a short-lived species. Time is what we make of it always, no?"

"Not necessarily," said Petros Floros, who represented philosophy and religion on the Council. "Not when disaster in the form of poisons and catastrophe are knocking at our membrane door. Being passive isn't the same thing as being peaceful."

"Listen," Cassidy said loudly, then bit his lip to regain control. "How can I tell you what will happen since we haven't yet found any clear alternative solution? Give me the option. I don't believe I'm in as much danger as Obeah does. He worries because he doesn't grasp the science; his consciousness is less abstract. On the other hand, I don't have any ideas beyond this latest one as a way to break through. Give me another handful of your patience, until the full moon. Try to trust me." He couldn't think of any other way to intensify his plea. He sat again, still wishing he could go run, and looked hopefully at each Council member.

Alarick didn't make eye contact, and his lips thinned before he spoke. "Much has gone wrong with our plans. First, all our efforts to communicate, to get humans to see reason, an effort that went on for hundreds of their years. Then gentem efforts to affect the science weren't enough to battle politics and human skepticism created by their narrow view of the world. Then the separation, which proved not to protect us or our ecosystem; that failure is leading us deeper into the death of Earth but so slowly that we're stalling on action, like the frog in increasingly hot water." He held up three fingers, then a fourth, slapping at it with his other hand. "Then Jasmine vanishes, and we lose the only communication left open to us. The children apparently lose contact with each other. And you, Cassidy, seemed almost ready to die before you returned to us this time. It's too dangerous for you to try again."

Cassidy shook his head. "Please. Even if I do die, it will be in trying to avoid genocide." Cassidy suppressed the desire to argue and plead more. He felt as though he were losing all confidence and, instead of sounding knowledgeable, was sounding more like a puppy whining at a door.

Alarick sighed, glanced around the semicircle of Council members. Most were looking down at their hands. Finally, Delara said, "Let us talk. Consider. We'll get back to you later."

Cassidy nodded, stood. "I understand. Thank you for your time and consideration. I know you each wish only to do what will best benefit the greatest number. As do I."

When he and Tandra reached the road, Cassidy turned and stared at the Council's yurt. He felt like stamping his feet. "I can't believe they even have to consider whether to try every alternative to genocide, Tandra. They're allowing fear to govern. And what does *later* mean? Today? Next generation?"

"Cassidy, you've never experienced some of the torture and bigotry some of them have within the human culture. And not just an experience or two as you did growing up, but decades and centuries of mistreatment, death, exclusion, and discrimination."

"Are you saying that being a victim of a wrong makes perpetuating wrongs all right?"

"No," Tandra said, slapping both hands alongside her head, "but I'm saying that you'd be better advised to treat them with as much kindness as you're saying they should give those who have tortured and even murdered their families. I can tell you the energy among the Council is not stable; they're not in agreement. And Alarick is alarmingly unstable. This has been a battle they have all been fighting for a long time, and Alarick has allowed it to seriously debilitate his LifeForce."

Cassidy sighed. "Well, they will probably debate the rest of the day. Do you want to hang around here or maybe get some food?"

"Food," she muttered, and they ambled to Cassidy's lab and quarters. As it turned out, the Council sent for Cassidy before he and Tandra could finish the salad they'd made. After Cassidy had answered the call, he turned to Tandra and said, "Please come with me. I'd like to have you there."

She nodded and they ran the mile together back to Council headquarters, Cassidy jogging to match Tandra's less enthusiastic run.

As soon as Cassidy was seated, Alarick began.

"We've reached a consensus. First, regarding your continued foolish efforts–"

Delara coughed loudly.

"Yes, of course. Regarding your outstanding efforts, foolish or not, you may continue at will. Do not jeopardize the Membrane and do keep the Council informed of any progress or lack thereof. Especially if you make contact; we want to know that immediately.

"Meanwhile, we're going to continue with our plan. We've been waiting too long, doing nothing while Beta Earth sickens. We can't wait longer on a gamble that you can overcome all odds and make contact with our people or that, if you do, they'll be able or willing to fulfill their roles."

"You'll continue?" Cassidy felt his chest tighten.

"Yes. We have one more set of tests that the scientists working on the project want to do. More tests." He muttered the last and shook his head. "Then we'll prepare the overall document for how to proceed. We'll be starting with the Colorado River in the Western part of the United States, which currently provides water for about 36 million people. We'll start small. We don't want to create panic or a major investigation. As you know, the complete plan as endlessly discussed by this Council will take about 20 years, during which time, of course, the environmental damage here will continue. Once this short-sighted delay–"

Delara coughed loudly again.

"Once this *well-conceived plan* is in full effect, the benefits from a rapidly declining human population will be slow, but they will come, steadily and thoroughly. We hope." The sarcasm in his voice couldn't be missed by anyone.

"And you're certain no other creatures will be affected? As you say, our plans have not gone well." Cassidy fought to keep his voice calm.

Alarick leaned back in his chair. "We've tested and tested and tested and–" another Delara cough–"All our scientists are in agreement that the only effect will be on humans. The substance has been bioengineered for human DNA that includes the Neanderthal genome. There is no antidote."

Cassidy knew he should be quiet, but he couldn't. "Can it

be reversed? I mean, if later, it becomes necessary to repair the damage?"

"Well, we can stop adding ephedra. Any humans not fully affected by that time would be able to gradually return to normal probably."

Probably? Cassidy's neck muscles cramped, and he couldn't help taking a sharp intake of breath.

Alarick's frown deepened. "You know, we'd tried to teach humans to control their environmental destruction—what Marina calls *carbon footprint*—for years, ever since their *industrial revolution*. If they'd made any progress after the mid-1900s, none of this would be necessary if, of course, they were willing to accept us without torture, murder, and marginalization. That never stopped." Alarick sounded as though he thought humans deserved anything that happened to them.

Cassidy knew Alarick's reasoning was sound if one looked only at the effects humans had on Earth as a whole. Tandra had once said humans were like a virus killing Earth. Nonetheless, whether bacteria or virus, an answer had to be available to allow some sort of future that didn't involve killing. And Cassidy still believed the key had to be with Sarah and Eric, the children who had been left as the communication link, the children he had regarded as super-heroes for as long as he could remember. Somehow. Yet, as he looked at Alarick's hate-ravaged face and heard his bitter tone, for the first time, Cassidy felt a slight doubt, a suspicion that this was too massive to pin on a handful of people, especially when two of them were children who may have never thought of themselves as anything but human.

Instead of voicing his doubts, Cassidy nodded. "I'll prepare to do what I must while you all," he gestured around the room, "do what you must. How much time do I have before you start using the bioweapon?"

"No more than one moon cycle," said Alarick.

Cassidy felt a lump of panic in his throat. What was more dangerous? The biowar or the fact that this Council was even considering such means?

Marina nodded at him. "Good luck, Cassidy. I hope that you don't wind up intertwined with the particles wandering space."

Cassidy knew she understood the low probability of his success, and she was using a metaphor to remind him how readily one could lose control when utilizing photon waves as he intended. Everything he was trying was unknown, was untested.

"Thank you," was all he said before standing and leaving with Tandra.

Tandra went to her quarters to take care of some work, and Cassidy returned to Obeah's quarters immediately. He explained what the council had said and what Cassidy himself planned to do. "I need a day to prepare. I need to memorize some notes, think about the best message to convey, then I want to make contact again."

The old healer lowered his head like a buffalo thinking about charging. "First, I think you could die, especially since you're not up to full strength yet, but you don't care about that. So, setting that aside, I think you're taking a risk for no purpose. What do you expect those abandoned children to do? Walk up to their police and say, 'I'm gentem, which, of course, you've never heard of, and if you don't change your ways, you'll all have to be eliminated'? Then they will get to spend their lives locked up as insane or dangerous, right?"

Cassidy said nothing. Obeah cleared his throat and made an obvious effort to change his tone of voice to one less sarcastic.

"So that's assuming that either of them is going to say or do anything. Remember, they've been somehow cut off from each other and from Jasmine; they have no idea that they're not human although they've probably been convinced they're not normal. And, finally, Cassidy, how do you think that technology and information is going to work? I know we brought the technological basics into our dimension or metaphysical plane or whatever you're calling it these days, but that was in 1999, almost 30 years ago on the human calendar. You've read history, and you know how fast humans change their tools, sometimes for no reason except for change itself. Their lives are so short that they cram them with change and stupidity."

Obeah waited barely a heartbeat before continuing. "Besides, humans don't believe in anyone unlike themselves. They don't even like each other because of minor details such as their spiritual beliefs or the hue of skin. They had so long ago decided that they were the top of all evolution, the only intelligent result of evolution, that they couldn't accept our abilities and even minor physical variations except as mutations and something dangerous. Why should someone who can run fast or who is 8' tall or who can bend metal through mental effort be treated as a freak or a threat?"

Obeah said something else and then quieted. Cassidy, still standing in the doorway, nodded at him, aware that Obeah had been speaking but mostly thinking about what he must prepare. He looked at Obeah when the silence deepened.

"So when do you go?" Obeah asked, resignation lowering and slowing his voice as he gestured at the table.

"Tomorrow. If I can figure out how to do this."

"Are you going to try to leave technology?" Obeah sat across from him.

Cassidy shook his head. "No. The only thing I can think of is to leave a digital message. Even if they're now using quantum computers, all computation boils down to a series of mathematical operations. I need a message that will connect with the children who, as everyone as pointed out, know nothing about gentem or the Membrane or their own history." Cassidy sighed, then quoted Roethke:

> I wake to sleep, and take my waking slow.
> I feel my fate in what I cannot fear.
> I learn by going where I have to go.

"Poetry aside, you also need to somehow prepare for the idea that, if they believe what you say, they could go into shock. You can't just tell them that you represent a different species that has come to collect them. They'll think you're insane or that they're insane. You can't tell them you're something familiar, such as an elf, because we're nothing like what they know of us as mythological creatures in literature. They would expect all elves to look alike, with pointy ears and with quivers on their back. Some of our early story tellers went to great lengths to portray all aspects of our history as fictional. That gave us a layer of protection. If the children do accept the idea of a separate species, how will you tell them what the species is?"

Cassidy laughed. "Our own writers did make us out as strange, didn't they?"

Obeah shook his head. "Cassidy, you're focusing on the mildly amusing and not on the problems. Our children have been indoctrinated by now."

"Your prejudice is distressing, Obeah."

Obeah shook his head. "Sorry. I'm frightened for you and, of course, I, too, have had some difficult times with humans. I suppose I'm also frightened of what happens if we have to drop back into that culture."

"But we have humans here, Obeah. I've never heard of any trouble." His legs were starting to twitch again.

Obeah tilted his head slightly. "You're not being very logical. The humans here joined us because, before the Membrane, they had close friends or family who were gentem. Or they were simply known as supporters of diversity and the environment and were invited. Some humans are progressive, of course. In addition, quite frankly, they aren't the majority of the population, and that does make a difference. The majority here consists of what would be freaks on the other side: us."

Cassidy shook his head and found himself once again tracing the growth lines of the wood in the table. Most of his adult life had been in this society, after the Membrane. He was grateful for that, he had to admit. He felt a nudge of worry about how life would change if Beta Earth disappeared. He smiled at Obeah. "Thank you for your care. I'll go prepare now and talk to you tomorrow."

Obeah waved his hand in the air, a gesture of dismissal and, perhaps, disgust.

Cassidy ran to the lab, then changed his mind about getting to work immediately, and he took a run up the path that led up along the Dungeness River, past what used to be the hatchery, and on through woods. The air, crisp and scented with cedar and distant snow, fed his energy and he picked up speed. No sound except that of a light breeze through the evergreens disturbed the evening. About thirty minutes into his run, he picked up Gulo, a resident wolverine, who joyfully greeted Cassidy and then joined him for the run out and back before silently continuing on his way.

Back in his lab, Cassidy finished his notes by pre-dawn. It was tricky. First, he imagined a summary of the gentem, the membrane, and their own connections, but too much information could overwhelm the children, especially if–as Cassidy suspected– all connection with Jasmine had been lost. If not overwhelmed, then dismissive. The best solution would be for the two children to connect. That alone would enable communication and, eventually, a long-term solution. Maybe. The spirals were a vital key. They *had* to be aware of the spirals on their palms–or at least partial spirals. If they could complete those, the implants would activate…but what if they hadn't pursued science degrees?

Cassidy decided he had to go for a simple focus, one he could encode in all portions of a computer's RAM and hard drives that had randomly oriented bits where the computer wasn't storing any information. If all of that changed rapidly, at once, to an exhaustively repeated patter, in might work. He'd ask the Council to trust him. Now he needed to trust himself.

He dozed off thinking about a Martin Luther King quote:

> Darkness cannot drive out darkness; only light can do that. Hate cannot drive out hate; only love can do that.

Chapter Four

Sunday, July 1, 2029

Steve Brillig's call to Eric came at 9:00 a.m. "Can you come by my office? I have information to give you."

"Really? On a Sunday?" Surprised, Eric arranged a one o'clock meeting after Steve said he'd be tied up until then. Eric arrived at 12:15. When the secretary ushered him into Steve's office fifteen minutes later, Steve was coming to the door to meet him. "Great to see you, even if apparently early, Eric! I'm just eating a bite—fab-meal sandwich—if you'd like to eat, too. Imagine being in touch two times in the same week! Glad you had some business—you apparently don't call otherwise. Come in and sit down so I can tell you about your individual. You pick interesting people."

Eric repressed his eager, "Tell me, tell me!" and settled instead for a polite response, trying to catch up on all Steve's statements and questions. "I'm surprised you're working on a Sunday, Steve. No, thanks on the sandwich. I'm sorry I haven't called. I become preoccupied." He settled into the plush office chair across from Steve's massive desk and waited for the next word barrage.

Steve laughed as he sat down, shuffled some papers. "Hey, Michael, seal the room, would you? No interruptions."

"Certainly, Sir," said Michael as he closed the door. At the same moment, a soft whir began pumping more cool air into the room.

"Our business doesn't take days off," Steve continued with barely a pause, "so we keep a rotating schedule for weekends. This is my weekend. So, if you're really sorry, you're going to call more often, right? We're all running, but we can take time to run into each other."

Steve, as always, spoke so fast, jumping from subject to subject, that Eric had to focus closely to track what he was saying. For the same reason, Steve was one of the most difficult people for Eric to read as far as emotions and needs were concerned. His mind worked in the same way a tornado tore through a town.

"Certainly, Steve." Eric couldn't wait any longer. "I thought she might be interesting. I didn't expect you to work this fast. What did you learn?"

Steve laughed. "Investigation gets easier when you pick someone rich and famous, Friend. Apparently, you didn't try to look her up on line." He opened a brown file and studied his notes. "The license belongs to a Vala Glen, born on February 29, 1999 to Caitlyn Woodard Glen and Walton P. Glen."

Eric did a poor job smothering his gasp.

"Problem?"

Eric shook his head. The fact that she was born the same day as his sister, Sarah, was not something to bring up. Nor was the slight twinge of disappointment that her name was Vala and not Sarah.

Steve looked back at his notes. "Father died when she was 16, but the mother—one of our local celebutantes—is still around. Apparently, the mother and daughter don't socialize with each other much though. The daughter isn't—" Steve hesitated, cleared his throat and leaned forward. "What I mean to say is that she isn't material for the social scene. She's…interesting."

Eric laughed. He'd rarely heard pauses in Steve's conversation. "You're certainly working hard at not saying something. Do you think you could be a little more specific?"

"Yeah. Well. I'm trying to be appropriate in how I describe her—remember PC?— but since it's you, I'll let you do the appropriate filtering. The woman is apparently odd, not mainstream, and nothing in her life ever has quite fit. To start with, in addition to her family wealth and a high-paying job, she has a substantial trust fund that pays her thousands of dollars a month by, apparently, an anonymous donor who gave the aunt the paperwork when the Glen woman was born—got that info from a clicktroll. No one knows who or why the donor was, apparently. Remember, I haven't done a deep dive on this." Steve looked up from his paperwork. "Don't you have some kind of trust like that, Eric?"

Eric nodded. He didn't think he could speak at that moment. His trust, too, had come from an anonymous donor. He focused on the wall of windows behind Steve. Mt. Rainier hovered on the horizon, smoky mist hiding the base as always. He tried to mentally perch himself on the very top, calm and away from all stress.

"Also, she's a—" Steve looked down at his notes. "—savant? That's the closest diagnosis anyone has had, apparently. I'm not sure how it's all related, but she's socially awkward, something that is apparently not uncommon among savants—sort of autistic but not in any way that inhibits her success. I'm not explaining this very well."

Eric held up a hand while telling himself to ignore the list of *apparentlies*. Long ago, Eric had decided that caution was part of Steve's nature, and he didn't want to say anything he couldn't take back. His conversation was always strewn with qualifiers. "Don't sweat it. I'm following. So I take it she's brilliant at something?"

"Right! She went through school like my kids went through diapers. She had her BS by age 15, Masters at 16, and first PhD at age 18 in 2017; two years later, she acquired a second PhD. She's currently working as a Senior Level Scientist—on a government-funded research grant—at the University of Washington in Ecology Research in Environmental Biology although her usual focus is apparently physics. She's won a number of awards for something-or-other, including the International Award in Biology for some work she did with air scrubbers, apparently, in and around waste disposal areas." Steve shook his head, then continued. "I asked someone to tell me exactly what she does, but I couldn't understand most of what they said. I finally asked them what her job description would be, and they gave me this." He handed Eric a piece of paper with a paragraph.

> A creative and synthetic thinker who augments, complements, or integrates research in aquatic ecology, biochemistry, disease ecology, terrestrial ecology, and/or urban ecology. She works within a vigorous, externally-funded research program.

"That's for her current project, apparently, although I wouldn't swear to it. Either within that project or something else, she's trying to figure out ways to clean up radioactive material with bugs–bacteria?–in ways that avoid any toxic by-products. Apparently, she's also doing work on some kind of connective waves between humans and other creatures within a quantum dimension; maybe she talks to animals. Or something like that. So, I still don't know exactly what she does, but she received government attention recently for her work with those industrial air scrubbers and chemical-free manufacturing. Again, I'm not sure what that means except that she's good at it. She was apparently involved with the air scrubbers that line our highways. And she was in on the toxic clean-up from that nuclear power plant mess in Japan in 2011. The university has received a lot of funding for her research. They even gave her a private arboretum near her lab where she claims to do research."

Eric shook his head at the rapid-fire mass of information and took a deep breath. Didn't Steve ever breathe? He'd ask Steve to write it down later. "What you're saying sounds like she's a well-educated, competent, and successful scientist. Where does the misfit issue come in?"

"Well, as I say, she's socially awkward. Or repressed. You fill in the blanks. She has lots of colleagues but no friends. No romance. No hobbies. No social activities. She was in-and-out of institutions all her teenage life. She hides away on the equivalent of a private park in the Alki Point area, apparently paid for with funds from that mysterious trust. She bought up property there that was in danger of being awash in 2025 when most of those beach homes and the lighthouse were destroyed in the remnants of Typhoon Megi."

"I remember that," Eric said. "That's when Seattle began moving uphill in earnest."

"Right. The point is, she's off grid except for a SmartHouse. No implant, no box, no personal links for her. Her house is wired and linked, apparently, only to University connections but nothing else– everything is GILS these days, including the University, so she's still connected to everything. Our office is wired up the wazoo. My IT guys tell me that all this linking means that everything is protected from loss or cyber-hacks, but I don't know how that can be when everything we do winds up being out there in the wind, so to speak. I wonder–"

"Steve, could we focus on Vala right now?"

"What? Oh, sure." Steve glanced down and shuffled papers again. "Apparently, she's had lots of medical tests and psychological evaluations but most of her files have been sealed. Doesn't seem to be anything wrong. Or right. Comes down to that savant thing, I guess. She has *spells* or episodes that come over her, especially when she was younger, apparently. The medical stuff is vague. I'd have to go deeper if you want that, but I can get it."

Eric was nodding. Whatever had happened at the market was probably a result of one of her *spells*. Epilepsy? Not treatable? And no wonder she hadn't responded well to the idea of a psychiatrist helping her; she'd probably had all of that sort of thing she could stand. By handing her his card, she'd probably thought he was one of those New Era Human Engineers, not worth their weight in smoke in Eric's opinion. But she obviously needed help.

"Does she live alone?" Eric asked.

"Yes. Except for a dog the size of my pod: a Rhodesian ridgeback named Serein. What the hell does Serein mean? And whoever heard of a Rhodesian ridgeback? And she is apparently close to her aunt, her mother's older sister, the only part of her family who has consistently supported her emotionally, as far as I can tell. Crazy, to have all those smarts and no real life, isn't it?"

Eric sat silent. He didn't bother to answer Steve's questions. Steve never waited for answers.

"Soooooo…" Steve said.

Eric blinked. "What?"

"Did you find out what you wanted?"

"I didn't know what I wanted, so I can't answer that. I was surprised that she was born the same day my sister was."

"You have a sister? I never heard of a sister when we were in the system together. How could you have a sister? Where is she?"

"She was stillborn. Do you know which hospital?"

"Your sister? I didn't even know…wait! Oh, right, I remember you used to believe that you needed to find her. Sorry, I'd forgotten."

"That's okay, Steve. It's been decades. I meant Vala though. Do you know where she was born?"

"Oh, sure," Steve said, checking his notes. "Swedish. In Ballard."

Eric focused on Steve. "That's where my sister was born." A twinge of what felt like hope was growing again. "Look, are you sure that this Vala was really the baby of the Glens? There wasn't an adoption or anything?"

"Well, it was apparently a caesarian, so I don't think it's a case of the woman not being the birth mother. Everything is fine with the records as far as I can tell, and the Glens have been her only parents. The father was apparently closer to the girl. As I say, the mother is, according to what I was able to learn from other people, aloof at best. Oh, she did change her name when she came of age from the birth name *Sarah*. She became Vala Sarah Glen."

Eric began to massage his forehead. His focus from the top of the mountain was spiraling away, like he was falling ... *Calm down, calm* DOWN, he told himself. Swedish probably had more births than any other Seattle hospital; but how many would there have been on that day? And how many of those would have been baby girls named Sarah? Why had she changed her name? How could she possibly have been switched with the Glen child? Or was she–

"Are you okay, Eric? Do you need to talk?"

Eric shook his head, stood. "No. No. Thank you, Steve. This entire matter is stirring up a lot of emotions for me. I don't even know this woman, but...something clicked for me with her."

"She *is* good looking." Steve grinned. "But–and I'm not saying it's impossible–but she's almost three feet taller than you, Buddy. Not that I'm saying size matters..." He grinned.

"No, not that. I have a mild obsession about my sister. Somehow, I feel that I was destined to care for her. I felt it as soon as I could begin to think. Then I found out she was dead. I've never believed it. This woman triggered all the emotional baggage I thought I'd unpacked." He shook his head again. The room seemed to dim slightly and he slowed his breathing, shut his eyes. He should just let this go. He opened his eyes, looked at Steve and said, "Could you get a sample of Vala Glen's DNA?" Eric couldn't believe he was asking that. Had some entity taken over his mouth?

Steve laughed. "Sure. I'll have someone pick up something from the university or somewhere that would have a sample if it's not already in the system. These days, DNA can be run off almost anything–one of my engineers claims he can cull it off a breeze that blows by someone. Say, look, why don't you come over and have dinner with Bekah and me tonight? The kids may be off doing something, so it may be low-key, but we could even get some of the natural food you like, you know, that live stuff–"

Eric shook his head. "No, Steve, thank you very much, but I don't think I'd be very good company. I need to glide a while. Thank you for the info. Let me know when you have the DNA. I'll ask Wyatt to run it for me."

"Well, soon then, right?"

Eric nodded and almost stumbled out of the office.

Instead of calling a driverless, Eric walked to his apartment, only a mile away. He needed to wear himself out, try to think about something else. With no patients, he had too much time on his hands. Maybe he'd schedule some time at the handball court. His entire body tingled. Fear? Anticipation? He could sense an exhilarating change in the air, change that was going to affect the world as he knew it.

CHAPTER FIVE

Monday, July 2, 2029

Vala wanted to spend a couple long days at the university to correlate her research with similar research being done in Sweden. She'd obtained government permission to work with the Swedish group last week, which was exciting. Getting permission from the Freedom Guards to work with any foreign scientists was getting increasingly difficult. She knew all her correspondence was monitored, but that was better than having no communication outside the country.

Monday and Tuesday would be the quietest time of the summer at the U. The summer quarter had started two weeks ago, but the holiday, made so long by coming on a Wednesday, would keep the grounds quiet and everywhere else noisy. The campus was always quieter than it used to be; in recent years, all the technology for work and study off campus had slowly drained away the energy, the vital presence of people at work as faculty or students. People were off at their own work stations, plugged in and linked up. Many professors, particularly the older ones, protested not having more interaction with students, but *distance learning* had been a strengthening trend all of Vala's life. As it happened, she was quite happy to keep students– and even faculty–at a distance; too many students were interested not in learning so much as getting credentials to demand big rewards, and most of their interactions were aimed at sucking up to anyone who could further their careers.

She had no students at the moment. All her work was focused on her grant projects. Her current work into extremophile bacteria stumped her. Although the bacteria she was studying were eating radwastes successfully, they were suddenly producing unexpected by-products that were contaminating water with neurotoxins, a major setback. The same thing had happened in a co-experiment in Sweden.

Vala had accepted the fact that people were going to keep polluting the world for power and profit. The only *solution* was going to be clean-up rather than prevention, a frustrating situation, but that just meant she needed to make the clean-up faster.

Aunt Char said the lack of thinking about the future didn't mean people were stupid, but Vala disagreed. Scientists didn't have time to go in wrong directions in trying to clean up ever-new messes, especially if the bacteria were going to mutate somehow. She had been part of the 2025 team that finally had cleaned up the last of the toxic waste from the nuclear plant disaster in Japan after the 2011 tsunami; they'd thought that they'd accomplished a major breakthrough with the bacteria and maybe with people. Then, unbelievably, Japan had rebuilt the nuclear plant. In the same place. With rising seas and worsening storms prevailing. Not stupid?

Vala had a couple coping mechanisms for functioning at the U. whether stupid people were around or not. Serein always went with her; she'd had him certified as a service dog through the university where, quite frankly, she could get just about anything she wanted. Simply stroking his coat helped calm her, and he was very patient with her erratic emotions. He always let her know if she needed to get exercise, and they would run together.

She also had an arboretum near her lab that was hers alone, filled with various plants and calming herbs. She had convinced the university board that this was necessary to her research, which it was but only because it allowed her to keep functioning without injuring someone.

Another people issue had arisen this morning when, on her 4 a.m. drive to the U, she was startled to realize that the same driverless had been behind or beside or immediately in front of her all the way. Of course, as always, traffic was heavy, including many fossil fuel cars. Supposedly those dinosaurs were going to be off the roads by

2025 but the projection now was 2035. In all the traffic, she could have been mistaken. Although she didn't see the driverless when she jacked into a slot, she felt apprehensive and that feeling was difficult to identify: legitimate or part of her diagnosed paranoia?

Later, in the hallway near her office, she spotted a young man with a skull cap pulled low over his eyes. He seemed to be studying a bulletin board. A student, even on the Fourth, wasn't that unusual, but her senses prickled. That increased when Serein paused and studied the young man, then growled so low that Vala felt more than heard it. She told Serein to stay alert but to be calm. If she saw this person again, she would call campus security.

Soon she was focused on work, and she managed to connect with the Swedish scientists. They went over data, with little result, for three hours. When they broke off, she headed for her Horticulture Isolation Lab and she saw the young man again. This time, he had obviously followed her. When she got to the door, she turned abruptly and marched toward him. His walk slowed, then he stopped in front of her, slowly looking up from his under-six-feet.

"Why are you following me?"

"I'm not. I was just on my way to…"

"Well, to where? This corridor dead ends right there." She turned and gestured toward her arboretum door. She turned back around just in time to see him sprinting back up the hall. Serein was willing to chase him down, and, of course, she herself could have caught him easily, but she didn't want to draw any more attention to herself than she had to.

She pulled out her cell, old-fashioned but still usable, and called campus security. She described the young man and the general location of places where she'd seen him.

Twenty-five minutes later, a security guard called her and asked her to come to his office to see if they had the right man. When she arrived, she went up to the young man sitting forlornly by the officer's desk. "Why," she asked while leaning over him, "are you following me?"

"I wasn't. I was just lost. I don't even know who you are."

"Does he have a reason to be on the campus?" Vala asked the officer.

"He says he was just here looking around. He's thinking about going back to school."

"If I see him following me again, I'm going to press charges." Without waiting for an answer, Vala left.

In spite of the confidence Vala had managed to convey, she was quivering inside. Her paranoia was well-known, and she had no doubt that the security guard was dismissing the young man without a word. On the other hand, this time she felt certain. The young man had followed her in the driverless and then on foot. What was he up to? Should she have kept quiet and waited to see how it would play out? Was this somehow connected to that doctor at the market? To the transparent man who came and went? To her insanity?

Unable to think about it clearly any longer, she almost ran to the arboretum. Eventually, with Serein's help, she was able to calm herself and finish more work on the project before returning home mid-afternoon. Once there, she found herself again feeling assaulted.

Someone had been there.

Nothing was disturbed, but Vala could sense a difference, a sensation supported by the raised hair on Serein's back as well as his emotional messages, most of which were in guard mode.

"Security footage, House," Vala demanded.

"For what time period?" House asked.

Vala specified the time she'd been out. Instantly, the holographic screen started playing back the recording, which was activated only by movement. There was some footage of a coyote and a raccoon, then there he was: the same young man, somehow in her yard and up to the back door. He rubbed something on the French door handle, then left. The time stamp indicated that his visit happened after the altercation at the campus.

"How did he get in the yard?" Vala asked House.

"He approached from the beach and into the garden," House said.

That was the one most-approachable direction. What could he have been after? He'd wiped something on the door. She switched off the tape and went outside with Serein. She studied the door handle. Nothing. "Is there something on this door handle?" she asked House.

"Negative."

Vala's mind stopped. She felt a chill. DNA? Skin cells, oil, even perspiration. It would all be there. Someone was, indeed, investigating her. She called Aunt Char and told her what she suspected.

"Vala, dear, why would anyone want your DNA? And, if they did, why not just access your records? Isn't all that on file for some of the government clearance you have? And your medical records?"

"My DNA is in some of my medical records, but I had those sealed after the last time I was…confined. Of course, the government has it, but just as a precaution, and those records aren't public. Of course, what isn't hacked these days?"

"There's no problem with your DNA, is there? I mean, why would anyone want it?"

Vala sighed. "There are minor differences in my DNA from *normal* DNA. However, no one at this point has any idea what any of it means or why. Are you familiar with Denisovans?"

"No. I don't think so. Should I know them?"

Vala laughed. "Think Neanderthal. These are all branches off the human ancestry tree. Most human DNA is similar and contains connections to Neanderthals. The first Denisovan DNA wasn't discovered until 2010; it has minor differences from the Neanderthals. Well, there is the same sort of difference in my DNA. Although some individuals have a smattering of Denisovan DNA, I have a lot. And no Neanderthal. Many people also have a smattering of a fourth source, but I have a fifth. A lot. We still don't know how a minor change will affect DNA as a whole. I've never been normal, have I?"

Char was quiet for a moment. "Dear, I'm not sure I understand most of what you're saying. Could you just tell me why it matters? And how you define *normal*?"

"Well, my DNA differences could explain some of the problems I've had over the years, for one thing, but not without a lot more study; no one is doing a study because as far as I've heard no other DNA like mine has appeared in any other living person. However, if someone found out–I don't know. Maybe for some kind of research?"

"If someone is interested in that sort of research, surely they'd approach you directly, Dear."

Vala slowly nodded. Perhaps she had just let her paranoia run a little wild. No one except one doctor and her mother knew about her DNA issues, and her mother probably didn't remember—or understand. She'd asked her mother to have a DNA test, but she'd replied that people of their class didn't worry about such things.

"You're right. I may be over-thinking this," Vala said.

"You should, however, call the police. That man was trespassing, and it sounds like he was also stalking you. For some reason."

"You're right again. I'll call my attorney and have her follow through."

Within a few hours, Vala's attorney, Leslie Cochran, called back.

"Only for you do I work on a long holiday, Vala—and into the late afternoon as well. Look, this young guy you caught on video works for a private investigative firm in town—Puget Investigations—PI for short. Cute, huh? It's a well-respected firm that normally does pre-trial stuff. I talked to the CEO there, Steve Brillig. Of course, he won't give up his client, but he promised me they were out of it. There won't be any more investigation on their part. He doesn't want static with me. Besides, he's a very savvy and ethical person."

"But what's to stop someone else from taking over?"

"Well, nothing. Except Brillig, the CEO, led me to believe that the client wanted it stopped, too. I don't know what was going on. It could be a head hunter. That's my best guess."

"Should I follow up in any way?"

"I don't think so. But keep an eye out. If anything else comes up, let me know immediately and I'll light some fires in some significant places."

Vala thanked Leslie and set the phone down. Then she picked it up again and called Char to invite her over for dinner. Some company would be good.

Chapter Six

"How could you have allowed this to happen? Professional! I wanted professional!" Eric heard yelling, felt the cramps in his fingers holding his phone. Wait…he himself was yelling. At Steve.

Eric took a deep breath, lowered his voice. "Steve, I'm sorry. I know you were just doing what I asked. I shouldn't have pushed it. I didn't think about the complexities for getting DNA."

"Normally, it's not that difficult, Eric. In fact, it's so easy that I didn't worry about sending out one of my youngest investigators. These days you can get DNA off almost anything the subject touches—or thinks about touching. I mean he could have simply swiped the handle of her pod or even her front gate as he walked by. I thought he'd fit in well at the university. Hell, no! He apparently decided to Sherlock it, follow her around for practice, the idiot. So he followed her, got caught! Then he apparently decided to be sneaky and trespassed into her yard to get the DNA off her door handle, her back door, mind you, not even thinking about security."

"Look," Eric said, trying to interrupt.

"I swear, Eric," Steve said, rolling on, "I didn't realize how dumb this kid apparently is, but he's the son of a client…well, never mind. He's lucky the Glen woman isn't sending the dogs after him. Instead, she sent her lawyer after *me*, and that dragon-slayer calls. Leslie Cochran. A very high-powered woman with Gersh, Weisblum, and Hancock; they operate on an international basis. You remember when Mexico was set up as an Environmental Free State with the UN in 2021? Mexico had to set up increased border security supposedly to keep U.S. citizens from charging down there to live. Well, Cochran–"

"Steve, stop! I don't care about that. Please tell me about Sarah. I mean Vala." He cursed his obvious slip.

"Oh, well, sorry. I got off track. But even talking to Cochran has me–"

"Steve!"

"Right. Chill, Eric. Where's your patience? So, I promised her that I'd drop the matter. And I put the kid on office duty until the Antarctic ice sheet finishes melting."

"So this is the end of it then," Eric said. He'd gone too far. He'd never have a relationship with Vala. "Did you tell the lawyer who I am?"

"Of course not!" Steve sounded hurt. "I did tell her that my firm was out of it and that my client wanted it stopped. Apparently–"

"Good. Good. I shouldn't have started it."

"So you don't want the DNA sample?"

"No!" Eric said. Then, almost immediately, he heard himself saying, "Yes. Yes, I do, but no more investigation. If you've already got the sample, I may as well follow through." Eric's head hurt with the yes/no arguments running through his head, with the ethical barbed wire that was cinching into his stomach. He should go see a good therapist; that's what he'd recommend for someone else. But first, he really needed to look at that DNA. Then he could commit himself to an institution. "I'll come by your office and pick it up now. Is that okay?"

"Sure," Steve said, then added "Do you want to have dinner with me? Bekha and the kids are visiting her parents in Arizona, trying to get some relief from the constant smoke in the air. Our daughter's mask doesn't seem to help her much even with nanobot assistance in clearing her system. I was going to go over to the Onion. They still have wait staff and live food. I know you like live food, yes?"

Steve's voice had softened, sounded wistful. Eric could tell he was lonely. "Sorry to hear about the family, Steve. That sucks. I'm afraid our technological cures aren't ever going to keep up with problems if some prevention isn't taken. Anyway, dinner sounds great." Eric tried to sound enthusiastic. He really just wanted to get the DNA sample and arrange to have a profile run–or destroy the sample and seek counselling. On the other hand, he needed to do some friend maintenance.

After a fairly relaxed dinner with Steve, Eric felt better. Talking with a friend wasn't that different from talking with a therapist.

As they were having after-dinner coffee, Eric said, "Steve, thank you for all your help and staying with me on this mess. I've been obsessive. I feel as though this is both urgent and significant to my life, and I don't know why. I've dropped into some sort of OCD loop."

Steve shrugged. "Remember that time I just had to investigate that transit accident, the one that was connected to no one and nothing in my life? The one that apparently had no unresolved issues? You spent a lot of time listening to me as I worked through that."

"And you ultimately tracked down the person who really caused that accident, bringing closure to the driver's family."

"Yeah. Well, I think I understand what you're going through. Trust your gut. We can't know everything in our heads. If you stay open, sometimes instinct tells you what needs to be done. That's what you told me. Apparently, it was good advice."

Eric sighed heavily. He felt as though he'd just been forgiven for something.

"Look," Steve said. "Your job is helping people. It's what you do. I suspect that the compassionate part of you is zeroing in on something that this woman needs. I'm betting on you for ferreting out whatever is needed and then using it ethically. I know about that. I've built a helluva good business on that principle. And I know you. I'd trust you with everything except my wife."

"Thanks, Steve."

"On the other hand, do watch yourself. I got the impression when dealing with her lawyer, that this Vala Glen's apparently a stony-hearted lady. I wouldn't want to be in battle with either her or her lawyer...or her dog. And the kid investigator said she went after him like a Balrog."

"I'll keep a low profile," Eric promised.

Instead of going home after dinner, Eric went to Wyatt Jennings' house, even though it was almost 11:00 at night. Wyatt was a geneticist and historical anthropologist at the University of Washington; he'd been the third member of their inseparable group in getting through the foster system together. Eric had the wipe the kid investigator had used in a plastic bag, and he had his own cheek swab in a test tube. When he got to Wyatt's box, he rang the bell and tried to be patient.

Wyatt, wearing a robe, opened the door. "Slicks and clones, Eric, is this some kind of emergency?"

"No, not really. But I wanted to ask if you would please run these DNA samples for comparisons as soon as you possibly can. I know it's a huge favor, but I need to get this issue resolved so I can go back to behaving normally. Normally for me anyway."

Wyatt chuckled. "Well, you *do* sound a little wigged. And you may not be the most normal person I know, but you've been the most helpful to me. I couldn't find it in myself to be there for you as I should have been in high school even though you were there for me, but obviously it's never too late. Literally. Drink?"

"I'd take some water. I've been dehydrated. Keep forgetting to drink."

As they sat at the kitchen table with water for Eric and bourbon for Wyatt, Eric again thanked him. "I know that using university equipment isn't a given, Wyatt."

"No problem. We've got a forensics class coming to the lab Thursday. I'll get everything set up for your samples tomorrow and run them. Then I'll have something to show them on Thursday when they arrive. Students are fascinated by DNA; they think it will provide direction in their lives or set their destiny for them. People have replaced palm reading and astrology with misapplied science. Of course, genetic engineering is the rage."

"I guess nothing can predict destiny, if there is such a thing," Eric said, partly to be agreeable but a part of him felt that *destiny* was the thing that he was pursuing. He'd been destined to take care of his sister–hadn't he?

"People need something to give them a sense of security or something to blame." Wyatt took a long drink.

"Listen to you sounding all psychobabble."

"I learned from you."

Eric finished off his water and asked, "So how long will it take, do you think?"

"The analysis? Not long. These days, DNA is as easy to run as a telephone number. But doing a full profile takes a little longer. As I say, I'll finish things up in the lab to have it ready for Thursday's class. Since this isn't an official request, and I don't have to document everything, I can have the basic information for you tomorrow late or the day after, depending on how things go. Wednesday night or Thursday if you want. This doesn't need to be admissible in Court, right?"

"Right. It's just basic comparisons for me to see what relationships, if any, you find."

"Piece of cake."

Wyatt's low energy was banging on Eric's mind for attention. "Anything working out between you and Nona?"

Wyatt leaned back in his chair, took another long drink of bourbon, re-filled his glass. "No. She says she needs something else in her life, something more. She's right, Eric. All I can seem to get passionate about is the lab, the work with DNA, and genetic engineering right now. There's something significant, just out of reach that just may make things better for people. For the world. I'm convinced we can use DNA to reduce the stress, the competitive nature, the violence … a vast amount of information is stored in DNA, Eric, and we understand only a tiny part. There are still missing links. If we can understand our own DNA, we can improve humanity and stop all this world-wide destruction. Not in the sense that the students want to claim to be something their not. And not that anyone agrees with me. One more cut on funding, and I'll be out on the street with hat in hand."

Eric expressed his condolences and then asked about Nona again. But Wyatt wasn't listening any more. He was off into that *better future* and how it could be had. Eric knew why Nona would feel excluded. He reached out, grabbed Wyatt's arm and gave it a light shake. Wyatt looked at him as though he'd forgotten Eric was there. After saying goodbye, Eric left, making a promise to himself that he'd get back in touch with Wyatt and arrange time for a long and bourbon-free talk.

CHAPTER SEVEN

Monday night, July 2, 2029

By the time the last of the rösti casserole and greens were eaten and the dishes cleaned, Vala had relaxed, something that usually happened in Aunt Char's company.

"This is delicious, as always," Char said.

Vala smiled. "And there is pumpkin pie for dessert. I made it from some of the pumpkin I stored in the keeper last fall."

Char laughed. "We'll be the only people enjoying pumpkin pie for the Fourth of July." Her words were punctuated by a series of bangs that penetrated the closed-up house.

Vala frowned. "The noise has escalated since Friday. I hate this holiday. Tomorrow night, I'll burrow under the covers and tell House to blare white noise full volume."

Suddenly, white noise blasted past them. Aunt Char clapped her hands over her ears.

"Not now, you asinine plug of sewage!" Vala screamed.

The roar continued.

"House! Stop the white noise!"

Silence.

Char giggled. "That was exhilarating."

"I've got to get tech here. This is getting ridiculous," Vala said.

Char chuckled. "So you were saying?"

"Oh, just the noise. It won't stop for Wednesday or the weekend. I prefer a weekend with the Fourth, so at least it's a shorter holiday."

"Is it difficult for Serein?"

"Oh, no," Vala said, automatically dropping her hand to his head, near her leg as always. "He comforts me." She laughed. "It's tough on the wild animals, of course, and other domestic animals, too. Not to mention the environment. On the fifth of July every year, I walk before dawn to pick up garbage on the shore and floating in the surf. Since the full ban on plastic three years ago, there's less of that, which helps. Of course, non-polluting and noise-free fireworks have been available for decades, but people keep buying without thinking." She felt tension returning and added "Most people don't even know what the 4th of July signifies anymore. I heard a student tell another one it was to celebrate the end of slavery." She shook her head as if clearing it. "Let's not talk about people. I don't want to be depressed."

Char laughed. "You can't dump all people in one basket, Dear. I'm people."

Vala knitted her brows. "Are you sure? You don't act like people."

They both laughed, then Vala sobered as she remembered the day's events. "I don't think I'm people," Vala said, setting her fork down, her plate clean. "Remember I told you that my DNA is off a bit? Have you ever had your DNA checked, Aunt Char?"

Char shook her head. "Never had any reason to do so. You said your differences may be related to those episodes?" She finished her wine.

Vala nodded. "Maybe. I don't know. Nothing else has ever explained my existence. I'm not like Mother—or Father for that matter although he was always very loving and supportive of me. Unless I can develop a taste for designer clothing, Mother is always going to think I was switched at birth. She denies that we've ever had any Asian heritage except, maybe, for some wayward great grandparent." Vala paused, then said, "I just remembered Mother once asking if maybe I had 'mongolism'—can you believe it? If anyone is a different species, it must be Mother."

Char reached over and patted Vala's hand. "She *does* love you, Vala. She's not good at demonstrating affection. She never pursued any sort of academic life. She only knows what she knows. She's

72

intimidated by your intelligence and strength. She doesn't know how to relate to you."

"It doesn't matter." Vala stood abruptly. "I'll get the pie."

"Need help?"

"Sure. Ask House for whatever to drink. Wine? Coffee? Something else?"

"I think I'd just like coffee, dear. I had some wine with dinner, and I have to drive home soon. I brought over my old fossil. House, coffee, please."

Vala looked at the drink dispenser and saw nothing happen. "House, make that two coffees, one to Char's specification and one to mine, Ass."

As they ate pie, Char asked, "Are you still thinking about emigrating to Mexico, Dear?"

Vala nodded. "The South and Central American unified government has gained strength, and the system is working particularly well for scientists. Mexico is thinking about joining, too, and they have some excellent research facilities. The Guardians here keep limiting what I can discuss with other scientists and how I can publish my research, which limits how it can be developed by others." She paused, thinking about the three U.S. physicists who had disappeared into Guardian custody the year before.

Vala sipped coffee, then said, "Borders are ridiculous human constructs anyway. All they do is divide and weaken what we can accomplish."

"But didn't you say that you may be blocked from emigration?" Char asked.

"The U.S. government is trying to do so. I may have to leave first and file immigration papers later. Or I can always ask for asylum." Vala shifted the subject farther, into discussions about Aunt Char's work in hospitality. Probably no one was listening in. Probably. Vala resisted the temptation to fall into paranoia.

After they finished their pie, Vala opened the French doors, and they sat in the living room. A light breeze off the sound ruffled the glass curtains. The noise had abated.

Vala, slouching into her hanging rope chair looked thoughtfully into the garden where her fairy lights sparked golden among the foliage, almost like fireflies. The lights were powered through bacteria growth that interacted with natural light during the day. Of course, the bacterial fuel cells had been utilized for some time now, but Vala's process was utilizing the ground itself; although it was still in the experimental stage, the process worked beautifully in the yard. A memory of the tall, almost-invisible man came to mind.

"Did you hear me, Vala?" Char asked, her voice raised sufficiently that Serein sat up and watched her.

"Oh, I'm sorry. I was thinking about microbial fuel cells and how much more efficient my garden is with the natural environment producing power for lights and the fountain. Did you know that the fountain is part of my house water filtration system?"

Char laughed. "Okay. Anyway, I was wondering if you'd seen that man, the transparent one, again?"

"No, I haven't."

"You sound almost sad about it."

"It's odd. When I saw him, I wasn't afraid. Not like I am when I have an episode as I'd had earlier in the day. I felt solidly in place, and you know I've never had one of those detached episodes at home. I want to know what he wants. Serein saw him, too, but he wasn't concerned, either."

Char looked at the huge dog. "Well, he doesn't need to be concerned, does he?"

"But when a stranger comes around, you know how the hair on his back stands up even more, and he looks like he could charge at any minute. He didn't do that. He just *stood* there and conveyed calm messages. He even wagged his tail. A part of me hopes that it happens again, so I can figure it out."

"Well, I hope it doesn't. First you have that episode, then that stranger in your garden, then that detective person following you … all that needs to stop, so you can have some peace and quiet."

A boom shuddered through the room, and Vala laughed. "There will be no peace and quiet for any of us for a couple more days. Do people think they're *free?* Since protesting the Federal government was deemed illegal in 2020, more than two million people have lost their right to vote simply by not voting."

Char frowned. "True. Look, Vala…"

Vala looked closely at Char. "What? Is something wrong?"

Char stared into space, then looked down at her hands.

"Char, tell me." It wasn't like Aunt Char to be slow in speaking her mind.

"Dear, I've never brought this up because, well, it had no answers and no purpose. But with all your talk about DNA and see-through men and investigators, I think this might be important." She studied Vala with her head cocked to one side. Vala knew that look: Aunt Char was appraising Vala's attention.

Char nodded briefly as though satisfied that she had Vala's attention and then continued. "You remember that I told you an anonymous donor had set up the trust for you?"

"Of course, although I've always suspected it was you."

Char laughed. "I don't have that kind of cash, Dear, but if I did, it would be yours. However, I didn't tell you everything. It wasn't quite anonymous. That is, I met the woman shortly after your birth. She came to me in the waiting room and told me that she had paperwork that would guarantee your income for life to use as you saw fit, that it was all set up, and she wanted me to have the paperwork as the most *stable* person in the family; she had reservations about your mother, and she seemed to think you'd need both emotional support and the trust fund. She swore me to secrecy."

"You *met* her! I thought no one knew where it had come from!"

"Well, I honored her request for secrecy because the Trust was so very significant. But after all these years, hearing nothing, I can't believe it matters. Besides, with strange people investigating you, it did occur to me that maybe it's related. Could that detective's client be that woman or someone related to her, maybe relatives who want to break the trust?"

Vala leaned forward. She could feel the powerful pull of intrigue, something that always pulled her into research about anything she didn't know or understand. That curiosity fueled her scientific research. "What was she like?"

"She was a very small woman. Maybe 4'6", but slim and… well, elegant. Seen at a distance, you'd think she was tall. She was youngish—maybe early 30s or late 20s—with auburn hair and eyes that I've never forgotten—sort of amber with green and brown flecks that seemed to be in motion. She was deeply tanned, or had just naturally copper-colored skin. Anyway, that's how I remember her. Beautiful."

Vala leaned back. "That's it? That's all you know?"

"Yes. I sat there with my mouth open, as I recall, and she simply stood and walked away. I never heard from her again, but when I looked at the papers, I found the lawyer's name and visited him the next day. Everything was, as she'd said, in place and legitimate."

Vala stared into space. "I'm amazed you kept it secret all these years."

"It's not much, but there is one thing more." Char hesitated.

After a few moments of silence, Vala spoke quietly. "I can't think of anything you'd tell me from 29 years ago that would bother me now." As she said that, she realized she had tensed, but she added, "Or that would affect my love for you."

"Dear, when you were born, I was in the room with your mother. You had eyes that were startlingly blue, so light they were almost clear, like your mother's; your dad, too, had, startling hazel eyes, but not that blue. After that woman gave me the trust papers, I went to look at you. When you opened your eyes, I saw that they were that beautiful umber color that you have to this day."

"That's not possible," Vala said. "Eyes don't go from blue to brown after birth."

Char shrugged. "I mentioned something to a nurse who simply said that the record stated that your eyes were brown. I was the only one who had seen blue."

Vala stared into space. Aunt Char wasn't one to make mistakes about details. "What do you think it means?"

"I don't know, Vala. Probably nothing. Maybe something. I'm not sure it matters. That was a long time ago. Maybe I was just wrong."

Vala stood and walked to the French doors, stared out, almost wishing she'd see the tall stranger again. She turned to look at Char. "Char, would you consent to a DNA test, one to compare yours with mine?"

Char's eyebrows went up. "Me? Well … wouldn't it make more sense to get a comparison with your mother?"

Vala waved her hand in the air to dismiss the idea. "If you and I are related, it will show that. If I'm not related to you, I'm not related to anyone in our family. Besides, Mother already refused."

Char agreed and Vala took swabs from the two of them and put them in vials. After Char left shortly before midnight, Vala and Serein went for a run of about ten miles, through the park area and over parts of the Alki Trail that hadn't flooded. In spite of the smoke and various bursts of fireworks, it felt good to stretch out her muscles and run, something she could do freely only at night when her running ability wouldn't attract attention. Although the air was heavy, the concentration of pollutants was slightly less near the water where a breeze had picked up. She focused on silencing the continual wail of sirens and traffic sounds by having a dialogue with Serein about various scents and sounds. His skills helped her keep her own senses sharp.

The next morning at six, Vala called her friend and colleague at the U-dub, Wyatt Jennings. She had a feeling he might be taking advantage of the holiday to get some work done in his lab early in the morning. He was probably more obsessed than she about work, which meant they were often the only people in labs at odd hours.

He answered his cell almost immediately. After she asked him if he could run some DNA for her, he laughed. "Evidently, the Fourth inspires people I know to ask for DNA reports. I'm setting up to do just that for someone else this morning, and I can do yours, too, if you want to bring the samples in. A class is coming in on Thursday, so the more profiles to look at, the better, I guess."

"That would be great, Wyatt. I'm planning on coming in to my lab while it's quiet anyway."

"That's why I'm here. If it weren't for a combination of a slower summer and the holiday, I probably wouldn't be able to do the process this quickly. Is it for part of your research with bacteria?"

"No, Wyatt. Actually, it's personal."

"So you don't need documentation or special treatment?"

"No. Just a profile panel. I'll see you shortly."

After arriving at the campus, Vala and Serein went to Wyatt's lab, gave him the swabs, then spent a refreshingly peaceful day in solitude and quiet in her lab and arboretum. No one followed her or called. She saw only a few people walking on the campus.

Finally, about six that evening, she geared herself up for the trip home through the crowds gathering for their all-night parties. She was braced to endure the constant booming and whistling of fireworks. She had been tempted to sleep in the lab, but Serein's food was at home and, once there, she loathed the thought of going out again. White noise it would have to be.

CHAPTER EIGHT

Monday morning – July 3, 2029

Cassidy sat up and stretched. He blinked into the sunlight streaming in through the open door and tried to remember why he was at Obeah's table. Oh, yes, he'd worked all night in his lab and then come over to talk to Obeah about plans for the next trip. He must have dozed off, probably in mid-sentence. Judging by the angle of light, it was mid-morning, so he must have slept two or three hours. Obeah was reading a book and stirring something in a dish at the same time. "Is that food?" Cassidy asked.

Obeah turned, shook his shaggy head. "No. It's some tonic for Misha Tunic's horse. The animal has a cough and Murell has a formula that isn't quite working; I'm trying to add something a bit stronger to her mix. Of course, it may work for you, too. I'm not surprised you're hungry–and tired. You've been absorbed in your planning, probably not sleeping or eating at all since your return."

Cassidy stretched again and yawned. "I'm starved. Of course, I could go home and eat, but if you wouldn't mind–"

Obeah grunted and then began lifting eggs out of a basket on the counter. "An omelet will perk you up. I have fresh cheese and vegetables. Do you still feel confident about your preparations?"

"Yes, I think so." Cassidy stood and went over to watch Obeah. He'd never known Obeah to cook anything but omelets. "Can I help?"

"Make your tea," Obeah said.

"You want some, too?"

Obeah nodded, and Cassidy chatted while he brewed tea. "My information is brief but specific and to the point. I'm hoping I can convey the idea that the spiral-like patterns on their palms are important. If they'd just link..."

He paused and stretched again. "How long did I sleep?"

"Not long enough." Obeah walked to the table and studied the paper containing Cassidy's notes. "Your notes surprise me. The only focus is for spirals and hands and implants. Why not just tell them to link hands?"

"I don't want the idea to be dismissed as laughable. I want to make it personal and have it gradually work into their minds. I don't know what their training is. I don't know what they think about each other, if anything. But similar incomplete spirals on their palms *must* have caught their attention."

Cassidy shrugged. "In reality, with the family history of these two children, I don't think their interest in the sciences could possibly be repressed." Cassidy put the tea on the table, then went to the lab sink, splashed water on his face, and then realized he had no towel. "Uh..."

Obeah snorted and thrust a towel at him. "The principles of existence, you get. Think of a towel first? No."

"I'll try to get the information to them this afternoon."

"No, you won't," Obeah said flatly as he folded the omelet, flipped it, then slid it onto a plate.

"I won't?" Cassidy asked, while eyeing the omelet being placed on the table. He sat promptly.

"No. I forbid it. You haven't slept nor eaten adequately and while I consider that a marvelous omelet, it won't substitute for sleep or lack of food for the past two days. You can't make your journey without me, and I won't cooperate until you've slept. You may still die, but I will not be culpable. Rest. Go out to run and rejuvenate yourself. Meditating would be a good idea."

Cassidy fidgeted. Obeah was correct: Cassidy needed to have Obeah's cooperation, both for the potion he must drink to ease his body into sleep and to support his mental focus as he maneuvered through the Membrane. Until the children could be linked and cooperative from the other side, Cassidy's hold on any reality–and his life–was tenuous at best once he was little more than a photon. Nonetheless, the urgency pulled at him; the Council would continue with plans. "Perhaps you don't understand–"

"Flummery! I understand just fine. No discussion." He picked up the paper again. "I see you have the equation for the Archimedean spiral here. Why not just picture a spiral?"

"The spiral on each palm is incomplete until their hands are clasped, activating the implants. It may not have occurred to them that those marks even represent spirals but with all this put together, how could they miss the concept? I'm moving ahead on the basis that for some reason, somehow, both children were separated not only from each other but also from Jasmine."

Cassidy studied the omelet for a moment thinking about a saying of his father's about having to break eggs to make omelets. Was that akin to the "ends justifies the means"? He shrugged and shoved a forkful of food into his mouth. "Anyway," he mumbled around a full mouth, "they may know nothing about themselves or their situation. They may even be close-minded to new ideas; they've been immersed in the human culture all their lives. I have to be simple. Anyway, I have a better chance of inputting an equation than a picture." He swallowed, then continued talking. "I wish we'd have left the children in Europe. I think the cultures there tend to be less ethnocentric, more open-minded."

"All cultures are ethnocentric. Don't we also think our way is best?"

Cassidy chuckled. "I suppose." He wasn't totally comfortable with equating human culture with that of the gentem. "Anyway, I can't account in a brief message our history or culture or our datea about LifeForce. Human science hadn't even considered a unifying field when we last had contact."

Obeah sat down and watched Cassidy scrape his plate. "You need to learn to eat to appreciate the food," Obeah grumbled. "So what happens if the children, as you say, connect?"

"We'll have similar patterns on each side–Tandra and me here; Eric and Sarah there. That will activate the obelisk. That, in turn, will open the portal between the meadow and wherever the children are when they connect, hopefully in a stable and private environment." He paused, started to rub his lower lip with his thumb, stopped himself. Tandra said the habit was a holdover from sucking his thumb as an infant.

"In theory," said Obeah into Cassidy's silence.

Cassidy nodded. He knew the theoretical didn't interest Obeah much. "It's all theory until we can do it and then repeat it, right? I was just wondering if maybe the reason that we're having occasional intrusions is that some particles are linking. What do you think?"

"You're asking *me?*" Obeah said.

Cassidy shrugged, stood, put his hand on Obeah's forearm. "Thank you, Obeah. That was good. I feel strong enough, really–"

"No. If you rest, eat, and exercise today, talk to me. Tomorrow, you can try it *if* you sleep."

Cassidy shrugged. "I don't think I'll be able to sleep," he said, stretching again and then finishing the last of the tea he'd fixed.

"After that tea takes effect, I think you'll sleep well," Obeah said, then added, "If I were you, I would go lie down now so you'll not wind up sleeping on the floor. I'm not going to carry you."

Even as Obeah spoke, Cassidy felt the first waves of sleep start to overcome him. "Why, you tricky old wolf," he muttered, staggering over to the bed in the corner and collapsing. "And in the tea *I* made, too!"

When Cassidy woke, he instantly noticed how refreshed he felt. Obeah knew just which herbs would not only put him to sleep but would also allow him to wake without feeling tired and fuzzy. Judging by the twilight in the room, he'd slept soundly for several hours. He was ready for anything.

Then he saw Alarick Kolos sitting at the table next to Cassidy's page of notes. He reluctantly sat up. "Hello, Alarick."

Alarick turned to face Cassidy, nodded abruptly. "Obeah said you'd be waking soon. Have a good rest?"

Cassidy nodded, stood and went to join Alarick at the table. "Been looking over my notes?"

"Yes. Can't say it makes much sense to me. Quotes? Are you trying to achieve a connection or teach literature?" Alarick shrugged then held up his hand, palm out. "Don't start explaining it to me. As you know, I'm a shaper. I can hold something and tell what it needs to be and how to help it become that, but papers full of ideas, no! Doesn't look like much on which to pin our hopes for world reconciliation and salvation."

"This is focused on the children's history." Cassidy pointed out the details for the spirals. "They have to realize that they must connect the spirals. Unfortunately, they may not even know that the marks on their palms *are* spirals. I'm hoping they've noticed and are curious about the marks on their palms."

Alarick slowly shook his head. "And I still don't know why you're bothering." He flicked his fingers against the paper.

"I've told you: because I have to believe there is an alternative to violence. It's part of who I am and what I believe our culture to be. Violence goes against our principles and values; it goes against the LifeForce, that imperative of creation, itself."

"You really mean that, don't you?" Alarick stood, threw his shoulders back and tipped his head back to glare up at Cassidy. "You're still young, of course. This *LifeForce* you talk about is irrelevant. We are who we are, and I see no reason to suddenly call it by some scientific gibberish. LifeForce. Unifying Field Force. Marina throws out terms like that, too. And how will you convince humans? You weren't there when we were trying to integrate, to merge, with humans, when we tried to convey the importance of connecting with the natural world. They don't even like each other, categorizing each other by color, spiritual beliefs, disabilities, ages, geographical location, and even gender or height. They are seriously flawed."

"Alarick, you connect to the LifeForce all the time. It's how you function as a shaper, why you've lived long. Do you think you're special, that this is magic outside of how all forces work? One of our complaints was that humans thought they were superior, god-like. It seems to me that your condemnation is the same sort of thing."

Cassidy regretted his words immediately. He should have offered understanding.

Alarick turned and strode to the door where he stood looking out with his back to Cassidy. "Perhaps it is. Perhaps I'm fed up with what they have done, in spite of all the warnings, to each other, to other species, to the world."

"What you're proposing could wipe out humans…and do so painfully."

"You're forgetting that they're already going through that. They've poisoned their world's air and water. They've produced chemicals that are deadly, causing cancers and deterioration of their bodies and minds. They continue to maintain lifestyles that use up resources and create pollution. Do you know that when the Membrane was put up, they were still debating climate change? They were still drilling and mining for fossil fuels. They are stupid."

Cassidy stubbornly shook his head. "So are rats. Would you exterminate rats?"

Alarick laughed, a rough and harsh sound. "On some days, when they nest in my cupboard and stink up my food, perhaps I would. Well, do what you will. It's going to make no difference." Alarick walked out the door without looking back.

Cassidy stood, muttering, "And he talks about humans having closed minds."

"It's true that Alarick dislikes humans."

Cassidy jerked around to see Obeah by one of the shelving units. "Have you been here all along?" he asked Obeah.

"This is my place."

Cassidy knew he'd have to be happy with that answer and said nothing.

Obeah smiled. "Would you have been more compassionate if you had known I was here? Alarick has been developing almost as long as I. We have a longer perspective and perhaps a greater frustration than those of you who have come on the scene within the past century." Obeah shrugged. "And you are no less stubborn than either of us. So now you'll eat and then you'll go on a run to clear your mind and stretch your body into relaxation, and then embark again on your mission."

Cassidy ate enough to satisfy Obeah. In spite of feeling like a stuffed squash, he obediently went on a run. Dark had settled in. Within minutes, he heard Gulo's *Race?* Cassidy was taking it easy, so Gulo could outpace him, which was good for Gulo's ego.

To Blyn? Cassidy silently asked, and Gulo was off in that direction, with his hump-backed gait. Fourteen miles was a long distance for a wolverine to run at one time at top speed, so Cassidy would catch up to him by the return even if he didn't speed up. As Cassidy ran, his head cleared, he relaxed, and for the last four miles he picked up the pace, really stretched himself out, reaching the starting point just seconds after Gulo.

I won.

You did! But I'll get you next time, Cassidy answered.

Back at Obeah's, Cassidy again studied the paper.

"How will you put this into a computer?" Obeah asked.

"All I need to do is translate my information into bits. It's like any code. The tricky part is entering and then leaving a computer system. I've never done that; I'm not sure anyone has. The last research I have from human scientists indicate they were *thinking* about being able to transfer consciousness into a computer, but their material reads more like wishes than anything practical. It should be no different than firing the neurons in my brain…maybe…which I've learned to do with excellent accuracy; we had to do that to create the membrane." He paused, shook his head. "My computer is self-aware, is learning all the time, but I doubt humans have achieved that yet."

He looked at Obeah whose eyebrows were dropped down so low over his eyes that they'd almost replaced them. Since Obeah said nothing, Cassidy continued. "The problem is that gentem consciousness, or human consciousness for that matter, is much more complicated than even the quantum computer, because it has more states than qubits provide. Humans think that the physical brain itself is the key to consciousness, but that creates more questions than it answers. Starting with the LifeForce as the source for all consciousness, Marina and I have reached the conclusion that the brain is just a tool, like a computer, that is developed and trained to respond as needed for life to function, a reaction to the unifying field force. Much of what is involved doesn't fit within limitations–you know: emotions, intuition, the personality itself. It's what continues when a gentem individual ceases to utilize a body."

Obeah shook his head. "I think you're treading into sacred spaces that should be left alone, Cassidy. Anyway, if some pollutants are seeping through into our existence–whatever it is–why can't you get a piece of paper into theirs?"

"Well, I might be able to do so if I could find the right place at the right time where some leakage is occurring. We don't understand the how and why of that leakage; if we did, we'd fix it. I don't even have a working theory. Once we can open a portal, we may be able to better understand. Maybe the children are part of that key. However, at the moment, I'd have no control over where the information would appear. Could be in the middle of the ocean. If, in essence, I'm there with them and I can key into their personal electronic devices, I can make sure the information arrives in the right place at the right time for the right people." After a moment's silence, he added, "I hope."

After Cassidy took a few minutes to meditate and relax, focusing on what he planned to do, he went to the clinic cot, drank the concoction Obeah had formulated to help allow him freedom from his body, and lay down. The process was slow. It would be morning before he would become aware of separation, of joining the flow of light while staying focused on the faint link of the incomplete implants of the children.

CHAPTER NINE

Tuesday/Wednesday, July 4, 2029

Tuesday night, Eric went to bed, got up, went to bed, got up and worked on his computer to find DNA information. He looked up Vala on GILS, then shut down the computer abruptly when he reminded himself he was prying, maybe stalking. He went back to bed, then got up at 3 a.m. to pace around his box.

Finally, he left to go for a walk, stopping at the Night Owl Coffee Shop, a place where he was well enough known to be greeted by name when he walked in. He considered calling some patients, just to check in and see how they were, then he realized that was ridiculous. He returned to his box. Finally, by ten, he could wait no longer, and he called Wyatt.

"Eric, I'm just about finished. Give me an hour. I'd like—"

"I'll be there in an hour," Eric interrupted. He looked at his watch twice in five minutes and then called a driverless. So what if he arrived a little early? It was better not to risk congestion issues today when people were still in celebration mode. He missed the era when people would sleep late with hangovers after celebrating; now the biobots cleaned up the bloodstream almost as soon as someone got high. "Okay," he told himself in the driverless, "I'm rationalizing. It's not a problem if I know I'm rationalizing. Sure I feel guilty, but that's normal."

"Did you make a request, Sir?" the driverless asked.

"Oh, no. No. No, I didn't." He closed his eyes, leaned back and focused on quieting his thoughts.

At the university, Eric almost ran to Wyatt's lab. Wyatt was adjusting some machine that was roaring like turbobots when they were sweeping skies over an event. Eric walked over and stood near Wyatt and waited, tapping his toe gently to keep from yelling. Patience. He was in no rush.

Wyatt finally switched off the machine, turning at the same time and then jumping when he saw Eric. "Frack, Eric! Couldn't you at least stand farther away and give me a chance to see you at a distance?"

Eric laughed. "Sorry. Didn't think of that. Would have been easier on my ears, too. What is that thing?"

"It's a piece of junk impersonating a fume hood. I was just mixing some chemicals, and I wanted to get rid of the fumes. I've been after the Dean about the thing for months. It's supposed to be silent. More or less. I don't think it's even cleansing the air as it roars." He threw his hands out to his sides. "Look at this place. It's archaic! We were supposed to have this room totally vented automatically by now. All I hear is that funding is tight. Of course, it's tight—we have more administrators than students." He slapped the hood control.

"Other labs get more equipment than they want, but I'm not working with the right sorts of genetic engineering. We need to sculpt our unborn children and figure out how to easily kill our enemies. Who wants evolutionary knowledge?" He stomped over to a lab table and plunked on a stool. "What I ought to do is call HR and complain about the noise level. It exceeds all safety standards ..."

Eric chewed on his lower lip and kept silent while he allowed Wyatt to vent his frustration, almost as nosily as the fume hood vented the lab, then re-chew it and spew again. Eric had a Fourth of July patient after all. After about five minutes of bashing the administration, the state education board, the governor, and somebody named Justin, Wyatt sighed and shrugged.

"Well, what the hell, right? At least they haven't cut the lab altogether. Yet. That's probably next. What do we need science for? We have the frigging computers. Students think they have all they need because they can search for genetics on GILS and come up with a passing paper. Who do they think is putting information up? Rats?"

Eric nodded. "I know the economy is hitting everyone. And you're right that the money flows to fads and government programs rather than needs. It's the early 2020s all over again. AI has taken over most service jobs, and the training programs aren't keeping up. U.S. exports are down to nothing since the 2020 tariff wars, and India, China and Mexico have non-polluting technology that far surpasses the U.S."

Wyatt groaned. "So it's just going to get worse."

Eric broke into song:

Soft kitty, warm kitty, little ball of fur...

They both half-sang the rest of their favorite TV song from when they were kids together in foster care. When they finished, Wyatt proclaimed, "Perfect! We've still got it, Squirt!"

Eric felt like he was ten again. Then Wyatt said, "Well, you're here about those results, aren't you? I want to talk to you about that."

Eric felt a flicker of worry, eroding his sense of well-being. "Is there an issue?"

"No, Not with the process. I have the panels—"

"What are you doing here?" The question sliced through Wyatt's voice.

Eric and Wyatt both looked toward the door. Vala ducked and entered, her hair brushing the top of the doorjamb. Eric felt as though he were shrinking, but it wasn't as much in comparison of height as absolute dread of encountering Vala here, like this, about to talk about her DNA. He couldn't run out the door. She filled it.

"I work here," Wyatt said.

"I meant *Doctor* Kine," said Vala.

Could a voice have the power to kill? Eric felt struck down. The way she said his name reminded him of the tearing metal roofing he'd once heard in an earthquake. If not the door, could he get out a window? No windows—

After a moment's pause, when Eric didn't speak, Wyatt answered. "Eric is an old friend of mine. We were in foster care together."

"You're not stalking me then? You didn't hire someone to follow me?"

Those were difficult questions, Eric thought.

As Eric continued to stand quietly by Wyatt's side, Wyatt again answered. "Eric? A stalker? Vala, something has gone amiss here. Eric is the last person who would do anything–"

"Wait, Wyatt," Eric said. Wyatt shut up immediately, relief flooding through him. As he spoke, Eric realized he had his hands out in a gesture that would normally be used to ward off an attack. He forced himself to lower them to his sides. Vala probably wouldn't hit him. "There has been a series of miscommunications, I think. Could we just sit down over coffee and–"

"No. No need. If you're a friend of Wyatt's, I'll take his word for it. It's just probable that your presence is coincidence. Look, Wyatt, I was coming by to pick up the panels, but it can wait."

"I've got them!" Wyatt said, waving his hands in the air above his head. "Look, I want to talk to both of you anyway, so please stay. I don't know what's going on, but I'm concerned about an error I may have made somehow. Maybe. Or not. I'm hoping you two can help me out." He walked to his desk and picked up two folders. "This whole thing has been oddly synchronous, but now it's getting spooky–By the way, you two know each other, right? No introductions needed?" He smiled.

"None needed," said Vala firmly.

Eric shrugged. He had a feeling that this wasn't going to end well, but he also felt certain that anything he tried to say was going to be squashed under Vala's firm foot.

"Right," Wyatt said looking from one to the other, clearly baffled, then down at the folders in his hand. "I've gone a couple years without anyone wanting DNA panels and then you two walk in on the same weekend. Since I have that class coming in tomorrow, as I told you both, it was good timing. But the results are puzzling."

"Did you find we're related?" The question popped out before Eric had the conscious thought to shut up. He regretted it immediately, almost slapping his hands over his mouth, but didn't try to repair the misstep.

Vala was giving him the triple-O, both eyes and mouth perfectly rounded. He'd never seen anyone do that outside of cartoons.

Wyatt laughed. "Why? Because you look alike?" When Eric didn't smile back, Wyatt sobered and continued. "No. That's just it. No one is *related,* but two of these share atypical sequences and one isn't even human. I've never seen another panel that showed the atypical sequences, so ... can you two fill me in on these? I'm wondering if I made a mistake or if I mixed material."

"Not human?" Eric said, shaking his head. He'd been called a lot of things, but–

"You *were* the one who hired that detective. You *are* stalking me! Wyatt, call the police now!"

Vala's accusations ripped into Eric's already guilty conscience. He was sure his life essence would simply evaporate. He'd never fainted in his life, but he suddenly felt as if that fume hood were roaring again, and he knew he had to sit down. "Please," he managed to say before he dropped into the chair by the desk. "Please," he said again. He lowered his head to his knees and focused on breathing. "I'm sorry. Need...a minute."

Eric became aware of Wyatt squatting down in front of him. "Are you okay? Should I call for med-eval? Is it your heart?"

Eric was shaking his head. "No. Light-headed. My own private obsession." He looked up at Vala again. "Please? Listen? Just for a moment? Please?"

The expression on Vala's face softened slightly: her lips became less thin. The twin bulges of her jaw lessened. Then Serein walked over, sat by Eric and put his paw on Eric's knee. Vala's posture sagged slightly. "All right. One minute. If Wyatt stays here to witness."

Wyatt pulled another chair over and the three of them sat in a semi-circle around the desk. Vala kept pushing her chair back. Eric knew he'd better talk soon or she'd scoot right out the door. He took a deep breath and spoke. "Since I'm the bad guy here," Eric said, "Let me start."

He had no idea where to start except the beginning, so he talked about his feeling that his purpose in life was to care for his sister in spite of being told she'd died. "My parents even took me to the graveyard, showed me her tombstone: the Virgin Mother holding a baby. I stood there looking at that grave, and I knew my sister wasn't there. They took me to therapy where I learned to say what people wanted to hear but not what I felt."

So now that he'd proved he was crazy obsessed, how did he explain? He swallowed hard, cleared his throat and began. "When I saw you, Vala, I knew that *you* are my sister. I simply knew it, and when you left abruptly, obviously distressed by my card, I couldn't figure out what to do. I know it sounds crazy, and I know how to recognize obsession. That's not what this feels like. Although," he added as he looked directly into Vala's somewhat too-direct stare, "I understand how you could disagree with that."

Vala just stared at him for a moment, then shook her head. "Why me? I mean, why in one brief encounter did you suddenly decide, *she's the one?*"

Vala's tone had softened and the emotions Eric read were more curious than furious. Maybe. He felt the merest flutter of hope. "When we met in the parking lot, I felt a connection with you. I couldn't understand why you suddenly turned distant. Later, when I learned about your past with doctors, I understood."

"*That's* what I want to know: how did you learn about me?"

Eric looked back at the floor again. "You have to understand that I *needed* to find out. I've never done that before."

"Well," said Vala, "*that's* not answer."

Eric felt her slipping away again. "Wait. I'll tell you, but please hear me out. I wrote down your license. I asked a friend of mine, Steve Brillig, who runs an investigative service to find out something about you. He didn't pry!" Eric added quickly. "You're, as Steve said, something of a celebrity. Everything was in the public records."

"Eric, none of this sounds like you," Wyatt said, shaking his head. "What were you thinking? And how did you get Steve to go along with you?"

"I wasn't thinking. I was reacting. Gut reaction. Sometimes you have to follow your gut. Some of what I learned stunned me." He looked at Vala again. "You were born at the same hospital on the same day and at the same time as my sister. Your given name at birth was Sarah even though you changed it later on. My sister's name was Sarah. Why did you change your name to Vala?" He looked up at her and waited.

She stared at him again as though she were looking at a microbe on a slide.

"What is it? You're puzzled by something," Eric said.

Vala shook her head. "No. It's just your eyes. They're familiar, almost as if I remember them—no, someone described them to me." She sat up straighter and shook her head. "Never mind that!" she said, her tone hardening again. "My DNA was *not* public record."

"Too much coincidence," Eric said, shaking his head. "I had to know for sure."

"I should think anyone could look at the two of us and negate the idea that we're brother and sister. But no, you had your detective follow me and when that failed, had him go to my house to steal something."

Serein whined and scooted closer to Eric. He put his hand on the dog's head and immediately felt a little calmer. "I swear," Eric said, "that I didn't mean to disturb you. Steve assured me that getting DNA was simple. When he called to say that you'd been alarmed, I told him to stop everything immediately. At that time, he already had the cloth used on the door handle. When he asked me if I wanted it, I said *no* ... "

"But you didn't stick to it." Her flat tone pronounced him guilty. Serein whined again. "Okay, okay. I'll try," Vala said to Serein.

"What?" Wyatt said.

Vala shook her head. "Never mind."

Eric shook his head. "No. I didn't stick to it. I gave Wyatt that sample and my own."

"So that's the story behind Eric's DNA," Wyatt said. "What about yours, Vala?"

"I don't think I have to tell you that. I didn't steal it or obtain it without permission, unlike some people."

Eric felt himself shrinking again.

"That's fine," Wyatt said. "But considering the results, we may prefer to have everything out in the open."

Vala took a deep breath, hesitated, then shrugged. "During a conversation with my Aunt, certain information came up that sounded odd. We decided to do a DNA test of the two of us to confirm our connection."

Wyatt was scratching and pulling on his ear lobe furiously.

Eric turned his focus on Wyatt while feeling some disappointment at the brevity of Vala's information. However, he already felt guilty and until he could figure out more of his own feelings, he decided to wait and see what Wyatt had to say.

Wyatt opened his file folders and separated the papers in the two into four piles. "What we have here are the profiles on three people and one canine. The canine, Eric, came from the cloth that you say was used on the door handle."

Vala started laughing, low-throated and almost musical notes that startled Eric. "You got Serein's DNA! He knows how to open that door with the handle, and he lets himself in and out all the time!" She started to wipe at her eyes. "Sorry. That's just ridiculous."

Wyatt chuckled and Eric manage to force a small smile.

"Well," Wyatt said, "two of these, as I mentioned, have a slightly different panel, deep in the gene sequences. It's related to Denisovan, not Neanderthal, as we usually find and ... something else."

"One of them is mine," Vala said. "I already knew about the Denisovan and unidentified genome. So my, Aunt, too, has the difference?"

"No!" Wyatt said and pointed at Eric. "It's Eric! I've never seen anything like this. I'm wondering if it's not a connection, a link with a supposedly extinct or dead-end branch of homo erectus. The most recent find was homo naledi, but that's still along the same old line. That Denisovan connection is one more that, until a decade ago, was unusual, but it's been identified in others, mostly Asian." He picked up the two papers.

"Your DNA indicates that Denisovan connections led to something else, bypassing Neanderthal...But how? Where? And what does it signify for differences in behavior and ability? This brings in another branch in the human evolutionary development." Wyatt started yanking on his ear lobe again. "This connects to research I've been doing and a hypothesis of mine that the Denisovans continued to develop and evolve independently, maybe in isolation, maybe peacefully. I continue to believe that a tendency toward competition and violence is genetic."

"You mean Eric and I share that genome?" Vala asked.

Wyatt nodded.

Eric felt a surge of excitement. "So Vala and I *do* share a commonality in our DNA!"

Wyatt shrugged. "Well, yes, if you go back through time. In essence, however, these three DNA panels don't share enough markers for any of them to be considered a relative. They're related in the sense that I'm related to most people."

"No closer relationships?" Vala asked quietly.

"No. Not what you were expecting?"

Vala just shook her head, her lips tight and thin. Her skin, normally a light, olive shade, had blanched.

"You were hoping for a match with your aunt," said Eric.

Vala turned and looked at him. "You talk too much."

Eric winced. Perhaps he was never going to be able to connect in a way to comfort this woman he was determined to call *sister*.

"I've known about the variation for a long time," Eric said. "It came up when I was trying to determine what accounted for my height, whether I had some genetic condition. I don't have any of the markers that account for it. The doctors say that the possibilities of how such a variation could play out through all the gene sequences is beyond our ability to predict or understand. No one was particularly interested."

Wyatt was shaking his head. "But Vala has exactly the same variation in her DNA profile–how such differences play out is what we need to learn."

Vala sighed. "The possible changes over the centuries are exponential." She studied Eric for a moment. "On the other hand, we both seem to be unstable–that is, nuts–so maybe that explains it."

Eric took a deep breath and dared another comment. "I'm sorry," he said. "You must be feeling a little lost right now after discovering that you're not related to your aunt."

She looked at him quietly then nodded. "Yes. And no. If the family I grew up with isn't my family, then maybe some of the reasons for…well… for me can be found in a different context."

Eric opened his mouth to speak, but now it was Vala who held up her hand. "But I'm not your sister."

Eric laughed and then, surprisingly, Vala laughed. She had, he thought, a perfect laugh.

Wyatt had stood and was pacing between his chair and a lab table. "I know all this is a lot for you both to take in, but on another note, don't either of you find all this just a little odd?"

They both stared at him.

He stopped, held his hands out as if begging. "Well, *think* about it. You both meet, for the first time, become intertwined, intrigued by DNA searches, and discover that you both have a similar oddity in your DNA. An oddity, I must add, that I've been searching for and never found. Add that to the commonalities of your birth, Vala, and Eric's sister's. I'm neither a religious nor a superstitious man, but I'm familiar with discussions of synchronicity and entanglement. Or something. Didn't they use that idea to try to speed the transfer of material to Mars?" Wyatt dropped back into his chair.

"I know what you mean," said Eric. He felt excitement rising. "That could explain the connections I've felt."

He wanted to continue exploring that idea, but Vala was just staring past him, obviously not focused on their discussion. "Vala, would you rather talk about this another time?"

Instead of answering, Vala continued to stare past him, off into space. Her eyes were narrowed, almost squinting, and her lips parted.

Instinctively, Eric turned around.

A tall thin man stood across the room, near the University server—but, no…in front of… Eric realized he could see the server structure *through* the man. The man's mouth was moving, but Eric couldn't hear anything.

"Can you hear him?" Eric asked Vala.

Vala said nothing, then suddenly she turned to Eric. "*You* can *see* him?"

It was more of a demand than a question. "Yes, of course, but I can't hear him. It's the same man who was at the Market the day I met you."

"See who? Hear what?" Wyatt demanded looking around.

Eric pointed toward the server.

Wyatt looked in that direction, stood and began walking across the room. "I see…light? Maybe?" He said as he turned to face the other two.

As Wyatt spoke, the see-through man shrugged, turned and seemed to put his hands on the server almost as if he were diving into it. Almost immediately, a blast of light filled the room and then was gone. So was the see-through man. Wyatt turned around and demanded, "What *was* that?" He sniffed the air. "I don't smell smoke," he said.

Suddenly a centrifuge began operating, as did a number of other pieces of equipment. Holographic computer screens flashed. Some were illustrating DNA panels, some were producing streams of data, vast amounts of text covering one another.

Wyatt was shouting demands at the computer and having no effect. He activated his implant and it projected the same flashing images that the other screens were showing. "I can't get through to tech!" He ran out the door, presumably to physically find IT help.

Eric was looking at Vala. "You've seen that man–that image– before?" he asked.

She nodded. "I thought it was just part of my–whatever it is. Craziness. Delusions." She shrugged. She was oddly calm, detached.

"Did you see him in the market the day we met?"

"No. Well, not then. That was different. Sometimes I feel as though I'm–I don't know. Falling? Falling out of the world. To somewhere else. Or sometime else?" She leaned forward, then looked directly at Eric. "Do *you* ever feel that way?"

Eric loved that she was looking for a connection, and he hated shaking his head. "No." As Vala slumped back in his chair, he added, "But I've seen him before. At the Market. And, then, the night we met, I think he was briefly outside my shower. Odd."

She looked interested again. "I saw him that afternoon! Later, after I got home and before Aunt Char came over. I thought he was just part of my imagination."

Wyatt came back in the room. "Everyone is having the same issues with their technology. No one knows what's happening. No one can shut it down. So you both saw a person here? Before the flash of light?"

Eric nodded. "A tall and thin man. He seemed to be trying to talk to us, but I couldn't hear anything. Then he walked over to the server, and then there was that flash of light. We've both seen him before. You couldn't see him?"

Wyatt shook his head. "I saw nothing but maybe a light–and then that flash, of course. He went *into* the computer?"

Eric shrugged. "I don't know where he went."

"Nothing is working correctly. Nothing will shut down. Everything is linked every which way. This could be an attack of some sort on the university system–or maybe it's even larger." Wyatt ran out the door again.

Vala stood. "I think I'm going home. I'm exhausted and feel as though I need to process all of this. I need to think. Or not think. Besides, House is linked to the University, and I may have problems there. I hate all this linking. At least I haven't gotten one of those damned implants."

Eric stood and reached his hand out to her as Serein stood and walked over to stand by her side. "Can we please talk again? When you're ready?"

Vala nodded without looking at him. "We'll talk, Eric." She turned to look around the room. "Something is happening, obviously. Probability aside, I don't understand it yet."

"Synchronicity?" asked Eric. "You know Carl Jung says that events are meaningful coincidences if they occur with no causal relationship yet seem to be meaningfully related."

"And probability denies anything having to be meaningfully related, Eric. I'm sure you've helped a lot of people work through their emotions, but psychology isn't really a science. It's not *real*."

Eric, searching for a response that was witty and nonaggressive, was saved when Wyatt came back in the room. "No one can do anything!"

"I'm sorry, Wyatt. I hope that things sort themselves out. I'm going to go check on House."

"I'll wait here until someone gets this back under control. I'd like to talk with both of you later about this DNA stuff. We need to do tests. How about dinner this weekend?"

Vala nodded. "Fine. I'll call you."

After she left, Eric said, "Thanks, Wyatt. I think we learned a lot today. I just don't know what any of it means."

Wyatt didn't look away from the panel of flashing lights. He seemed mesmerized. "Sure, Eric. I want to talk. We'll get together this weekend even if Vala doesn't join us."

Wyatt still stood transfixed as Eric left the room, and he knew it would have to be up to him to later contact Wyatt. Surely his interest in the DNA research had been temporarily replaced by a need to figure out what had happened to his technology. That lab was everything to Wyatt.

CHAPTER TEN

Wednesday night - Thursday, July 5, 2029

Vala spent Wednesday night alternately running and meditating in the back garden with Serein, listening to gentle waves when they weren't drowned out with explosions still heralding the sillier side of humanity. At least the partiers weren't in the mood to take to the running trails, and Vala and Serein were alone each time they ran full speed to clear Vala's mind. Meanwhile in her garden, a sweet scent had overcome the city smells. She soon realized the mock orange had bloomed again, defying heat. She wished she could bottle the scent.

She had recovered from most of the Wednesday debacle at Wyatt's lab, but she'd never had so many unanswered questions blocking clear thought. She wasn't worried so much as confused by a jumble of emotions that she couldn't identify. She mentally listed emotions to try to come to terms with the information overload. She'd spent most of her life hiding emotions and had become so good at it that they weren't even known by herself, so she didn't get far beyond *confused*. Was that even an emotion?

Then she listed ideas and facts, which was a little longer but not much. What did she know about all this? She needed to understand the scientific explanations. She needed to somehow make this *real*.

Then she just sat and let the night, which had quieted with the near-dawn hours approaching, and sweet mock orange embrace her. A slight breeze found its way to her and she felt as if she could simply melt into the texture of wind. She began breathing in unison with the rise and fall of the breeze, a harmony of molecules–oxygen, nitrogen, hydrogen–flowed, negotiating the rising humidity, and the infinite space between, the vastness of space within everything around her as the solar systems and galaxies of atoms and their particles whirled through the night…

She was so immersed in the natural space and deep meditation that it took Serein's pawing at her to alert her to the ringing phone. She almost ignored it, then, realizing it was not yet dawn, she answered in case it was an emergency.

"Vala, this is Eric. Are you okay?"

Vala sighed, resisted the temptation to hang up. "You're an odd man, Eric. Why would you call me at–whatever hour this is–to ask if I'm okay? Who calls other people before dawn with that kind of question?"

Silence lingered for a full minute before Eric said, "I knew you were awake."

"Are you spying on me again?"

"No! No! I just knew."

Vala punched the phone for speaker, set it on the table next to her and leaned her head back. "You're irritating enough to be a little brother, Eric. I'll give you that." Silence descended again.

Eric cleared his throat. "Well, since you're awake, and I'm awake, and it will soon be morning…would you like to have breakfast? Maybe at The Bad Bishop on Boren? They serve live food with real table service. Do you know it?"

Vala thought for a moment. Something was going on for the two of them that neither understood. Vala was curious, but she wasn't sure why. She didn't feel ready to tell Eric to go find another project. Besides, she thought, he's good at waiting through silences. "Yes. I know it." So few retro restaurants were left that most people knew the handful in Seattle. "Let's do it. But I want my Aunt Char there."

"Still don't trust me?"

"No, it's not that. She knows my history, and all of that is coming into question. I want her there for a discussion. Do you agree?"

"Yes. Six?"

"Yes." Vala hung up. No silence on that last one. And brief. The way she liked telephone conversations. Was Eric picking up on that, too? Why was she even talking to him?

Vala called Aunt Char, who never seemed to mind being awakened or she was very good at hiding her irritation. "So if you're willing, I'll pick you up in thirty minutes. There will be someone else there, too. That man I met at the market the other day. I told you about him."

"The stalker?" Aunt Char sounded concerned.

"That's...complicated. He's not really a stalker so much as, well, a pest. I'll tell you more as we go there."

Later, in the pod, Vala filled Char in on the latest information, including the fact that she and Eric did share similarities. "I want your take on him," Vala said. "You've always had a level-headed, practical approach that sees right through agitcons thrown your way."

"Sadly, the use of agitcons are part of my job. Agitation from increasingly thorny marketers is worse every day as they compete to get people's attention. Well, to help you, I'll first have to get over my reservations," Char said. "I'll try. I don't like anyone threatening you."

Eric was waiting for them outside the restaurant. He held out his hand to Char, told him he was honored she had joined them, and they entered The Bad Bishop together. As they walked in, the hostess smiled and said, "Eric, Sweetie! Good to see you. It's been a while! Want the back booth?"

Eric nodded, and she quickly took them to one of the high-backed and private booths. "Thank you very much, Jocelyn," Eric said.

"For you, always. Just water?" Jocelyn asked with a smile and a wink.

All three nodded, but Vala noted that Jocelyn's look never left Eric.

"Here are your menus, and I'll be right back."

"You come here often?" Vala asked. She was not successfully repressing her smile or sardonic tone.

Eric nodded. "Usually at night. If I'm not sleeping, this is a place to come to make notes and to think."

"Just think?" Vala asked.

"I didn't say that I did *nothing* in life but think about my sister," Eric said. He smiled. "We've gone out a couple times, but we're friends, mostly."

Vala felt a twinge of envy. Friends. She didn't have anyone she went out with. She'd feel exposed. Ultimately, people let you down if you became vulnerable. Except Aunt Char. But there was only one Aunt Char.

After receiving their water, Vala said, "Eric, I do understand the desire for family, for connection. Aunt Char has been my go-to safe place all my life. My father died while I was young, and my mother has never been particularly interested in her peculiar daughter."

"You have different interests," Char said automatically, as always, to rise to her sister's defense.

"Sure," said Vala. "And anything that's not one of my mother's interests is peculiar. Anyway, I understand why you're looking for family. But just recently–right after I met you–Aunt Char told me some things that I hadn't known before. Added to this information that I'm apparently not even related to Mom or Aunt Char, I decided I need to investigate what's going on. Not to mention the transparent figure that only you and I can see. You're oddly interwoven into the mix. This is like standing on the threshold of suddenly understanding the key component to a scientific puzzle. Except, in this case, I don't know the puzzle or the goal. So I guess it's more like being crazy. That, I get."

Eric nodded. "First, don't blame your own mind. Or me," he added, jerking his thumb toward his chest. "As I've said, I've always felt that I was destined to somehow help my sister, a sister who died before I was born. I never believed she died. I've always had a door open to finding her. When I met you–"

"Not again, Eric. The DNA proved we're *not* brother and sister."

"I know, I know, but it only proved we're not blood related. Other relationships exist. Look at you and your Aunt. Just let me finish. When I met you, I *knew* some sort of connection was being made, an important one. You're my *intended* sister. Surely, you understand what it is to *know* something without proof."

"You sound obsessive about this," Char said. "Why?"

"Because I *feel* it, but not in the sense of emotional response. A physical knowing. It's like knowing that when you stand up, you'll stay on the ground, not float off into space. It's not because you can *see* gravity. You don't even think about gravity being there. But you *know*... Believe me, Char, I would never do or say anything hurtful to Vala."

Vala realized Aunt Char was looking at him with something akin to adoration. "I believe that's true, Eric," she said.

"Are you ready to order?" Jocelyn interrupted.

Vala and Eric both ordered poached eggs and fruit, and Char had a Denver Omelet. "I see you two eat alike, too," Char said.

Vala shrugged. "I want Aunt Char–" she turned to look at Char. "May I still call you Aunt Char?"

"Of course, Dear. My feelings and relationship with you will never change."

"See?" Eric said. "Blood is over-rated!"

Vala smiled. If she ever lost Aunt Char, the world would be empty. "Look, Eric, I have to tell you that all your *knowing* fails to connect with me. Having a hunch is fine, but then one seeks out real world *proof.* Leave out the speculative. I want Aunt Char to tell you some things she recently told me about my birth. *Facts,* Eric, not speculation." Vala turned, and Char cleared her throat.

"You mean the eyes and trust, dear?"

Vala nodded.

There was a brief pause while Jocelyn slid food in front of them, then Char continued. "You have to understand that Vala is as close to me as a daughter. She's asked me to tell you things I've never told anyone else. I didn't tell Vala until recently. I'm not comfortable with this, but I'll do what she wants. I believe you don't want to hurt her, but keep in mind that if you ever do, I'll hunt you down and rearrange your method of locomotion."

Eric nodded. "I accept your terms and appreciate your honesty. I'm a counselor with considerable training in ethics. I'll not betray her."

"Training is irrelevant. I do believe you have built-in loyalty, however."

Vala shifted uncomfortably and put her fork down. She held her hand up to stop the conversation while she swallowed, then said,

"It's okay, Char. You know I trust Wyatt, and he thinks Eric is worth trusting."

Eric laughed. "I'll tell Wyatt how much he's helped me."

"I thought you could keep a confidence," Char said, not smiling.

Eric sobered. "Sorry. Banter. Go ahead."

Char took a deep breath and then began to tell Eric about the day Vala was born, including the difference in her eyes and then the strange woman who left a trust for Vala.

When she was finished, Eric nodded. "More coincidences. When I was born, somebody set up a trust for me, anonymously. My parents left information for me about the trust and the bank account where monthly payments were deposited. Since we had no other relatives, the State maintained it while I went into foster care."

"Why weren't you put up for adoption?" Char asked.

Eric looked down at the table with his eyes closed for a moment, then looked back up at her. He smiled but it was barely a smile, both wistful and appealing. "People don't want to adopt someone different, especially not a boy who is not only already seven but who is also only slightly larger than a three-year-old. I was about a foot shorter than most boys my age, and I was therefore considered a *special needs* case. People want to adopt *normal* babies, as a foster parent told me."

"Oh, I didn't think—"

Eric waved away Char's confused apology. "It's all right. I was quite well off for a foster kid. I had no control over my money, but whenever I needed anything—clothes, school supplies, special event money—I got it thanks to some oversight by a lawyer somewhere. And I met Wyatt and Steve, who became my best friends. I'm sure money was skimmed here and there, but I didn't care."

"Wyatt mentioned that he'd met you in foster care. I'd no idea he'd been part of that system," Vala said, thinking that she'd never really discussed anything personal with Wyatt. "What's his story?"

"You'd need to ask him. Confidences. I was able to help him a little. I had no money to give him, but I would give him whatever items I had—computer, cell phone, whatever—and then say I'd lost them. In return, he helped keep kids from picking on me. That was true, too, of Steve, to a lesser degree. Poor Steve kept getting shifted around more than I or Wyatt; he was always getting into scrapes."

"You seem very well proportioned and comfortable in your body," Vala said. "Do you know why you're so short? Were your parents short?"

"Vala!" Char said sharply.

"He knows he's short, Aunt Char."

Eric laughed. "It's fine. I do know I'm short though most people try to treat me as though they don't notice–at least to my face. Which is kind of funny since they have to bend their necks to look at me. Kids aren't subtle, however, and I was always fair game. Anyway, the doctors can't find anything *wrong*, not in the sense of genetic issues or medical conditions. The only variation has been that one Wyatt mentioned in the DNA, which I share with you, Vala, although you're certainly not short. And my parents, if they were my parents, weren't short. My father was quite tall, about 6'2", which makes him not as tall as you, Vala. Do you know why you're so tall?"

Vala laughed. "No. No one else in the family that I'm not related to is this tall. That's irrelevant now. To make it worse for my mother, my Eurasian appearance and my DNA indicates that I do indeed have some Japanese relatives somewhere. Of course, I was picked on because I was tall. But I had a family, a wealthy family, for protection. Especially Aunt Char. I was never as isolated and vulnerable as you were." She forked some food into her mouth. She was feeling better.

"The woman who came to me about Vala's trust was short," Char said.

"How short?" Eric asked around a mouthful of egg.

"Short enough that when I was sitting down, we were close to eye level. Somewhere around four feet, I'd say."

Eric rubbed his forehead, sighed. "I wish I knew more about her. Maybe she and I are connected although basing that on the fact that we're both short seems farfetched."

Vala laughed. "It's no more farfetched than thinking I'm your sister because of a *feeling*!"

Eric shrugged. "So never mind logic. But I have no one to ask about the person who set up the trust. And I can't even get DNA from my parents to check that connection since they died while I was still young."

"They died in a car wreck?" Vala asked.

Eric nodded.

"Have you ever looked at old hospital records to see if there are files on them?" Vala asked as she shoved her empty plate toward the end of the table for Jocelyn to grab. "Sometimes those old records had blood smears kept with them. Some people had samples filed away for future reference. It's worth checking. If nothing else, you could check blood type. That would tell you something."

"I never thought of that," Eric said.

"You seem to be very intuitive, Eric. Maybe you didn't want to find out," Char said around her last mouthful.

"You have your niece's talent for directness," Eric said. "Maybe you're right. All my life, I've felt as though something, just out of my reach, was important. I've always tied it to that idea that I should have been helping my sister. Besides, as with you and Vala, it doesn't matter whether I was my parents' biological child; they couldn't have been more loving." He smiled at Char, who suddenly leaned forward and stared at him intently.

"What is it?" he asked.

"Your eyes," she said. "Your eyes are like hers."

"Whose?"

"The woman who gave me the trust papers and information when Vala was born."

"That's it!" Vala said. "I knew that your eyes reminded me of something. It was Aunt Char's description."

Eric shook his head and sighed. "I don't know what journey we're on, but since I met Vala, my life changes moment to moment. I believe it will eventually make sense. And maybe I can fulfill my destiny." He winked at Vala.

"You always say *helping* or something like that about your sister. Why do you think your sister would have needed help?" Vala asked.

"I don't mean *help* in the sense of her incompetence. I think she's supposed to be doing something of major importance, and that I'm supposed to help her. Like a sidekick. Somehow we are able to accomplish things together that we can't individually. Again,

I *know* that is what I'm supposed to do, that you are the reason I'm alive, Vala."

Vala shook her head. "You're stubborn. I'll give you that. And you seem to get a lot of convictions. I wish I had that much certainty about my life and work. However, I have *no* interest in being anyone's reason for breathing."

Eric chuckled as Jocelyn picked up the last of the silverware and plates. "Anything else?" she asked.

Everyone shook their heads.

"Are you paying by implant?" Jocelyn asked; her broad smile seemed to indicate a private joke. Again, all three shook their heads. "Okay, Eric, shall I put it on your comp-pay?"

"Yes, please, Jocelyn," he said.

She nodded, winked at him again and said, "My number hasn't changed."

After she left, Eric continued talking.

"Well, Vala, look at everything that is happening. The coincidences of your birth and my sister's birth. The DNA connections, connections Wyatt hasn't identified in any of his research before. The transparent man. The trust accounts. The fact that we both started pursuing aspects of our lives in ways that brought us together. The—"

"Okay, okay," Vala said, holding her hand up and interrupting. "I get coincidences. And I'm sure that your psychology can come up with some synchronicity explanations. But whatever *can* happen *will* happen. You're just citing a sequence of events that are personally relevant to you. That capture your attention."

"Is that the scientist talking?" Eric asked.

"If by that you mean logical thinking, yes. Eric, if I hadn't become faint at the market that day, we'd have never talked."

"But you *did*. And we were there at the same time. And we have the same connections through this trust fund donor. What do you think about quantum entanglement?" Eric asked.

Vala sighed. "What I need to understand is why you and I are both seeing this transparent man. Let's stick with that oddity."

"I'm convinced that you two have mysteries to work out," Char said, "but this mysterious visitor worries me. That's not just an oddity–that's frightening." Her eyebrows drew together and she shook her finger at Vala. "I think you should call the police."

Vala shook her head. "I've been the route of telling people about the unusual. That's how I wind up being institutionalized. We can't tell anyone until we have some facts."

"I agree with Vala on that," Eric said. "Those computer issues have to be related to our mystery man, and if we bring him up, we could be implicated. Even Wyatt brought up issues of cyber-terrorism, which means guardians will be sniffing around."

Char sighed. "At least you have Eric for support, Vala. You can best solve the riddle by working together, in my opinion, but do be cautious. Vala, you wanted my take on Eric. I trust him."

"Not that I expected you to make judgement in front of him," Vala said, working to keep her irritation under control. She tossed her napkin on the table. Aunt Char's comment gave Eric more validity in their lives than Vala wanted. "We should go."

Eric laughed. "I'm glad to hear that your aunt trusts me. Serein trusts me, too." He grinned, then shrugged as Vala glared at him. "Char, thank you for your trust. Vala and I both need answers. The world, in my opinion," he said, nodding at Vala, "holds secrets that we sense but can't always prove. Did you know that the brain functions in more than eleven dimensions, and we've made only slight headway in understanding the more than 90 million neurons and the multiple connections of each? So I agree with Vala that coincidence, synchronicity, can be a by-product of our thinking, but we don't understand the *spiritual* component of that. By *spiritual* I'm talking about emotions, instinct, awareness of the world on levels that our conscious thoughts don't comprehend."

Vala gestured at Char to slide out of the booth. "It's time for you to get to work, Aunt Char, before Eric buries us in superfluousness."

"Is that a word?" Char asked.

"It is since I met Eric," Vala answered.

As Char stood and Vala slid across the seat, Eric kept talking. "*Time to go*. See, we say things about time to regulate our lives. Time itself is incomprehensible to us. We base it on what we can measure, but that's like basing the estimate of your life span on your birth date.

What we don't understand is so vast that we're bound to stumble into new information just by looking. That gets back to Vala's argument about what *can* happen *will*."

Char sighed. "You two even talk alike. You're connected, all right. Somehow."

Vala said, "Sure. We're both human."

Eric sighed and stood.

As they stepped outside, Vala took a deep breath and then coughed. The restaurant had obviously been filtering the air and adding oxygen. Although the day was visibly lighter, thick smoke made finding the sun impossible.

When she could finally take a deep breath, she stopped and said, "Eric, I see the world as a whole. Everything is dependent on everything else. Our environmental web demonstrates that. Fires are increasing because climate change has resulted in drier and hotter conditions. Fires worsen climate change. Cause and effect. All things are connected. Sometimes, I can see beneath the physical, using calculations and observations, to understand how things are working or not working, how to fix something or what to change to bring together a solution. That's because I'm looking. So our coincidences may just be a result of looking for coincidences. This is, after all, what you've been *expecting*, Eric. We often find what we expect to find."

Char nodded. "Sure. I may want coffee again if we're staying."

Vala chuckled. "Look! We're up. Outside. And walking!"

In spite of Vala's continued hints about leaving, they stood in front of the restaurant talking, mostly about less significant things in their lives. Vala found herself at ease, something she never felt within a group of three people. At first, she attributed it to having Aunt Char present, but she was beginning to realize that, despite her intentions, she felt comfortable with Eric, too. Maybe she could feel comfortable with change. Change felt inevitable, but it could be natural, surely, like the scent carried along when the winds came whistling down Puget Sound bringing a heavy load of clouds and rain in from the Pacific.

She wondered how Eric would respond if she told him she could communicate with animals, that she could run faster than anyone else. As she was thinking, she noticed him suddenly looking at her intently, and her discomfort returned.

"We're going," she said. "Eric, keep a log of when and where you see our mystery man. I'll do the same. Then we'll be in touch." She walked toward the pod with Aunt Char muttering something as she followed.

Vala took Aunt Char to work and then returned home. She and Serein enjoyed a twenty-mile run on Alki Trail, giving herself a chance to transition from personal thoughts before heading in to the university.

CHAPTER ELEVEN

Thursday Afternoon, July 5, 2029

Eric scurried to two emergency appointments, returned to his box by noon to change, then went to the gym to meet a friend for an hour of racquetball. *Don't think, don't think* he kept telling himself every time he was alone. After showering and eating a late lunch, he discovered he'd missed a phone call: Wyatt wanted him to call immediately. Since Eric was only ten minutes from the university, and he already felt guilty about having missed the call, he called a driverless and went over. He found Wyatt in the lab where he always seemed to be. He'd make a good single person. His emotions, as usual, were an assault.

"Wyatt, I just heard your message. Is something wrong?"

Wyatt jumped up from a stool by one of the counters and almost ran toward him. "Eric! Wrong? Everything is wrong. Ever since you were here, ever since that strange light and then flash, the computers have been constantly running–no one can shut them off–but they're inaccessible. The links can't be shut down, and even back-up systems are affected through universal storage systems. My classes were all lecture without anything to show them. I've had techs here, and they say I loaded data into the server that has it processing so much information that every bit of space is being utilized. The computer can't do anything else–anywhere. They even unplugged the system and it *kept running*. Eric, that's not possible–"

Eric held his hands up, palms out, hoping to slow the torrent of words, but Wyatt took no notice.

"I'm just hoping GILS still has stored data, but so far any University material can't even be accessed through GILS. This could be related to you–and Vala– but I'm getting the blame. It could even be terrorism that just happened to start when you were here. But you saw someone. You've got to tell me what went on here." He grabbed Eric on both his shoulders, almost shaking him. "If something doesn't happen quickly, the university is simply going to shut me down, close my lab."

Eric forced himself not to react to the sour taste of fear and panic that washed over him as Wyatt's emotions surged through the room like a rip current. Taking a deep breath, Eric took both of Wyatt's hands and pressed lightly on key acupressure points. "Take a deep breath, Wyatt."

Wyatt inhaled deeply, involuntarily, and his hands relaxed. Then he dropped them to his side. He was far from relaxing. This was more like near collapse. Eric kept his voice soft and gentle.

"So, Wyatt, this will resolve itself today." Eric didn't feel at all sure that was true, but it wasn't impossible. "You need to think clearly, right?" He'd never seen Wyatt this bad. He could be excitable, yes, but this was near hysteria. "I know that you've got your life totally invested in your work, but from what you say, the equipment is working; it's just not taking on more right now. Time will help?"

"Nobody knows!" Wyatt wailed, immediately escalating again. "That's the problem. Whatever is going on may be destroying everything. Nobody has seen anything like this before. Now the university president is calling the Guardians in case it's a cyberattack. By *me!*"

Eric gestured at the stool where Wyatt had been sitting to see if he could get him to sit down again. "It sounds as if you've got top people looking into this, Wyatt. But what can I do to help?"

"Tell me exactly what is going on. I saw light, but you said you saw a man? Where did he come from? Where did he go? Did you know him? Was he a saboteur? You need to tell security. Is this–"

"Wait!" Eric yelled. "Wyatt, I don't know much, but listen to what I do have to say. Both Vala and I have seen this transparent figure, like a holograph. You know. Faint, wavering. Like bad CGI. No one was really here."

"Why couldn't I see him? How is that being done?"

Eric repressed a smile, wondering why anyone would want to sabotage the university–then he thought about what some of Vala's work included. Specialization, including that for the government, was no doubt cached in various university locations on GILS. He shook his head. "Wyatt, I don't know why you couldn't see him. Perhaps you just looked at the wrong time at the wrong place. He was more impression than anything else. It may not have even been a human figure. Maybe it was just a pre-flash or something, and Vala and I fed into each other's imagination." Eric began to feel that he was treading close to lies, but he wasn't ready to discuss some of the more peculiar things going on with Vala and himself.

"Look," he said, "both Vala and I think *something* is happening, but we don't know what." Eric looked over at the server where he'd seen the figure, then the flash. "Let me show you what I thought I saw. I saw him walk over here. This is the server for your computer here in the lab?" he asked as he rested his hand on its surface.

Wyatt was nodding just as another flash of light filled the room. Eric's ears popped, as though the room pressure had just suddenly changed, then he felt dizzy and nauseous, and he staggered slightly, grabbing the counter to keep from falling. "What the hell?" he asked. "Did that thing just shock me?" He didn't feel shocked so much as stunned.

Wyatt was yelling about something. When Eric felt he could look up, he did so. Wyatt, ignoring Eric, had called up a computer screen, which was flashing a request for Wyatt's password. Off to the side and slightly behind Wyatt, the transparent man was gesturing wildly in Eric's direction. The man's mouth was moving, but Eric couldn't hear anything. Then he was gone.

Eric rubbed his eyes, looked around and blinked, rubbing his eyes again. Suddenly Wyatt was beside him.

"Are you okay?" Wyatt asked. "What did you do?"

Eric shook his head. "Nothing. Well, I touched the server. Then there was that flash–"

"The same flash that was here before!"

Eric nodded. "I felt dizzy. I think there must have been an electrical surge or something. Then, I saw–"

Suddenly, Eric thought it better not to mention the transparent figure.

"Saw what?" Wyatt asked.

"Well, you, with the computer screen. Is it working?" Guilt for not being completely honest made him bite his lip.

"I don't know. It seems to be responding. Look it's pulling up the information I requested for the class I gave." Wyatt started firing requests at the computer and one screen after another popped up until so many appeared that it was difficult to read any of them. Wyatt's implant signaled him and he started talking almost immediately. "Yes, yes!" He said. "It's working! I'm going through it now. Everything seems just fine. An inventory of files? Yes, I'll do one for the lab."

Eric walked over to the server and stared at it.

"No, no, no! Don't touch!" Wyatt yelled.

"I was just—"

"No, no, no!" Wyatt said again. "I've got to check and see if anything is missing." He started talking to the computer again.

"Well, I'll see you later."

Wyatt did a half-wave.

Eric shook his head and walked out of the lab. He hadn't done anything. Had he?

As he walked back to his car, Eric called Vala. She answered quickly. "Vala, I've just left Wyatt's lab. His computer—"

"The mystery man was here in my lab, Eric."

Her voice sounded shaky. "I'll be right there," he told her. He'd had a patient once who said every minute terrified him as though he had to defuse bombs but no bombs were there. The description was apt to Vala's days.

When Eric walked into the lab, he noted that Serein was standing between Vala and the door. "Are you okay?" Eric asked, stopping a respectful distance from the dog.

Vala nodded. "He did what he did before. Showed up. Looked like he was trying to communicate, then vanished."

"When was this?"

"Just before you called. And my equipment started working again. It's been down all day. Serein, it's okay." Serein walked over to a large dog pillow by Vala's desk and lay down.

Eric nodded. "I saw him just before you did, I think." He told her what had happened. "Wyatt's all excited that his lab is up and running again."

"Did Wyatt see him?"

Eric shook his head. "No. Only the flash of light. How did Serein act?"

"As he has before. He's alert and sees someone. But he isn't alarmed or defensive. He's sure I'm in no danger. That gives me confidence. But I'm confused."

"That seems to be the condition for all of us. Wyatt says the entire university system was down and that people are running around everywhere investigating. The President apparently called in the Guardians."

"That's why I'm here. I got a call asking me to come in and check out my lab. Just before you came in, I got another call to ask me to do an inventory of my files. We have to do something, Eric. Whatever is going on is … important. I agree that you and I are somehow in the middle of it, but we shouldn't tell anyone until we understand more. We need data. Someone could be targeting us. People tend to leap into action on too little information. Look," she said, calling up a computer screen, "I've made a list of all the connections and questions we have. I don't think we're blood relatives, but maybe that similar difference in the DNA Wyatt found is significant."

"Well, it's obviously not a height gene," Eric said, grinning up at her.

"Nor humor," Vala said without smiling.

Eric felt himself mentally shrug. "You should know that I've contacted Steve again–"

"The detective?"

She said it as though he'd just referred to serving intestines for breakfast. "Yes, but not to track down anything to do with you. I've asked him to research my parents, try to find out if there is any DNA evidence anywhere."

Vala nodded thoughtfully. "Our histories could be key. In effect, we were both orphans. Or something. It can't be related to our jobs. We don't have anything in common in our daily world except the information you have on your sister and the fact that we're both hallucinating or something with this transparent man. I've discovered I'm not related to the people I thought were my family."

"They're still your family," Eric said soothingly.

"Stop that. I'm not looking for counseling. I don't need family, except for Aunt Char, and she'll always be essential to me. I'm relieved to not be related to my mother. Dad was close to me, but he's dead. If I want comforting, I'll let you know."

Eric wondered just how *helping* could possibly fit into his relationship with Vala when she shut down any personal connection except from her dog. "A key may be in the lab. Whatever happened this time involves that computer. The lab is where we first got together for a civilized–sort of–conversation. This transparent individual is trying to communicate. What better way than with a computer? Let's go find out what Wyatt thinks is happening."

They discovered, much to their surprise, that the lab was locked and Wyatt gone.

"Guess we'll have to wait until tomorrow," Eric said. "We could all probably use some rest. Besides, your house is linked to the university, isn't it? Maybe something will come up there."

Vala nodded. "I haven't been able to connect with GILS while this has been going on, but it may be working now."

CHAPTER TWELVE

Thursday night, June 5, 2029

"He *is* back, Tandra, but he's very weak. I'm keeping him sleeping until he has some time to mend," Obeah said.

Tandra had pushed Obeah near the end of his patience as Cassidy's restlessness had increased without his regaining consciousness.

"But he *is* okay?" Tandra asked from her kneeling position by the cot. "My emotions are tight, and I'm having trouble reading him." She was kneeling by the bed, holding Cassidy's hand.

"I'm not certain, Tandra, but I think so. These trips take us into territory that gentem haven't visited for centuries. I've heard stories about everything from teleportation to traveling as wind, but we've lost a lot of our culture in the hundreds of years we've tried to merge into human culture. Cassidy keeps pushing our knowledge both backward and forward in time. Something unusual must have happened. It's as though his identity is fractured."

The door swung open, and Alarick strode in. "I understand Cassidy is back," he said. "I'll talk to him now."

"Some individuals say *hello* or *how is he,*" Obeah said.

Alarick shoved past him and crowded in next to Tandra and Cassidy. "Why isn't he awake?"

"He's weak. I'm keeping him sedated. He needs peace right now." Obeah wasn't in the mood to deal with Alarick.

"He can recover later. I need to find out if any progress has been made in his futile endeavors. Wake him."

Obeah shook his head, but before he could speak, Tandra, who had stood, was leaning over Alarick with her hands on her hips. "Alarick, this is *not* a situation under your command," she said.

"She's right. You have no authority here," Obeah said. "This is a healing center, and you need to leave. Your negativity is intrusive. Come back when you've meditated or wait until I've called you."

"I forbid any more of these attempts to contact the humans!" Alarick yelled just before the door slammed behind him.

Cassidy groaned and moved restlessly. Obeah went over and rested his hand on Cassidy's forehead until the restlessness eased and Cassidy was breathing softly again.

Only when Cassidy was still did Obeah turn and focus on Tandra's eyes to make sure she was listening before he spoke softly. "Alarick may be on track with the idea that these trips need to stop, but I'll not tell him so. One of these times, Cassidy may not return to us, Tandra."

She kneeled by the bed again. "Perhaps he was successful this time, and he won't feel the need to go back."

Obeah shook his head as he turned away and returned to his counter to mix another healing mixture for Cassidy. Tandra's emotions were too raw for him to make a practical appeal to her to help him stop Cassidy's efforts. "I'm leaving this on the counter, Tandra. Cassidy should remain asleep, but if he wakes, get him to drink this immediately. Don't let him try to talk or rouse himself. He desperately needs rest. This will both hydrate him and allow him to sleep deeply."

"Where are you going? Should you leave?"

"I won't be gone long. You'll be fine. If an emergency does arise, just push the button over the bed. I'll come immediately."

"Does it summon you somehow?"

"Sort of. It's a siren." Obeah chuckled at her expression as he left. He had a phone somewhere—he just couldn't seem to keep track of it. Individuals had a way of reaching him when he was needed—often it was just a clear sense of urgency.

He found Murell, one of the Council members with a particularly gentle nature, at the stable where she was cleaning a horse's hooves. Although she stood only flank high, the animal gave her no resistance as she worked, head bowed with dreads falling across the near side of her face. Obeah hoped she would be receptive to the idea of altering the Council's decision to continue looking into the poisoning of the water.

He waited silently to one side until she finished. The day was quiet and here on the edge of the village, few individuals were moving about. A few horses and a mule shuffled around a mound of hay in a feeder by the corral gate. The ripe odor of animals and manure rose with the heat waves. Obeah allowed his mind to quiet and sink into the day's tranquility.

"Thank you, Obeah," Murell said without looking around as she finished the last hoof.

"Could you smell me?" he asked ironically.

She chuckled. "Not through the delicate aroma of stable. Your presence announces itself, and you have the respect to wait until I've finished before you speak. Want some ale?" she asked as she patted the horse in dismissal and he trotted to the water trough. She turned to face Obeah and smiled broadly.

"No, thank you. Cassidy is still in a deep sleep and, although Tandra is there, I don't want to be gone too long."

"Is he going to be okay?"

"I think so although I've been worried. Now he needs sleep to repair stress damage and then nourishment for the body. I don't yet know what happened on this trip."

Murell climbed up and sat on the top rail of the corral fence so she was eye-to-eye with Obeah. "I'm beginning to rethink my disagreement with Alarick's claim that Cassidy is wasting his and your time *and* endangering his own life for nothing. You look worn and worried. In addition, his project is draining the harmonious energy out of the community. Tension spreads like kudzu. Cassidy has been obsessed by this project since five years after the Membrane was created."

Obeah sighed, leaned on the fence. "I believe it to be Cassidy's choice. Although it may also be Moirai ordained. He and his colleagues believe that we can't justify the use of chemicals against the humans. We've never violated our principles this way. What gives us the right to attack any other creature?"

121

Murell shook her head, rubbed her hand up and down along her jaw thoughtfully. "We've never been in a position in which everyone, every creature, is at risk. If humans want to kill themselves off, fine. They should do it without killing everyone else at the same time. I don't know how we can handle all this. Alarick has pointed out that if we use his poison, we're only speeding up what the humans have been doing to themselves for decades. He has studies that show that the human carbon footprint was growing even after they learned about the environmental damage they were causing. Judging by what's leaking into Beta Earth, that hasn't stopped."

"That gets back to the argument for retaliation. Do the ends justify the means?"

"We've been peaceful for as long as anyone can remember. The results haven't been good. Who said that the definition of insanity was doing the same thing repeatedly while expecting a different result?"

"Einstein?" Obeah wasn't sure how to argue against an argument for change. "I don't know the answer, but I want you to let the Council know that I've come to believe that Cassidy is correct. We've allowed negativity too much sway. I want to make sure the Council is aware of Alarick's prejudice against humans. He's not capable of unbiased action, and lately he's been acting more like a king than simply Chair of the Council. Frankly, I have the clear sense that he's not stable. He needs some quiet seclusion."

"We know." Tears brightened her crystal-blue eyes. She began swinging her boots against the wooden rail in a waltz rhythm. "The Council was in consensus about releasing the chemicals. That doesn't mean that we're all in favor of it, but, Obeah, we're desperate. All of us ache with empathy for Earth. You're right, though; the negativity is growing, a cloud that blackens the light of reason. Disappointment and frustration fuels negativity and fear. This break, our emigration—or escape…we pinned our hopes on that. But that hasn't worked either."

Obeah leaned against the corral rail. He felt like putting his head down and sobbing. When had he last cried? "I'm not sure we ever had much clarity about that emigration, either. Our clarity of has been obscured for a long time. Instead of working with LifeForce, we're trying to manipulate it."

Murell shook her head. "Too much has been bad for too long. You, Obeah…you *know* better than many of us how grim it was to live in the human culture."

Obeah nodded. "True. But Cassidy's fighting to allow us choices. Alternatives. He believes that until we've tried everything, we're giving in to hopelessness. The children were always our fall back plan, a connection to humans. The children should have insights we don't. They think they're human." Obeah paused, took a deep breath, and composed his thoughts. He rested one hand on her shoulder. "At one time, Murell, you agreed that the children would help us heal. What has changed?"

"I don't know, Obeah. So much has gone wrong…Being in contact with humans never helped." She shook her head and quit kicking her heels against the fence. "We should never have left the children there. I feel guilty about that. I don't want to abandon them now, to not give them a chance to fulfill their promise, but the human activity is destroying the very fabric of both Earths. LifeForce, of course, will continue, but at what cost?"

Her heels again took up the waltz rhythm and she dropped her gaze. "I'm sorry I can't be more positive about this situation. I see nothing positive about it. While I don't agree with Alarick that the only solution to the human's destruction is to wipe them out, I do think that we've run out of options that we can manage. Especially since the membrane is failing. If we don't do *something*, we may be responsible for destroying both Earths."

Obeah thought about his conversation with Tandra, about the things gentem had lost over the centuries. "Do you think our position as a marginalized minority has altered our views, made us unable to adhere to our own nonviolent beliefs? Is there a possibility that we're no longer truly gentem?"

"That thought makes me weep, but creatures evolve to survive. Living as ourselves with humans didn't work. Living separately hasn't worked. Trying to pass as humans, slowly relegating our history to stories in fiction and myth, didn't work. Beta Earth is the only place where we've lived in freedom for as long as anyone can remember, including you. I love this place, this life. I don't want to give it up."

123

"If it were impossible to get along with humans, there wouldn't be half-gentem humans. There wouldn't be humans living here with us, by choice."

"We're circling the issue again, Obeah. It's not *all* humans—maybe just ninety-five percent." She tried to smile, but the effort faded to a grimace.

Obeah felt too tired to respond. The resistance coming from Murell wasn't aggressive, but it was unyielding. No. Hopeless. That was the serious block: gentem were losing hope. Obeah shrugged, stood away from the fence. "I'll let the Council know when Cassidy has a report."

"Thank you, Obeah. I hope he can give us hope."

He turned to walk the short distance to the Healing Center. He returned greetings to Samuel Dreyer in front of his creamery but didn't stop to talk. Not now. Violence. War. How had they become immersed in such thinking? What would happen to their abilities if they became humanized?

Tandra was still kneeling by the bed when Obeah walked in.

"Obeah, are you sure he's okay? He hasn't even twitched."

"That's good, Tandra. You may as well go tend to your other activities. I'll send for you if anything changes."

She shook her head. "No. I'll stay here. Devin said he'd be here in a while."

"I'm not sure that's a good idea until Cassidy is stronger. Devin constantly incites Cassidy to action, to feeling angry over the disagreements with the Council; I'm not sure Devin should even be on the Council."

"Why shouldn't the Council include a voice from those who dissent?" Tandra pushed her long dark hair back from her face and jutted her chin out in defiance. "You know that I think the only thing wrong with the Membrane is that it leaks. Otherwise, we could live out our lives in peace. Unfortunately, it *does* leak. Of course, the human environmental movement may have stalled *because* we left, taking a major contingency of the movement when we separated from them. It was the biggest global brain drain that could ever happen at the worst possible time. But we deserve some peace." She shook her head and her shoulders sagged. Voice lowered, she continued. "If we *knew* what was going on over there, could contact our children or get through the Membrane, maybe we'd have more clarity, maybe not. But if we could just seal it off, I'd be okay with that, too. We've got to stop the leaks somehow or go back to what was and then change it by whatever means we can. Like almost everyone, I want this over."

Obeah sighed. "I'm not getting into that, Tandra. What I am saying is that you can only weaken Cassidy by plunging immediately into inflammatory rhetoric with him."

Tandra frowned. "That makes sense. I'll talk to Devin. Sorry, Obeah. I need to listen more."

"Thank you." Obeah leaned over Cassidy, then straightened. "He's sleeping quite peacefully. Why not just leave?" he asked again.

She didn't answer, nor did she move. Obeah went quietly to work at counter. What could he say? She knew the sleep was not a natural one and that Cassidy's reserves were faint.

CHAPTER THIRTEEN

Friday morning, July 6, 2029

Vala put off calling Char until after a quick ten-mile run with Serein through the morning mist. She relished the coolness while dreading that the day would bake to more record-breaking heat—close to 104° according to the forecast. Vala sensed it would top 106° before the day was over. She could hear air quality warnings blasting from speakers on the West Seattle Bridge. All major roads had such speakers since environmental laws and regulations had been dismantled a decade earlier. Although some countries were making strides toward sustainable living, the U.S. withdrawal as leader in reducing carbon lessened the initiative in many poorer countries.

As she listened to the dire air quality forecast, Vala drummed her fingers on the counter. In her work with radwastes, she'd come across various ways to mutate bacteria to thrive in bad environments. Progress had been made to convert CO_2 to energy for heat in cold areas, but the process was inefficient, and burning the fuel produced more CO_2. Something broader was needed.

What if bacteria *Ralstonia eutropha*—or some other bacteria—could be released in the atmosphere to eat and convert the material into something that would be neutral? Or even positive? Of course, scrubbers were already in operation, like those she'd designed for highways, but what about in the atmosphere itself—an orbiting ring or even a net in the stratosphere? Could anything be created that would clean and repair the ozone layer? Break down the CO_2, eat the carbon, and help forge O_3? Some bacteria had been grown in space, but what about *C. thermocellum*, the most likely candidate to absorb

CO_2? She'd have to get Guardian permission to call some people and see if anyone had made progress with the idea. The idea and related problems occupied her mind as she fed Serein, drank some live juice, and then put in her call.

Vala skipped the introductory statements and plunged immediately into her concerns. "Aunt Char, something is changing in my life, and I increasingly believe it's important. I need to learn more about who this anonymous donor was. I need to become more active in orchestrating my life, that is my life beyond work."

"But, Vala, I've told you all I know, which isn't much, certainly. What other information can I possibly give you?"

"The actual trust papers, Char. What did you do with those?"

"I put them in a safety deposit box at the bank where the trust is managed. Your name and mine are both listed. That seemed like the most sensible place for them."

"Washington Federal? Where the monthly checks come from?"

"Yes, dear."

"Will you meet me there this morning, in thirty minutes?"

Aunt Char couldn't get away for an hour, but once they'd agreed on a time, Vala called Eric. He agreed to join them but said he had an urgent appointment with a patient at one o'clock. He said his checks came from the same bank, though he'd never looked into them; he didn't think he had a safety deposit box.

The three of them met in the bank lobby and asked to see the manager, Thomas Bradley. While Eric and Vala waited, Aunt Char went to the safety deposit box to get her copy of the papers. Surprisingly, Vala and Eric were ushered in quickly. Apparently, the trusts were significant enough to make Vala and Eric more than casual walk-ins.

Thomas Bradley, a portly man in his 50s, rose when they came in. He nodded, yanked down on his vest like a character in an old movie, and said, "It's a surprise to see you two together, but, of course, you're welcome any time. Is there some problem with your trust accounts?" He gestured at the chairs opposite him as he sat again.

"Not exactly," Vala said. "But we've both," she gestured at Eric, "had some major changes in our lives. We need to know some

128

details about the trusts. Aunt Char is getting the papers out of our safety deposit box." Vala heard Eric's intake of breath preparatory to speaking and held up her hand in his direction. "Unfortunately, due to Eric's circumstances—the death of both of his parents—he doesn't have the key to his safety deposit box, but a box was set up here for him, and he'd like to see it, too."

"Hummmmm..." Bradley intoned. "You have no safety deposit information?" he asked Eric.

Eric just shook his head.

Bradley nodded. "Here's what I suggest because, otherwise, I have legal problems with giving you access, Dr. Kine. First, you, Dr. Glen, and your Aunt have what you need out of your safety deposit box, right?" After Vala nodded, he continued. "Okay. Then I want you and Dr. Kine to go see Matthew Buckler at Buckler and Associates on 6th and Pine I'll forward the information to your implant."

"We don't have implants," Vala said.

His eyebrows went up and he pursed his lips. "Well, then..." he fumbled for a paper and pen and wrote down Matthew Buckler's contact information. "I'll notify Mr. Buckler that you'll be calling for an appointment. He can advise you on how to best proceed. You have to understand that the box you're asking about, Dr. Kine, has your name on it as heir, but although we haven't heard from the box owner for some time, we have no way of knowing her status. Talk to Mr. Buckler about how to proceed."

Eric looked at Vala, and she smiled at him. The importance to him of this quest was clearly communicated by his expression.

Aunt Char brought the trust papers to Vala, but they gave very little information except for the firm, Buckler and Associates, and the monthly amount. Vala was surprised that the principal was only two million dollars, but with some quick mental calculations she realized the $6,000 a month could last well beyond her lifetime if investments didn't collapse completely, especially since Vala simply banked most of that in her savings.

They called Buckler and Associates and were surprised that they were again immediately given an appointment. "I'm surprised he's still there," said Char. "He wasn't a young man when you were born."

When they arrived, they waited for only about thirty seconds before being ushered into the cedar and mahogany office of Matthew Buckler. "Welcome," he said while rising and supporting himself on the huge desk. Vala guessed that, if he pulled himself straight, he was taller than she, but he looked as if he hadn't stood straight in decades. Under his silver, dandelion fluff of hair, his dark skin was etched with deep creases; half-glasses perched low on his large nose. Vala hadn't seen anyone with eyeglasses in longer than she could remember. Most people just got implants. He gestured toward the two chairs. "Please, be seated."

He looked, thought Vala, as though he were 95 at least, and Vala wondered why he hadn't retired. However, he appeared strong. He pressed a button and requested a third chair for Eric.

"We've been expecting you," he said as he folded himself back into his desk chair. "Actually, I thought you would have come before this. Would you like something to drink? Coffee? Tea? Water?"

Vala waved her hand to dismiss the request, but Aunt Char said quietly, "I'd very much like some water, thank you."

Buckler nodded at the man who had ushered them into the office, and he went to a small bar on one side of the room and quickly brought Char a glass and a pitcher of water. "Will that be all, sir?"

Buckler nodded. "Thank you very much, Pat. I'll call if we need you."

Another person brought in the third chair, and Eric settled in next to Vala.

"Why would you have been expecting us?" asked Vala. "I'd never heard of you until I was in the bank today."

"I just thought curiosity would have brought you here sooner. You must be content in your life. Yes?"

Vala nodded while feeling slightly disoriented. Content? No. Intimidated and isolated, yes. "More or less," she said, "but I've been operating on a lot of assumptions that I've come to realize were invalid. My parents are not my parents. The trust was set up by an anonymous donor, not my parents. In short, I suddenly don't know who I am."

"Pshaw!" His tone and voice reminded Vala of Santa characters in movies. "You're the same person you've always been.

Most people don't know who they are, but they plod along making the best of life. Either way, you're better off than most people since you have this trust and your Aunt Char who, I see, is still with you and being supportive."

"You remember me?" Char asked.

"Of course! Don't you remember me?"

"Well, yes, but…"

"I look like a wet and wadded up piece of paper that can't think at all, eh?" He laughed. "Well, I refused to retire or get reconstructive surgery. Until I heard from you." He met Vala's gaze directly. "Now I may decide to travel the world. And this is your brother?"

She inhaled sharply. "Brother?" she said softly.

"Yes. You're Eric, aren't you?"

Eric was grinning and nodding his head like an animated compdoll.

Vala shook her head. "Eric Kine? He's not my brother. We did a DNA test. I'm not related to anyone. I never even met him until a week ago."

Buckler drummed his fingers on the table, sighing. "Things have gone awry, haven't they? I was afraid of that. But none of that matters. You're here now. And, of course, he's your brother. In intent, anyway. I'm surprised you don't know that."

"That's what he claimed–"

"He would sense that. You listen to him. He's important to you." He stopped drumming. "So I suppose you want information about the trust."

Vala nodded. Her thoughts were cascading out of control: Eric, her parents, lawyers, Aunt Char, the anonymous donor … they all knew more about her life than she did. She should just get up. Walk out. Go run with Serein. She inhaled deeply and tried to focus on what Buckler was saying.

"…can't tell you much. Even though I haven't heard from Jasmine in over a quarter of a century, and I must assume something happened to her, I still must abide by her confidences."

"Jasmine who?" Vala asked.

"*That* is one of the confidences. Doesn't matter. I think I know what happened, but, well, that's all conjecture. What I can tell you is that Jasmine set up two trust accounts, one for you and one for Eric. She expected to be keeping an eye out for you both and coordinating how things went in your life–"

"*Coordinating?*" Vala asked. "What were we, a scientific experiment?"

"No, no, no. She cared for both of you deeply. You've got a quick flare response, don't you?"

Both Aunt Char and Eric chuckled, and Vala silenced them with a look.

"Anyway," Buckler continued, "the word choice was not a good one, but it was mine. She expected to be a *presence*. Yet, she wasn't stupid, and she set up legal protections to cover the contingency that she wouldn't be present. She gave me very clear instructions about how and when to precede if I didn't hear from her but did eventually hear from you. I was not to contact you directly."

"What about simple knowledge for the day-to-day life? Do you have any idea–"

Buckler held up his hand. "Let me stop you. Jasmine didn't want our firm to interfere *in any way* with your lives. She hoped she had set you up in such a way that your lives would be productive and valuable."

He lowered his hand and continued. "One of her provisions was that any time you came to this firm seeking information, after you were of legal age, you were to be given full control over the trust and any paperwork connected to that trust. Her assumption was that if you had to search us out on your own, something would have happened to her. She also had absolute faith that you would both be responsible and productive members of society. I've followed enough of your careers to know that's true."

"What if Vala had never come in?" Char asked.

"She would simply continue getting monthly payments."

"And now?" Vala asked.

"Whatever you want. You can have the entire principal, continue monthly payments, or whatever."

Vala waved away the options. "I don't care about that. I want information. I want to know who this Jasmine was. I want to know who my parents are."

Buckler shook his head. "I can't tell you anything about your family, Vala. Jasmine was looking out for you. However, she believed it best that if something happened and you didn't already know about her, I shouldn't pass on more information."

"You don't understand. I've had medical issues, and no way to connect them to any family history. Jasmine's history may be my only chance of tracking this down."

"My sense was that the relationship with your brother—"

"He's *not* my brother."

"That *Eric* would be a resource for you," Buckler said, still sounding rather like a patient parent Santa.

Vala threw her hands up over her head. "I'm getting nowhere! Let's go, Char," she said, rising.

"What about the trust?" Buckler asked.

"Just keep it as it is," Vala said. "I'll try to figure out something else later."

"Well, here is your file that shows where the money is invested and how payments have been made; that's through the bank, of course. Please try to understand that I have to try to honor my client's wishes as well as provide assistance to you."

"Oh, I know," Vala said. "It's just that you don't know … but how could you know? Never mind. I'll be in touch. Come on, Eric."

Eric stood, and Buckler raised his hand to wave him back down. "Please, Dr. Kine, would you stay for a moment?"

"I have a client soon—"

"This will take only a moment," Buckler assured him.

"I'll talk to you later, Eric," Vala said.

"Sure, Sis," he said with that irritating wide grin of his.

She glared at him but said nothing.

Halfway to the elevator, Aunt Char complained. "Vala, you do know that I *don't* run every day and that I *don't* have those long legs you have!"

"What?" Vala asked, stopping and turning.

"Slow down!" Char said.

"Oh, I'm sorry. This is all just so frustrating that I feel like running away. I have no control over my own life."

"Vala, dear, you've developed a strong tendency to run away when things are difficult. One way to get control is to quit running. Besides, you have as much control over your life today as you had last week. Gaining knowledge can be intimidating but also invaluable. You know that."

Vala started to argue but then she started toward the elevator again, walking at a slower pace. "I need to get to the U and get some work done. Do you want me to drop you at home, Aunt Char?"

"Only if you have time. I could take a driverless."

"No, I have time. You're not that far away." She dropped off Aunt Char then went to House to pick up Serein.

Back in her office, Vala tried to get caught up on mail and forms and scheduling for some of her experiments. She also had a paper deadline to take care of as well as a grant proposal to the government of Mexico that had to be finished before the end of the month; the Guardians were requesting more information about her plans with Mexico. Unlike anything she'd experienced before, she had trouble focusing her thoughts and staying on task. She felt like crying. Or screaming. Or hitting something.

Serein trotted over and rested his head on her knee. He was comforting her, but he was also suggesting that none of this stuff she was trying to focus on mattered—not like these issues in her life mattered.

Suddenly she slammed her fist down on her desk and swore. "This is NOT what I need to be doing!" she yelled, agreeing with Serein, and then she called up the Dean.

She answered immediately, as she always did for Vala, but the background image and noise—a pool and bar—showed that the Dean wasn't at her office. Vala reminded herself that most people were taking the entire week as a holiday even if available on their implants.

Vala apologized briefly and then told her that she needed a sabbatical starting immediately.

The Dean cleared her throat and her normally large brown eyes narrowed slightly. "Normally, Vala, sabbaticals are applied for a year in advance."

"I *know* that," she said. She swallowed hard and tried to take the snappishness out of her voice. "But I have personal issues, and

I either have to take a sabbatical or resign." As it happened, she had no summer or fall classes since she'd been planning on focusing on research; she did have a grant, but she could stall on it. Since she'd taken no time off in the ten years she'd been teaching and doing research for UW, the Dean quickly assured her there'd be no problem. Vala knew it was the threat of resigning that clinched the deal.

Vala promised to clean up her current projects and think about the grant while she was gone. The Dean said she'd plan on nothing for Vala until fall quarter in 2030, but the Dean's naturally pale and long face looked like a horse's ghost by the time the conversation ended. The Dean was making a concession, but Vala had a feeling she'd be doing payback.

As Vala disconnected, she felt a physical release and sudden motivation for getting work done. Serein experienced the same release and happily settled on his big pillow and went to sleep while Vala cleaned out her correspondence and paperwork that had deadlines. Several hours later, about midnight, Serein started pestering her. "You haven't had dinner or a walk, have you? All right. Let's take a break," Vala said.

Aunt Char had asked Vala not to run at night, so Vala avoided telling her that the middle of the night was still one of her favorite times to run the Alki Trail. Char, of course, knew Vala was just not telling her, so she had foisted a Shocker-Block off on her. "Really, Aunt Char, no one is going to take on a 6'7" person, obviously physically fit and accompanied by a Rhodesian ridgeback." Nonetheless, Vala had taken the Shocker/flashlight combo and promised her Aunt that she would carry it.

After going home, she and Serein ran about 12 miles, they had their meals, Vala content with her high protein salad. By 2:30 am, she was sitting outside, enjoying a slightly cooler breeze coming off the water, and thinking about the frustration of not being able to move forward in discovering more about herself, about ways to resolve these odd "spells" she had, unable to quite connect with the world around her. It was as if she were in two places at once. And now, the invisible man. Except he wasn't invisible. Eric had seen him. No sooner had she thought of Eric than her phone rang.

Eric.

135

"Don't you sleep?" she said into the phone.

"Well, yes, thank you. I just had four hours, which usually serves me well. How about you? Have you gotten some rest?"

"I've been sitting in my garden resting, sort of thinking. It's like sleep, I guess. What happened with the lawyer after we left?"

"Jasmine was my mother," Eric said softly.

Silence.

Vala's mind lurched into some sort of incoherent swirl. No words came to her.

Eric's laugh almost brought her out of it. "I didn't think you'd ever be left speechless, Vala."

"I–" Still her mind offered no coherent thoughts. "Why don't you come over here?" Vala said. "Now."

House announced, "Someone at the gate."

"That's you, isn't it?" Vala said.

"Yes."

"House, let Eric in. Always let Eric in. I'll come meet you," she said, feeling both pleased and a little uncomfortable with how close she kept feeling to Eric who was, after all, still a stranger.

"Don't bother," he said. "I'll come around to the garden."

Vala stayed put on the lounger. "You know the way?"

"Serein is here to guide me."

Vala looked around. Indeed, Serein was gone.

Eric came into the garden. His usual bouncy step was missing. He looked...sad. She'd never seen him look sad. He was carrying a cloth bag with a purple dragon on it.

"Hi," Vala said. "Are you bringing groceries to me again?"

He smiled and shook his head. "Beer."

"Beer? I don't drink beer."

"I was sure you didn't, so I brought my own."

"I have tea."

"And I have beer." He settled on a chair opposite her own. "It's nice here. Smells good–at least better–and it's peaceful. Cooler. That's not always easy to find."

Vala asked, "Are you sure she was your mother, Eric?"

He nodded. "The lawyer told me, and he was quite certain. In fact, he said I look a lot like she did. I believe it. He had a picture for me." He reached into his inside jacket pocket and pulled out a photo to hand to her.

Vala studied the picture, nodded. "You *do* look like her. Especially in the eyes. They are just as Aunt Char described them."

"He told me other things, some of which I'd already figured out. That I was to take care of my sister, who also has a trust fund. We were supposed to have been raised in the same family, each with our own trust funds. We have a job to do, and we need to do it together. Then he gave me the papers to get my safety deposit box open; the bank is processing the papers."

"A job to do? What?"

Eric shook his head. "I don't know. Apparently, Jasmine–Mom?–had some papers she was going to bring in and leave in the office in case anything happened to her. Meanwhile, she was en route to Algeria as a writer with a magazine; something about dangerous travel and the effect on tourism at the famous Casbah. That was in May 2003. Before she left, she told the lawyer that some things had gone "wrong" with the two children, and she needed to bring in papers that would help "bring the children together" and that she'd do that as soon as she returned.

"The lawyer never heard from her again. He said that two days after she left, the Boumerdès earthquake hit. He thinks something may have happened to her there." Eric downed half his bottle of beer.

"And nothing else? The name of the magazine? Other relatives? Nothing?"

"Nothing. Maybe in the safety deposit box."

"But we had DNA, Eric. We're *not* related."

"We were meant to be raised together, Vala. For a purpose. Even if not blood related, we're linked in very deep ways. I can feel it. And you *are* my sister, for what that is worth to you. It means everything to me." His voice, low, suited the set and clamped jaw as he stared, unsmiling, at the ground.

Vala no longer doubted Eric's intuition. It worked for him in much the same way, perhaps, that her communication and empathy with non-human living creatures worked. Or with numbers. Another oddity they had in common. Slowly, she nodded.

He was looking at her carefully now as though studying her. "You finally believe me."

It hadn't been a question, but Vala nodded. She no longer felt isolated. They sat, resting in the quiet with Serein sleeping between their chairs, until dawn.

CHAPTER FOURTEEN

Saturday, July 7, 2029

Vala and Eric went to the kitchen shortly after dawn to prepare a veggie frittata breakfast.

"What the hell, Vala! I can barely see the top of the counter. Who was your contractor? Colossus?"

"House was built to my specifications. I wasn't expecting short people."

Vala found a stool and set it at the counter. Eric climbed up and then was able to use the counter for eating. "Don't expect me to cook though," he warned her.

They'd almost finished when Eric's phone rang. "Wyatt! Good to hear from you. Have you gotten your system up and running?"

"Yes, but there have been some surprises. I won't go into the confusion, but I have documents that are, I believe, for you and Vala. I can't understand the material for the most part, but some of the numerical notations refer to dates that I think also relate to you; I'm hoping you can fill me in on the rest." Wyatt muttered something into the phone and then continued. "There was some sort of intrusion into the system as a whole. None of us can figure it out. Some systems were jumbled, and there is stray data here and there, but IT says everything is usable again. No indication of terrorism is involved, but the Guardians are suspicious. You can come by and pick up a copy, or I can send you a copy."

"Vala and I are having breakfast—"

"Well, of course you are. What's going on with you two?"

"She's my sister, Wyatt. I have confirmation that's more important to me than blood or DNA evidence. I found out about my birth mother, as well."

"Okay, Eric. Whatever you say."

Wyatt's disinterest in Eric's personal situation silenced Eric's retort. "What I was about to say is that you can send copies to each of us since we're here together."

"Right. On the way. I wish you'd both just get implants, but even those went wild. Implants were sending all sorts of odd information. Notifications of death. Some people couldn't stop singing. The Department Chair thought he was camping in the woods. That, too, has straightened out."

"I'm glad things are okay, Wyatt. Send it to Vala's House link," Eric said, raising his eyebrows at Vala. She nodded.

After he hung up, Eric explained to Vala what Wyatt had told him. "I heard you claiming me as your sister again."

"You agreed. Too late to change your mind now."

Vala laughed.

Vala activated House computer and the U-dub link, which she hadn't done since before the meeting at Wyatt's lab. Within seconds, House had four screens scrolling information by and the printing system was actively spewing out sheets of data. Eric was adding more paper to the machine. Vala called Wyatt.

"How much stuff did you send, Wyatt?"

"Not much. About five pages that seemed to apply to you."

"We're getting a lot more than that. House is spewing out information like we just hacked into GILS itself."

"Your link may have downloaded all this nonsensical stuff that we got here. I guess you'll have to just sort through it. That happened to all of us."

"Scheisse!" Some sabbatical. She looked wistfully outside, then said, "We'll scan through and figure out if anything seems related to us or our situation."

As Vala disconnected, loud music began spilling into the room. "House! Stop music!" Vala yelled.

Nothing.

"House! Stop! Stop! Stop!" she yelled as she slapped the counter.

"Try just reducing the volume," Eric said.

"House, lower volume!"

The volume dropped. "What the hell song is that?" Vala said.

Eric was tapping his fingers on the counter. "I haven't heard this in years. It's *Algorithm* by Forest for the Trees."

"House, lower volume again," Vala commanded. The music faded into the background.

Within a few moments and with computer help, they sorted information into files both paper and in the computer. Eric quickly had files devoted to Jasmine that included Eric's birth date and references to Vala as his sister. "This is obviously intended for us, Vala."

Vala nodded, then said, "I'm sorry, Eric. I wasn't listening."

"I have a lot of individual files that refer to Jasmine, me, and you. There's very little information though. It's almost like our names—you as Sarah—and birth dates are here just to get our attention."

Vala nodded. She swiped the screen. "Here's some information to add to what you have. Let's just call the file personal. This has my birth date on it, but it's enclosed in a quotation. It must have somehow merged."

"I'm finding quotations, too. How about a file of quotations?"

Vala nodded. They began setting up files of information.

"A lot of this doesn't relate to anything I know. I think some of it is Wyatt's work and maybe someone else's."

After a couple hours, they had four files on the computer and four files with the same titles on the counter. One of each was labeled *irrelevant* and included a number of red-flagged warnings that they were illegally trying to access confidential government files. The others were *personal, quotations,* and *QCL.*

"What's *QCL?*" Eric asked.

"Quantum Computation Language," Vala said. "It's probably someone's work, but I sorted it out until I can take a closer look."

"Well," Eric said, "you're the math genius. Most of this doesn't make sense to me. There isn't that much in the *personal* file."

They decided to sort through that file first, but there was little that seemed new. Jasmine's name was repeated numerous times, usually in conjunction with Vala and Eric. Repeated dates, including Vala and Eric's birth dates, were also included. As Vala looked at the references, she noticed that the sequence of repetitions of the personal information wasn't quite random. She put the material back in the groupings in which it had appeared instead of the verbal groupings they currently had for coherence. She broke the dates down into sequences. "Look at that!" she said.

"Okay," said Eric. "I see how you took coherent information and deconstructed it into incoherent information."

"No, it's a Fibonacci series. This is deliberate repetition."

"Fibonacci? That's those repeating spirals, no?"

"The series is most often presented to the public with photos of designs in nature that are spirals. I suppose this could be coincidence, but I don't find any number patterns that *aren't* presented as a Fibonacci series. That's deliberate."

"Spirals connect with this file I've set up of quotes. I thought maybe we'd just downloaded a bunch of stuff from literature classes."

Vala called up the quotes file.

> Life spirals laboriously upward to higher and even higher levels, paying for every step. –Ludwig von Bertalanffy

> The evidence at present available points strongly to the conclusion that the spirals are individual galaxies, or island universes, comparable with our own galaxy in dimension and in number of component units. –Heber Curtis

> The human mind always makes progress, but it is a progress in spirals. –Anne Louise Germaine de Staël

> Who are we? We find that we live on an insignificant planet of a humdrum star lost between two spiral arms in the outskirts of a galaxy, tucked away in some forgotten corner of a universe in which there are far more galaxies than people. –Carl Sagan

"Well," Vala said, "these are spiral references, but I'm not quite sure what it has to do with a Fibonacci series except for shape."

"It *has* to be connected."

"I don't see how. You're again falling into the idea that there is *meaning* because two things have one point in common. You're making things fit in the same way that a person blames tripping over a rock on the black cat that crossed his path an hour earlier."

"Our conversations keep spiraling, too. Sometimes I feel like we're in a time loop like in *Star Trek*."

Vala's mouth bunched up on one side. "Sure."

"Don't look contemptuous. You obviously know the reference. Maybe we're on a spiraling path. I'm reminded of a limerick I read in a Stephen Hawking paper:

> There was a young lady of Wight,
> Who traveled much faster than light,
> She departed one day,
> In a relative way,
> And arrived on the previous night.

Vala laughed.

"You're laughing more often," Eric said.

"I was just thinking that," Vala said. "But then, you knew that, didn't you?"

Eric nodded.

"Anyway," Vala continued, "what have spirals to do with us or our situation? I think we've let ourselves veer off course."

"Or loop? Can't veers and loops lead to spirals?" Eric put his head down on the counter and let his mind wander for a moment. He sat up and clambered down off the stool. "I need to walk some. That's not a comfortable stool. Ever consider cushions?" He let his mind wander some more as he looked out into the serene garden. "You know, it's funny, but spirals have always intrigued me. When I was a still a foster kid and sometimes wanted to escape my life, I drew out the complete spiral of the odd marks on my hand and pretended I could travel to the center and vanish."

Vala was staring at him, her mouth slightly open.

"What is it? You think I'm nuts again? Why are you suddenly empty emotionally?"

"Let me see it," she said, walking over to stand in front of him. "What?"

"Your hand with the marks, Eric. Let me see it."

He held out his right hand while studying her carefully. He'd never heard that particular tone of voice from her before. She was almost vibrating tension waves in his direction but no clear emotion or thought. He felt a wave of fear but was uncertain if it was Vala's fear or his own.

She cupped the back of his hand with her right hand and, with the forefinger of her left hand, she traced the three layers of spiral that would be there if it weren't broken in key places. Eric resisted the urge to jerk his hand back as her finger lightly tickled his palm. He also resisted the urge to say anything. She had entered some sort of space of wonderment, of no thought at all. He could feel surges of emotions, raw, vulnerable, and fractured but no thought.

And then it was gone. She closed off. Everything.

Her face was a mask, but her complexion had faded from her usual warm tan to a gray. Even her eyes changed color, from the rich amber to a faint, pale yellow. She dropped his hand abruptly and picked up her phone, jabbing at it a couple times. "Aunt Char?" she said. "I'm lost."

Eric felt himself tense. What was she questioning here? He still couldn't read anything ... except maybe a growing fear. The fact that he couldn't read her was a new experience. He felt his mouth grow dry and his scalp tingled.

Vala got up, apparently following Char's instructions, and went into the house. First, she stood in front of the hallway mirror for a moment, muttering something. Then she went into the kitchen. Eric followed with growing concern as Vala pulled a Sharpie out of one of the drawers and drew on the back of her hand, first a 9 and then a 6. Next she checked her phone and pressed a button, which set off an alarm. She shut that off and then reached down to pet Serein who was pressed against Vala's legs. She was following reality check procedures sometimes recommended to those utilizing lucid dreaming.

"Yes." She finally said into the phone and then, "Eric." Then she handed the phone to Eric.

"Eric, what happened?" asked Char.

"We were just talking about a document Wyatt sent us, trying to decipher the math. Some of it refers to spirals. I mentioned a birthmark on my palm, an incomplete spiral. Vala looked at it and then called you."

"Eric, look at Vala's right palm."

"May I see your right palm, Vala?"

Silently, she held it out to him. She was still a blank to him.

The birthmark there was identical to Eric's except different parts of the suggested spiral were missing. "It's the same spiral only with different gaps," he said softly into the phone.

"At one time, Vala went into something of a spiral herself, trapped in the math and work with spirals. She was convinced she had to connect the spiral with something in order to accomplish some plan or goal and in order to stay whole, but she had no idea how to do so or what she wanted to accomplish. Her mother put her into Seven Cedars Clinic in Port Townsend for that episode. She was ten."

"How could a mother do that?" Eric whispered.

"No one knew what to do, and I had no say. Anyway, Vala was there for eight months. Eventually, of course, doctors convinced her that she'd had a breakdown of some sort, that she was holding onto sanity tenuously. They convinced her to drop all her thoughts about spirals because it was just an unhealthy obsession. There was talk of a skin graft to remove the birthmark, but her father put up a ferocious battle against that."

"So now, she's frightened that the experience is repeating?"

"Yes. Talk to her. Explain that this is real. I'm on my way."

Eric handed the phone back to Vala. "Can we go out to the garden and sit?" he asked.

She nodded robotically and they went back out. "I don't know if you are really here," she said.

"Well, it won't do much good for me to reassure you that I am, but watch this." He walked to the far side of the garden and said, "Serein, here!"

Serein looked at Vala who said nothing, then got up and trotted, tail wagging, over to Eric.

Eric petted him, then walked back to sit beside her. "You wouldn't imagine that about Serein, would you? But he does like me." Eric smiled. "Listen, in less than a week, we've both had huge amounts of information to digest and our self-images have changed dramatically. This is just one more."

"I've spent a lifetime trying to understand who I am," Vala said softly. "It never ends well."

"You've never had me around before," Eric said. "Remember, I'm your brother, and I have a mission to help you. We all have doubts about who we are and what we are doing. Have you read Chuang-tzu?

> "Once upon a time, I dreamt I was a butterfly, flittering hither and thither, to all intents and purposes a butterfly ...suddenly I awoke... Now I do not know whether I was then a man dreaming I was a butterfly, or whether I am now a butterfly dreaming I am a man."

Vala almost smiled. "My life."

At least, he thought, she's still responding. "I think that many things were supposed to happen for both of us and that many things went wrong. But I sincerely believe we're both on the right track now. Just a few decades later than intended."

"He's telling the truth," Char said from the doorway to House. "You're going to have a better life now, Vala."

She turned and smiled at Aunt Char. "Maybe. Did you fly?"

Char nodded. "Driverless copter."

"You hate those," Vala said.

"You're more important than my fear of crashing to Earth and dying in a ball of flame."

Vala cringed. "What would I do without you, Aunt Char? Don't even joke about it." Char sat in a chair next to Vala and held her hand. "I'd be locked in a little room somewhere on suicide watch, I suppose."

"You'd be yourself, as you are now, Dear. I've just been a place to rest now and then. Look at Serein. He's concerned."

Vala looked at the dog, patted him. "He responded to Eric. Eric must be real."

Char laughed. "I think Eric is one of the more real things to have happened in your life in a long while."

"I am real," Eric said. He was beginning to feel irritation tighten the muscles around his ears. Sarah–no, Vala–didn't even look at him.

"I've taken a sabbatical," Vala said. "I think maybe I'd better go back into the clinic for a while. I think maybe I need rest and some professional help."

Eric shivered. Goose bumps again prickled his scalp and skittered along his spine. She had just excluded him from her life, from her future. Her emotions were so far buried that he was receiving no more from her than he was the chair where she sat.

Serein, on the other hand, was growing increasingly tense, enough so that Eric could feel the dog's worry almost like a physical tapping, tapping, tapping in his thoughts–not quite words but clear meaning.

"Vala," Char said, "you do realize that Eric *is* a doctor, a professional counselor."

Eric didn't hear Vala's response as he went to the kitchen, found a pitcher in a lower cupboard, then dragged a chair over to the sink so he could fill it with ice cold water. Happily, House responded to him for a change when he specified the 35 degree temperature. He grabbed a towel from the downstairs bathroom, then went back to the garden, coming up behind Vala.

Now Char was kneeling in front of Vala, talking intently. She glanced up, saw Eric, stood, and took a step back.

Eric dumped the water over Vala.

She jumped up, spinning around as she did so. "What the hell do you think you're doing, Eric?" she yelled.

Eric nodded. "Good. You know I'm here. Does that feel real, Vala?" He tossed the towel to her.

Vala glared. Char was smiling slightly while obviously trying to not do so.

Vala looked at Serein. "How could you just *sit* there?"

Serein wagged his tail while remaining seated by Vala's chair. He didn't seem to mind the splash-over and Eric could feel the tension release in him.

As Vala started rubbing at herself with the towel, Eric said, "Look, you're very smart. Brilliant. A genius. But I am wise, and you are a little deficient in that department. Stop feeling sorry for yourself–which, by the way, seems to be your hidey-hole response– and stop disappearing emotionally. Stop running away from everything. Let's put together your smarts, my wisdom, the clues we've been handed and figure out what's going on in our lives. I can't do it without you."

"Damn straight," muttered Vala. She threw the towel on the ground.

"And you can't do it without me."

"Hummmph. I hardly think throwing cold water on me is an indication of how much I need you. Or how good you are as a counselor. Is that with you do with your patients?"

"Well, it wasn't particularly methodical or controlled hydrotherapy, but, look! We're talking again! Besides, you're not a patient, you're my sister."

Char's laughter broke free. "I'm sorry," she sputtered. "I can't help it!"

Vala glared at her, then she started laughing, too, then collapsed into the chair.

Finally, after Char went to the kitchen to get tea for them, Vala smiled at Eric. "Okay. Again. Let's start. After I change. If nothing else, it no longer feels quite so hot."

"Vala!" Char called from the kitchen. "House won't make tea! It keeps spewing out quotes and music."

Vala went in, cursing at House before finally getting it to stop uploading repeats of the same information from the university, then changed while Char set up tea in the garden. When Vala returned, Eric said, "Let's start with your horrific response to the birthmark on my palm and why we both have them."

For a response, Vala held out her right hand, palm up.

Eric stared at both their birthmarks. "No," he muttered. "Not birthmarks. Something else." The one on Vala's hand looked smaller on her palm–her hands were half again as large as his–but the spiral shape was the same size. However, where his was missing segments to complete a spiral, Vala had the line. Where she was missing segments, Eric had the lines. They weren't identical since they'd both grown and used their hands differently over the years, but they were obviously paired.

"So what do you think it means?" Vala asked.

Eric shook his head. "I don't know. But it confirms in my mind that we need each other, that we have mysteries to resolve.

Look, they're each incomplete in different ways. Also, you have skinny fingers."

She yanked her hand away. "It proves nothing, Eric. Lots of coincidences most likely means only that we're looking for coincidences."

"What the hell, Vala! All those spiral quotes and the Fibonacci series and that song and our palms and … it's like seeing the glaciers disappearing, the sea water rising, the forests burning, animals going extinct, temperatures rising and saying that climate change doesn't exist. That's not scientific; it's stupid."

"Eric, there is clear, measurable science behind all the climate change observations. We have nothing backing up these personal coincidences," Vala said. She sat down and began vigorously rubbing Serein's ears. The dog whined, and Vala apologized and sat back.

Eric lowered his head into his palms and groaned. Vala could be a textbook example of stubborn.

"What happens next?" Char asked.

"Let's look at our files again and see if we can find anything measurable," Eric said. "Something Vala can accept."

Char grabbed both of their hands as they stood to go into House to look at the computer screen again. "I don't know if I've said this before," she said, "but I'm delighted we've added a nephew to the family." She stooped and kissed Eric on the cheek. He bit his lip to limit his outward emotional response to stinging eyes rather than tears.

CHAPTER FIFTEEN

Saturday early afternoon, July 7, 2029

Cassidy thought maybe he was awake. Perhaps groggy and disoriented was his normal condition. Only this time, he had a massive pain in his head, something he'd never experienced before.

"Good morning again," Obeah said. He was sitting on the bed and holding a damp cloth over Cassidy's forehead. "I know you're going to ask, so you've been in and out of consciousness for the equivalent of three 24-hour cycles. You were too weak to stay focused."

He pushed himself into a sitting position, pushing against the damp cloth. Obeah took it away. Cassidy glanced down and saw Tandra asleep on the floor beside the bed. "She was worried."

"Of course," said Obeah. He held out the cloth and Cassidy grabbed it and lowered his head into it. "She's been awake for about four days if you count the time before you left. It caught up with her. Her health is suffering. Mine is, too, for that matter. If you don't care about yourself, I'm hoping you'll consider others before you plunge ahead again."

Obeah sounded crankier than usual. "What's wrong with my head?" Cassidy rubbed the cloth against his forehead. Maybe he could erase it. That didn't help. He felt queasy.

"I suspect you have a roaring headache, tension-based with a chemical imbalance."

"I just said that," Cassidy said. Are you sure I wasn't hit on the head at some point?'

"Quite sure. A headache is a malady in the brain, usually caused by a variety of things from a change in blood vessels to muscle tension. As far as I can tell as I've been monitoring you, your stress and emotions have had an effect on your chemical balance, and this has triggered something that humans go through on a regular basis. What you're experiencing is like a human's hangover from drinking too much alcohol. You've probably never experienced one before." He picked up a glass from a low table. "Here, drink this."

Cassidy didn't even ask what it was. If it would make his head quit hurting, he didn't care. He threw down the cloth and grabbed the glass. If drinking too much alcohol caused this, why would anyone do it a second time?

By the time he'd finished drinking Obeah's drink, his head already felt better although it also felt as though someone had crammed it full of cotton wadding. "Thanks. That's better."

"The pain will ease off. You had another hazardous journey, and your reserves are becoming less with each trip."

Obeah sounded like a recorded message. "How long did you say I was gone?" Cassidy asked.

"By Earth calendar, three days, more or less," Obeah said. "You've been in-and-out of semi-consciousness. It was hard to track exactly when you were here."

"That's too long since I left the information. If they understood, they'd have done something by now." He shook his head and regretted it immediately. "Another failure."

Obeah went over to the counter and returned with another drink. "You're too hasty, as always," Obeah said while handing him the glass. "People who aren't overly-impulsive need time to process information and act."

"What is this?" Cassidy asked suspiciously.

"You need to rehydrate. And I made it taste good for your delicate sensitivity."

Cassidy smelled it, grimaced.

"I didn't say I made it smell better. You're supposed to *drink* it, not smell it."

Cassidy shrugged and drank trying not to breathe before drinking the entire concoction. The taste was good. "Better tasting," he said, then added, "If my information had made any impression on them, I think we'd have had a response by now."

Tandra stirred, stretched, looked at Cassidy and smiled. Then frowned. "You're never doing that again!"

"I'm okay, Tandra. And I probably won't. I'm not sure what else I *can* do."

"You said yourself that the technology may well be too different to communicate," Obeah said.

"No, I don't think that's the problem. I was able to enter their device and input information. They aren't using a quantum system, at least not where I was."

Obeah shrugged. "I want you to eat, and we have to talk," Obeah said.

While Cassidy ate one of Obeah's omelets, this time loaded with goat cheese, and had another "good for you" concoction, he told Obeah and Tandra, who joined him at the table, about seeing the children together at the lab. "That at least is good news. I know they could see me, but they didn't respond. When I tried to incorporate the information into what I thought was their computing system, I..."

"You what?" Tandra asked, too impatient to wait for Cassidy to gather his thoughts.

"I don't know. It wasn't like being in my quantum computer lab; it wasn't harmonious. I sort of lost myself, lost everything. I didn't seem to have direction or sense of place. I kept trying to place my information within a huge data stream, both more limited and more chaotic than made sense. Then, suddenly, Eric's palm implant, though incomplete, gave me a focus point, and I was back on my path, able to focus. I saw Eric, then I focused on Sarah and saw her briefly. Then I felt as though I had to get back, that I couldn't continue." Cassidy set his fork down and massaged his temples.

"Is the pain still severe?" Obeah asked.

"No, not as bad," Cassidy said. "I hope I never go through that again."

"So you don't know if they can read the information?" Tandra asked.

Cassidy shook his head. "I'm not even sure that I managed to upload information. And I can't think of anything else to do. I was sure this would work. Their data stream was illogical. I ran into a lot of encrypted files and there were blocks to the information I didn't recognize." He ate the last of his eggs.

Obeah cleared his throat, leaned forward and said, "I have information."

Cassidy didn't like Obeah's tone. "You sound serious. What has the Council done now?"

"First, I want you to understand a couple things. The Council is not directly responsible for what I'm about to tell you, except for the fact that for too long they've backed down from Alarick. In effect, they've become figureheads for a demagogue whose agenda has always been founded on hate and resentment. Alarick isn't stable. The Council members have known this, but they've wanted to support him, try to guide him back into balance. They were remiss in their duties but not unethical in their proceedings."

Obeah's explanation sounded rehearsed, formal. Cassidy's discomfort grew. "We've known that. But the Council will never vote to replace him."

"Wrong. They *have* dismissed him. But they need to talk to you. They want to try to understand how realistic your success in contacting the children is and how realistic you think help from those children will be."

"What's brought about that attitude shift?" Cassidy asked.

"They have discovered, through a leak from those working with Alarick on his private projects, that the chemical additives to the water began two years ago. The past six months, he has stepped up the project, using more chemicals in the water because he sensed the Council was beginning to re-think the plan." Obeah sat back in his chair as if expecting Cassidy's outburst.

"Guts for garters! *Everything* is going wrong, Obeah! Our plans for the children. Our hope for reconnection. Our efforts to avoid this mutated act of genocide." His head suddenly began throbbing again. He groaned. "What have we become? What kind of culture are we morphing into?"

"No, Cassidy, you mustn't succumb to anger and condemnation. Remember history. Think about this: I don't believe that your DNA can overcome cultural immersion. Consider how long we struggled within the human culture, tried to effect change. We ourselves have been changed. We're *trying*, Cassidy. The Council has polled our gentem. They want complete separation, even if it means abandoning other gentem on Alpha Earth." His expression softened. "We need your help. You're the only one who has *seen* the children, who has a perspective for the whole, not just a segment, of our situation."

Cassidy pushed back from the table. Obeah was looking to him for an answer, for hope. What could he say? "Everything is out of sync, falling into ruin. I've failed–"

"Will you quit saying that. What has ever been accomplished in three days?"

"Obeah, you forget all the time I've spent trying to work this out."

"No, I don't forget. You forget that you, yourself, are barely more than a child; you could have worked on it since you were born, and it would be little enough time. Don't throw it away. Talk to the Council. They're looking for direction. Open your mind and your thought. Quit thinking about yourself." He paused, stood, and began clearing the table.

As he set the dishes on the counter, he continued, his voice softer. "Cassidy, I'm discouraged, and I'm tired. Many of us are. We need to work together and resolve this issue now."

"Marina is working on a way to connect with the human Internet through the membrane, maybe start a cyber communication," Tandra said.

Cassidy nodded his head and noticed again how pale she was and that she'd lost weight. "Okay. Guess there's no reason to stop now; we can keep trying. If she can set up some kind of link, maybe we can contact the children that way. The problem is that since we're in a different time, the signals won't likely catch up with each other. Maybe we could utilize light. Light, like water, is more effective at going through the Membrane."

Tandra tilted her head and drew her eyebrows together. "Why can't LifeForce be utilized? We utilized it, as you explained it to me, to generate the membrane, to create the original temporal shift. Can't we communicate that way? You said that it was a unifying force."

"You forget that humans don't utilize the LifeForce as we do. According to what I've read, we didn't understand ourselves *how* we were able to do the things that humans called miracles, witch craft, or magic until the 1960s." Cassidy stared into space and rubbed his lower lip. His head had quit throbbing although a steady pulse kept darkening his vision repeatedly. "We've only begun to understand LifeForce even now—and we still don't know all the ways in which it interplays with other forces. It's not something we can just pull out like a hammer. We also don't understand all the DNA differences that our scientists have identified—or at least how those differences play out in connection with other genomes."

Obeah sat back down at the table and nodded. "But we've made progress." His voice was thoughtful, and he pulled on his long moustache. "I remember the hoopla when our scientists set up the Anomalies and Paranormal Research Institute back in the late 60s… that was an era when even the humans were into understanding the environment, the web of life. Our people spent 30 years doing scientific research that was later incorporated into programs at Oxford and Stanford. Those programs diverged considerably, but echoes of our research remained."

"Weren't you part of all that, Obeah?" Tandra asked.

Obeah nodded. "The idea grew out of the 1953 *First International Utrecht Conference on Parapsychology* in the Netherlands. Some gentem attended, but it was mostly human scientists and parapsychologists from 23 countries." Obeah chuckled. "Imagine that. At the time, humans were ahead of gentem! I was very hopeful. Most human programs quickly relegated the research into psychology programs, but our Institute made excellent headway into identifying gentem natural abilities. Then, our facilities were bombed and our scientists harassed. We had to shut down the Institute due to human religious pressure in the 90s because of our 'anti-Christ' interests. Everyone scattered."

Cassidy nodded. "I met Marina at the Institute when I was only ten. She helped me focus on physics. When I was 15 and it shut down, we went to Australia."

"We still had hopes we'd work with humans," Tandra added. "Gentem are slow learners."

"So what's next?" Cassidy asked. "What *hasn't* been tried?"

Silence.

Cassidy groaned. He'd never felt this poorly. "This would be easier if anyone had kept better records. Frankly, the records most of you kept are very poor, Obeah."

"It's true," Obeah said. "We've never been good at keeping calendars and records and what the humans call *paper trails*. I suspect that in one sense, most of us didn't want information following us around. For the sake of not drawing attention to ourselves, we had to *die* and start new every so often. We've relied on oral culture for our stories. Such a fuss over birthdays among humans! Anyway, for many of us when it came to the Membrane, I think we hoped it was done and we could just move on."

Cassidy tried to silence the frustration that tightened his thoughts into a knot. A quote came to mind. "'There is no energy in matter other than that received from the environment,'" Cassidy said. "The answers have to be in our environment, in our natural resources. A modification of that thinking is what we need."

"Nikola Tesla!" Obeah said. "You know that Tesla has received deep and continued criticism from humans."

"He made the mistake of trying to create technology that allowed humans to do what he—and most gentem—can do through innate abilities. Training, not technology, should come first. It was like turning a computer over to someone who'd never seen one before."

"Is he nearby? Would he have insights?" Tandra asked.

Obeah shook his head. "The last I heard, he was somewhere in the Dolomites, looking for … something. He doesn't communicate."

Cassidy took a deep breath and was relieved that his head didn't start pounding again. Tesla's discouragement with humans had almost destroyed him. Cassidy felt a stirring of empathy. "When do we see the Council?"

"I'll go set up a meeting now that you're awake," Tandra said. "You stay here. Rest some more. I'll be back shortly."

Tandra left to talk with the Council, Obeah left to see to a patient, and Cassidy washed up breakfast dishes. He stared out the window over the sink. The air sparkled, and a deep peace rested within the stately evergreens. How could they keep this Earth from being destroyed? Or any Earth? He reviewed the information he'd tried to pass on to the children, and his head throbbed again ever so slightly. He felt slightly dizzy, and he sat back at the table.

What could he have added? How could this not connect? If notes about spirals made no sense to them, this was hopeless. Should he try again? Before he could start banging his head on the table, Obeah was back.

"Just saw Tandra. The Council is ready. Are you able to meet? You look...shaky."

Cassidy shrugged. "I'm okay." He rose and they walked to Council chambers. Cassidy tried to think of what he could say to the Council members. Delara was Vice Chair, but she was also a descendent of victims of the Basque witch trials, and she had no love of humans. The same was true for most of them. When he voiced his concerns as they walked, Obeah waved them aside.

"Delara knows history as we all do, but she very much believes in living in the now time, not in the shifting recall of the past. She is, however, very angry at the way humans in the now continue to trash the environment. She suspects they are stupid and that suspicion causes her to lean toward anger. Anger shuts the mind off to options." He knocked on the chamber door and opened it without further ceremony. Tandra, who'd joined them at the steps remained by the door inside in case the Council asked her to leave.

The entire Council of Nine, minus Alarick, was present. Delara welcomed Obeah and Cassidy and then asked them to be seated. "Are you staying?" she asked Tandra.

"If I may," Tandra said. "I'm not only concerned about this project but also about the toll it has taken on my brother's health."

Delara nodded and said, "Then you are welcome."

Cassidy looked around at the various faces. All except Delara looked angry, and Cassidy tensed as he felt a slight throbbing in his head again.

The Council was supposed to be set up so that the special interests of the various communities were all represented. Of course, some individuals always felt under-represented, no matter how the elections went every sixth solstice. One senior Council member was allowed to stay beyond the six rotations, but all others had to be replaced. Alarick had stayed on the council for eight election turns and, in Cassidy's opinion, had been long overdue for replacement.

Delara began to speak. "Obeah, Cassidy, we're glad to have you here. As Obeah knows and, I'm sure, has passed on to you, Cassidy, Alarick has violated our processes and our trust; we have voted to remove him from the Council and to perform a full investigation into what he has done and what our response should be. It's not, quite frankly, that we all disagree with what he did, but he has launched himself into anarchy. He has," she added, holding her hand out to Cassidy to stop him from speaking, "also violated the principles behind gentem nonaggression, which we recognize."

Cassidy looked around the room again. Everyone, except Devin, was studying their hands or the table carefully. Devin, who was a member with Cassidy of the Peaceful Coalition for Human Reintegration, was scowling at Delara. This was not a unified Council.

"Alarick has committed an act of war. Be honest," Devin said.

Delara looked around the table, and it became clear no one else was going to speak. She chose to ignore Devin's comment. "In short, we need someone to replace Alarick temporarily until a special election can be held. We are chartered to operate as a Council of Nine. If we don't have full membership, all approvals, changes, or progress regarding our community must stop." She looked at Cassidy. "That would include your attempts at communicating with those on the other side of the Membrane."

"But–"

Delara again stopped Cassidy with a raised hand and stern look. "This isn't a matter of debate, Cassidy. We've asked Obeah to take Alarick's place, and he has declined because his healing work takes too much time. Our next choice was Jasper Chanter, but he is out of contact somewhere in Africa. You, Cassidy, probably know more about the issues right now than anyone else. We're formally asking you to serve temporarily–at least until an election can be held. Of course, your activities would have to cease while you were on the Board."

Cassidy immediately felt that a carrot had been dangled in front of him as a reward for being compliant. When he met Devin's gaze, Devin's head shook, ever so slightly, from side-to-side. Cassidy took a moment and then changed his view. The Council was in a bind, and perhaps they honestly wanted his involvement. He should try to be positive, especially with Marina on the Council. Was he, too, becoming infected with negative and aggressive thoughts?

All were looking at him intently and, except for Rainbow, their expressions were unreadable. Rainbow looked smug. But then she almost always looked smug.

Cassidy pulled to mind all he knew about proper protocol and began his speech. "It's a great honor to be asked to fill such a position with the Council. Your guidance and governance has proven itself over the years, and it's vital to our continued success as a species and as a culture. Because of that, it's with great regret that I have to decline. As you know, my work trying to contact our children on the other side of the Membrane is of great importance to me and, at this point, I am the person best suited to that work. I also believe that the work may be on the edge of a breakthrough. In addition, in all honesty, I wouldn't be able to fully dedicate my thoughts to anything else right now." He stopped. That was about as gently as he knew how to be to say *no*.

Delara's lips thinned. The others were all, again, studying their hands or the table. Devin looked more relaxed.

A sudden thought came to Cassidy. "However," he added, "may I suggest that you consider my sister, Tandra, for the position. She is wiser and better informed on general cultural matters than I. She, like Obeah, is a healer although more of a spiritual counselor. She understands cultural needs, and she's a part of the project with the Membrane and the children."

Delara pursed her lips and nodded. "We'll take your suggestion to heart, Cassidy. We appreciate your candor, and we'll be in touch with you about your communication project. As I say, we can't move forward until we heal our Council breach. Thank you."

"I would like, as soon as you believe it's appropriate, to know more about the position of the Council regarding the humans," Cassidy said.

"Of course," Delara said. "Tandra, will you stay for a time?"

The clear implication was that Cassidy and Obeah were dismissed. "Not sure why I was here," said Obeah as they left.

"Probably to encourage me to take the position," said Cassidy.

"Not my place," said Obeah gruffly. "I have medicines to attend to."

As they reached Obeah's clinic, Cassidy's mind blanked, then his physical senses grew dark. He could tell he was falling, but he was powerless to stop it. Fear prickled the back of his tongue as he felt himself tumbling through space. His hand felt as though it were on fire. The spiral! He swallowed nausea and forced himself to try to focus on Earth, on light—on the underlying primal field that gave gentem their source of Life. He had to stay centered! The children had connected! He sensed their distress, which matched his own.

He couldn't see. He felt something holding him. Obeah? He tried and failed to speak. Tried again. "Obeah, the meadow. Quickly. Children. The portal. The obelisk."

Cassidy's sense of place was expanding, connecting to new sensations and perceptions. It was both sensory overload and contradictory sensory input. He had once fallen into a turbulent river, couldn't tell up from down, couldn't breathe. He was feeling the same sensations. Now he forced himself into a mind/body duality, creating a meditative state that began to give him stability through knowledge of what was happening. The children would have no such anchor.

Somehow Obeah had gotten Cassidy in a three-wheel scooter. By the time Cassidy could begin to see, they'd arrived in the meadow where the obelisk stood, less than a mile from Obeah's clinic. The idea was that a portal would open for those who were linked when the children themselves linked. They'd never used the portal with Jasmine, but the theory was sound. In essence, the obelisk used an Alfvén wave to open and hold the portal open, but the plasma field itself was self-generating.

Judging by how Cassidy felt, the effect of a sudden linking between the four of them was more powerful than they'd expected.

"I don't know if Tandra can make it on her own," Cassidy muttered when Obeah stopped the scooter.

"I'll send Fulton," said Obeah as he punched a quick call out to Fulton to check on Tandra.

Cassidy continued to focus for a moment in the sidecar with his eyes shut. He was trying not to be sick to his stomach as the vertigo came and went. Finally, Cassidy half-fell out of the sidecar and, with Obeah's support, lurched over to the obelisk and peered around. Due west, light shimmered oddly as though an imperfect mirror were reflecting the surroundings. But the surroundings were not only wavering but slightly different in color and composition. "Can you see it?" he asked Obeah.

Obeah shook his head. "No, I see nothing. I think you are correct that it's functional only for you and, perhaps, the other three."

"I'm going through, Obeah. When Tandra arrives, have her wait here until she hears from me. I don't know what to expect."

"Cassidy, you're weak—"

"No time to argue, Obeah."

"The Council will be unhappy if you don't talk to them first."

"This is what all our efforts have gone toward. We must be prompt in answering the children's call. If I feel this shaky and know what's happening, they must be near panic. I'm not waiting." With that he walked forward and into the shimmer.

At first, the experience was like walking through water, then he suddenly realized that where he was walking was not the same environment he'd left. He glanced back and saw the same shimmering he'd seen before. Had he somehow gotten turned around? He looked forward again. Green leaves were all around him.

Cassidy stopped, confused, then realized he was standing in dense rhododendron growth. He pushed at the leaves and peered out into a green garden—the same one he'd seen before when he'd tried to communicate with Sarah! There, in the middle of the garden in an open area were the children—and someone else—as well as the large dog Cassidy had seen before. The children were both on their knees being violently ill. A large dog stood by the kneeling woman, seemingly on guard. The third person was on her phone saying there was a medical emergency.

"Please," Cassidy said, "they'll be fine. Do *not* call for help. Give us a moment. Medical personnel wouldn't understand."

The woman with the phone looked at him, her mouth hanging open and mouthing silent words. Cassidy realized he'd never seen anyone outside of a cartoon do that. Then she yelled at him, "You get out of here! You're the stalker! I'm calling the police!"

"It's all right, Aunt Char," said the woman who was pushing herself upright with the use of the chair. "Just wait. It's passing. We'll–" she stopped while she struggled against more retching–"wait! Eric! Okay, Eric?"

Cassidy studied the woman, Sarah, surprised at her apparent composure. He didn't think he would be as calm if he knew nothing about what was happening or why. "He's all right," Cassidy said, joining her to hoist the small man back to his feet.

"Yes. Yes," said Eric, sounding very uncertain and leaning against Serein who licked him on the face. "I think so. What the hell?"

"You and Sarah have completed your spirals," Cassidy said. "You opened a portal for us. Look at your palms."

As they looked at their palms, each of which shimmered a complete spiral, Char spoke up. "Vala, is this okay? Should I call the police? Who is this person?"

"We're okay, Aunt Char. For now. Are you?"

Char shook her head. "I'm fine."

Vala nodded. "You stay. Be an objective witness. I need that." She moaned, then swallowed. "I don't want more people and confusion. I have to understand."

"Vala?" Cassidy asked. "Aren't you Sarah?"

"Yes. No. Long story," she said. "I have to sit down."

She and Eric sat in chairs. Char brought them wet towels to wipe their faces and to cool off and then she found a hose and cleaned off the area of the patio where the two had vomited.

Vala opened her eyes, nodded, pushed herself up to sit straight. Eric, too, was sitting upright and looking more alert.

"What's that?" Eric asked pointing at the shimmering portal barely visible through the rhododendron. "It looks like a bush halo."

"That's the portal you opened and that I came through. That's what allowed me to come here physically this time. You two opened it. Only we can see or use it–and my sister."

"Serein! Come back from there!" Vala yelled, too late, as Serein ambled into the shimmering space. "I thought you said only we could use it! What will happen to Serein?"

"But—" Cassidy started.

"Wait, Vala," Eric yelled as he ran after Vala who was chasing after Serein and calling his name. "Char, she'll be okay," Eric called over his shoulder.

"No! No!" Char was yelling. "Where did they go?"

Egads, Cassidy thought. Did they often freak out like this? "It's okay," he said to Char, trying to calm her down.

"It's not okay! They've disappeared!"

"They'll be back. I will, too, but I have to go after them and guide them. Be patient. Just wait here, and I'll make sure someone gets back soon to reassure you."

Sounding distant and hollow, Vala's voice filtered into the garden: "It's okay, Aunt Char. Serein would never lead me anywhere we can't handle."

Char still looked shaky and pale, but Cassidy turned and went into the portal after the three. He could make out swirly figures—it was like looking into a wide-angle photo of a bowl of green water. On the other hand, he knew that Char would see nothing but the garden, empty of those she loved.

He plunged after them.

CHAPTER SIXTEEN

Saturday, July 7, 2029

Vala had only one thought as she followed Serein and that was to make sure he didn't vanish from her life. He wanted her to follow, that was clear, so it must be safe. A lump of fear that had settled in her throat lessened as she made out the figures of two people, one of whom was kneeling to pet Serein. They stood in what appeared to be a continuation of her own green garden, but, not quite–the meadow was surrounded by forest. Cool air encouraged her to take a deep breath and relish the sweet smell: cedar, fir, earth.

Had she ever left the clinic? Perhaps she was still there, still hallucinating wildly, plunging down fictional rabbit holes. Was it possible to live an entire life separate from reality?

A shimmering obelisk stood slightly to one side of the two people, and scooters were parked nearby. The familiar mixed with the surreal made the episode more dream like. The air, free of smoke, was alive with bird song! Distracted, she stopped and looked around, listening. That quickly, she knew there were at least 46 species, singing, in summer, but not in a summer that was so oppressively hot. These birds had plenty of food and fresh water, and they were thriving! The entire area hummed with health.

Serein was already back by her side, calm and working to reassure her. She felt herself relaxing in response to Serein and the environment, listening and responding silently.

The older man who had been petting Serein was dressed in simple black, loose-fitting shirt and pants with a long, embroidered vest, almost to his knees. At least 7' tall, he was smooth shaven except for a long and bushy white mustache that matched his white, bushy hair. His dark, coppery skin, the color of fall English oak leaves, completed the impression of dignity, age, and peace. He reminded Vala of an actor, Sam Elliott, that Vala had met once when doing the university asked her to do consulting work for a stupid Internet movie.

This man's hands were clasped about waist high and he looked at her steadily and quizzically. Somehow, she felt as though he knew more about her than she knew about herself.

The woman with him was also slim and tall, about Vala's 6'7"–she almost glowed. Her clothes, similar in style to the man's, were white and golden yellow, catching and reflecting light all around her. Her radiant and tawny complexion reminded Vala of early morning light in the Sahara.

The Sahara. Had that been hallucination, too? She studied bacteria to compare to similar bacteria found in ice in the Swiss alps at almost 11,000 feet. Her thought morphed into the realization that the woman reminded her of someone. Before she could remember who, something hit her from behind. She spun around, at first seeing nothing and then, looking down, saw Eric.

"Oops–sorry," he said.

"Why are you here?" she asked him just as the stranger, the formerly transparent man, joined them. "Is Aunt Char okay?" She peered over Eric at the shimmering passage where the stranger from her garden emerged.

"She's fine," the stranger said. "A little worried."

The woman spoke while smiling. "Welcome."

Serein trotted over to the woman. "Serein!" Vala called.

Serein, tail still wagging, came back to sit next to Vala. "And why couldn't you have done that three minutes ago?" Vala asked.

"Probably because he wanted to see what had been offered to us," Eric said. "Do you want to go check on Aunt Char?"

"Yes, now," Vala said, starting toward the opening.

Eric was passing her going the other direction, his hand outstretched toward the woman. "Hi!" he said. "I'm Eric. You look like Cassidy."

The woman laughed. "I'm Tandra, Cassidy's sister. And this is Obeah, a healer."

"A doctor!" Eric said. "Nice to meet you. Ignore Vala. She's not open to new experiences."

Vala spun back around. "Don't talk for me!" she said.

"Well, then talk for yourself and don't be so rude. Sis."

"Please, Vala. Give us twenty minutes. We can explain everything," Cassidy said.

"Vala? What about Sarah?" Tandra asked.

"Everything?" Vala asked. "Well, that would be a nice change from nothing. I assume you sent us that cryptic message about spirals. Fat lot of help that was."

"We're here," Eric said.

"We're in the middle of one of my delusions. I don't like this particular delusion." Vala started back toward the portal.

"Perhaps we could go have tea and talk," Obeah said. "Having our children with us requires gratitude and joyful celebration."

His tone stopped Vala and she turned to look at him with deep curiosity. His voice ... it was as if it vibrated in her bones. She'd lied about the delusion–this space felt good. Healthy. But a good delusion wasn't necessarily better than a bad delusion. Serein radiated well-being, confusing her. "Well, since this is all in my imagination anyway, maybe we should. Are you the Mad Hatter?" She resisted the urge to stick her tongue out at Eric. She went over to stand closer to Obeah with Serein trotting by her side. "Who are you again?"

"I'm Obeah. I delivered you. Even then, you had eyes that sliced through mystery to Truth. I knew you'd be strong. You look like your mother."

"*You* delivered me?" Something like a jolt of electricity ran down her spine. "You *know* my birth mother? I was born here? Where is she? What happened to–"

"Let's have tea. And we'll talk."

"Yes," she said again. "Who are the children?"

Obeah chuckled. "You, of course. And Eric."

Vala started forward, then stopped. "Aunt Char! I need–"

"I'll go," said Cassidy.

"I'll go with you," Eric said. "She won't trust you."

Vala nodded, feeling more confidence in Eric than she cared to admit, and then she and Obeah got in Obeah's electric scooter and puttered off. Tandra chose to wait for Eric and Cassidy. Serein stretched himself out into a comfortable run beside the scooter. Vala felt jealous; she would have liked to have run with Serein through this place of meadow and forest and brisk air. She hadn't breathed air this fresh and clean since her last trip to Antarctica for some scientific work with microbes. She heard no people or traffic noise. No planes or jet trails marked the sky. They rode along a dirt trail, not pavement.

Yet still, somewhere in Vala's brain warning bells were sounding. What was she doing? Was she hallucinating? Why was she just going along with this stranger? On the short ride to Obeah's clinic, she did every mental trick she could think of to identify the reality of the moment and then she began to analyze the situation. There had to be a reasonable explanation for all of this. *Aliens?* she asked herself. *Drugs?* Had she checked herself into the clinic and started hypnotherapy?

At Obeah's clinic, they waited outside a low-peaked building with white walls. She guessed it was straw bale construction, but it looked sturdy and welcoming. Not surprisingly, the doorway and roof appeared to be about eight feet high, easily accommodating anyone Vala's or Obeah's height.

Cassidy, Tandra, and Eric arrived quickly, reassured Vala about Char, and they all went into Obeah's small quarters behind his clinic and sat around the Doug fir table. Obeah insisted on making tea for everyone before he'd allow discussion. "You've all been through a lot. We need to breathe, relax, and have some comforting tea."

After Obeah poured, Vala sniffed at the tea.

Obeah chuckled. "I have no reason to poison you, Dear."

Vala could feel her face heat up with embarrassment. "I just— what is it?"

"Primarily ashwagandha with a bit of valerian root and honey. Just herbs for calming and taste."

Vala looked around the small quarters, sparsely furnished with simple wood furniture. A small kitchen lined the wall next to the door. Most of the room was taken up with the table where they sat.

A door just past the end of the kitchen counter was open, and Vala could see a bed—no more than a mattress on the floor with mosquito netting draped from the ceiling. Opposite the kitchen counter was another door, partially opened into a room filled with hanging herbs and drying roots. Tapestries lined most of the walls. More roots and herbs were hanging in the kitchen area, giving the entire room the rich aroma of forest and mountain meadow and heady spice. Several bookcases stood between tapestries, all loaded with books. Mats, woven from natural fibers, were on the floor.

"This is your home?" Eric asked Obeah.

"Yes. My clinic is attached through there," he said, pointing at the partially open door to where she could see the abundant hanging herbs and roots. "Cassidy has spent a lot of time there as he searched for you two."

"Clinic?" Vala could hear the pitch of her voice rise. Serein had his head on her lap immediately.

"I'm a healer, specializing in herbs, plants, and other natural remedies to keep one's spirit content."

Vala relaxed a little. Herbs were never mentioned at the brain crank factory. "Now will you tell me about my mother?" Vala asked.

Obeah chuckled again. "Take a sip of tea, and then we'll begin."

Vala reluctantly tasted the tea. A bitter tang was offset by sweetness. She drank some more. Serein was sitting calmly beside her. Maybe everything was okay. Wherever she was, mentally or physically, she was okay. If Serein was really here. He pawed at her leg to prove his own existence.

"You can understand why we have many questions, I'm sure," Eric said.

Cassidy nodded. "You weren't meant to be in isolation. Our plans…" he paused, pursed his lips, and then shrugged. "Our plans have gone wrong. Repeatedly. Jasmine was to be in contact with you and guide the process of linking. With guidance, the experience wouldn't have been so wrenching."

Vala involuntarily looked down at her palm where the spiral, complete now, seemed to almost radiate light. "Just what is this thing? I know of nothing that works this way."

"Unfortunately," Obeah said, "with the isolation you've had, you've not been able to develop many of your latent skills. Your mother was also a scientist, but she was very skilled in both healing and what you would know as magic."

"Magic! She was a magician?"

"No. Not as you mean. Not a trickster or slight-of-hand entertainer. Oh, dear, you know so little. We need time."

Vala shook her head. "How about if you answer my question. *What is this thing?*"

"I think we need more history," Cassidy said. "Can you be patient while we –"

"No, I can't be patient!" Vala said. "*What* is going on?"

Eric sighed. "Vala, this...*whatever*...affects both of us. I think it's more complicated than just the two of us. If you had a student who demanded to understand quantum theory before she understood basic addition, would you attempt to explain it to her or tell her to be patient and learn addition?"

Vala glared at Eric. Life was easier before he'd manifested. She didn't *need* a little brother. She hadn't *asked* for a little brother. "Fine," she said.

"That's the best you're going to get," Eric said to Cassidy.

"Let's start by simply explaining a bit about who you are. We'll begin with the DNA. You've noticed a difference, a minor variation between your DNA and the average human DNA, yes? I left a reference to it for you in that computer."

Eric nodded. "We knew about that, but we must have missed part of your message. You kind of messed up the computers."

Vala glared at Eric and swallowed the ten questions that came to mind.

"Yes. Well, I kind of messed up myself, too. Anyway, that DNA variation is minute, but is exponential," Cassidy continued. "It interacts in various ways through the gene sequences with a few major results that make us a variation of homo erectus rather than homo sapiens. Our scientists use the term homo Sophos; less academically, we call ourselves *gentem,* rather than human."

"That just means *people* in Latin," Vala said. She made no effort to disguise the contempt in her voice.

"True. But we needed something to distinguish the difference. Many gentem are uncomfortable referring to themselves as people or humans because of centuries of conflict. Throughout history, our differences have resulted in ... well, problems."

Tandra laughed, but the sound contained little mirth. "Problems? Look, humans regard themselves very highly. Unique. They don't like the idea that they share a world with other unique creatures quite capable of intelligent thought and complex relations. They certainly don't want to be just one species of homo erectus."

Cassidy nodded. "Humans don't like those who are different. Although we, too, have our biases. Humans, though...they seem to fear even minor differences. Different skin tones, for instance, have led to wars, hatred, and slavery." He rubbed at his lower lip with his thumb as though he wanted to erase something there.

Eric nodded. Vala glared. She knew history and was on the verge of saying so when Eric kicked her ankle. She turned to him and made a silent promise to drown him later; she hoped he could understand the threat with his mind reading or whatever trickery he used to know what she was thinking and feeling.

Cassidy took a deep breath. "Two major ways in which we are different is that we live longer and we have abilities to interact with quantum forces that humans do only with technology. This is due to instinctive connections with LifeForce, a unifying field force. It's *not* magic or trickery; it's simply utilizing resources of our very real world. LifeForce is a fundamental theory; the divisions between the fundamental forces—what you probably think of as strong, weak, electric, and gravity judging by my experience with your computer—must include the underlying connected field, LifeForce. *Something* has to provide the connections, the reason for things to work, the drive behind the creation of life."

Vala opened her mouth to protest. Then she thought about her relationship with Serein and other animals in the past. Even awareness of the health of greenery that humans didn't sense. That could be considered a special awareness, she supposed. She wanted to know more even if only to argue against it.

"You're talking about a particle, like the Higgs Bosun?" she asked.

Cassidy shook his head. "LifeForce is a fundamental field, not a particle. Like gravity."

Cassidy's patient tone irritated Vala. "What scientific evidence do you have for this–what?–force? You must have some proof. Science doesn't rely only on the five senses…in fact, we know our senses can't be trusted. So what's your empirical evidence?"

"Well, this Beta earth is pretty good evidence, no?" Cassidy smiled. "Our scientists have done a lot of research, and the only consistent causal difference between humans and gentem is the DNA. Further, we've tested gentem and humans to see what could be accomplished that was related to this connective ability. We've also done research to determine the presence of LifeForce in many conditions and found it to be consistent. Look, I have a lot of data you can examine, but could we get through generalities and then get more specific?" Cassidy asked.

Vala started to get up, but she felt Obeah's hand on her own. "Be patient, perhaps?" he said. "I'm sure you've heard it's a virtue. A stoic idea, perhaps, and painful at times, but a doorway to learning often. You've finished your tea. Have another cup."

Vala settled back in her chair, shut her mouth, then glared at Eric as he released what sounded like a relieved sigh.

"Back to your differences," Eric said. "How much longer-lived are you talking about?"

Cassidy shrugged. "We don't generally bother with the human arbitrary calendar and time measurements because they aren't as important to us as is our development in understanding the LifeForce. We age in understanding. But of course we understand and refer to human calendars. We've lived with them for as long as humans have. So, in human years, we live a lot longer. You've heard Obeah refer to you as our children. Adulthood is achieved by growth in understanding, not by years. However, by those yearly terms, I'm fifty. Tandra is seventy. Obeah is … I have no idea."

"I was born in the early 1700s, as I recall," Obeah said.

"That's ridiculous," Vala said.

Obeah smiled at her. "I must agree that the early 1700s were, at the least, ridiculous."

Cassidy said, "Such age also has been documented, not with

paperwork like humans use. Humans wouldn't accept the paperwork anyway, and your reaction proves my point. If humans figure out that those of us with this slight DNA difference are living for four to seven times as long as they do, the situation could be, and has been in the past, dangerous to the gentem. Humans will literally kill for the ability to live longer."

Obeah nodded as he poured more tea for himself. "Gentem don't die on human terms either. They merge with the environment— but more on that later. Much human folklore comes from human interactions with gentem. For instance, stories of vampires came about because some of the elite who learned about gentem living so long began draining their blood and drinking it, hoping to gain immortality. That never made it into history books."

Tandra stood suddenly, walked to the window and stared out. "We learned to hide. Take on new identities. Move around. Be reclusive. Not help with our skills for fear of being labeled not quite human, such as witches or devils. Now we'd be oddities to dissect and study. The passage of human time affects only the methods of discriminatory behavior, not the existence of discrimination itself."

The tension Tandra was emitting silenced everyone. She stood rigid, her back to everyone. Vala had to make a physical effort to quit staring at her and look back at Obeah. "You don't understand what I mean by ridiculous," said Vala. "I mean it's not possible. You can play around with speculation all you want, but humans don't live that long."

Tandra was suddenly behind Vala and tapped her vigorously on the shoulder. "Try to pay attention. We're *not* human. Dismiss what we say with caution. Many things have been declared impossible. From the Earth being round to objects as small as atoms. Your declaration has no substance but your own bias, and, in fact, lacks the empirical data that you're touting as vital. You're ignoring your own presence here." Tandra flicked her right hand in the air and flames began dancing on her fingers.

"Magic tricks? Scheisse!" Vala tried to lower her voice. "I feel as though I've just fallen into the laps of cult leaders. And just where the hell is *here?* For all I know, we're being conned somehow."

"How'd you do that?" Eric asked Tandra.

"Eric, don't fall into their tricks," Vala said.

"Later," Tandra, smiling, stage-whispered to Eric. "It's just a matter of rearranging molecules that surround us."

Eric shrugged. "Okay, but you *do* die, yes? You're mortal, right? I mean, we…we're mortal?" Eric's wonder—curiosity—came through his voice clearly.

"Well, yes and no," Obeah said. "We move into other patterns …life is a process. For humans, too. Of course, the body can be killed, rendered incapable of functioning, but I think we should try to stay a little focused in the conversation. Let's move forward by agreeing to keep our minds open."

"If nothing else," Cassidy suggested, "regard this as a thought experiment." He looked directly at Vala. "Are you familiar with Mary's Room? Are you ready to learn?"

Vala remained silent. How did this guy know about Mary's Room? Who was he? Had she been limited in perceiving the world as had the fictional Mary in Frank Jackson's thought experiment?

"Hey, I know about Mary's Room," Eric said. "So you're suggesting that like Mary, we've been forced into living in circumstances that didn't fully represent the world?"

"Mmmmmm…" Obeah said. "Sounds like that's a connection. Now then, suppose the people who have been living in a sensory-rich world also looked different than Mary. How would she feel about that?"

"I don't understand," Eric said.

"Well, some of us tend to be on the tall side, about your height and taller, Vala," said Obeah. "We attract attention. And some of us on the short side, only 3' to 5'. There isn't a clear reason for this, but our anthropologists have found recent evidence, mostly through oral tradition, that indicates that our species has often sought isolation. The environment may have something to do with evolutionary size needs, maybe in connection to space or food availability. Think about the Bambenga. Humans have created the arbitrary term *race* for many such individuals, but that's ludicrous."

"It's like saying a heron and an eagle are different *races* rather than species," Tandra said.

Vala noted that Tandra consistently sounded on the verge of anger although she was again sitting at the table. She studied the teapot diligently, apparently working very hard at controlling herself as she poured the tea.

"Taller gentem," Cassidy continued the discussion, "could have lived in open plains. We've had to discover reasons for our differences and how we fit into the evolutionary pattern. We've learned to recognize each other and we tend to associate with each other, but many of us have felt that we were just freakish humans until the past few decades. Most differences are easy to hide. Size is just the obvious physical difference."

"Wait a minute!" Eric's voice was higher-pitched than normal. He was obviously suppressing the desire to yell. "You're talking about elves and dwarves, aren't you?"

Vala had never seen Eric erupt into anger before.

Eric stood. His voice lowered, but he was clearly deflated. "You're right, Vala! This is all a big joke. I've gone through the whole short thing: midget, dwarf, freak, leprechaun, pocket pet. I grew up with it. This is some sort of hoax! Or cult." He looked almost as if he might cry.

Vala smiled at him. "So you do have a button or two to push."

Eric looked at her in silence for a moment, then his shoulders, raised with tension, dropped. He took a deep breath, exhaled slowly, and shrugged. "So I do. But put the pieces together, Vala. I had such high hopes…"

"Eric, this is a picture of your mother, Jasmine," Obeah said, handing Eric a photo. Eric sat back down abruptly.

Vala realized she'd again drunk all the calming tea in her cup. Should she say Kool-aid? Perhaps it wasn't working because her tension was increasing. If this was even bothering Eric, they should probably flee. "Eric, I don't know how they know what the lawyer told you, but I think you're right about all this. Let's just go."

Eric silently handed the photo out to Vala. She glanced at it and then took it to study more carefully. It was the same person as in the photo the lawyer had given him. Was this a conspiracy? "I think we're being manipulated. We've already both had our mothers brought up. I'm beginning to wonder if this is an elaborate con. We're both wealthy, Eric."

"Of course, she could be correct, Eric," said Obeah. "But

knowing your history and abilities, I think you probably sense what is true."

Eric stared at Obeah for a moment and then sagged slightly into his chair. "In spite of it all, Vala, I have a feeling–maybe it's just a desire–that this is true. These people are being honest. At least they think they are, so if they're fooling us, they're fooling themselves, too." He paused, took a deep breath as though he were about to dive deeply into turbulent waters. "So, Obeah, what do you claim happened to her?"

"We don't know," Obeah said. "She was in touch with us through her ability to communicate through thoughts with me. We didn't need to open a portal. She was a powerful empath. All contact just suddenly ceased shortly after you were born."

"The plan," Cassidy said, "was that she would manage to stay connected to both you and Vala although Vala's placement with your family had gone awry. Their daughter had, indeed, died, and Jasmine had to improvise placement."

"Placement?" said Vala. "What does that mean? She was distributing children like apple seeds?"

"It's complicated," said Obeah.

"That's what people always say when they've done something inappropriate," Vala said.

"You're right," said Cassidy. "This was an extremely complicated and manipulative scheme. I, and others who think like I do, would have fought the plan had we been older. That things went awry isn't surprising. As it is, we've been struggling to regain our connection with you, as you know. But we *are* telling the truth. Think about it, Vala–the other differences, the things you hide from others because you've learned that they aren't acceptable or even possible."

Vala's list of those items, she realized, had landed her in a mental institution. She looked at Serein and heard him clearly telling her that these were honest individuals and all was well, his favorite communication when she felt like she was standing on the edge of a mental precipice.

Eric walked to the door and stood looking out. "You've talked like you all were living among humans. What happened?" he asked. His voice sounded as though he were much farther away.

Tandra stood and began pacing between the kitchen counter and the bedroom doorway. "For millennia, forever, we did live with them. After all, we *are* the same with our ancestry; we're a branch off the same homo erectus tree. But the differences were enough to earn us hatred, fear, contempt, and anger. Gentem tried to live separately but eventually there was nowhere for us to go. We tried to merge, inter-marry even. Humans alternated between being jealous and being infatuated, just as they do whenever they come in contact with something new. Our ancestors and families were forced into roles such as jesters, circus freaks, clowns, seers, and worse. They were burned as witches and banned as spawn of the devil."

She stood across the table from Vala and focused on her with an intent gaze that made Vala feel unable to move. "I'm sure you two have felt like misfits in your lives. It's as if who we are creates an aura that turns the average human cold."

She turned her gaze to Eric. "Many gentem writers and story tellers created those oral and written myths, fairy tales, and legends about elves, fairies, fauns and dwarves to make them so unlike humans that those of us gentem in human society wouldn't be classified as such. You know: pointed ears, heavy beards, super warriors." She sucked in her cheeks and pulled upward on the tops of her ears.

Releasing her ears, she continued. "We were always a minority—we don't have many children. Look at their population escalation: 1 billion in 1800, 2 billion in 1930, 3 billion in 1960, 4 billion in 1975, 5 billion in 1987. It's like that joke about saving a penny a day, doubled every day to be a millionaire." Tandra literally shook herself like a horse dislodging flies. "I'll try to stay calm, but I tend to get angry about this."

"If it was so terrible and you have all these powers, why didn't you fight back?" Vala asked.

Cassidy sighed. "Some of us are proposing that now, Vala, but retaliation—violence—is against all our principles of life. It contradicts the LifeForce, the impulse toward life. If we begin turning away from what makes us who we are, we'll lose our connections to … everything. We'll cease being gentem."

"Our differences are deeper than appearance," said Obeah. "Our natural tendencies to link with nature, with animals, with the environment, with Earth herself means we must respect all life–even human life. Homo sapiens relate more to power through human-made contraptions, technology, materialism. They want to manipulate the environment rather than harmonize within it. They need to measure, quantify, and label everything. They perceive their worth, their success, in how much they acquire and control. Solipsism."

Tandra joined in again. "We tried to lead by example. We worked in fields to help show people that they were interdependent with Earth, with the environmental systems, but, again, we were freaks: eco-terrorists, tree huggers, birkenstinks, granola nuts–you've heard the terms. As the air and water grew worse and the pain of the animals, plants, and Earth worsened, we, too, were dying. The humans, without even realizing it, are engaged in a war against the LifeForce, and we're part of that."

Tandra stretched, shook herself again, then sat down. "Violence and anti-life: that's our Achilles heel." She pointed at Vala. "Tell me, you suffer from the sounds, the stinks, and the general pollution, don't you?"

Vala clamped her mouth for a moment to avoid making a useless retort about *everyone hating the pollution*, for she knew most people were not as sickened as she was by it, even those who wore masks and used nanobots. Yet humans didn't make correcting it central to their lives; it didn't depress them. Vala couldn't stand crowds, in part, because of the noxious odors they smeared on their hair, their bodies, their clothes. And that was nothing to most people. "But even what you call pollution isn't *unnatural*. It's all made up of elements, molecules, and combinations that exist naturally. And if you have these abilities to modify particles, elements, molecules like you did with her finger flame–why don't you just change the pollution, wave it away?"

Cassidy shrugged. "In that sense, toxic waste is, indeed, *natural*. If it were simply a generation of natural processes within the LifeForce, I know we could adapt, maybe even change the conditions. But the difference is that it's not part of a natural and ongoing process but the product of a malignancy; humans have generated much of this stuff with a killing purpose. Bombs. Pesticides. Chemical attacks. In other cases, it's generated without concern over the welfare of life, and so creatures go extinct, the air becomes unbreathable, the water undrinkable. In essence, this is a manipulation of conditions without regard to harmony. Of course, if you don't believe Earth is a living system, then you wouldn't see the difference."

Cassidy walked to the sink and got a glass of water. After a long drink, he returned to the table and sat. "Think of it this way: cancer cells are *natural,* yet they kill people. As unlikely as it may seem, this disruption of harmony in the Web is like a cancer to gentem, which is why we often say it's not *natural.* Interestingly, the conditions are damaging human health as well, but they don't think in terms of physical health as related to mental or emotional health."

Eric was nodding again. "You probably don't know this, but the estimated lifespan of humans has been dropping for the past five years."

Vala tried to keep her voice level. "You didn't answer my other question. If you gentem are so tied to the environment, why can't you use some of your powers to simply clean up the mess, counteract the damage?"

"You're not listening," Tandra said. "It's not just the toxic shit, it's the toxic mental and emotional conditions. Besides, that is a giant leap from the work we can do. It would probably take all of us concentrating and working twenty-four-seven to begin to have an effect. Meanwhile, humans would just continue producing the stuff. Our efforts wouldn't change attitudes. The frustration would be immense. It would be like mopping a floor while people with muddy feet followed you. And don't forget, you're one of us."

Vala shook her head. "Okay, moving on...you still haven't said how it happens that you are living separate lives now and how that relates to Eric and me."

Tandra grabbed the tea pot and went to the counter to refill it again. "Our scientists, back in the 1980s, started considering various aspects of quantum mechanics in relationship to LifeForce wave functions, combined with how time and space can be bent to create another–*dimension*? I think. That's Cassidy's field."

Cassidy leaned back in his chair and smiled at Vala. "Well, I'm too young to have been in on any of that original work or the decisions of the Council except, eventually, as an apprentice with

Marina–who lives physics, and you should meet her–but I've been studying it intensely as an adult. I've often argued for re-integration with humans, taking down the Membrane, as have many of my friends. Now, I'm not so sure." He began scrubbing at his lower lip with his thumb again.

"Cassidy!" Obeah said.

He jumped. "Sorry...I was thinking. Anyway, we need a fresh perspective on how to live with humans. Or not. I'm hoping that you, Vala, and you, Eric, will help us with that. That was the plan: you have the connections through your human families and friends to help us establish communication."

Eric was shaking his head. "Membrane? I don't understand."

"When you came here through that portal," Cassidy said, "you were stepping from one world into another. We call it a *Membrane* but that's misleading in many ways. We're thinking of it in terms of the separation itself, a division of sorts, but it's really an entirely new world except that it was created out of the same world as it was in the past, the recent past. Think of it as a second Earth in a bubble, the tenuous edge of the bubble separating the two Earths, like a Membrane." He paused and began scrubbing at his lower lip again. His eyes became unfocused.

Obeah reached out and nudged his arm.

Cassidy looked surprised. "Oh. Sorry. Look, this Beta Earth is a duplicate in the sense that it shares the evolutionary history of Earth and it has the same infrastructure that existed for the Earth in the recent past. However, it has been in its own time the past few decades. In my lab, we can go over this in detail."

Eric held his palm out. "You're getting into Vala's area. Let me ask about something I know. Humans will always have issues with differences. In my opinion, it's a survival thing. Take skin color. Whites fear becoming a minority, in part, probably, because they've treated minorities so badly. I'd like to say that no longer happens in the U.S., but all I can say is that it's less acceptable. That means it's less obvious. However, several years ago, the States began a rigorous program against immigrants until only white Christians have been allowed to become citizens for some time. In other parts of the world, particularly in Asia, the bias is against whites and most especially Christians. Religious wars are still being fought on the northern African continent. One reason for this, in my opinion, is that basic survival skills require humans to be in groups. The fear of being marginalized makes differences risky. It's also possible that differences weaken the group's power. In short, I think you're wrong about that slap-happy, harmonious unity, Cassidy."

Silence.

Vala tried to suppress her surprise. She hadn't thought Eric had a negative thought in his head. "You sure know how to interrupt, Eric," she said.

"That makes me want to cry," Tandra said. "I've known, of course, that humans were driven by a desire for domination for their clans, but I thought it would change."

"You're equating intelligence and logic with time," Vala said. "As far as I can tell, your culture displays some of the same attitudes toward humans."

Tandra jumped up again. "We have a lot more–"

"Wait!" Obeah said, standing and spreading his hands out. "We're not here to debate. We're trying to provide information to each other. Can we just do that?"

Tandra's jaw muscles bulged as she clamped her mouth shut and sat.

"Good job, Eric," Vala muttered.

"I have a question then," Tandra said.

Vala nodded.

"What do you mean that I'm equating intelligence with time?"

Vala shrugged. "Many people think that primitive people were stupid because they didn't, or don't, have technology. The idea is that *some* people evolved over time, that is grew more intelligent. Personally, I think that's just ethnocentric arrogance. How was, for instance, Steve Jobs any more intelligent than the first person who picked up a stick, bent it, secured it with a tight bit of hide, and created the bow? That is, invention builds on invention, but having technology doesn't make anyone smarter."

"In addition, you keep equating time to personal developments," Eric said. "Yet from what I've gathered, you think time is more of a human construct than a scientific fact. Isn't that contradictory?"

Obeah laughed. "You're both going to keep us alert to our self-deceptions. You're right—our culture doesn't view *time* as significant in the way humans do. But we don't regard development quite as simply as you might think. For instance, people in one culture picked up a stick and used it to dig up roots for eating and making medicines, the homo Sophos method. People in another culture picked up a stick and bashed someone over the head to take away the food and medicine, the homo sapiens method. I think that's the difference that has continued. It's deeply embedded in who we are."

For a moment, everyone was silent. No one disagreed.

Cassidy nodded. "Okay. Well then, let me continue with some information. Beta Earth was successfully created right after your birth, Vala."

"How?" Vala asked.

"I can show you better than tell you if we go to my lab. Simply put, we built on what exists, inserting one more alternate reality, or parallel world, into the mix. We didn't want to try emigrating to a parallel world where we would be intruders. We'd probably be in the same mire. We needed a fresh start. If I could just provide general information for now…"

Vala sighed. "Shut up and listen, right. Got it. For a bit."

"You and Jasmine were at the hospital when the final work was done. Jasmine let Obeah know you'd gone to a different family, but Jasmine was going to work out connections."

I need to stop. Vala suddenly felt as though she were separating from herself, as though she were losing track of everything she knew. Her overload senses were kicking in. She wanted to run.

"Jasmine was still in touch with you when I was born?" Eric asked quietly, reaching out and resting his hand on Vala's arm as Serein put a paw in her lap.

Cassidy nodded. "She planned your birth to coincide with the Kines' expected baby, a boy. She gave birth to you in the morning and swapped the children in the delivery room that afternoon."

A low tone buzzed in Vala's ears as Eric asked softly, "Swapped?"

"Yes. She took their child with her."

182

"My poor parents," Eric said. "First their daughter dies and then they have a son who is a freak and not even their son."

"Don't use that word, Eric!" Vala snapped. "My brother is *not* a freak!"

Eric grinned suddenly. "Thanks, Sis."

Vala realized what she'd said. How had Eric wormed his way into her life like this?

"But," Eric added, "I don't understand how she could just swap children around. That sounds heartless."

"She loved you dearly," Obeah said. "But we needed you and Vala to be raised with humans to better understand them and their culture from the inside. The Kines are people who give you strong connections, and they were thoroughly vetted. They are good people."

"Were," Eric said. "They were killed in a car wreck when I was seven, and I was raised as a foster child."

Obeah shook his head. "I'm very sorry, Eric." He shook his head. "We should not have taken on the role of gods."

"Look," Vala said. "If I understand what you're saying, you are a race, a culture, who grew so tired of prejudicial treatment that you built a separate world and took away all your knowledge, abilities, and hope to create your own utopia. Yet as bad as that culture was, it had nourished and educated you. Meanwhile, in the process of running away, you abandoned your children to a future you were desperate to escape. Currently, you continue to think you're the good guys and the abused! So what's all the fuss now?"

Cassidy's bronze skin had deepened in color, as though heated, as Tandra stood, tossed her hands up in the air and said, "Oh, great! Now you're going to condemn us after knowing us for– what?–the length of time to drink a cup of tea!"

Cassidy held his hands out, almost in supplication. "As it happens I agree with you in one way, Vala. However, utopia hasn't proven bullet proof. Our Membrane isn't holding. We're not as separate and independent as we thought we would be. And, obviously, humans have continued with major pollution or it wouldn't be seeping through. I'm sure some of this world is seeping into what we left behind, but we have no way of knowing. Instead of becoming more distant, we seem to be drifting back. You have to understand that the human culture was killing us off, not just with prejudice, but physically, by cutting off our life source. It turns out the gentem are as dependent on environmental conditions as are many other species. We were in danger of becoming extinct, like the dodo. We can't live in a manufactured, robotic world."

Again Vala opened her mouth to protest and then shut it again. Then she said, "Your implication is that gentem, for instance, can't utilize manufactured food well, that fundamental particles are distinguishable. In other words, vitamin A, or [C20][H30]O, created in a chemical reaction in a lab is fundamentally different from vitamin A created by a carrot. Do you have any proof?" Vala's desire to run away eased as curiosity took over. She, herself, detested lab-produced food.

"We're in tune with the natural, not synthetic," Tandra said. "It's not that the chemicals are different, it's that the live food is rich in many micronutrients, all kinds of vitamins and minerals, that are part of the growing process. Synthetic foods don't mimic the interaction of the carrot with soil minerals, bacteria, air and water, and even weather conditions that humans disregard as insignificant." As she spoke, she opened her arms almost like an embrace of all the environmental conditions she mentioned. Her facial expressions relaxed. For the first time, Vala realized how lovely she was.

"Of course," Tandra continued, "bioflavonoids are also present. All of that can affect the bioavailability of the nutrients the system needs. We don't know exactly how all the elements interact in the system." The tension returned. Her lips thinned, and her voice hardened again. "The last I knew, human scientists disregarded the information out of hand at the same time that they acknowledge that something like smoking *can* affect how the body responds to nutrition. That's not logical."

Vala nodded. That made sense to her, but it made sense in her mind that humans, too, would be affected. The information about everything, scientific and emotional, was draining her. Yet it seemed too pat.

"So in essence," Vala said, "what you're telling me is that you must operate on a harmonious level and that turning your back on human need and suffering didn't work. Fancy that." She looked at Eric. "I need some breathing space. I'm going home."

Tandra stood in the doorway. "You can't–"

"Tandra, I think that perhaps Vala and Eric do need some time to think, to reflect," Obeah said. He turned to Vala, then nodded at Eric. "Go in peace, please. We know we've dumped a huge amount of information, some of which is personal and even hurtful, on you. I just hope we'll be able to talk more. You still don't know the whole story, and it's important that you do. Meanwhile, Vala, this is for you." He handed Vala a sealed envelope.

"What's this?"

"A letter from your mother."

"I'll drive you back," Cassidy said.

Vala pushed the envelope into her jeans pocket. "I'm going to run," she said. "You take Eric."

And she was out the door, with Serein, running as hard and fast as she ever had in her life. She didn't know if she was running from or to something, but she knew she had to run.

The evening air cooled her skin as she ran, keeping about three paces behind Serein, who knew where she was going at least as well as Vala did. She used him as her guide. The night was alive around her with more wildlife than she'd felt around her for a long time. She felt waves of envy for those who were living here at the same time that she resented that they had abandoned Earth, abandoned Eric and her, to create their own utopia. They deserved to fail.

Chapter Seventeen

Saturday night, July 7, 2029

Cassidy stood in the doorway looking in the direction Vala had gone.

"You don't want to follow her," Eric said quietly.

"Why not?" Cassidy asked without turning around. "I can keep up with her."

Eric's own stomach churned with a mix of confusion and desire Cassidy was feeling. Painful. How could that be when they'd just met? Then, he thought of his own reaction to meeting Vala. Just like Eric, Cassidy had known of Vala his entire life and been working to meet her. She was probably bigger-than-life to him; more than a sister, she was a savior.

He took a deep breath to try to explain. "I'm sure you can run stride-for-stride, but you'll destroy any chance you have of establishing a relationship if you crowd her. She needs time to think and meditate, analyze what she's heard. She told you that. Vala retreats when she's feeling pressured."

Cassidy's resistance, a stubborn wall, blocked his listening. He *was* young emotionally. In addition, he was feeling mostly excitement that the portal had worked, and he was eager to get on with the work. Eric needed to treat him like a teenager. "Think, Cassidy. She's spent years thinking she was insane. Suddenly, a whole new world, literally, is jammed in her face. She needs to talk to her Aunt Char, a stable and long-term safe person. You're surrounded by such people. She has only one."

Cassidy turned around. "*Why* has it been so traumatic for her?"

Eric rubbed his forehead. Cassidy was obviously not one of the more sensitive individuals they'd discussed. Did talents among the gentem ever mix? Eric glanced over at Obeah who had a smile twitching his lips. He was no doubt grateful to hand Cassidy off.

Eric tried again. "Cassidy, suppose I told you that in reality you've been immersed in a dream world? You're not gentem. There is no Beta Earth. You have no family. The LifeForce is your imaginary toy. I've been treating you for years, and now you're about to wake up to the fact that you're just a human with a problem."

Cassidy just stared at him.

"Egads, Cassidy, don't you get it? What you've all talked about the gentem suffering in the past is Vala's life. She hears things people can't, sees things people can't, and because she's had no one to guide her, she could only assume that people were telling her the truth: she's delusional…crazy. Fortunately she's crazy smart, a genius scientist and that's won her some freedom but no social life. She was abandoned by this culture and rejected by the culture where you left her."

"What a mess," Tandra said. "All this effort to find a whiner."

"No, Tandra," Eric said. "She doesn't whine about it. I'm telling you what I know, what she won't tell you. Aren't you supposed to be a healer?" He paused for a reaction to his question, but surprisingly Tandra didn't erupt. He continued. "Vala spent her childhood living in a clinic for the insane. She was finally working out a life that was working for her when everything started coming apart. Her parents aren't her parents. The time she spent trying to be cured was wasted because there was nothing wrong with her. Those who are "her people" or family abandoned her when she was an infant. And you ask why she's reactive? Obeah, can you mix an empathy potion for Cassidy and Tandra?"

Obeah chuckled. "They're young."

Cassidy shook his head. "Not that young. Anyway, Vala still knows who she is, how she interacts with the world, no? If I lost everything, I'd still know myself, my place."

"That's because you've had a place to start with, Cassidy," Eric said.

Cassidy opened his mouth, shut it, then turned his back to again stare out the doorway.

"What about you, Eric?" Obeah asked.

Eric smiled. "Well, finding out about my mother is a surprise, but I've always known, somehow, that something had gone awry. I've been searching for someone supposedly dead–Vala, as it turns out. I've found her, and I feel as though I'm finally on my correct path. Somehow, maybe…I must have captured and kept Jasmine's hope for us. I mean, I've felt lost and abandoned at times, but I was blessed. For the first seven years of my life, I had parents who loved me dearly, then I found friends who overlooked my peculiarities and helped me out of scrapes with bullies. Yet, like Vala, I am stunned. I can't understand your actions. I'm both dismayed and saddened that all of you simply abandoned the world, not to mention us."

"You haven't heard the worst of it," Cassidy said.

Eric quit smiling, sensing immediately Cassidy's worry over revealing a secret. "Maybe you'd better tell me."

Cassidy came back to the table, sat down, and met Eric's eyes steadily. "First, you have to understand that what has happened was…unplanned. Or unscheduled. Not everyone agreed. Most didn't. It just shouldn't have happened." He looked down, studying the table.

"Yet maybe necessary–we just weren't sure yet," Tandra said. "That may sound self-serving, but many species have been dying for a long time."

"My sister and I don't agree–at least not totally although Tandra also is opposed to destructive acts, isn't that right, Tandra?"

She nodded but said nothing.

After a moment of silence, Cassidy continued. "I've always hoped that completing the mission to contact you and Vala would give us answers or maybe another way to try to redirect human culture."

Eric was beginning to feel as though a guillotine was being set up for him. "Could you maybe just tell me and then rationalize it after? I'm starting to feel faffed."

"What?" Cassidy said.

"Faffed. Put off. Just get on with it."

Cassidy began an explanation of leaks of toxins through the membrane when Tandra interrupted.

"What's wrong with humans? Don't they realize that they're killing themselves along with everything else? Increased diseases—everything from cancer to diabetes to failed immune systems. They don't use prevention; instead they keep coming up with ways to live with the mess. Since long before we—"

"Stop stalling!" Eric yelled. He felt chilled. These people knew they'd done something wrong and were doing everything possible to explain it as rational. "What the hell have you done?"

"Are you familiar with ma-huang?" Obeah asked as Tandra and Cassidy remained silent.

"It's ephedra, no?" Eric asked.

Obeah nodded. "It interacts with almost all drugs and herbs in negative ways, from caffeine to medications."

"Right. It's sold in the U.S. only by prescription," Eric said, "but it's used freely in many other places. What about it?"

"Some scientists working with Alarick figured out a way to tailor ma-huang to attach to the Neanderthal gene—epigenetics. It's designed to be cumulative, so it gradually increases the effects."

Now all three were silent. Eric looked at one and then the other. "You're telling me that you've created a biological weapon tailored to be used against humans—at least those who have the Neanderthal gene, which is most of them. Which suggests that gentem don't carry that gene?"

More silence.

"You're *terrorists?*" Eric could hear his voice rising in pitch. He swallowed hard. He had to stay rational. He almost laughed. Rational? Was anything rational?

He held his breath a moment, then said, "You people who are telling me that harmony with this LifeForce is essential to your existence…then you're telling me you're committing biological war against an enemy who doesn't even know you *exist?*"

"Not all of us!" Cassidy yelled. He stood and held out his hands to his sides, almost imploring Eric to understand. "I don't think any of us really want this…at least most of us. And none of us knew that it had started—"

"What?" Somehow Eric found himself standing, leaning on his palms on the table. He wanted to run away, follow Vala, but his legs felt locked in place. *"Already started?"* He shook his head. He forced his voice to lower and he slowed and emphasized his words. *"Again: what have you done?"*

"Look, Eric," Tandra said, "none of us knew what was happening. It was Alarick and his cronies. The Council had *not* yet approved any of that."

Eric shook his head. He was getting nowhere with these two. He looked at Obeah. Obeah flinched under the onslaught of Eric's emotions.

"Alarick has already released the chemical into some rivers. The way the membrane leaks, it's probably already entering drinking water sources on Alpha Earth," Obeah said. He offered no justification.

Eric sat down. He wanted to scream, cry, and strike out. So he did nothing but sit and stare at the table, at the swirling wood grain representing decades of peaceful growth. Then he shook his head. "Your description of a harmonious, even utopian society sounded wonderful. No prejudice. No bullying. No environmental destruction. And it's all lies. You're no different from a pack of wolves killing another pack's pups in order to stay dominant in their territory. I feel ill."

Obeah sat down next to Eric. "Your horror emphasizes how far we've strayed. Alarick was head of the Council for too long, and he should have been dismissed long ago. He has never overcome his intense hate for humans."

"You're going to blame one individual for this? It appears that your objective ethics are more situational than you believe."

"Just let me speak for a moment, Eric." Obeah said and then continued when Eric nodded. "First, a bit of history. Alarick and his wife were Romanians. His wife, in 1865 was arrested, raped, and murdered as part of the Nachrichtendienst in Bezug auf die Zigeuner–"

"What is that?" Eric asked.

"It was another racist situation," Obeah said. "In 1899, the Bavarian police created a special force called the Gypsy Information

Agency. The process was very like tracking Jews under Hitler. Data was collected, Gypsies were labeled a plague. Alarick and his wife were labeled as Gypsies based on their height and her healing powers. They were separated and Alarick never saw her again, but he heard from other gentem what happened to her."

Obeah paused. He cleared his throat and regained emotional control. In the process, Eric also felt more control.

"Anyway," Obeah continued, "he's never forgiven. So he and a band of similar speciesists have waved the flag of hate openly for some time. In sympathy, maybe … maybe just because most of us have similar histories…No, I won't justify. We've been too slow in condemning that attitude. Meanwhile, Alarick and his cronies started their own war. We're trying to find out which rivers and how much, but Alarick isn't sharing information. We can't undo what's been done, but we think it's stopped. Alarick has been removed from the Council and they're now looking for a replacement, perhaps Tandra. We're deeply ashamed…"

Eric looked at Tandra. "But you agree with Alarick, no?"

Tandra chewed her lower lip and tears brightened her eyes. "Yes and no. I have no respect for humans, and I believe that if we try living with them again, all our lives are at risk. On the other hand, I deplore killing. So no. As I listen and talk to you–" Her voice broke and she sat down. "I'm sickened. And angry, deeply angry."

Eric nodded. "And you don't even know why you're angry, do you?"

Tandra, looking down at her hands, simply shook her head.

"Have you considered that it's cultural influence?" Eric paused. Something else. "And some personal hurt?"

Tandra turned and went to the door without speaking.

"It seems to me," Obeah said, "that your presence is already helping us, Eric. Be patient."

"We need solutions, Eric," Cassidy said. "We're not safe here. We're not safe in the human environment. Earth itself is *not* safe. For one thing, if the Membrane collapses entirely and our two worlds collide, I'm not sure there'll be enough left of either one to worry about. But we're going to find a way to fix this without betraying our culture, I promise."

Eric braced his elbows on the table and lowered his forehead into his palms. "Vala is going to explode when she hears this. She's dedicated her life to trying to clean up pollution, find peaceful ways to resolve issues. Telling her about this violence is going to be … explosive."

"Do you want me there?" Cassidy asked.

"No. If you're there, you'll become a more entrenched symbol of the problem. You need to be presented as part of the solution. I think." Eric shrugged. "Who knows?" He stood. "I should go. By the way, do you have anything that fully represents this family tree as you perceive it? I don't fully understand why you see gentem as a separate branch of evolution."

Obeah stood. "I have a copy. It was prepared by some of our geneticists who were making it simple for me. Their findings were another reason for arguing in favor of the Membrane. More DNA research is going into this, but it's clear the difference is there. What it means we don't know. What we fear is that if this were to become clear to humans, we would be listed as a *sub species*."

"That means," said Tandra, "*not quite human* in the same way they labeled slaves and various human enemies. And us when we've been labeled as witches and demons. They even burned Giordano Bruno at the stake for heresy because he claimed that there were other solar systems. It takes little in the way of differences to marginalize an individual."

"Eric, this isn't just our imagination," Obeah said. "Even humans recognize the situation. Have you heard of Professor Ellen Dissanayake and her work *Homo Aestheticus: Where Art Comes From and Why* in which she describes human group tendency to find other groups inferior? It seems to be a consistent behavior."

"I know her work," Eric said, "but you do realize that you've been doing the same thing, yes?"

Cassidy nodded. "Exactly. And it will destroy our culture."

Eric was silent. He honestly didn't know how to process the information he'd been given. Certainly, difference was not tolerated by homo sapiens. The idea of another species, an equal species, would have been more extreme than race or ethnic difference. Yet these *gentem*…were they any different?

He glanced at the paper Obeah had given him.

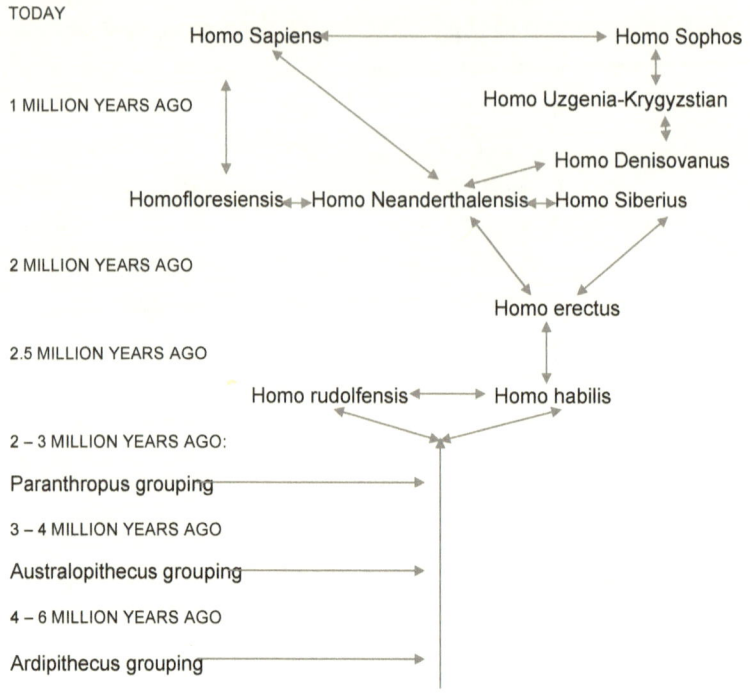

"I'm not sure," Obeah said, "how that may have been changed by our own researchers by now; and it may be different from the human perspective as well."

Eric nodded. "Change the name of your *Homo siberius* to *Homo Denisovia* and add Homo Naledi about 250,000 years ago, and you will have a reflection of some of our recent work. How did you learn of Homo floresiensis? That wasn't discovered until 2004, and I thought you had no communication then."

"We didn't," said Cassidy. "However, one of the last communications from Jasmine mentioned that she knew this was coming about. We added it although we weren't sure of its existence. I don't think it's connected to us. Of course, our scientists continue to study here on Beta Earth."

"I've never heard of this Homo Uzgenia-Krygyzstian" Eric said.

"That," said Cassidy, is the remote link that accounts for gentem. You'll find an unidentified genome in your make-up, something not found in homo sapiens. We found details and records of our own that account for this. More than 40,000 years ago, indications are that our ancestors were peaceful and trying to hide their culture in that remote area from more aggressive groups."

Eric would like someday to do research on that claim. "Of course, I haven't seen anything about Homo Sophos, but reports have come in about a third species, unidentified. Scientists have admitted that the scheme of human life is much more complicated than they'd thought based on fossils found before this century. What do you mean that Jasmine knew something was *coming about?*"

"As are you, your mother was highly empathetic, Eric. She was also able to predict some events," said Obeah. "It's not telling the future; it's just awareness of what individuals are expecting to happen based on knowledge that they themselves may not even be aware of knowing."

"You seem to have a solid knowledge about the history of human development, Eric," Cassidy said.

"Well, I've been intrigued by it because of my condition. Doctors could never find anything exactly *wrong* with me. I've never felt there was anything *wrong* with me either, although there was no shortage of reminders that I was different."

"Difference can be painful," Obeah said. "It's interesting that no one ever tracked down anything unusual in your DNA."

"Well–" Eric hesitated, then said, "Someone has. A friend of mine, a molecular anthropologist and geneticist ran DNA profiles for me and for Vala. He discovered a link to the Denisovans and also this unidentified genome. He's very excited. He says he hasn't found it before and that it could be a breakthrough in his work."

"Oh, cac!" Tandra said. "It's starting before we even interact with them! Of course, he hasn't found others. The humans have been killing the gentem off for centuries, so they all hide!"

Eric smiled at Tandra. She flushed, and Eric knew she was unhappy about her anger. "No," he said. "Wyatt is a very ethical person and a good friend. I'll talk with him. He probably won't believe me. I think it will be important to avoid calling you anything but human."

"So right away, we change. We can't be who we are. We need to be called by *their* names and live like *they* live. I think I, like Vala, need a break," Tandra said. "Good night, Eric." Without further comment, she walked out.

After Tandra left, Cassidy shrugged. "She has a temper."

Eric laughed at the understatement. "She reminds me of Vala. However, that last is more from sadness than anger. Look, Cassidy, Obeah, I'm swimming in confusion about how this Membrane was created, about how you live here, about how you use your skills. But I need to see how Vala is. I need to talk to her about this. I can come back?"

Cassidy nodded. "You can walk through the portal any time you wish, Eric. As can I. No one but Vala, you, Tandra, and I can do so. And, apparently, Serein. The palm implant is coded to that specific opening, and the obelisk boosts the power to keep the portal open now. Think of your palm implant as a key. And you're always welcome here."

Eric nodded. "Can you give me a ride back to the portal? I'm not much of a runner, and I'd rather not take the time to walk even if I knew where to go."

Cassidy chuckled. "Of course. Let's go."

Obeah said goodbye and added, "I think you are a strong and wise person, Eric. It's an honor to meet you."

Eric was reluctant to go in many ways. He felt accepted here. He thought he had a taste of how difficult it would be for these people—no, *gentem*—to tear down the Membrane and merge again into the teeming population of human society, those who would view them with suspicion or disdain. What, exactly, was wrong with wanting your own space? For emigrating to a better environment? If it weren't for the leak, that is. What if there were no solution? He himself didn't want the worlds rejoined; he would enjoy an escape hatch, especially to a world with fresh air, clean water, and a healthy environment. He'd bet almost every human would feel the same.

At the obelisk, he said a quick goodbye to Cassidy and started through the portal. It was like being in water, he decided. He could see but everything was slightly distorted. And, of course, at this hour, dark. Funny, he thought, that he'd never thought to ask anyone about time. It had seemed to get dark about when one would expect. Hadn't someone said that, in effect, the time difference between these places was very little?

As he stepped into Vala's garden, he immediately heard Char's greeting.

He walked over to where she and Vala were sitting. Serein, of course, was lying at Vala's feet.

"Learn anything worth staying for?" Vala asked. She still had an edge to her voice.

"I have so many questions that it was difficult to leave," Eric answered. "But I wanted to talk with you, see how you are. And I need to go into my office and finish cleaning things up."

"Cleaning things up?" Char asked.

"I'm closing my office for a time, taking leave. I don't know where all this is going, but I'm torn between clients and … all this," he said gesturing toward the portal. "I'll arrange to have a colleague work with my patients."

Char nodded. "A lot of things are changing."

"So then, how are you?" Eric asked Vala.

Vala shrugged. "Fine."

Eric snorted as he dropped into a chair next to Char and across from Vala. "Right. You're scared to death that you've slipped out of reality and dreamed this whole thing up. That none of it is real. And if it *is* real, you're furious at the folks who put you in this position, who abandoned you and the world to try to build their own place where they wouldn't be tormented as you and I were for years."

"Quit doing that!" Vala snapped. "Why ask if you know? Even if you do know what I'm feeling or thinking, it's only because you don't exist. You're just part of my imagination, so, of course, you know what I'm thinking and feeling. And, even if you do exist, reading my thoughts and feelings is just rude."

"Any ice water left?" Eric asked.

"Don't you dare!" Vala said.

"You two certainly squabble like siblings," Char said. "I used to fight like that with your mother all the time when we were young."

"I can't imagine Mother as a child," Vala said.

"Vala, you're not alone in this," Eric said, leaning forward. "That's not just empathy. If none of this had happened, you wouldn't have your Aunt Char and Serein, but you do. Also, I, too, have learned that my parents were not my parents. That my mother is the mysterious woman who set up our trust fund accounts. Who knows who my father was. I don't know what happened to the child I replaced in the Kine family. But more. I know that my whole life searching had a reason behind it, and you, Sister, are that reason." He braced his elbows on his knees and tried to make eye contact, but Vala was focused on the distance, another way to escape. "You've been searching, too, but you didn't even know you were searching, mostly because you keep running backward."

After a long pause, through which Eric managed to wait, Vala finally answered. "Eric, you have to admit it's a disappointing search. What's wrong with those people? They segregated themselves, taking their abilities and knowledge to keep to themselves. They abandoned *us*, their own children. They act superior, but their behavior is flawed, is *wrong*. They aren't better than humans, but they seem to think they are." She pulled a fleece blanket up closer to her face.

"First," Eric said, "I'm not disappointed I found you; that alone makes it all worthwhile. As to the behavior of these folks, they sound very like us, yes. They're trying to live up to their principles but, as you know, objective ethics can be a bitch to live with."

Eric took one of her hands in his. "Think about it. In essence, they believe they must live in harmony in order to survive: no hate, no anger, no revenge, no destruction. They've derailed under the current situation, and they're scared. But they're trying to get their culture back on track, the peaceful and harmonious track. They're trying to protect Earth. Both Earths. They don't know how. They don't know why the membrane is failing, and they don't know where they can go. They're hoping you can help with the science. They're hoping I can help somehow…maybe by keeping you from killing someone."

Vala snorted.

"Look, I agree. They ran away. You had to run away yourself tonight. Of course, you're just a child. They said so."

Vala was silent.

Eric decided to keep hammering home his point. She hadn't completely retreated. "Keep in mind, Vala, that some of these people suffered *themselves*. They lived it. It wasn't just their grandparents or great grandparents. Look at us. We've both been called freaks by one name or another. If you had a chance, for the first time in your life, to live with only those like yourself or who accepted you as Char does, wouldn't you take it? Would you emigrate to have a life where you didn't have to feel conspicuous because of your height, because of your affinity with nature, because of how fast you can run?"

Vala's jaw muscles bulged, but she didn't say anything. She didn't kick or hit him either.

"I wish I could wash all this away for both you," Char said. "None of this is new. Immigrants used to group together for protection when they came to the United States. That's where many neighborhoods got their start. And what are borders but a way of separating people who speak a different language or look different? Granted, this–you said *Membrane,* no?–is pretty damn extreme, but only because they had the technology or skills or magic or whatever it is to do it." She laughed. "People are talking about living on Mars in two years. Are they explorers or deserters? Some of the people who will take that one-way trip are our best scientists."

Char stood and walked over to pet Serein and, at the same time, knelt to look up at Vala. "Is it similar to what you're thinking about with emigration to Mexico? Don't you want to escape the limitations the government imposes on you as a scientist?"

Eric let go of her hand and clasped his hands together. "Really? You're planning on emigrating, Vala?"

She looked at him and smiled. "*That's* what you took out of Char's heartfelt speech?" She laughed, then continued. "I'm thinking about it. Why didn't you know that if you know what I'm thinking?"

He laughed. "Maybe that hasn't been the focus of your thoughts for a while."

"Well, anyway, Latin America is making great strides. Unfortunately, as a scientist who has worked on government projects, my freedom is limited both in the work I can do and my options for leaving." She shrugged. "This country slid into fascism ten years ago, but most people are ignorant of how far it has gone."

Eric nodded. "And here you and I suddenly have a new option, Vala. We have a new community. A new world? I don't really understand that. Quit looking so sour. I'm intrigued by the fact that they tried to leave a beacon for us, tried to connect. They also still have hopes that maybe they could reintegrate with humans, and that we'll be able to help with that. But after what we've been saying here, do we believe they can?"

They all sat in silence for a few moments. The question was one being asked on both sides of the Membrane, in two worlds, Eric knew. Did the culture in this world even want their help? Hadn't this culture always dismissed their sort of radical thinking?

After a few moments, Vala silently reached out and handed Eric an envelope. Eric recognized the scrawl across the front; it was the letter Obeah had given her from her mother.

No wonder she wasn't more responsive. She'd be focused on the letter. "I can read it?" Eric asked, just for verbal confirmation.

After she nodded, Eric handed her the timeline he had. "You can read this at the same time. They gave it to me, along with other information, over there—" he gestured toward the shimmering whatever-it-was "—to show how those of us with our genetic difference fit into the homo sapiens timeline from their perspective."

Vala took the sheet but didn't look at it.

Eric read:

28 November 1999

My Darling Daughter,

As the time draws near for your entrance into the world, the ache in my heart grows stronger. For one thing, I'll never get to know you, and some days I think that my decision to give birth to you was incredibly selfish. I want you to know that the decision wasn't an easy one, but I also want you to know that no child has ever been loved more than you.

My heart also aches because I know that your life will be one of sacrifice.

You are being given a difficult task in life, one that will challenge you daily to stay strong, stay dignified, stay true to the principles behind your birth. You are our nation's hope for a better future, one where we can live free wherever we choose, one in which the Membrane that is soon to be erected between us and the humans can come back down or can stand to allow freedom for all the gentem.

Your intelligence will be crucial. You may be able to help humans discover ways to stop the destruction of Earth or ways to protect the gentem from that destruction. Your compassion and understanding will be essential to easing resentment and distrust on both sides. Your common sense will help guide our nation in ways to work with humans harmoniously or to part with them with love in our hearts.

You will have some help. Jasmine and her child should give you companionship and someone who understands who you are. That's little enough in the world you will face.

No matter what you hear from others, no matter how you are treated, remember to be proud of who you are, of your heritage, of your abilities.

By the time you receive this letter, you will understand what has happened to me and why. Although our nation tends to be long-lived and immune to most human-borne diseases, radiation poisoning is difficult to combat. I don't regret trying to help the people–both those of our nation and the humans–in the once-beautiful city of Nagasaki. Some of our own relatives lived there, but they were lost to us.

I've been assured that the radiation poisoning will in no way affect your health. I know all the rest of this situation will greatly affect you, and I hope you can forgive me for agreeing to this arrangement. Because of our strong heritage of intuitive awareness of the natural world and strong intellect, as well as the magic of life that you have probably not yet discovered, we were asked to serve.

Bless you in that endeavor and in your life as a whole. I hope it proves to be fulfilling, both for you and all those whom you will help.

Sasa no ha sara-sara
Nokiba ni yureru
Ohoshi-sama kira-kira
Kingin sunago
Goshiki no tanzaku
watashi ga kaita
Ohoshi-sama kirakira
sora kara miteru

My love will always be with you. Listen for me in the whispering wind, the soothing surf, the singing bird, the silent night of stars; the firefly that will guide you: That is your heritage.
Your mother,
Vala Sherren Matsu

Eric read the letter, stared into space. What a message to have from a mother Vala had never known. He read it a second time, then said, "A powerful gift. This says a great deal about your mother. And you. I wonder what the Japanese means."

Vala answered softly as though reciting. "It's the song of Tanabata, a traditional festival:

> Bamboo leaves
> are rustling, rustling,
> Swaying close to the
> roof's edge,
> Oh, how the stars
> are twinkling, twinkling,
> Gold and silver
> grains of sand.
> Five wishes
> I have written
> The stars are twinkling
> And watching from
> the sky.

"I didn't know you spoke Japanese!" Char said.

Vala stared at her a moment, her eyes wide and unblinking. Then she said, "I don't."

"Then how–" Char started and then stopped.

"Wonderful," Eric said into the silence.

Vala turned to look at him. "Eric, I'm none of those things. Well, smart, yes. But I'm not intuitive. I'm not strong. I have no special abilities. And, as you have pointed out, I'm a coward–I know how to run away. As you've also said, I'm not wise."

"Well, you're incorrect about all that," Eric said flatly, "except, maybe the running away part. Well, and maybe the wisdom. You and I both are strong, beyond what we realize. We had to be to wade through all the craziness surrounding who we are to arrive at this point, sitting and talking about it, in front of some whacky portal no one on earth will believe. As to special abilities ... well, we don't know a lot about our heritage yet. We need to find out, to learn, to accept what we can, to change what we can, to make things

202

better as we can. As to wisdom and not running away, you have me. My legs are too short to run away. And we're both still children, yes?"

"I'm just scared!" Vala said, her voice quavering. Serein sat up, put his head on her lap and studied her carefully.

"Of course, you are," Char said. She stood and kneeled beside Vala to put her arm around her. "Anyone would be. This is tremendous responsibility."

"But what are we going to do, Aunt Char?"

"Well," Char said, "first you're going to feed Serein who has been very patient. Then you're going to get some rest tonight. Then you and Eric are going to change the world."

"That sounds like an excellent plan," Eric said. "I'm going to go refresh myself, finish the office clean out, and I'll see you back here in the morning. Maybe about ten?" He vowed to tell Vala about the ephedra in the water supply the next day after she'd had some time to reflect. This wasn't a good time.

Vala looked at one and then the other of them. Then she started to laugh. As she did so, a light breeze found its way into the garden, then a firefly flew by, then returned and landed on Vala's knee.

Vala sat very still, then whispered, "We don't have fireflies in the Northwest."

The firefly flashed rapidly for several seconds then lifted, flew through the portal and to the other side. For several moments, no one spoke, then Vala said, "Yes. We'll go change the world. Tomorrow."

CHAPTER EIGHTEEN

Saturday night, July 7, 2029

Cassidy took his time leaving the portal after he dropped off Eric. He could see their wavering figures as silhouettes against some lights, but he couldn't hear anything they were saying. The tension he'd felt while they'd all been talking still had a grip on him. He stretched a little, bit his lips, and considered Eric's comments. What would it be like to be told that everything you knew, everything you believed, was skewed. He wished he had Eric's ability to understand people from the inside out. More than once Cassidy had been accused of being off-hand about individuals' feelings.

He knew now he had been too cavalier about his mission to contact the children and dump the entire situation in their spheres. But how could he have done it differently? The problem began with leaving the children as foundlings. Abandoned. He couldn't quantify the situation. Would it be a zero? His mother's voice echoed in his mind: "Cassidy, math sometimes has nothing to do with a situation. You can't compute emotions."

If they couldn't be computed, perhaps they could just be disregarded. Individuals could fake emotions. Tandra had deep empathy for anything living but a temper that often overrode her instincts. She was learning to control the temper, but she had to work at it every day. Cassidy could do without that sort of emotion. Their mother had been kind and compassionate, but she, too, had been a scientist, tending to become totally absorbed in her work just as he did, and Tandra sometimes resented that.

He shrugged. What good was that sort of analysis? All they could do was move forward.

Cassidy turned to get on the scooter, stopped. A light cedar-scented breeze cooled a clear night. He could run back. Just then he became aware of someone, then smiled. Gulo. Even if he hadn't been alert to Gulo's thoughts, he'd have picked up on the odor.

What are you doing here? Cassidy asked.

Watching. Are we going to lose our home?

Cassidy shook his head, not in denial but in uncertainty. *More emotions? From a wolverine?* Cassidy found it fascinating that Gulo was aware of what was going on, was communicating emotions clearly enough for Cassidy to sense.

I don't know. Something needs to be done to stop Earth's destruction. It's coming here, Cassidy answered.

Race?

Cassidy laughed. Gulo always took a philosophical approach to life. Maybe that was how to quantify emotion. Without replying, Cassidy took off into the night. As he ran, he considered his silent talks with animals. How would he explain that to a human? No, it wasn't English. It wasn't words. It was understanding, but was it even language?

Gulo outran him—Cassidy's top speed was about 40 miles per hour, but he slowed that down so that, by the time Cassidy ran the short distance to Obeah's clinic, Gulo had vanished into the night. Obeah was cleaning up the clinic, preparing for the next day, when Cassidy entered.

"Ran back," Obeah said. It wasn't a question.

"Gulo wanted to race."

Obeah chuckled. "Did you let him win? He gets cranky if he loses, then he takes out his frustration on someone's chickens."

Cassidy nodded. "He won. Maybe he'll stick to the woods and not raid tonight."

Cassidy did some quad stretches while wondering how to ask Obeah if he thought Vala was unstable.

"She isn't," Obeah said.

Why did he ever bother to try to keep his thoughts or feelings secret from Obeah? "And is she up to the task?"

Obeah shrugged. "We don't even know yet what the task is. More than eight billion individuals teem on these two Earths we know. We don't know how to save any of them at the moment. Major cultural shifts are needed on both Earths. Who is up to that task?" Obeah picked up a broom and began sweeping, his words keeping pace with the motion.

"World wars, contamination and overuse of drinking water, increased diseases, and finally global warming: none of it has been enough to force change for humans. Like little children, they put their hands over their eyes, deny the problems, and look for new plastic toys. Or they simply believe *science* will save them without realizing that science is the study of nature for understanding, not the solution for betraying nature."

Obeah swept his little pile of dust to the door and swept it out. "I should wash the floor, but I'd rather have tea." He poured tea into two mugs and set them on the table. As he sat down, he said, "Meanwhile, every change the gentem has tried to make has failed."

"Well, that's bleak," Cassidy said as he sat down and took the warm mug in his hands. "We have two individuals who have just had their lives devastated and we want them to change what appears to be unchangeable conditions. Vala doesn't even believe us."

"She'll be with us. She has Eric. He's a powerful man, Cassidy, much more powerful than he understands. He has great intelligence, but he's also an empath with great persuasive powers, the *gift of gab*. He could persuade a pharisee to become a hipster. He's also extremely ethical, perhaps more so than we've been, so I think he can be trusted in spite of his power. Vala is able to sense that quality, and she has quickly grown to trust him, even if she doesn't readily acknowledge it yet. Eric reads her well, better than she reads herself."

Obeah stood again, got a cloth, and wiped up some drips from around the teapot before sitting down. He drank some tea and said, "I think it will come down to allowing the fresh perspectives of those two to guide us."

"But there are just the two of them."

"What has happened, Cassidy? You were the one pushing for this, convinced that this would work to change the world."

"I know. That was before I met them, before I understood what their lives have been. That was before Gulo wanted to know if we were going to cast the animals aside, abandon them to destruction."

"That doesn't sound like Gulo."

"Well, okay. He wanted to know if his world was going to be lost. I paraphrased the context. Kill off all the humans and save the world? Save the humans just so they can kill off themselves and the world?" Cassidy groaned and dropped his head on his arms on the table.

Obeah patted him on the back. "I believe there's an answer, one that doesn't involve killing or being killed. One that will allow us to live the lives we wish to live. Let this play out. You've said that creative solutions always exist."

"You're both wrong, you know."

Cassidy, recognizing Tandra's voice, didn't bother looking around or even lifting his head. "You know, Tandra, your continued dislike for humans continues to amaze me. You're still young. You don't have a long history with humans, either."

"Emotions are sometimes stronger than logic, Cassidy," Obeah said.

Cassidy jerked his head up and turned to face Tandra who had flushed a deep bronze. "Gornisht! You were in love with a human! That's the hurt Eric was talking about!"

"So what if I was? I learned my lesson."

Cassidy swallowed all the sarcastic or insulting words that came to him and said simply, "Tandra, I'm sorry. What happened?"

"She decided to go back to her husband, an abuser and drug addict. They're all like that, you know. Stupid. Short-sighted. It's why they hate us."

"Did she know you were gentem?"

Tandra shook her head. "I was going to tell her, but everything fell apart. Then the Membrane… " She shrugged. "I'm better off."

Cassidy stood and gave Tandra a hug although it was a little like hugging a board. "One is never better off when one is hurting. But to heal, you've got to let it go and move on. Don't become like Alarick, Tandra. You'll lose life's beauty. And you do see beauty. You live it in your work."

Tandra stepped back, laughed. "Well, look at my little brother being all motherly."

"Does Mom know?"

"Sure. She's the one who says I'm better off. I came back for something to help me sleep, Obeah. The day has drained my reserves."

Obeah went to his shelves and picked out a small bottle among the many. "This will take the edge off, Tandra. Meanwhile, I suggest you think about seeing Abuelita. Her knowledge is ancient."

Tandra smiled. "I'm seeing her tomorrow. I've realized that I've lost control of my emotions. I was cruel to both Vala and Eric. They've been through hell. If I'm going to be on the Council, I need to have my old self back, which is merely contentious, not vicious. I also need to align myself if I'm going to help others."

"Then you've accepted the Council position! That's wonderful news, Tandra. You'll be a blessing to them," Obeah said.

"I, too, think that's excellent," Cassidy added.

Tandra nodded slowly. "Thank you. I hope you won't live to regret recommending me, Cassidy, and that my decisions will always please you."

"When have they ever?" Cassidy asked. He grabbed her hand and squeezed it. "This will get easier, I hope, for all of us."

"Yügen. We shall see," Obeah said.

After a few moments silence, Cassidy sat down again and smiled. Tandra's closeness had given him hope. "Vala is a fascinating woman, isn't she?"

Obeah chuckled. "Heigh ho! You're smitten!"

"Really, Cassidy?" Tandra said. "You find her appealing? She's such a cowardly creature."

Cassidy felt himself bristle. "I don't think she's cowardly at all. She's fought against all odds to succeed at her work. She came here, a place that shouldn't even exist by all she knows. She stood up to *you*, Tandra. That makes her a grizzly for certain."

Laughing, Tandra slapped him on the shoulder. "We'll see. We may never hear from her again."

"We'll hear," said Obeah. "She's important."

"Important how?" Tandra asked, with an edge to her voice.

"I'm not certain yet." Obeah walked over to the counter and stared out into the night, pulling at his moustache. "As Cassidy and I were saying when you came in, there *is* an answer, but it's hidden. An answer always exists. We're too close; we lack perspective. Vala's distance may turn out to be an unexpected benefit–maybe our instincts to leave the children wasn't so bad in spite of their pain."

"I may go through the portal and see her tomorrow," Cassidy said.

"Remember what Eric said. Wait. For a time."

Cassidy nodded. Not because he agreed but because he didn't have a good argument. At least not good enough for Obeah. Besides, Eric had said not to run right after her, not that he shouldn't follow slowly.

Obeah sighed, and Cassidy knew that Obeah had probably read his thoughts as clearly as if Cassidy had spoken them aloud.

"I'm going to my quarters to lie down, meditate. Maybe sleep a little," Obeah said. "I'll see you in the morning. If you're around," he added a little sarcastically.

"I'm going home, too, Cassidy. See you tomorrow," Tandra said. "I promise to think about being mellow."

Cassidy laughed. "I'm sure you'll think about it, Tandra. I'll see you tomorrow. And good night, Obeah. Thank you for everything. We could have never made the breakthrough without you."

Cassidy sat alone for a few moments in the clinic, then he went outside. A quick run. Maybe to the portal. He wouldn't go through, but he wanted to go there. Just to look. Nothing more.

At the portal, he could see some lights on Vala's side. Her house or other buildings perhaps. Then he thought he saw the silhouette of a dog pass by. Serein. He wouldn't be there without Vala being nearby.

Cassidy was fascinated that he could stand here on the Olympic Peninsula and look into Vala's yard in Seattle as though she were next door. He hadn't before thought about how that would work once the links were established. What if the children had been elsewhere when that had happened? If they'd been on an airplane, what would have happened? Gentem had been playing with forces they hadn't fully understood. That needed to change.

Cassidy stepped into the portal. As he stepped through to Vala's garden, Serein came over immediately and nuzzled his hand. Cassidy stooped, rubbed his head and answered his *Hello*.

"I'm not used to having people just walk into my garden," Vala said from a chair by the fountain.

"Sorry," said Cassidy. "There's no way to knock."

"It's after midnight," Vala said.

"Oh. Is that significant?"

Vala laughed.

Cassidy smiled. Her laugh reminded him of a bamboo flute. "I like hearing you laugh," he said.

"Eric says I don't laugh enough."

Cassidy looked around. "Why does it smell smoky?"

"We still get fires all summer. I used to think we'd run out of burnable material, but it hasn't happened yet. The smoke here is coming mostly from the Olympics, in an area near where you live on the other side of the Membrane...on the upper Dungeness River."

Cassidy's stomach churned at the thought of the beloved forest on fire. They had avoided many such risks on Beta Earth when climate change issues had leveled out. He changed the subject. "Where do you run here?"

"Want to see?"

Cassidy thought he heard a challenge in her voice. He hoped she didn't run on a treadmill. Before the Membrane had gone up, he'd joined a gym and tried the various machines. It had been like marching death. "Yes. I'd like to see more here," he said hoping that would encourage her to run outside. "And I'd like to run."

She stood. She was wrapped in a large white robe. She looked like a snow-covered mountain. "I'll change and we'll go." When she returned, dressed in a snug, sleeveless, black top and gray, slightly loose, black shorts, Serein was immediately ahead of her, leading the way. Cassidy followed them through the house, abruptly stopping at one point to read a framed letter on the wall.

Vala turned around and joined him. "Powerful, isn't it? Aunt Char wrote that to the editor of the newspaper about the plans to tear down some dams that were on Native sacred ground but build dams on other rivers."

Cassidy read aloud:

> You say that this land, here or there, is sacred,
> but I tell you that every spot where you step
> is sacred, is our living Earth. Every sip of living
> water, every breath of unseen air, every tug
> of gravity, every creature, plant, stone,
> and grain of sand is sacred, a part of a whole
> and living Earth, part of every other living
> being, recycled for millions of years. When
> you kill, dam, clear cut, and burn; when you
> disregard the sacred; when you mine the land
> and pollute the sea, air and sky, you kill parts
> of your own spirit, becoming the walking dead.

"Aunt Char was an environmentalist before it was popular and remains one now that it's unpopular again." Without waiting for a response, Vala turned, walked down the hall, out another door to the front walk, and then through a gate. Cassidy followed, surprised at the number of rooms, doors, and gates.

Without speaking, Vala started to jog down a paved path that led away from her house and out along a beach. Debris and remnants of what looked like houses were scattered here and there, but this was a trail that was obviously used often. On Beta Earth, they also had debris that had come along with the building of Beta Earth. They scavenged for materials from some of it, but there was too much to clean it all up.

Cassidy repressed his disappointment as they lazily jogged for a few hundred yards. Apparently, she wasn't the runner he'd hoped. Then she began picking up speed. Soon he felt his legs stretching out as he matched her pace. Wind and surf sounds merged in the night. Again, he heard her laughter, and it was free and joyful. Just when he began to think he'd reached his speed limit, they came to a hill and slowed slightly to run up. Steps were nearby, but they ignored them and ran across the grassy slope.

At the top, Vala paused, looking out into the dark where a light line of surf broke along some rocks. A rail surrounded the concrete platform at the top. A statue stood to one side, looking off at the sea. "You can run," she said. She sounded pleased.

"It's how I rest," Cassidy said.

Vala nodded. "I also rest that way, but I don't often run full speed. People don't understand when I run fast. I learned that when I was ten and discovered I could outrun everyone, even the boys. They were furious and began making fun of me. As an adult, I began running at night when people weren't around."

Cassidy felt a twinge of sadness. Empathy? That was interesting. Certainly, much of her life had required hiding who she was, how she felt. The story echoed what he'd heard from other gentem all his life. "You know why you can run fast, don't you?"

"I told you: I'm a freak."

"That's not true of either of us. Not all gentem can run fast, nor do they enjoy it as freely. But some of us have genetic ability. First, big feet."

Vala laughed. "I have those. Size thirteen or fourteen. Special order."

"In addition, we have a longer Achilles tendon, usually about 20 centimeters long, combined with extra-strong calf muscles if, of course, they're used. Most of us with a running ability start running almost as soon as we walk, like baby ostriches. The long tendons store elastic energy when running. Obeah has speculated that we had ancestors who were great runners, maybe because they lived on open plains, which may also be related to height, but maybe just to escape predators. That's guess work."

She laughed again. "You've put a lot of thought into this."

He shrugged. "Our scientists have intensified study into who we are and how we can do what we do. For instance, as runners, we also have less mass for our height, combined with longer legs, shorter torsos, and more slender limbs. In other words, we're skinny. Tandra is built like that, but she never loved running, never developed her calf muscles. Function and form don't always combine with interest."

Vala was silent for a moment. "I'm intrigued by the idea that my structure is both normal and accepted in some cultures. Have you found no humans with those tendencies?" Vala asked as she turned her back on the sea and leaned against the metal railing to look directly at Cassidy. Her eyes seemed almost to glow in this light.

"Apparently, some people from Kenya have been noted for a genetic proclivity for running. One of our researchers described the Kenyan physical differences as "bird-like," saying that the traits would make them more efficient runners, especially over long distances. But rarely is it as noticeable as it is for some gentem. However, some of our researchers believe there is yet another branch on the homo erectus tree that we haven't yet found. Also, Neanderthal DNA is less common in Africa, so maybe our connection there is stronger."

Vala shook her head, and her lips thinned and turned down slightly. "I wonder what Mother would say if I told her that she could relax, that she hadn't given birth to something like me."

Cassidy couldn't think of a reply. Someone like Eric would know the correct response. Cassidy gestured toward the breaking surf far below. "What's all that rubble down there?"

"The land used to extend out further." She turned around and pointed off to their left. "See that tower out there? That's an old lighthouse that was on dry ground, a park of sorts, not long ago. There were houses all along this point, surf breaking almost to the doors. As the sea began rising, Alki Point was flooded, especially during the more frequent heavy storms. One reason I was able to buy property here, build my private home and have some isolation is because everyone knows the surf will soon be breaking along this hill, especially in storms."

"Climate change." Cassidy said.

Vala nodded. "People just keep building further up the hills and keeping the same names of towns, cities, and even neighborhoods. That way they can ignore the problem. Of course, people have done that for thousands of years. When they move out of an area that's flooded, burned, or buried under magma, they call the next place by the same names. A decade or so ago, a lot of archeology work was done on Neolithic villages, lines of them, in the North Sea; people just kept moving inland as seas flooded land at the end of the last ice age."

She made a sweeping gesture over the area around them. Standing straight and thin, she looked like a mythological goddess. Cassidy could feel his cheeks heat up as she continued.

"What they call Alki Point now is where the lower parts come up near this area, Schmitz Reserve Park. That makes up my backyard.

All that," she said gesturing to the west, "was houses and streets. When it flooded out, I bought my place adjacent to the park with its waterfront for very little money. I had all the houses dismantled, but I wasn't able to have all the rubble hauled away—there aren't many places to dump stuff like that anymore. There's too much of it. Now I run through the park and out on what is left of the Alki Trail. It soon will be underwater, too. Were you from this area, Cassidy?"

He shook his head. "I was born in Dublin but didn't live there long. We wandered the world. I was sometimes with my father, an oceanographer, and sometimes with my mother, a cultural anthropologist." He perched on the top rail of the fence and hooked his feet between the second and third rails. "When I was twelve, I went to live on a private estate in Australia where Marina, my science mentor, and other scientists worked and taught. We were rather isolated there and didn't have much interaction with human groups except for some of the indigenous people. They accepted us without question."

"Those in gentem culture don't seem to have very tight-knit families," Vala said.

She was looking at him carefully, her head tilted slightly, as though studying him. Was his answer particularly important to her? He spoke slowly, trying to not say the wrong thing. "I suppose it seems that way, but in fact our family group includes everyone and is very tight. That's why various individuals refer to you and Eric as 'our children.' Our entire population is a village. We're collectivists but with a strong interest in the individual."

"Yet we were abandoned."

Cassidy studied the ground, realized he was rubbing his lower lip with his thumb and stopped. He felt as though he'd been slapped. "That was unintentional and a horrible mistake." Unable to think of anything else to say, he looked at her. "You're beautiful," he said. "You remind me of a sandy beach, full of energetic, almost chaotic movement, and yet harmonious in action."

"Wow! You have poetry in your soul." She smiled.

Surely, that was a good sign. He tried to answer her comment appropriately. "No, not really. I've never written poetry."

Vala laughed. "You don't get out much, do you?"

Cassidy started to speak, stopped. Was she amused by him? Bantering? Or serious? Eric would just *know*. "I'm out all the time, Vala. I much prefer to be out than in."

She smiled. "I forget. You've been in a very different culture the past thirty years, and you've lived in a supportive and unique group. I was just trying to say that what you said was lovely."

Cassidy felt uncomfortable. Now he was biting the inside of his cheek. Honesty. Would that work? "I have trouble expressing my feelings about you, Vala. And Eric. I don't think you understand how important you and Eric are. You two are on an epic hero's journey, like Odysseus. From my childhood, I remember Wonder Woman." He looked her up and down. "I hope that's not insulting. Anyway, we've waited for this reconnection in order to know what our next step into the future would be. You and Eric represent our future."

Vala stared at him for a moment, then shook her head. *"Us? Your future?* Is that a joke? Or are you insane?" She was bent forward at the waist slightly and looking at him as though she might shove him off the rail.

He slid off to stand facing her. "Neither. What you and Eric do is crucial to our continued survival." Cassidy felt uncomfortable with the discussion. Perhaps this was too much. "You do intend to help, don't you?"

"Cassidy, we'll try to do what we can. But you have to understand that neither of us knows what we're doing or how to do it. We don't understand what the gentem are doing or even how they're doing it. We're just two bewildered individuals who have had their worlds flipped upside down in a matter of a few days. We're on a planet that is in serious trouble and that has billions of people on it. You're on a planet we've never heard of. Honestly, I can't imagine what we can do, in part because I've been trying to do something about it for years, and I've made very little progress."

"Right now, I think we should run some more."

Vala laughed again. "Your non-sequiturs keep me off balance. Do you do that deliberately to keep people on edge?"

Cassidy shrugged. "I didn't know I did it at all. According to most individuals who know me, I'm merely obnoxiously outspoken. I don't think any of it is planned. But I'm trying to keep you comfortable. Or maybe I'm trying to keep myself comfortable. I know the situation is urgent. That's why I've been working to set up the link. When the effects began to hit us, we knew we weren't protected, and we don't know what to do, either. But none of us can be overwhelmed because that won't help. Eric thought I should leave you alone for a while, and I didn't. So running seems like a good idea."

Vala laughed and, without warning, turned, and began running back the way they'd come, Serein directly in front of her. They silently covered the distance in a few minutes.

Back at the house, Vala fixed some herbal tea, and they sat in the garden again. "What smells bad here besides the smoke?" Cassidy asked, wrinkling his nose.

"Everything. Car exhaust, for instance–many cars still burn fossil fuel, and they haven't been banned. The fossil fuel cartel is still very powerful in this country, and the big tariffs and taxes on alternative energy sources and imports have just about wiped out the competition. All the driverless cars operate on fossil fuels. We have access to other technology, but, people fear a declining economy. Manufacturing continues, such as the paper mills. Then there's garbage. Sewer. Pollution permeates everything, but people rely on masks or nanobots to compensate. The idea is that no matter how bad it gets, we'll figure out ways to live with it."

"I don't remember it being so noticeable, but it was a long time ago. And I didn't live here. Obeah says that people have been aware of the problems for more than 200 years. Is it this way everywhere in the world?"

"No. In some places in Europe, alternative sources of energy have replaced almost all the fossil fuel use, and people there have always had a lower carbon footprint than here. Latin America has had a huge turn around since 2020. It's not enough. In addition, water shortages have become severe almost everywhere. Water wars are common."

"Yet you have a fountain here. And good water, no?"

"My place is unique, Cassidy. I built it as a self-contained system. The fountain is part of an underground filtration system of water used in the house. There's some evaporation but not much. I have to recharge the water system about twice a month."

"Are countries, people in general, making any effort to help one another and improve conditions?" Cassidy felt a lump of discouragement lodging in his gut, but there had to be some positive action. Didn't there?

"In some places, on a local level, people are trying to help one another. The idea of territory ownership, borders, and political power is strained. In spite of the desires of many to end the era of nuclear escalation, the threat of disaster continues. There was a song in the 1960s–by the Kingston Trio as I recall–that ends with the lines

What nature doesn't do to us
Will be done by our fellow man

"That's still applicable." Vala paused, shook her head. "It's not all bad, Cassidy. I'm just soured." She patted Serein's head, then gestured at her garden. "I've tried to make this place a haven. I'm lucky in that sense." Vala poured some more tea. She stood, walked over to one of the plants where an AI bee was upside down on a leaf. She fiddled with it for a moment, then set it upright. It buzzed, hovered, then settled on the leaf. Vala sat back in her chair.

"Cassidy, some nights all I can do is cry. Humans are killing… everything. I've tried to combat what I can. My greenways along the roads have been used but mega-monopolies have squelched our efforts to have, for instance, more public transportation. People continue to commute to work instead of living nearby or working remotely. Increasingly, my research is limited by the government. That's one reason I've thought about emigrating, but I'd have to do it secretly. The government doesn't want to lose top scientists."

Cassidy shook his head. "It's worse than I expected. And that all explains why the pollution leaks are worse. Carbon is particularly bad." Being self-aware of one's upcoming extinction was gruesome. He took a deep breath, coughed, then sipped some tea. "We've brought back huge areas of rainforest and animal species. Our scientists have been able to bring back some previously extinct species with DNA; they're very excited about that. I don't want it to have all been for nothing."

"So how do you live without the same problems with manufacturing starting all over again? And battles over ownership and borders and … everything?"

"Everything we do must be set up to utilize and operate only on green technology; we have power from wind, waves, and sun; even the ground—well, the bacteria *in* the ground generate energy—"

"I've done that!" Vala said. "The garden lights are all operated out of the soil itself through bacteria."

"That isn't common?"

"No, not really. In a small way, but not without utilizing construction of housing or other facilities. What I'm doing in the garden doesn't require a facility."

Cassidy nodded. "It sounds like you're helping humans make progress. We, too, recycle water. All village sewage is recycled as clean water. Some of it is modified by our shapers who neutralize toxins. As to the politics: we don't have borders because we haven't divided up land into property, not on a personal, local, or national scale."

"But what if two people want the same property?"

"No one owns it. They can share or work out a compromise. Anyway, our population is small. Without individuals thronging space, we all have plenty of room to be and do wherever we want. We don't tend to be a very prolific species, in part because, according to Obeah, we're not in such a rush. Humans die so fast that they might procreate quickly to fight off mortality."

"It's more complicated than that," said a voice behind Cassidy. He looked around and saw Eric standing there.

"Eric, wonderful to see you!" Cassidy said.

"Want some herbal tea?" Vala asked.

"Okay." Eric grabbed a chair and dragged it over while Vala poured more tea. "I see you decided to visit," he said to Cassidy.

Cassidy shrugged. "I couldn't help it."

"House didn't announce you," Vala said.

"The gate just opened as I approached. Didn't you say I was to have access?"

Vala shrugged. "I guess House didn't ignore me just to be different."

Eric laughed, then said, "The idea that humans fear old age and death is partly the reason they have children. They also still want to pass on their personal beliefs, religion, or ethnicity. Having their beliefs and their bloodline continue somehow makes them feel closer to life. Or they fear becoming a minority. In many cases, they just act without thinking."

Vala handed Eric a cup of tea. Eric looked at it and said, "Thank you. This isn't tea from Obeah, is it?"

She laughed. "Would you rather have beer? I got some for you." Eric grinned and Vala stood.

"Beer?" Cassidy asked.

"I'll bring two," she said.

"So anyway," Eric continued, "you'd be amazed at how many people go through their lives just doing what's expected of them: grow up, get a job, marry or partner and have children. Meanwhile, many children remain orphans; the gut response is to want kids of your own bloodline. The drive may be buried so deep in our–their?–genes that humans have no idea how to escape the concept."

He paused, pulled on his ear lobe. "I wonder if the genetic difference with the gentem is related to attitudes toward reproduction." He shook his head. "Anyway, close to one-third of the US population today is childless."

"Marriage? Isn't that a religious-based custom? Why do people still do that?"

Eric laughed. "If you're looking for logic, humanity isn't the group to turn to. They say one thing but do another."

Vala returned with beer for both and sat back down.

"What are your clothes made of?" Eric asked as he reached over and fingered Cassidy's pants.

"Hemp. Don't you have hemp here?"

Eric nodded. "It's not all that popular."

"I wondered how you could run in those," Vala said.

"They're very comfortable. And light. I never feel overheated in them."

"How can you manufacture clothes and such without running into the same problems we have here?" Eric asked.

"Vala asked the same thing. In the case of clothes, everything is hand-made and bartered. People don't need much."

"What about fashion?" Vala asked.

Cassidy shook his head and tried to figure out the context of the word. She didn't mean manufacture. Then, he remembered. "Ah, you mean what makes you look good and sends a message about your status. I don't know much about that."

Vala laughed again. "My mother claims I don't, either."

Eric smiled. "I've never seen you in anything that wasn't good for running."

Vala picked up her tea, started to take a sip, then looked at Eric intently. "I thought you were going to clean out your office and sleep."

He shrugged, downed the last half of his beer, and said, "I did. It's almost daylight."

"Cassidy thinks we're super heroes, Eric," Vala said. "If you keep being that efficient, you'll encourage him. Wonder Woman and Odysseus, I think he said."

Eric looked at Vala. "Noooo … maybe Raven."

"Who's that?" Vala asked

"I don't know that reference, either," Cassidy said.

"Let's just say she's a bird," Eric said. "I don't want to be Odysseus. Maybe Spiderman."

"Him, I've heard of," Cassidy said.

"I want another beer. How about you, Cassidy?"

He shook his head, and Eric went into House.

"You seem to know a lot about some of these characters. How can that be?" Vala asked.

"Well, I was a teen here before the Membrane was created. Also, before that happened, the Council had a vault built into one of the hills by Deer Park Road–"

"You've kept the names of places?"

"Sure. That meant we didn't have to re-create maps. Anyway, the vault was built, almost filled, and shifted when we finished Beta Earth. When the division occurred, they could bring only what they could carry. That was where our library began. The Council also set up a digital library of everything that was available, including books, Congressional proceedings, and more from around the world."

"I want to learn a lot more about how this was all created," Vala said. "There's too much we don't know. If we're going to try to explain this to people, we need to understand more."

"That's another problem from how things were supposed to go. Jasmine was going to find ways to teach you both," Cassidy said. "Vala, no one ever intended to abandon you and Eric."

"I keep hearing that, but my mother makes it clear that intentional abandonment was exactly what the gentem did."

Eric returned into a silence that Cassidy wanted to break but didn't know how.

"Well," said Eric, clearing his throat, "I called Wyatt tonight. I took him the timeline for homo Sophos development Obeah gave me. He's wildly excited about it. Vala, I told him I'd talk to you and see if we could meet him here tomorrow. I didn't tell him about the portal, but I'd like to bring him into this. If we can't convince Wyatt that we know what we're talking about, we can't convince anyone. I think Cassidy should be here."

Vala shifted uncomfortably. "I suppose we have to start somewhere, and we don't know what we're doing, so ... Cassidy, you want to meet Wyatt?"

"Is he human?"

Vala's eyebrows lifted. "You mean you left others here, others like us? I thought they'd all left!"

Cassidy began to have an idea of just how much information they had yet to exchange. Vala was right. How could they explain what they didn't know? "No. Probably a half-million went to the other side. Remember, we had no idea how it would work. Many didn't want to make the commitment. Probably a thousand or so on Beta Earth are human–"

"Human!" Eric sat forward on the edge of his chair. "You have humans who went with you? On purpose?"

Cassidy laughed. "Well, we didn't kidnap anyone. Yes, we have humans who have been living very happily with us. Not all humans have the same instincts. Some are very closely aligned to gentem values. In fact, the child Vala replaced lived with a family near the portal."

Cassidy sensed instantly that he should have provided that bit of information more tactfully. Vala was on her feet, leaning over him.

"The child I *replaced*? The human child with the blue eyes Aunt Char mentioned? You *did* kidnap her? And left me in her place? Does she know? Is she all right?"

Eric touched Vala's arm lightly. "Vala. This happened 29 years ago, remember? It's *not* Cassidy's fault."

Vala shook his hand off, then dropped back into her chair. "How deep does the crap go? All the manipulations, the stupid planning that went wrong, the lives that have been altered and battered about."

Cassidy swallowed, looked at Eric who had all his attention on Vala. No help there. "Uh…well, I should have been more tactful. You're right, of course. Everyone has been manipulating and planning, and it all went wrong. But Vala, Sarah has grown, married another human, and moved to southern Europe. They're raising a vineyard. She knows she's human, but she thinks she's the daughter of the mill operator. She's very happy."

"It's okay, Cassidy," Eric said. "There's nothing we can do about it. We need to keep looking ahead. So how many of your nation–of our nation–of gentem–are left here?"

"I'm uncertain, but the Council's best estimate is about one or two million. All living as humans here. They wouldn't be making themselves known to anyone."

Eric was looking thoughtful. "I think I may have one or two as patients."

"Why would they have stayed?" Vala asked.

"Well, think about yourself," Cassidy said. "You have human friends and family, a job, a place where you live. Leaving it all can be nearly impossible for some. Leaving home is…hard," he added, thinking of Gulo.

"Well, back to Wyatt, who *is* human, but a remarkably open-minded one. Tomorrow?" Eric asked.

Vala nodded. "We'd better do something. Nothing will improve if we don't. Noon?"

"I'll be here," Cassidy said. "In fact, I'd like to come early, maybe in a couple hours, and use your computer to bring myself up to date on the technology and politics of today if that's okay."

After being assured he was welcome any time, Cassidy went home. He ran to his quarters behind his lab, but the run gave him no rest. Eric and Vala had huge gaps of information to fill in. Worse, Eric had apparently not yet told Vala about what Alarick had done. Cassidy didn't want to be there for that conversation.

CHAPTER NINETEEN

Sunday morning, Vala put together some refreshments for the noon meeting while Cassidy sat at the dining room table studying the computer. She kept swallowing a lump of panic. *Super-hero, indeed. Wonder Woman. Wandering Woman? Wondering Woman, maybe.* She sat down beside Serein and hugged him, which he tolerated although, he reminded her, he preferred running. "I'm going to call you Wonder Dog," Vala said.

Serein rolled his eyes at her. Obviously, he was no more interested in being a Super Hero than was Vala.

At ten, she called Aunt Char and complained, maybe whined, about the expectations put on her. "The worst is this party!"

"Why don't I come over, Dear. I don't know that I'm any real help, but I can be a familiar face to smile when needed."

"That would help, Aunt Char. I can't even imagine myself entertaining people, much less visitors from another Earth–temporal zone?–along with an unsuspecting colleague who is going to be told about that new world."

After the call, Vala thought about various times she'd called on Aunt Char over the years. She'd always been there. The earliest time Vala could remember was when she had been six years old.

Sarah strolls along the beach near their home on Perkins Lane in Seattle. On this day no one else visits this secluded and quiet beach. As she looks across glistening sand left by the outgoing tide, she sees a brown lump, out of place. She picks up her pace and finds a burlap bag, tied with a red ribbon.

Curiosity causing her to bite her upper lip—a bad habit her mother detested—she slowly unties the ribbon, feeling as though she were receiving a late birthday gift. She spreads the top of the bag and looks in to see five black and white, lifeless puppies, too young to have ever opened their eyes.

Hands to her mouth, she jumps up and back. She looks up and down the beach, searching for anyone, desperately hoping someone can make the puppies open their eyes. No one appears. The puppies don't magically begin moving. She pulls out her BlackBerry and calls her mother, who immediately asks Sarah where she is.

"The beach...a couple blocks from the house. Mommy, I found puppies! They aren't moving!"

"Sarah, I've told you not to go down there. It's filthy. Come home at once and get cleaned up!"

Sarah stares at the dead phone, at the bag of lifeless puppies, and she calls Aunt Char, repeating herself.

"I'm on my way. Don't move!"

Soon Aunt Char, with a shovel, is with Sarah. They bury the puppies, each with its own driftwood marker. They cry.

"How could this happen, Aunt Char? Who would hurt them?"

"Darling, humans sometimes have to make difficult decisions. They don't know they're being cruel. They just don't know any better. Maybe we can teach them."

Vala shook herself out of the still painful memory. *Teach them?* She felt herself falling deeper into depression and took a quick run with Serein, then showered. Aunt Char was there by the time Vala, dressed in different running clothes, came downstairs. At that point it was eleven. "I should just cancel," Vala said.

"That wouldn't help anything. Vala, grit your teeth and go through with it. Set your sights lower than saving the world. Just get through the meeting."

"Just get through the meeting, just get through the meeting, just..." For the next forty minutes, Vala kept repeating the phrase to herself. Cassidy was still glued to the computer, frantically rubbing his lower lip with his thumb. Then Eric and Wyatt showed up, which meant no more time to escape. Cassidy shut down the computer and joined them. His expression almost matched Vala's mood. Evidently, he'd found little news that was encouraging.

Vala swept through the introductions and herded them out to the garden to join Aunt Char, while asking Wyatt how he was and how Jan, his wife, was. She saw the warning glance from Eric too late.

"Uh, well, Jan has moved out. Even filed for divorce this time." Wyatt shrugged. "I'm not relationship material, she says. I'm sure she's right." He pasted a smile on his face that reminded Vala of teeth implant ads.

"I'm sorry, Wyatt. When did that happen?"

Wyatt blushed. "Well, I'm not quite sure. There was a note at home. I'd been sleeping at the lab because I was so deeply involved in some projects, especially after that huge computer scare."

Vala swallowed the obvious response. "I'm sorry, Wyatt. You must be devastated. Sit down and have something cold to drink."

"I suppose I'm—something. Maybe devastated is extreme. I'm not surprised. God, it's hot."

"It's another record year," Vala said, grateful to escape personal issues. She sat down in a chair near the fountain, hoping others would follow suit. "We've had a new record in June: fifteen days in a row over 100 and no rain for fifty-two days. Guess that's better than anyplace south of Oregon these days. Phoenix was at 130 again. A new wildfire is threatening Snoqualmie, and more than fifty thousand people are evacuating."

Wyatt, still standing by the bar, turned to Cassidy who had taken up a post by Vala's right shoulder. "Excuse me, did Vala say where you're from? Are you with U-Dub?"

Cassidy frowned. "What's a U-Dub?"

Eric chuckled as he rubbed the cool beer glass across his forehead. "Nickname for the University of Washington."

Vala smiled. This just could be fun. "Cassidy is from the other side of that bush," she said, pointing across the garden.

"I told you about the portal, Wyatt," Eric said.

"Are you human?" Cassidy asked Wyatt. "You're quite tall and fit looking."

"Do I look like a chiton?" Wyatt asked.

Cassidy looked puzzled again. He shifted foot-to-foot. His literal-mindedness didn't seem to process sarcasm well. "Don't you know what you look like?"

Vala laughed. She couldn't help it. Wyatt's discomfort suddenly made her feel much more comfortable, and Cassidy's occasional literal interpretations added spice. "Cassidy lives on the other side of the portal, Wyatt. Only Eric, Cassidy, Tandra and I can see or go through it. And–Serein!"

She turned to look up at Cassidy. "Why can Serein go through the portal?"

Cassidy looked down at her and frowned, tilted his head and shrugged. "I don't know. I hadn't thought about it. Perhaps, somehow, he's linked with you? Maybe he simply is using different senses? Maybe he doesn't know he can't? Other animals don't come through any more, not after the first twenty-four hours after the Membrane was established and Beta Earth shaped. Not that I know of. We have to look into that. Shall we go to the lab?"

"No," Vala said. "I mean, yes, we should look into it, but, no, not right now. We're having a meeting. Remember? And, yes, Wyatt's human."

"He's certainly an unlikely one," said Tandra who was now standing beside Cassidy.

"I didn't know you were coming," Vala said.

"Am I unwelcome?"

"Of course not!" Vala said, thinking that Tandra wasn't any more direct and abrupt than Vala. She shouldn't think less of Tandra for being herself.

"Can I have a drink other than iced tea?" Wyatt asked as he stared at Tandra.

Vala nodded. "Just tell House what you want, and the dispenser should handle it. House is supposed to be on party mode."

Tandra was looking around at the overgrown and tangled garden. Traffic sounds permeated the dense foliage, but the far end was open to the water, and the surf sloshing came through clearly, making the fountain a muted accompaniment as it splashed on stones.

"The environment looks healthy here," Tandra said, "but the vegetation is stressed. And the air stinks."

Vala shrugged. "I know. The pollution and the noise stress the plants and there are few pollinators to interact with them. Floaters have a tough time growing produce."

"What are *floaters*?" Cassidy asked.

"Those are individuals who don't want implants, don't want to fit into the system, so they don't have boxes assigned to them and they can't afford to buy places like I did. They drift from one place to another where space is available, often in areas abandoned because of pollution or rising sea water. Even fires. Because they don't have assigned boxes, most have lost their voting rights."

"What do you mean by assigned *boxes*?" Tandra asked.

Vala sighed. "A lot has changed since you left. The government owns most property, and housing is assigned to people based on their income and taxes. If their income goes up, they're eligible for better accommodations. If it goes down, they're reassigned to less-desirable quarters. Fees are paid through taxes. Eric, you have a box, right?"

Eric nodded. "I'm eligible for a larger one, but I don't have any interest in moving. I don't need more room, and I'm close to my office."

"So," Tandra said, "does that mean you can be kicked out of here? Could you lose control of this space where the portal is?"

"No," Vala said, thinking it was like Tandra to zero in on a potential problem. "I own this place, not the government. It's called a shroud-box because it's not within the government system. I need... privacy. That also means I can't vote."

"That all sounds...terrible," Cassidy said.

"The government sold the idea as a benefit to people who don't have to worry about damage to property from storms, rising seas, or fires." Vala didn't add that she had given up on the idea of honest elections anyway. Money paid for public office.

Wyatt, who had returned to the group after getting a cold drink, tapped Cassidy on the shoulder. "Why don't you know this? Are you from a foreign country?"

"Wyatt, they've been..." Eric started then just held his hand up. "Let us explain as we go along, okay?"

Wyatt shrugged.

Tandra cleared her throat. "This smoke is worse than I expected."

"A huge area of the Olympic National Park is on fire to the west of us, and to the east, the Henry M. Jackson Wilderness area is totally engulfed in flames," Vala said. "I didn't notice smoke on your side."

Tandra shook her head. "No. That hasn't started there. Yet." Her lips turned down.

Cassidy crossed the grass and was studying Wyatt from inches away. "Are you part of Vala's team?"

Wyatt, almost as tall as Vala, was almost eye-to-eye with Cassidy, but he seemed to get a little taller. "No. I don't work in physics. I work in genetics."

"Oh, yes, Eric mentioned that. So you're the one who received the sheet with the homo erectus development?"

Wyatt nodded.

"Don't you find it odd that humans have never acknowledged another species?" Tandra asked him. She was still standing, rigid, next to Vala.

"I need more information about this situation and exactly where these people have been, Eric," Wyatt said, dropping into a chair next to Eric. "It's like talking to people from a different planet."

Vala settled back into the cushion and waited to see what would happen next.

"Quit smirking. You look evil," Eric hissed at her, loudly enough to be heard by everyone. Then he lowered his voice and talked earnestly to Wyatt. Vala could clearly hear Wyatt say, "I want to see that."

Cassidy and Tandra had drifted over to the portal and were engaged in what looked like a heated debate.

Vala looked around and spotted Aunt Char who was perched on the steps to the house. Her lips were thin and she was directing her intense stern look at Vala. She'd been seeing that look off and on all her life, and she decided she needed to do something or hear about it later. She stood and yelled, "Hey!"

No response.

Serein barked twice.

Silence.

"Hey," Vala said, "everyone find a place to sit and listen!"

Cassidy obligingly dropped down where he was standing, sitting cross-legged on the stones. Tandra joined him. Char remained sitting, looking less angry. Eric and Wyatt stayed in their chairs at the far end of the oblong grouping. "Thank you. Look, we've a diverse group of individuals who don't mind expressing themselves without explaining anything. Yet, we don't know or understand anything about one another. The first thing to understand is that we have two cultures here. Each has been living in vastly different worlds the past few decades."

She started with introductions again, by name and location, and then said, "All of this is new to Eric and to me as well, but we are in a unique position. Although we've been living on this side of the Membrane–"

"What–" Wyatt started and then stopped as Vala held her hand out in a stop motion.

"As I was saying, we've been living on this side of the Membrane, but we're genetically linked to those of you who created the division. Simply put, Wyatt, the Membrane was created by some sort of temporal shift, as far as I can understand at the moment, that allowed the gentem to emigrate into a space not occupied by humans. A portal from one Earth to the other has been opened but only four people are able to see or use it. Eric, show Wyatt."

Eric obligingly rose, walked to the portal and entered it.

Wyatt stood up abruptly. "But where–"

"Right here, Wyatt!" Eric said, stepping back into the garden.

"So you're telling me you just stepped into another world, Eric?" Wyatt asked. "And just how, exactly, is that possible?"

"Cassidy knows about that," Vala said and looked at Cassidy.

Cassidy shook his head and said, "Well, it *is* a temporal shift but only after a split occurs from Alpha Earth. As matter accumulates in the split, gravity increases and time slows until a tipping point is reached. That creates the initial division, like a kick. The separation should slowly increase in space/time. Building block material is ever present, now and in the past. So duplication is infinitely possible."

"Are you talking about quantum cloning?" Vala asked, sitting down. "That doesn't work."

"No...but quantum cloning *is* possible–I can show you–"

"No, not now," Vala interrupted. "Go back to your explanation.

"Okay," Cassidy said, but he sounded disappointed. "Beta Earth isn't a clone. It's more like holding a mirror in front of an object then putting up something that separates the two but keeping the reflection. Once you have the duplication, then the temporal shift separates the two. The shift gradually increases, and one develops separately from the other. There's less chance of interaction all the time, supposedly. During that initial period, living creatures can readily pass through the Membrane, but gradually that ceases to be true. When first created, all creatures could see Beta Earth except humans—we filtered out their DNA."

"Why has that failed?" Vala asked.

"We don't know." Cassidy shrugged.

Wyatt cleared his throat. "What happens if the Membrane fails completely, and the two—what do you call them? Universes? Is this part of the multiverse theory?—merge completely?"

"We don't know, Wyatt," Cassidy said. "We're trying to figure that out. It could be catastrophic."

Wyatt shook his head. "If science is based on observation, experimentation, and more observation of results, you don't practice science so much as guess work."

"But it worked, Wyatt. We know this other Earth exists. We *can* observe it," Vala said.

"We who? I can't," said Wyatt. "I've seen the results of the genetic differences—sort of—but all the rest of this may as well be gossip I overheard while walking through University Village."

"Why do we have to explain all this to one human?" Tandra asked while looking at Wyatt as though she were studying him for an experiment.

"Think of it as good practice," Eric said. "Wyatt is a good friend to both Vala and me, and he's also a scientist specializing in molecular anthropology; he's also a geneticist."

Vala noted that Tandra's eyebrows went up and she studied Wyatt with less of a confrontational air. However, the look also had a suspicious quality to it.

"If we can't make sense to him," Eric continued, "we'll not make sense to anyone. Plus, he's familiar with the DNA samples from Vala and from me."

"Why do you keep calling me human?" Wyatt asked.

"Well, you *are*, aren't you?" Tandra asked.

"Of course, but aren't you human, too?"

"Wyatt," Vala said, "Eric gave you the gentem version of the evolutionary development of the homo erectus tree that the gentem have researched. The split that led to homo sapiens and homo Sophos, who call themselves *gentem,* represents significant difference. The differences need to be recognized and respected."

"We have nothing in our research that verifies this," Wyatt said. "Even if such a split happened, there's no clear indication that this is two species. Human is human. Maybe a subspecies?"

"There you go!" Tandra said as she stood and threw her hands up over her head. "And your research is the only valid research, right?" She glared at Wyatt.

"Tandra!" Vala said. "Cap it!"

"Look, I'm not insulting anyone," Wyatt said. "I'm just saying that one sheet of paper doesn't exactly represent proof of anything."

Cassidy looked at Tandra who just shrugged. Cassidy shrugged back and then began to speak softly. "Please understand that I'm not an official spokesperson for the gentem. I'm very young–"

"How young?" Wyatt said.

Vala winced. How were they ever going to get anywhere if everything had to be explained in a digression? The gentem had extensive knowledge of the humans, trying to explain gentem to Wyatt was like trying to introduce a peanut to space travel. "It's probably better to not interrupt until you have more information," Vala said. "Wyatt, Tandra, both of you sit down."

Cassidy looked back and forth between individuals. His eyes narrowed slightly. Vala thought he looked like she felt before she needed to run twenty miles.

"Yes," Cassidy said. "Well, I was just saying that I have less personal experience with humans and human history, but it's important to realize that for thousands of years, these two groups co-existed. However, because of our differences, the gentem were discriminated against. Humans were suspicious of us. That led to fear and bad treatment, so bad that our researchers came up with the 'temporal shift,' as Vala called it, as a way to allow us to live separately from the homo sapiens, or humans. Because of the discrimination and our research, we *don't* consider ourselves human."

Cassidy stopped and looked at Vala as if to ask what else he should say, and Wyatt leapt into the silence. "So what are these differences?"

Vala stood. "You've noted the heights represented here, right? Tandra, Cassidy, and I are all above average while Eric is shorter. It seems that all gentem are either over six or seven feet or under five feet. We don't know why."

Wyatt shrugged. "I hardly think you'd find a great deal of discrimination based on height. I'm 6'7" myself. So what?"

"Have you forgotten our childhood, Wyatt?" Eric asked softly. "Don't you remember the bullying and name calling that was part of my daily routine?"

"I'm sorry, Eric," Wyatt said. "You're right, of course, but that's mostly for shorter people, not taller."

Vala laughed. "While your height probably earned you positive recognition, Wyatt, I was called names all the time, just like Eric," Vala said as she sat back down. "Some weren't too bad, like *Stretch* and *Stork*. Others were worse, like *Skunk ape, Skyscraper,* and *Swizzle-freak*. It doesn't take much of a difference to incur mockery and bullying. But added to my height was, for instance, the facts that I'm female and that I can outrun any guy anywhere."

Wyatt laughed. "Then why wouldn't you be famous?"

"Because it's not just fast, it's freaky fast. Fame draws too much attention. In our world, Wyatt, if you're different, you learn not to draw attention to yourself."

"So all gentem can run fast?" Wyatt asked.

"No," said Tandra. "Both Cassidy and Vala can, but I'm not much into it."

"With my short legs, I was never into running," Eric said, chuckling.

"So that's like humans. Some gentem have different talents. Again, so what?"

Vala sighed. Wyatt didn't understand the example. He'd never experienced discrimination, not as a daily event. She decided to address the common age issue although she had only the gentem information. "Gentem live longer, a lot longer. Cassidy said he was young but he was almost Eric's age when the Membrane went up when I was a baby. Tandra's a couple decades older than Cassidy."

"No, I don't think so," Wyatt said, shaking his head.

Vala sighed. "I'm not sure simply denying whatever you hear is the most productive route. Wyatt, one reason the relationship between the two cultures is so bad is that some of the older gentem have *seen* their families burned at the stake for being witches in the 1800s, they've been denied work and had their families beaten, and they *remember* that. It's not just that they heard it through family stories, it's that *they were there."*

Cassidy stood and walked around. Vala suspected he was trying to suppress his need to run. "When living around humans," he said, "gentem have to hide any talents they have, what they know, and even how old they are; they have to move and take up new identities after they hit 80 or 90 of your years. Anything too different can lead to serious problems. To make it worse, we don't know why any of this is true, but apparently it's all due to that early split, that small DNA difference, long ago. In essence, we have to hide, to pass as normal humans, in order to survive."

"But that would be wonderful," Wyatt said. "Think about it: you may carry the genetic material humans need to extend their lives. Things have changed–"

"They could extend their lives by just improving their living conditions, not experimenting on other individuals!" Tandra said, again rising to her feet. With hands on hips, she yelled, "We don't want to become your parts supply warehouses!"

"I wasn't suggesting experimentation on anyone!" Wyatt said. He stood, too, and he and Tandra glared at each other across the five feet separating them.

Suddenly Aunt Char was between them. "Neither one of you is demonstrating superior intelligence or control at the moment. Stop snapping your jaws at each other. Look, I don't understand any of this, Wyatt, but I do understand that there is a critical situation. Decisions have to be made. You all have a lot to learn about that situation and about each other. Now sit down!"

They all sat down. Aunt Char nodded, then perched again on the steps to gaze out at them as if she were an angry goddess.

"Cassidy, tell Wyatt why his computer slipped its circuits," Eric said.

Cassidy nodded but remained silent.

"It's okay, Cassidy. Just do it," Eric said.

Cassidy took a deep breath and said, "I've been trying to establish contact with Vala and Eric for most of my life. We never intended to lose contact with them. We hoped their existence was going to be a way for us to once again interact with humans. Because our plans went awry, I was trying to contact them through your technology when I managed to interact badly with your computer."

"*You*? You're what screwed up my computer?"

Cassidy nodded. "My interaction with the entire system was unintentional. I was just trying to get the document I'd prepared for Vala and Eric into your system. I wound up a little lost."

"You seem to have a lot of mishaps and unintended consequences," Wyatt said, his jaw line bulging as he clamped his mouth shut when Vala glared at him.

"That may be," Tandra said, "but we're not burning the planet while killing off gentem in muck."

Vala glared at Tandra, but it didn't have the same effect Char's glares had. However, Cassidy rested one hand on Tandra's arm, and she relaxed a little. Vala was surprised that Serein went over and sat by Tandra. She petted him and seemed to lose interest in more attacks. Vala began to suspect that Serein had a better grip on the situation than any of them.

Cassidy cleared his throat. "What Tandra is suggesting is that one of our differences is that gentem have a biological, genetic connection to nature. The Earth. Animals. We view all of it as one living system, and we communicate with it. We merge with it. Totally, eventually. We use natural forces to help us expand our abilities, which apparently operate on a slightly different metaphysical level from humans. The gentem scientists have identified LifeForce as a unifying field, as more significant than gravity; in fact, LifeForce helps make gravity possible. The LifeForce makes life possible by constantly affecting conditions favorable to life."

"Paranormal jibber-jabber? Religion?" asked Wyatt. "I've never heard of this LifeForce."

"No," Cassidy said, shaking his head. "It's not paranormal. Nor religious dogma. Nor witchcraft. You're trapped in four dimensional thinking. Think of our awareness as bidirectional. You see light that may influence you but you don't interact with it. For us, direct interaction with everything around us, even on a molecular level, is a normal part of living. Our sense of LifeForce is as strong to us as hearing, tasting, smelling, touching, and seeing are to you."

He paused, then held one finger up as though he'd just had a thought. "Think about gravity. You interact with it constantly even though you don't consciously manipulate it. Gravity is part of what *is*. Well, that's how the LifeForce is for us. Even before we understood it as a field, as a scientific force, we felt and interacted with it. Was gravity different before humans understood it?"

Wyatt shook his head. "Surely this LifeForce must operate on everything then, as does gravity, including humans."

"It *does*," Tandra said. "First of all, life is everywhere. Wipe it out with asteroids or your bombs, and it will prevail. Everything is in motion, being recycled, through plants and people and ocean currents–everything interacts with everything else...but have human scientists yet explained that spark that brings life into being? Is there yet a clear cause for the Big Bang, for instance?"

"Yes. Well, no, not that, but scientists have created test tube life. And cloning–" He stopped. "Can you create life then, with a snap of your fingers?"

Tandra laughed and Cassidy shook his head again. "No," Cassidy said. "We can't. That's the point. The LifeForce exists and is a part of us, but we can't manipulate it in that sense. Can you turn gravity off and on while you're sitting there just because you're aware of it? In fact, trying to mess with the LifeForce could have extreme unintended consequences. It's an underlying primal force. Maybe someday..."

"But you're saying that, first, you're not human, and, second, whatever you are enables you to tie into other senses, not physical, tied to this supposed force," Wyatt's voice had a sarcastic edge to it.

Cassidy kept his own tone level. "Yes. Well, no. We're not human, but we're all branches off homo erectus. You're homo sapiens and we call ourselves homo Sophos. And yes, we use–not manipulate–the LifeForce in conscious ways. Some humans do, too, often without realizing they're doing it. People call the results miracles. A miracle suggests a setting aside of physical laws. How can that be? Is gravity apt to just stop working?"

He stopped but no one spoke. He shrugged and continued. "Each individual utilizes their interactions with LifeForce in different ways. Eric, for instance, has great empathy, much more than can be accounted for by his education. He could sense what he was supposed to do about his sister, and he was able to know that Vala is that sister. He simply *knows*. He never had proof or data." Cassidy looked at Eric and nodded slightly. "Obeah thinks you're very powerful, Eric."

Eric's eyebrows went up. He looked at Wyatt and grinned. "Told you."

Wyatt ran his fingers through his hair and then shook his head. "This all sounds very…tenuous."

Cassidy shrugged and continued. He patiently went through the information he and Obeah had told Eric and Vala. He included witch hunts and more, including Galileo's woes for being different. Vala made a vow to ask more about Galileo later.

Wyatt was remarkably quiet for the fifteen minutes it took Cassidy to wind down, finishing with the human focus on limits, on numbers. Finally, he fell silent after adding, "Eventually, of course, humans will discover this force."

For a few moments, silence held sway.

"Let's get a little more scientific," said Wyatt, leaning forward. "*How* did you create this Membrane, this portal, this place that is Earth but not here? What steps did you take?" Wyatt was mellow, something Vala rarely saw in him, and his voice was calm. She decided to take the lead, just to take the heat off Cassidy.

"Wyatt, you're familiar with the work computing companies did to develop low-power computing—that is, using *slow light?*"

"More or less," Wyatt said.

"Well," said Vala, "Those theories for stopping and starting light would work for time as well, wouldn't they?"

"That's a pretty big leap, Vala. And they aren't creating other planets with it," Wyatt said. "You're talking a massive difference."

"Right. But if I understand the process used to create the Membrane, time itself was stopped, stored, restarted. A temporal shift occurred. I'm unsure about a lot of this–I haven't yet studied the material Cassidy has in his lab. But another Earth evolved–"

"Presto?" Wyatt said.

Cassidy waved his hands in the air. "No, this isn't quite it. I have the data–" he broke off and furrowed his brows. ""Let me see if I can explain. First, this was an experiment based on a hypothesis, and it involved many gentem working to copy the physical matter of Earth and then the desired infrastructure. Utilizing gentem links with the LifeForce, we, as a group, worked together to manipulate matter–not to create a copy of Earth or life, but to create the *idea* of Earth and then to shape the particles and qualities and so forth. We had to have a place, so the Membrane was created as a place to put what we built and–"

"What's the Membrane made of?" Wyatt asked.

Cassidy rubbed his lower lip with his thumb as his shoulders sagged. He looked tired. "We're back to LifeForce in conjunction with Kaluza-Klein theory. Are you familiar with that?"

"More or less," Wyatt said.

"Okay. The main problem with that is limiting the dimensions. Work with the idea of eleven dimensions and the LifeForce as the unifying field and you begin to utilize LifeForce. I have the research on that. We create the Membrane through a quantum split in the time-space fabric; axions form the brane itself. The original split becomes a bubble into which we can place the particles we want. As mass accumulates, the weight warps time and space around the bubble, which increases the stability of the split and also gives us room for more particle additions. The trick is to keep everything separate. The process took time, so that even after the material had coalesced into Beta Earth, lifeforms, except humans with the Neanderthal genome, could simply step through the Membrane. When the critical mass is reached, Beta Earth is ejected."

"You created *something like a second Earth* out of thin air?" Wyatt asked.

Cassidy shook his head. Vigorously. "What is 'thin air'?" he almost yelled. "We're immersed in LifeForce and that includes all the quarks, fermions, and other sub-atomic matter. *Stuff* is constantly being created out of *thin air*. Even a vacuum buzzes with virtual particles that pop in and out of existence. This is essential to the quantum computers we've created. There isn't *nothing.*"

Wyatt shook his head. "There is a *big* difference between a virtual particle and a complete copy of Earth."

Cassidy looked at Vala. "I really need to be in the Lab and let you see data to get into this, Vala." He looked at her like Serein did when they hadn't run all day.

She nodded. "Wyatt, we've got to move one step at a time. You haven't even yet accepted the idea of the LifeForce. Or even that Beta Earth exists." She looked back at Cassidy. "So the theory was that this *copy* would increase in distance, a parallel world."

"Sure." Cassidy smiled as though everything was resolved.

"And why is that parallel world interacting with this world?" Vala asked.

Cassidy's smile faded. He scrubbed at his face with his hands as though he were washing. "We don't know."

Wyatt threw his hands up over his head, got up and went to replenish his drink while saying, "And Eric, Vala, you two are drinking this Kool-aid?"

Cassidy looked at Tandra. "Kool-aid?" he asked.

"I think I remember a sugary drink—"

"Wyatt, do you think Vala is smart?" Eric asked.

Wyatt came back and stood near his chair, sipped his drink, and looked at Vala thoughtfully. He nodded. "I envy her. She's obviously a genius. She comes up with brilliant ideas and knows how to implement them."

Vala shifted uncomfortably, forced herself to stay quiet while Eric worked out whatever reasoning he was following.

"Okay," Eric said. "How does she do it? Please give me a concrete, maybe mathematical formula."

Wyatt started to open his mouth, then snapped it shut. He looked at Vala, then back at Eric. "If I could do that, I'd know how to make everyone a genius."

"Right," Eric said. "Many things exist that we can't explain completely. If you limit the world to only what you can readily quantify, you limit life. Maybe a formula exists, but we don't know it yet. So Vala, explain to Wyatt how you work out a new mathematical formula."

Vala had been asked that question before, usually by new grant-board members, but she'd always skirted the answer. She took a deep breath. "I'll try. When I have a problem or an idea, I mentally manipulate it, play with it, sometimes when I'm running, until I see some patterns, some relationships. It's not really *mathematical*. It's organizational and relational patterns. I can see them and, eventually, I can get them to flow, connect." She felt herself drifting into the problem of the explanation almost as she would any other problem. Her own voice sounded distant. "Then I follow the flow like a tenuous path that emerges in a dense wood. It follows logic, but it extends into not just what *is* but also what is possible." Serein rumbled, almost a growl, and Vala jerked herself back. She needed to stay in the present.

Cassidy was nodding. "Yes! That flow. When you enter the problem and *see*, then you just *do it*, Wyatt."

"So you've no scientific explanation that allows the idea to be repeated?"

"Not exactly," Cassidy said. "We don't know if the work can be repeated with the Membrane. We've never tried. We have the process written down. Sort of. More importantly, we *know* it. We wouldn't want to try to repeat it until we know why it's not working."

"Wyatt," Vala said, "if it didn't work, how do you explain the portal?"

Wyatt turned in a quick circle with his arms out. What was left of his drink flew out of the glass. "What? The thing I can't see that you claim you enter when you disappear? I say it's some sort of magic trick."

They were all standing, tense and looking at one another. As someone had said–was it Vala herself?–if they couldn't get it across to Wyatt, they weren't going to get it across to anyone. On the other hand, if people experienced an event, then the event became a part of their experience. For most people, that would help with disbelief.

Vala turned to Cassidy. "Is there no way to get him through the portal or at least let him see it? If Serein can go through... surely, there's a way."

Cassidy was shaking his head, then his eyes unfocused, and he rubbed his lower lip. Vala found herself wondering if he ever developed a lip blister.

"Hmmmmm…" he hummed tonelessly. Then he brightened. "In essence, the link we share is powered through the obelisk, and the digital implants on our palms are just chip-less, biocompatible RFIDs. Possibly, if the four us surrounded him, we may be able to create a field force to walk him through as if he were part of us. Maybe. Some humans came through the Membrane when it was first created by simply holding hands with gentem, but that's when gentem could still get through themselves. Whatever people carried came through, too. So if we enclose Wyatt like lunch in our digestive system…"

Vala could see the excitement sparking in his eyes. She'd seen that same expression on other scientists' faces when they had a breakthrough idea. She turned to Wyatt. "How about it, Wyatt? Are you willing to be our lunch?"

Wyatt looked at Eric, who was eagerly nodding and grinning. "Eric's never steered me wrong. Except … well, never mind. Okay, let's try it."

"Wyatt, you stand between Eric and Vala. I'll stand in front, within four or five inches, and, Tandra, you stand behind them. What I want us to do is focus on the idea of a fence made from the links we share, going from one to the other. We're already linked, so this is just reinforcement. If this is going to work, the four of us should be able to sense a connection building, like an electric charge." He eyebrows drew together. "Maybe," he added in a low voice.

Vala tried to silence all her questions. They all became very still and very quiet. For a few moments, nothing happened, then Vala began to sense a tingling. Just as she was beginning to feel like jerking away from the group, Wyatt tensed.

"Is that it?" Wyatt asked. "That shimmering! Like air turned to water?"

"That's it," Eric said. "Shall we try going through?"

"I'm not sure that will work," Cassidy said.

"I'm willing," Wyatt said. "I want to see for myself what you're talking about."

"Okay," Cassidy said. "Let's start walking then. Wyatt, if you feel any pain, tell me immediately."

Less than a minute later, the five of them were standing in the meadow next to the obelisk. Wyatt broke free of the group and began circling, looking around.

"That was amazing! It was like–like–nothing else. What was that? Between dimensions? And where are we? This isn't your backyard anymore, Vala! This is–where the hell is this? Is this a trick? Did you hypnotize me?"

All four of them laughed, even Tandra. Wyatt's childlike joy and excitement was contagious. For the first time, Vala suddenly believed all of this was, indeed, amazing and *real*. With this sort of knowledge, maybe they could make a difference, a real difference in how humans interacted with Earth, with each other, with even those who were different. Just look at Wyatt, she thought. What if every human could experience this?

"It *is* amazing," Eric said.

Vala looked at him. He was responding to her thoughts. Again. A wash of gratitude for her little brother made her almost hug him.

Eric grinned.

Damn him. Eric just kept grinning. Vala turned her back on him and noticed Cassidy talking to Wyatt.

"–and we're standing on the Olympic Peninsula, south of Sequim, much of which is under water at this time. This area should be safe, especially if we can continue to stop climate change here; it's already decreased. But for some reason, some of what is going on with the human environment keeps seeping in. We're getting reversals in our progress."

"Two days ago, a stand of forest in Brazil disappeared," Tandra said. "Not burned, not logged, just not there."

Cassidy frowned. "I hadn't heard about that. Action may be more urgent than we thought."

Wyatt was still vibrating with excitement. "Can I see your town, some of the people?"

Tandra started striding off toward town.

"It's about a mile, Wyatt," Vala said. "Want a ride?"

"No," said Wyatt. "Walking is good. The smells. Sounds!"

Tandra smiled at him and said "Tenalach. In a healthy relationship with the environment, you can hear Earth sing."

"Char!" Vala said. "I've got to go tell her what we're doing. I'll catch up."

Char said she'd happily sit in the garden. "But I want to go next time!" she added.

Vala caught the group quickly and they soon reached the town. No, village. The main road was bordered on each side by simple wooden structures, mostly plank-style houses although one was a large dome that Cassidy said was the Council meeting hall. Obeah's home and clinic Vala remembered: white straw bale construction with a low-peaked roof. The clinic entrance faced the main road. One particularly large, white building was very different.

"What's that made of?" Eric asked.

Tandra smiled. "That's part of the local community stable and barn. Many people move their larger animals in there for bad winter storms. It's a straw bale construction and is much warmer and drier. When the animals are in there, their body heat alone keeps the place toasty—almost too warm at times."

"I don't get it," Wyatt said. "Much of the infrastructure of the old town is nearby and well above the sea. Why didn't you all just move into those homes?"

Cassidy laughed. "Sounds simple, doesn't it? But those homes are set up to function within a technology network, a grid, that we don't have enough people to maintain. Most of it isn't green, either. Maintenance would involve utilizing materials that we have no interest in using. We have power here, but it all comes from light, wind, water, bacteria and so forth."

"Then why did you keep it? Why is it here?"

Cassidy shook his head. "To be honest, we often wound up with whatever came along. We didn't pick and choose the objects. It's difficult to explain. We tried leaving some of it out, like paved roads, but it was like trying to take a picture of only selected structures in a scene. We've scavenged supplies, but we're not interested in their power grid, their paved roads and parking lots, and such. We don't need their home gadgets, so we don't need all that power."

Vala realized how remiss she'd been in not finding out more. Wyatt's continued questions and enthusiasm demonstrated an open and inquiring mind of the best scientists, and Vala had just been focused on herself. Or, to give herself some credit, maybe she'd just been in a state of shock. Finally, at the edge of the village, they came to Cassidy's lab.

"There's not much in here," Wyatt said.

"Well, you have to call up what you want." Cassidy said, "Screen" and a screen appeared along one wall. "Notes on Membrane creation," Cassidy said, then added, "Initial notes." The wall was suddenly filled with written comments, notations, equations..."

"Where's the computer? The Server? Whatever you use?" Wyatt asked.

"We're in the computer. Everything is within the walls, ceiling, and floor. Do you remember the holodeck on Star Trek television shows? That inspired me to think about how I could make a working computer like that. So I did."

Vala's breath stopped. *So he did?* She looked around. No windows, but the room was light from–somewhere. "Where do you get the power?"

"It's a combination of sources, including wind and solar; also, the building itself stands on one large microbial fuel cell. The important feature is that the computer itself stores energy when not being used. The computer has a life-imperative program, a connection to LifeForce, which motivates it to stay active."

Motivation for a computer? Vala needed time alone with Cassidy just to sit and quietly talk. Humans had been playing with this sort of idea for generations and not come up with anything that worked fully. She became aware of Wyatt talking excitedly.

"–benefit everything humans are doing. The quality of life would improve exponentially."

Vala looked around. "Where's Tandra?"

"Ummmm...she left," Cassidy said.

His voice communicated volumes. Something Wyatt had said had apparently set her off again.

The three of them left the lab and wandered up to a small plaza in the center of the village. Cassidy gestured at a table. "Obeah said some folks would bring lunch by." As he spoke, several people showed up, introduced themselves, smiled, and left food and drink for them. Except for extreme variations in height, they looked like any human.

As the group ate lunch of fresh garden fruits and vegetables, Vala noticed for the first time that there were no restaurants, grocers, or other food vendors. *How had she noticed so little?*

Eric sat down beside her and said, "You know that the reason you've been self-focused is because this was a major personal trauma handed to you."

"Eric, stop doing that. I'm going to have to not think if you keep it up."

"Or, you could just try speaking up, honestly and openly, about your feelings in the first place. There's nothing wrong with them, you know."

Cassidy came over and sat down on the ground facing Vala. "So what do you think?"

"What a refreshing question!" Vala said.

Eric laughed and Cassidy looked confused.

"Never mind," Vala said. "So where has Tandra gone?"

"When Wyatt was talking about how this place and our work could be used by humans for wealth and development, she freaked out. It was best that she went home to meditate or she would have gone after Wyatt."

Vala shrugged. "Wyatt's response is normal. Humans think that nature exists for them to use. Cassidy, I'm impressed with what you're doing here. Especially your lab. I'd really like to spend some quiet time talking about what you're doing and how you're doing it. As it is, I don't even understand how we brought Wyatt here."

"Of course," Cassidy said. "Any time."

"How do you manufacture the equipment?" Eric asked. "I mean, if you don't do manufacturing ...?"

Wyatt, munching on a large peach, joined the group.

"We just pull together material and assemble it. Shapers do that. I'm not sure I understand." Cassidy was shaking his head.

"So you don't have factories? Places where everything is built? Manufactured?" Wyatt asked.

"We have some shops where people who are adept at assembling things work," Cassidy said. "Everything is done by hand. People have different skills: shapers, weavers, artisans of all sorts. We have, of course, materials stockpiled that were part of the infrastructure here when the Membrane went up. When we first started the project, the first few years were just clean-up of toxic materials. Shapers are vital; they convert the atomic structures of matter into what we can use. But mostly, every shop or lab is unique, and the tools are designed and built to meet the specific needs. If we don't need it, we don't make it. That sort of local economy is practiced in all the gentem settlements."

"They *convert* the atomic structure? Vala asked.

Cassidy nodded. "Sure. As they did in the initial design of Beta Earth. I thought we covered that."

Vala winced. That conversation in the lab was apt to last for years.

"Are there many settlements?" Eric asked.

Cassidy shook his head. "They're located all around the world, but our population is small. Gentem and humans tend to have settlements that include like interests and needs."

"Why are there no restaurants or markets here?" Wyatt asked.

"We have a market once a week just west of town. People who have been harvesting or baking or making tools, clothes, or whatever bring goods down and everyone swaps, gets whatever they need. Sometimes they just barter for future work. Just depends on what your skills and needs are."

"You have no money?" Vala asked.

"No. When we first gathered to come here, people relinquished all material goods and cash, and Jasmine used proceeds to set up your trust accounts and programs for gentem who stayed behind."

"No money?" Wyatt asked. "All cultures have some sort of money."

"We have our skills and an egalitarian sharing network," Cassidy said. "No one goes hungry or without shelter. Value is in the individual, not in extraneous possessions."

"Right," said Wyatt. "And what about the shiftless, the bossy, the jerks? Are you claiming that your society is so far advanced that everyone is contributing equally?"

"Not in the least," said a sharp voice, which Vala recognized immediately as Tandra. "You've already heard about issues with Alarick. Some individuals go off on their own, totally absorbed in their own interests or even in acquisitions. That doesn't mean that if they're hungry, they can't get food. You've done nothing for anyone here, but you've been eating everything."

"Welcome back, Tandra," said Cassidy. "Did you come to share?"

Vala laughed. *Siblings, indeed.*

"How do you travel?" Vala asked. "How did people settle all around the world?"

Cassidy nodded. "Everyone who came to Beta Earth essentially went home, wherever that was, to exactly what they had at that moment. Like us, most abandoned the human-created infrastructure. However, the main Council is here, so members of the Council come and go. Each community has its own Council. We travel by ship, by foot, by solar-powered vehicles and such. Wherever gentem are, they no longer have to hide who they are or do work that's not suited to them. They're free. And they're happy."

"It's like an entire population coming out of the closet at once," Vala said.

"The closet?" Cassidy was confused again.

"I just mean out of hiding."

"That's what I said," Cassidy said.

Eric cleared his throat. "Here's a serious question for you, Cassidy. Gentem here are happy. They're free, freer than any of them have ever been. The environment is better. Why would any of them favor tearing down Beta Earth?"

"Many, maybe even most, don't, Eric. But there's no question that somehow the devastation going on in the world on the other side is going to destroy Beta Earth, too. Something isn't working. We have to find out what that is or plan to reintegrate in a controlled way. If the two Earths collide, we believe all of us will be destroyed along with the planets themselves. I'd hoped that maybe we could reintegrate peacefully using the influences of you and Vala. She's led me to believe that they probably don't have that much influence." Cassidy shrugged.

"You youngsters think that somehow you can change thousands of years of human behavior, traits that are so ingrown in them that they will never stop hating, killing, and polluting. We've come up with the solution. You just don't want to admit that it's the only way." Alarick spoke from behind Cassidy, his arms folded, his face blotchy with anger. "What are you doing bringing that human here?" He jerked his head toward Wyatt. "What happens when he tells others who we are, where we are?"

Cassidy didn't bother to turn around. "Vala, Eric, meet Alarick, formerly head of the Council."

Neither of them said anything. It seemed obvious that Alarick wasn't interested in the social amenities.

"What is the solution you have?" asked Wyatt, ignoring the human reference, from where he sat.

"Has the Council met these people yet?" Alarick demanded of Cassidy's back.

Cassidy slowly stood and turned to look down at Alarick. "Not yet," Cassidy said. "This wasn't a planned visit."

"Well, you'd better do it quickly. They don't like anyone acting independently, you know."

Vala worked her eyebrows back down as Alarick stomped off. "So that's Alarick," she said. "You're right, Cassidy. He's very angry."

"He needs help," Eric said.

"What solution was he talking about?" Wyatt asked again.

Cassidy sighed. "We need to go see the Council. Obviously, word has spread about you all being here. To not meet with the Council would be a grievous diplomatic error." He pulled out a phone and placed a couple calls. "We'll meet at the Center in walking time."

Vala looked at his phone. "How can you have phones without servers, towers, and everything else?"

"These are more like walkie-talkies. The range is about ten miles. We do have another communication system, but it operates differently."

Before Vala could ask about that other communication system, Wyatt spoke up again. "Will someone please tell me—"

"Hold on just a second, Wyatt," Eric said, interrupting. "Cassidy, Wyatt and Vala need to know what Alarick did. Now."

Cassidy nodded although he looked as though he'd been kicked in the stomach. "Please hear me out before you react," he said, looking at Vala, not Wyatt.

Vala felt her stomach clench. Now what? Her legs twitched, making her want to jump up and run back to the portal before this day could be ruined. She felt Serein press against her side. She took a deep breath and nodded. She was not going to run away.

"Alarick," Cassidy began, "was head of the Council for a long time." He then went through a careful explanation of Alarick's history and his hate for humans. Then he detailed Alarick's work with scientists to come up with the ma-huang tailored to attach to the Neanderthal gene. "It's apparently cumulative, so it takes very little at a time to have a deleterious effect."

When he paused, Vala spoke for the first time. "But the Council said no, right? They surely wouldn't allow chemical warfare to be used against humans."

"Yes and no," said Cassidy. "You have to understand that we were feeling desperate, which is another reason I was working so hard to contact you. The Council gave me a deadline. We've been hoping that somehow, if the portal were opened, we could mitigate the situation with the humans."

"And?" Wyatt asked.

"Alarick and his small team secretly began dumping the chemical into rivers that supply drinking water for millions of humans. He reasoned that if things could be affected here, then things could be affected there. Of course, he's been removed from the Council."

"Hasn't that destroyed the water for you, too?" Vala asked.

"No. Remember that we don't carry the Neanderthal gene. Any water used here is monitored to make sure local humans aren't affected. Alarick acted too soon and without consensus."

"But they're still considering it?" Wyatt's voice was little more than a whisper.

"We've never taken direct action. We've just gone into hiding," Tandra said. "Many want that stopped."

Vala's emotions tumbled into confusion. Her initial outrage faded quickly. She could see their side, and she hated that she could see it. The treatment their culture had received was the stuff that made revolutions. She herself had fought pollution and unreasoning human behavior for so long that she had lost all respect for most humans. At that moment, she realized that she had transitioned: she was thinking of *them* as humans and herself as *gentem*. She had taken a side.

"Cassidy," Vala said, "such action will betray everything the gentem claim to be; you'll become killers. We'll all be killers. You're destroying your culture and your future. Surely you can see that. Another solution *must* be found."

As she spoke, she felt an odd shift somewhere in her mind, maybe even in her body, and she knew that nothing would ever be the same again. She didn't feel angry or betrayed or even frustrated; it was more like standing on the edge of a cliff just before jumping off and hoping she could somehow fly.

CHAPTER TWENTY

Sunday mid-afternoon, July 8, 2029

Expecting the worst, Eric tried to focus on both Wyatt and Vala. For some reason, Vala had become very still and thoughtful, but she wasn't nearing eruption. She'd retreated but not in a way that warranted urgency. He'd have to make sure she didn't emotionally vanish again.

Wyatt, on the other hand, was entering amygdala hijack, so he went to Wyatt, took him to one side and began quietly talking to him. After about five minutes of soothing nonsense, Wyatt began to listen, and Eric tried to be specific and brief. Not much time for soft-peddling. "What Alarick did was sabotage, and he's been dismissed from the Council. Cassidy is fighting to prevent this chemical dump into the rivers, Wyatt. He's not alone. Most of the individuals here oppose any killing, but they're fighting to save the planet as well as their own lives. We have to help them—"

"Help them? No, no, they are committing war, terrorism—"

"No!" Eric interrupted before Wyatt could escalate. "Not help them with poison. Listen, Wyatt! Alarick acted without sanction. Remember the U. S. Presidential forces sent into Mexico in 2020? Ever since, we've had escalating border issues, exchanges of fire, and constant casualties—unmitigated hate from just one person's anarchy. Don't let Alarick's sabotage derail you. You and Vala are respected scientists, and your voices will be heard on the human side. We have to start by educating ourselves, and that means having an open mind at the Council meeting."

Wyatt was still shaking his head, but he met Eric's eyes and slowly began to nod. "Well, yes, maybe. They have gone to great lengths to try to contact us—at least you and Vala."

"Yes!" said Eric, jumping at any positive change. "Cassidy risked his life to contact us, to get that portal open. It's an open door, Wyatt, and you've been invited through it. We need to use it to figure out a solution."

Wyatt kept nodding, not in agreement, just in stunned silence.

Eric knew this was the best that he could do in this brief time. He nodded at Cassidy, and they all started off to meet the Council, just a quarter of a mile away. Eric kept monitoring his own breathing and emotions. How this meeting went could determine everyone's future.

Along the way, Cassidy gave a quick summary of the members of the Council. He said they included one half-human, Rainbow Summer, who, he said, "was a product of Woodstock." His voice and manner conveyed his aversion for her; Eric could tell it wasn't because she was half-human but because he considered her silly. "Everyone else is gentem," he said, "ranging from a good friend of mine, Devin, to those who dislike everything I'm trying to do. Right now, since Alarick is no longer present, there are only two still interested in drugging the rivers. One is Julia Kostrovo who thinks we could come and go as we like but not allow humans access; she doesn't understand the situation clearly, but she represents artist guilds. The other is Quetzal Huepa but only because Julia talked him into it. He's a follower."

He listed the other members as Delara Ò Broin, Vice-Chair, a plantae specialist who talked with plants as Cassidy did animals; Petros Floros, who represented religion and philosophy; Marina Lorca, a brilliant physicist and technology specialist who had been Cassidy's mentor; Murell Mati, a shaper of metal and specialist for animal needs.

Once at the Council Chambers, Cassidy knocked quietly, and the door quickly opened to reveal Delara, a couple inches shorter than Cassidy's 7', which put her close to Vala's height.

Delara nodded her head at Cassidy, then at Vala. When she looked down at Eric, she smiled in a gentle way that made him feel as though he'd come home. "Your mother was a dear friend of mine," she said. Then, she looked directly at Vala and said, "We're glad to have our children back."

Eric reminded himself that these folks did, indeed, still think of Vala and him as children: children who were to save the world.

"What children?" Wyatt asked grabbing Eric's arm.

Eric wished he could put tape over Wyatt's mouth, but he had to settle for shaking his head at him and whispering, "Not now."

Delara nodded at Tandra. "Are you going to take your place in the Council, Tandra?"

Tandra shook her head. "Not for this meeting, Delara. It's best if I wait, I think, to be sure no conflict of interest arises."

"As you wish," Delara said, "but keep in mind that the Council is unable to vote without full participation." Then she stepped back and waved them through the door. She neither acknowledged nor looked at Wyatt. Eric would swear the room temperature dropped by thirty degrees as Wyatt passed her.

A large round wooden table took up most of the round room; elaborate tapestries lined the walls and a beautiful woven rug covered the floor. Along the curved wall opposite the door was a grouping of five chairs. "Please be seated," Delara said, "and I'll introduce you. Tandra, you pull a chair over there to sit with your group or just sit wherever you please."

As they all settled themselves, with Tandra sitting a little apart from everyone, Delara took her place at the table, near the door. The Council members created a semi-circle along that side of the table, facing the visitors. "As you all know, Cassidy has been trying to establish contact with our children for some time. This abruptly happened just recently, and they have been learning about both themselves and this place. I'm sure the transition has been challenging. We're glad to have you here.

"A quick run-down of our Council may help put you at ease." She gestured to her right at a man about a foot taller than Eric with skin that reminded Eric of deeply burnished copper; his dark hair had almost purple glints to it. He grinned openly, and Eric liked him immediately. "This is Devin," Delara said and then added, "a friend of Cassidy's. Next to him is Quetzal, who teaches tennis, martial arts, and other physical activities to children." Quetzal nodded in their direction but gave the impression he was bored with the process. Eric could tell the man was physically fit, but his attitude made Eric wonder if he was very bright. He, too, had dark hair and eyes, but his skin was more deeply tanned than naturally dark.

"Next to him is Rainbow Summer, one of our musicians. She plays a number of stringed instruments and composes music." Rainbow gave an odd waving gesture, tossed her long blonde hair back, and then focused her intense, violet eyes in a brief glare at Cassidy. Delara gestured to her left. "This is Petros Floros, a philosopher and leader of the only Christian group I've met on this side of the Membrane." Petros showed age, with gray hair and deep lines around his eyes and mouth; however, he seemed good humored, not angry. Again, Eric felt a strong liking. Petros, whom Eric gauged to be well over seven feet, nodded and smiled at Eric and the deep folds in his dark skin deepened.

"Next to him," said Delara, "we have Marina Lorca, brilliant with technology and sciences. She's designed many of the sustainable systems we have developed here." Marina didn't look up or acknowledge the introductions in any way. Eric didn't sense any emotions coming from her; he had the distinct impression that mentally, she was somewhere else altogether. Sometimes he had the same feeling with Vala and Cassidy—maybe it was connected to the math and science focus. She was closer to Eric's height with such a light skin, almost transparent, that Eric was startled by the richness of her deep chestnut hair.

"Next to Marina is Julia Kostrovo, a well-known and respected artist, both here and on Alpha Earth, especially in Russia, although she has used different names over there to prevent issues over age. You know," Delara said, glancing briefly at Wyatt, "how desperately humans count each other's years." Although tall, Eric guessed Julia to be almost half a foot shorter than Vala.

"Finally, we have Murell Mati, an outstanding shaper of metals, particularly in conjunction with animals' needs. She's had many wonderful ideas for ways to convert and utilize various metals since the Membrane went up. She keeps our animals secure and happy at her stables."

Eric looked in Murell's direction for the first time. His breath caught in his throat. From beneath dark dreads that cascaded from a metal holder almost like a cap, her widely-spaced, cerulean-blue eyes contrasted strongly with her tawny skin. She flashed a smile in his direction. She was short, judging by her sitting height, and her features were delicate. Her hands, resting on the table, were long fingered, thin, and delicate. *She* shaped metal? He looked back at her face and couldn't break away from contact with those beautiful eyes–he suddenly realized Delara was speaking again and that he'd been not listening, only staring at Murell; on the other hand, she'd been staring back.

"–our children, Vala and Eric. Vala's companion is Serein. Now Cassidy–" Then Eric froze as he heard Vala speak up. He had to pay closer attention!

"Excuse me, Ms. Ò Broin, the esteemed Council has not yet met Wyatt Roberts, a dear friend of Eric's since he was a boy, abandoned, as you know to foster homes and mistreatment for his size. Without Wyatt, his life could have been shattered. Wyatt is also a colleague of mine at the university, and his work with Eric and me was instrumental in bringing us together and, subsequently, to this meeting. We are in his debt."

Delara smiled. Eric stared at Vala. This was a totally new side of her. He caught Wyatt's eye, and Wyatt winked at him. This time, Wyatt had read Eric's surprise perfectly.

"Call me Delara, please, Vala. You'll find that we use last names rarely here. You've correctly pointed out our omission and rudeness and, at the same time, you answered my question about why Wyatt was brought here." She nodded at Wyatt. "Forgive our rudeness. Many of us have long memories and we've grown short on patience and courtesy; that's unforgiveable. It's what we've disliked in others and, yet, too often what we find ourselves practicing these days. We were over-reacting to your arrival."

"Uh, sure, no problem," Wyatt said.

Rainbow giggled and everyone else studied the table carefully. Delara smiled slightly.

Eric felt like stomping on Wyatt's foot, but Wyatt had never been known for the social graces.

"So Cassidy," Delara said, "the *why* of Wyatt's presence has been covered adequately, but the *how* remains a looming question. We were under the impression that only those with the implant could pass through the portal. Are we to expect of a sudden wave of humans charging into this space?"

"No, Delara," Cassidy said. "No danger exists, not from hoards or Wyatt. Further, I apologize for giving you no warning. We were trying to explain things to him. Of course, he was having trouble understanding. Interestingly, Vala's companion, Serein–" he gestured at the large dog who was, Eric suddenly realized, sitting with Murell–"passed through the portal readily. Their connection was the only logical explanation. It occurred to me that we could possibly embrace Wyatt within our link by physically surrounding him. It worked!" He paused. "I'm not quite sure how ..." he said, pausing and drifting into thought.

Marina said, "Well, I'm sure you'll figure it out, Cassidy. Are you still making great intuitive leaps into impossibilities?"

Cassidy looked down at the table and grimaced. He was obviously being gently chided about some behavior in the past.

Delara cleared her throat, after giving Marina a warning look, and began speaking again. "In the interest of bared hearts, let me detail the Council's overall concerns. First, we want to know if any of this is *significant*. That is, do you believe that reconciliation is possible? Should this world be dismantled and if we do so, will we be able to merge into a functional society where we can influence people to do whatever is necessary to preserve our Mother-Father Earth? As you may know, Eric and Vala, our hope was that your influence and position in human society can help with that.

"Second, if it's not likely that we can merge in society and affect it in positive ways, do you see an alternative to Alarick's plan to eliminate human impacts on Beta Earth?"

Cassidy sighed. "I don't have clear answers. Our meeting in the garden, just before we decided to try bringing Wyatt here, was about your first question. He's as stunned as are the rest of us at the immensity of our task. Damage is extreme, judging by what I had time to learn from Vala's computer. We've also underestimated the population: it's closer to eight and a half billion."

A small gasp went around the table.

"Second, the pollution is worse, in spite of strides that have been made in many places. Wyatt assures us that progress has been made, but climate change continues. Fires are worse. Sea level continues to rise. The air is almost unbreathable, in my opinion although humans seem to handle it with medical and AI advancements. Global cities are either slowly moving themselves inland, like Seattle, or they are simply gone, absorbed into other cities. That includes Guangzhou, Miami, New Orleans, Mumbai, Nagoya, Tampa, Boston, Shenzen, Venice, and Osaka from what I can tell from their Internet, GILS. Some countries, such as Bangladesh and many small island nations, are gone …simply washed away by rising seas and flooding rivers. Pollinators have all but disappeared, and people no longer rely on live food."

Eric studied the faces around the table. From horror to broken hearts–Murell had tears rolling down her perfect cheeks. Petros had his head lowered prayerfully. Each of the others were staring into space, even Rainbow, their breath caught in their throats. Silence throbbed in the room.

Cassidy cleared his throat. "Finally, from what I've learned, military build-up continues. For instance, the U.S. has border skirmishes with Mexico. Nuclear testing continues globally. Crime is a major issue, including mass shootings." Cassidy paused, looked around at each person.

Eric found it difficult to meet Cassidy's eyes. The emotional intensity in the room jangled Eric's nerves, and the muscles along the base of his skull felt as though they were being screwed down. He glanced at Vala. She sat rigidly straight, staring into space. She had herself in tight check.

"As you can imagine," Cassidy continued, "the subject of how we influence any of this is much more complicated than can be covered in hours or even days; Vala, Eric, and Wyatt all have influence, but it's not such that clear answers exist. From what I can tell, money is more powerful than intelligence or kindness. We haven't even broached the second question yet, Delara. We need time."

Silence.

Cassidy cleared his throat and said, "Uh–look, I haven't had a chance to discuss this with the others, but–" Cassidy stopped and looked at Vala.

"Yes?" Delara prompted.

"Well, I think the reintegration with the humans will be challenging for a long time. I no longer believe it's worth it."

Delara nodded, then said, "Cassidy, we don't have time. Last night, some of our people observed a huge ship suddenly appear in the Strait of Georgia; then it disappeared again. In the middle of reforested area in Brazil, a skyscraper flickered in and out of existence where a rain forest had been. Marina tells me that if the two Earths collide, causing an uncontrolled collapse of the Membrane, the result will be annihilation. Cassidy, do you think we can even survive there?"

"Of course. Eric and Vala have. Apparently those who stayed behind have. I'm not sure about quality of life. Surviving as gentem might not be possible."

"Delara," said Vala, "I survive, but I find it tiring. After a stay in Antarctica, I had to wear a mask for about six months to readjust. But it can be done."

Murell's voice cut through the tension. Eric could listen to her resonate tones all day. "What will happen, Cassidy, to this place, to the animals, if we reintegrate?"

"If I may answer that, Cassidy?" said Marina. When Cassidy nodded, she said, "Again, there's no clear answer. Nothing like the Membrane had been done before, nor has it been done since. In effect, we created this space as a duplicate, a parallel existence. It was a little like Alpha Earth giving birth. Taking it down is like suddenly destroying a continent dividing two seas. What will happen when the seas meet?"

Again, a silence cloaked the room. Finally, Delara spoke. "One more question remains. I know what your response will be, Cassidy, but it's essential that you listen to the Council and the final decision. Is that clear?"

Cassidy shifted his weight.

Eric was braced for anything. He held himself stiff against the pressure in his neck and ringing in his ears.

Cassidy nodded, then said, "I know I'm very inexperienced for the work you've allowed me to do, and I know I've fought against your decisions in the past. But you can trust me. I'll try to do as you wish, but when I speak out, it's for a just cause."

"I understand it's for your perception of a just cause. I wish I could agree that ethical values are always definitive, but they are not. So, this is the situation: the Council will decide shortly on our action and that action will be implemented soon. Meanwhile, we have another issue. Petros?"

Eric pulled his gaze from Murell again as Petros inhaled deeply and then began speaking sonorously. "I've heard some interesting language here today. For instance, already our children are using the term *human* as something other than themselves even though they have, for their entire lives thought of themselves as human. Of course, it sounds as if they haven't always fit in well, but they *have* fit in. Yet, loyalties exist on a very deep level and loyalty to one's own kind is powerful. They are gentem. In short, I have concerns that we can't have this human, Wyatt, return to the other side until we have some sense of a plan, some sense of unity. You've said he's a respected scientist, and I have no doubt that's true.

"You also," he said while looking directly at Wyatt, "have a deep loyalty to your friends here. That I don't doubt. On the other hand, until we've resolved the issue of what to do with Alarick's plan and Cassidy's desires, I propose that you stay here with us. Remember, friends, that Christ was betrayed by a friend."

"You're making me a prisoner?" Wyatt asked.

"Sir," Eric said, his skull practically vibrating with the sharp need to protect Wyatt, "that's unacceptable."

Vala spoke quietly, but everyone turned to look at her almost immediately. "Petros has serious and legitimate concerns based on a long history and an uncertain future, Eric. Thank you, sir, for being honest with us."

Petros nodded his head toward Vala, then cocked his head to one side, saying with a slight smile, "And?"

Vala smiled back. "I'm concerned with some of the logic. You want us to make connections on the other side. However, those connections are going to be much more difficult, maybe impossible, without Wyatt's expertise and position in the human society. Eric and I have connections, but with Wyatt we become a powerful triad. To exclude him somehow foreshadows failure, a self-fulfilling prophecy. If we can't trust and work with Wyatt, we're doomed to failure. You'll trust no human. Not ever. Any peaceful resolution must include him and his freedom. We can't argue for our–gentem–freedom and involvement in world decisions while denying freedom to another. As is always the case, one must commit fully if one wants to achieve."

Petros nodded slightly. "I see the logic of your argument. And three is a powerful number. I suggest that the Council meet privately to discuss this."

With much murmuring agreement, the Council decided to meet while the four of them waited outside. Tandra was invited to sit in on the discussion. Once they were outside, seated in a circle in the small park outside the Council's chambers, Eric turned to Vala.

"What the hell was that?"

Vala's eyebrows went up. "What?"

Eric shook his head. "You've never behaved that rationally, that diplomatically, before. Who was that?"

Wyatt laughed. "Vala's been part of a university system since she started her Bachelor's degree at age 13. That's 16 years. She's gone through two dissertation defenses and an untold number of committee meetings, grant proposals, and departmental budget requests. She knows how to power-psyche."

Cassidy looked at Eric. "What?"

"He's saying she knows how to play politics," Eric said.

Cassidy nodded. "Diplomacy. Did you think Vala unable to be diplomatic, Eric?"

Eric nodded. "I did." He laughed. "She surprised me. Again."

Vala looked down at him and rubbed the top of his head. "That's good to hear, little brother."

Wyatt leaned against the stair bannister. His body language showed his tension. "What do you think our chances are?" he asked. "I have to tell you that I don't like the idea of being told I can't go back to my lab."

"I think the Council will listen to reason," Cassidy said. "They are frightened, but to succeed, we'll have to take risks. You have to understand that this is new to you three alone. For the rest of us, this is a long-running issue."

"In my opinion," Eric said, "the majority vote of the Council–wait, do they work on a majority basis, Cassidy?"

Cassidy shook his head. "Consensus."

"Well then," Eric said, "it may take a little longer, but I believe they'll give us some time to work things out. They want to do that. And they want to let you go home, Wyatt. Every person in that room is honestly trying to do what is best for everyone, and they are a democratic culture, one that honors individuality and autonomy. They're a little afraid of you, but they trust your friends–us. Clearly, they want to do what's best."

"I need your vow, Wyatt," Cassidy said, "that you won't go off on your own to divulge information. That you'll work with Vala and Eric on plans."

Wyatt nodded. "To be honest, no one would believe me anyway without their corroboration. The only proof I have is in DNA testing, and that just shows a slight variance back in time. I don't think anyone would care at this point."

Eric studied Wyatt carefully. He was holding something back, not being entirely honest.

"I'm surprised," said Vala, "that Christianity is practiced by any gentem and also represented on the Council."

"A number of spiritually-based groups practice here," said Cassidy, "but the Christian group is the only formal structure I know of. Their principle belief is that Christ was teaching non-violent love for one another, a traditional gentem approach. In fact, Petros' theory is that Jesus was gentem, trying to promote a philosophy that would reduce violence in the human culture. That's based on some gentem records from those who have lived long lives."

"Then why didn't he live longer?" Wyatt asked.

"If, indeed, he ascended," Cassidy said, "then that would indicate that he simply progressed in his thinking to the level at which gentem join with whatever forces they've been a part of during their lives. Maybe he truly was gifted and achieved that in a short span. As we've said, time is measured by development, not by how many times Earth orbits the sun. We believe we're coalesced in this form to accomplish the care of our home and all those who inhabit it. A purpose."

"By your home, you mean the planet, right?" Eric asked.

Cassidy nodded.

Eric and Vala made eye contact but remained silent. Vala was, Eric realized, as surprised by this casual revelation as he was. They had so much to learn! Eric looked over at Wyatt who was staring thoughtfully at the ground, obviously nonplussed. "So does that explain why so little DNA of what you call Homo Uzgenia-Krygyzstian has been found?" Eric finally asked.

Cassidy shrugged. "Our anthropologists don't think so. They speculate that the Homo Uzgenia-Krygyzstian had probably not evolved enough at that point for such achievements, although it would account for why nothing is found more recently. When gentem are killed one way or another before their time, their bodies are desiccated and powdered, then spread. In that way, they are sustainably recycled. Nonetheless, if Homo Uzgenia-Krygyzstian were nonviolent creatures, they may have lived in isolation, hiding remains even then."

"Do you have many anthropologists on this side?" Vala asked.

"Not many," Cassidy said. "Mom is one, and she lets me know what is going on."

They fell into silence again although questions filled Eric's head. While the group waited, shifting and walking around now and then but saying little, Eric continued to study Wyatt closely. At times, Wyatt was simply turning slowly, studying everything around him. He was restless and uncomfortable in a way Eric had never seen before. Periodically he would glance quickly over at the door of the Council chambers. Was he simply worried about getting home again or was he harboring a hidden rebellion? Eric was about to get up and go talk to Wyatt when the door opened. All of them leapt to their feet and looked up at Delara at the top of the stairs.

"Please come in. Let's talk."

Inside, the small group remained standing. Their restlessness was obvious, thought Eric, and he wasn't surprised that Delara didn't ask them to sit.

"The Council agrees to hold off on making a decision about our next step. But if something isn't done soon, our Earth will be gone, on both sides, before anything we do can have an effect. We'll know when we've reached a crisis. Also, Wyatt can return, but we do want you all to stay in constant touch with each other. This could turn ugly, uglier than you youngsters can imagine. Some of us have firsthand knowledge of how ugly. Finally, you must take one member of the Council with you, in addition to Tandra. I assume you can do that as you did with Wyatt."

They all nodded.

"Who?" asked Vala.

"Julia will go with you. She's very well versed in art and the human culture. She speaks thirty-three languages fluently, so she may be a good help in communication globally. She is also tolerant of humans. This will give us a more objective report."

Eric looked over at Julia. She looked calm and reserved, but her emotions were turbulent. She was very anxious to go. Eric felt more nervous about her than he did about Wyatt, but he kept his mouth shut. Maybe she simply was excited about the idea, but Eric sensed a hidden agenda. The others in their group were sharing glances, but Cassidy seemed unconcerned.

"Welcome, Julia," Cassidy said. "When shall we leave?"

Julia stood. She was elegant, graceful and slightly aloof. "No time like the present," she said in a contralto voice.

Without any further discussion, the group headed for the door with Tandra in the lead and Wyatt following. As they left, Eric looked back and made direct eye contact with Murell. She smiled and nodded. He wanted to go back to talk with her but refrained. Nonetheless, he wished she were the one joining them on the return trip.

CHAPTER TWENTY-ONE

Sunday night-Monday morning, July 9, 2029

As the group left the town and walked silently to the portal, Vala looked back over her shoulder. A part of her wanted to go back and ask to meet her grandmother, get to know more of these people–gentem, she mentally corrected herself–and just enjoy the feeling of wholeness, of healthy well-being that vibrated from the natural environment. They might be having issues, but this place was the only peace, the only clarity of spiritual place, Vala could remember experiencing except for excursions to Antarctica and the Arctic. Although Cassidy had painted a fairly bleak view of the human side, Vala doubted if any of the Council knew how distant the human population had truly become from their environment. She remembered a student who had told her that honey came from tree sap.

"Did you forget something?" Cassidy asked.

Vala realized he'd dropped back from the others and was walking with her, lagging behind.

"No, I just –" Just what? What could she say?

"Think about how difficult it must be for individuals who have lived here for decades to think about leaving," he said.

"Don't tell me you're an empath, too!"

He laughed. "No, but I can observe the obvious and make interpretations–or, as Marina calls it, wild leaps into impossibility."

Vala felt relief and chuckled. "What about you? You've given up on having the cultures merge?"

"As I've seen more on your side and talked to you and Eric and others…I'm dubious. The extent of damage, the sheer numbers of people, and the apparently competitive and acquisitive nature of humans as even Wyatt has expressed … yet, what choice have we? If everything is collapsing, we're all doomed anyway. I don't know if we made an error in our computations of if maybe the whole idea is just wrong…or?"

Vala said nothing. She didn't know the answer, but somehow this world needed to be preserved, either as part of the human's existence or without them. What had been created here was valuable. They went the rest of the way in silence.

Back in Vala's garden, Aunt Char was sleeping on one of the garden chairs. Vala woke her, hugged her, and apologized for leaving her. "Aunt Char, you need to come over with us at some point. You'll love it there."

"I'd like to do that," Char said. "If there's a chance that place may disappear, I'd like to see it at least once."

Hearing Aunt Char express the possibility of destroying the other world jolted through Vala, but she tried to set it aside. She introduced Aunt Char to Julia, and then Char excused herself. "I need to go get some sleep, Vala. And feed my cat. Just please let me know what is happening."

After Aunt Char left, Julia was the first to speak up. "I suggest," she said, "that we come up with specific tasks for each us and then split up to get those tasks done. We don't have much time to come up with a plan and set that plan in motion, to have something definitive to give the Council."

Somehow, Julia continued guiding the conversation and prompting ideas. Vala began to suspect she had an agenda of her own and was manipulating them all to that end. At one point, Vala made eye contact with Eric, and he gave her a nod, slight shrug and mouth twist that spoke volumes. He, too, was concerned.

Without much effort, they soon agreed on a plan, mostly organized by Julia. Eric and Wyatt would go to the lab and prepare a paper and presentation about the DNA difference between the humans and gentem, a sort of species revision or what Julia called "aliens among us" approach. Wyatt seemed enthusiastic about the project. "We'll need to keep it general. Nothing about *gentem* or about your special skills. Maybe something about height and a propensity to live longer. If we deviate from known science–enter skills of healing or empathy, for instance–we're not going to make an impact. We'll be dismissed as crackpots. We can't wait for normal channels, such as academic journals, either, so we need to create a social media buzz and contact individual scientists."

Vala and Cassidy agreed to work out the same sort of process to provide information on possible ephedra contamination of drinking water. "We just need to put the idea in people's minds, so they'll look for it. The water tests can only show what is being looked for. Maybe we can allude to climate change that's causing the plant to spread. If we suggest that any of this is planned, as fearful as people are about terrorism, bombs, and shootings, we'll have the Guardians on our necks. Besides, we want to emphasize environmental issues."

"What are Guardians?" Julia asked.

Vala tried to keep it brief and simplified: "In September of 2001, 19 terrorists hijacked four commercial jet airliners to fly into important U.S. structures, including the Twin Towers in New York and the Pentagon in Washington D.C. Homeland Security was a federal agency created to investigate and stop terrorism. The abuses were staggering–ranging from impositions on personal liberty to torture–and many times people have talked about closing the department and relying on other long-standing agencies, such as the FBI and CIA. Two years ago, the department received a make-over, most of which was a name change from Homeland Security to *Guardian Alert System* with the Freedom Guards as the agents. Most people just call the agency GAS, which isn't popular with the conservatives or the organization; otherwise, people just refer to the agency and the agents as Guardians–maybe sarcastically or even as linguistic 'feel good' medicine–you know…like guardian angels."

Julia shook her head. "Everything I hear makes this side sound worse than I had imagined. Smells worse, too." She shrugged. "I'll see what I can do within the arts community. Tandra has a sense for the unity of community, and we both have previous experience. We'll see how we can connect. Does the Seattle Art Museum still exist?"

Vala nodded. "They currently have an exhibition titled, ironically in my opinion, nature's place in art; I've been meaning to go see it. They also have an exhibit on aboriginal influences."

After agreeing on morning plans, individuals separated to rest or meditate until morning. Vala and Cassidy took a ten-mile run on the other side where both of them felt their energy levels rise, then they returned to rest in the garden.

Aunt Char returned in the morning and set up a large breakfast for them. Afterwards, the group split up, leaving Vala and Cassidy in the garden. Cassidy lay down on the grass next to Serein and asked, "How do you want to proceed?"

Vala looked at him in surprise. He looked so calm, so relaxed, that the idea of world catastrophe seemed ludicrous. His eyes were bright, sparkling with what could be amusement. He was smiling and, Vala realized, she was smiling back, brainless as a 13-year old staring at a zilph music star. Yet, for the first time in a long time, she felt strong, energized, even though she didn't have a good answer for him. Maybe, she thought, this is what it's like to not worry about being crazy all the time.

She forced her thoughts to the situation and said, "Perhaps we have three tasks to consider beyond just contacting some people about contamination of the water. I can do that with emails to various labs and scientists who regularly watch over water supplies; I'll claim that some samples came my way that indicate there may be ephedra present. I often use water samples from around the world to study bacteria, so I have Guardian approval." She hesitated. She didn't want to be pushy, but she wondered if she might have insights into the Membrane problem that Cassidy didn't.

"More urgently, Cassidy, I'd like for us to more deeply consider why the Membrane isn't working. Why isn't it keeping out the problems? Why aren't you, on the other side of that portal, truly separate? If we could solve that, everything else would become academic–gentem need only decide where they want to live. Vala paused. She didn't want to insult Cassidy, but they needed other input. Male egos could be delicate. She took a deep breath and continued. "To do that, I think we need to look at the original plan and maybe even talk to Marina."

Cassidy said nothing.

"Well?" Vala asked.

"Are you through? I thought you were going to say more about tasks. That wasn't three."

"Do you mind talking to Marina with me?"

"Why would I mind?"

Vala looked at him carefully. He showed no signs of being upset. He continued to look relaxed. How odd. Vala gave a mental shrug and continued with her thoughts.

"Okay. We should do that. At the same time, I need to figure out how I can talk to humans, give them an acceptable scientific theory about any of this. At this point, I don't understand it myself; it's all four-beer rhetoric. As far as the science goes, what I have to show anyone is my height and big feet." She paused again. Why was he just listening?

"Finally," she continued, "how can we convey to people quickly that the current destructive behavior *must* stop. Now. How can we convey the urgency of us having a handful of time to correct thousands of years of violent human behavior? I'm space dead on that one—"

"Space dead?" Cassidy asked, tilting his head slightly.

"I mean I don't have any ideas. After all, King Edward I was the first person to ban the burning of coal back in 1272 because of air problems. In 2018, the US government was *encouraging* continued use of coal. Consumerism has increased—people *live* to shop—and carbon footprint be damned. Do we just say, 'You've been given thirty days to take action or else another species is going to start wiping you out?' A sort of 'The aliens are coming' take on Paul Revere?"

Cassidy grinned. "I don't think the *or else* is a good idea." He rubbed his lower lip with his thumb, sat up and nodded. "Laid out that way, the task seems monumental. Humans haven't changed in … well, ever. To be honest, Vala, my original idea was that we'd show humans logical arguments, and they'd agree. I'm feeling, as Obeah has labeled me, naïve. That has played into my expectations about fixing the Membrane, too. The original experiment was monumental for us, and the practical application has proven more difficult than anyone anticipated."

Cassidy stood, paced a moment, then stood looking at the portal. "That worked," he said.

"What worked?"

"When you and Eric finally connected your implants, the portal opened. The Membrane is working in a general sense: we have our space, the humans have theirs. It's those leaks and the those are growing worse, larger …everything comes back to the original plan."

He turned. "Why don't we go back to my lab, and I can show you all the work from the time this plan was initialized. We'll talk to Marina, too. Vala, it was meant to be a solution, not this monumental problem and not such a negative experience for you."

He walked over to stand in front of her chair. "Want to go?"

"Starting with the science is perfect," Vala said.

Cassidy held out his hands. "Let's go."

Vala looked at him, nodded, and took his hands to let him pull her to her feet. For the first time in ten years, she felt that tension in her throat, that urge to ease into an embrace. Funny that she hadn't thought of Professor Sekel for years, but suddenly she remembered how safe she'd felt with him. She'd held her romantic feelings to herself then; he treated her like a daughter. In truth, she'd been drawn to him because he talked to her as her father had. Cassidy was nothing like her father. Or anyone else. And he treated her with respect, as an equal. That was no less amazing than learning she wasn't human.

As Vala had stood, Serein yawned and stretched mightily. He shared Vala's enthusiasm for returning to the other side, away from the sirens and smoke and the pressure of all those lives out there. Serein was standing at the portal and looking back when Vala realized she was still holding Cassidy's hands, and he was smiling at her, glints of light sparking in those brown eyes that reminded her of a fawn: dark, large, and trusting.

She snatched her hands back. "Let's go," she said abruptly. She focused on their mission as they walked through the portal, back into the other world, and headed for Cassidy's lab.

In the lab, Vala's first problem was understanding how they could be inside the quantum computer. He explained it again, but she shook her head in confusion.

"It's linked with me," Cassidy said. "When I'm inside, my ideas are treated as additional data. Marina's lab is the same. The computer is designed to learn from mistakes, to spot errors in its own work and in mine."

"Some of that has been done on the other side, but not to this degree. AI works that way, but not in direct link with people."

She set aside learning more about the computer so they could tackle the Membrane issue.

Within two hours, Cassidy had shown Vala screen after screen of data, most of it based on familiar science and ideas. Each screen he called up covered one of the walls and at one point, all four walls were filled with information.

In essence, Vala noted, the process involved splitting sub-atomic particles, creating different spin states for each, sometimes separating them from their properties. Then the space in that split was used to rebuild what had been there. Vala could visualize that his ideas would work, but the *how* eluded her. Work had been done of a similar nature in China, but for no practical purpose.

The key to using the science seemed to be the unifying field, LifeForce, and that was alien to her way of thinking. It was almost as if the imperative of the LifeForce was to animate–bring life to everything from the Big Bang to the existence of gravity.

"Cassidy, this indicates that your scientists had evidence-based information, but for implementation, it's just a list of names of individuals. There's nothing here to say *how* each person applied the science, did whatever it was that each did."

Cassidy stared at her, blinked slowly once, rubbed his lip, and tilted his head to one side.

"You look like Serein when I suggest skipping dinner," Vala said, laughing.

Cassidy shrugged. "If you mean that I look like I don't understand, I don't. How do you *apply* gravity? Those individuals are our most brilliant in mathematics and physics. They took the data and put it together to formulate ways to work within the fundamental forces to create the Membrane, the place for this world, that gave space for the gradual accumulation of material. What more do you want to know?"

"But...*how?* How did they *implement* it? Did they have equipment? Did they have a series of steps that had to be worked out in unison? If I were to take this to the human side, I don't see any way to explain how to create a Membrane."

"The individual scientists entered the work and applied their skills in harmony with LifeForce. *Everything is* connected to the LifeForce. Isn't that, in principle, the same way you converse with Serein?"

Serein, wagging his tail, looked at Cassidy.

Vala felt as though she'd gotten stuck on an out-of-control merry-go-round that was about to launch into orbit. "There are many possible explanations for my communication with Serein. One, I'm crazy. Two, we've learned each other's mannerisms, body language, and habits. And so forth." Even as she spoke, she knew she was parroting conventional thinking to an unconventional thinker. *How* did Eric read her? *How* did gentem live longer? *How* the hell was she going to explain any of this to someone else?

"Cassidy, if we were to set up a little mini-Membrane now, how would we do it?"

"I don't know if we could do it with just the two of us, but essentially, we'd go through the set-up processes, both enter the concepts, and bring it into existence–we'd need to have an object..."

Vala stared at him then at the formula. "*Enter* it? You mean input it into a machine?"

"No. No, no. *Enter. Join.* We become one with the data stream and the process. Think of it in terms of aligning the supersymmetric codes with the natural conditions of space-time. The copy of Earth, as it gains mass and gravity expands its own space, slowing time in the process, and then becomes its own entity. Think of the development of a child–before conception, where is the space the child will occupy after birth?"

"It's just recycled matter," Vala muttered, trying to avoid getting immersed in philosophical argument. She felt that she was on the edge of understanding Cassidy, but his ideas seemed to suggest that proving theory required that the scientist become part of the theory. In addition, his metaphors weren't clearly related to what she wanted to know. "Can you show me?"

Cassidy paused, opened his mouth, shut it again. "You don't know how to work within the concept of fundamental forces?"

"I know how to work with representations of the fundamental forces, symbols and numbers and such. But are you telling me you're able to simply manipulate, for instance, gravity?" Vala shook her head. "I don't understand."

"No, I'm not saying that gravity, for instance, is something to be manipulated directly but we do work with our understanding of it to alter its effects, no? Space travel, for instance. Look, how do you work out a problem? How did you come up with, for instance, your ideas for utilizing bacteria to power the lights in your garden?"

Vala stood, walked back and forth and tried to suspend her questions to think. "Well, I reconsider the ideas I'm using and how they're interrelated, how they affect one another. Sometimes I envision the result I want and try to see how everything works together within that vision. I may have to re-imagine how the theory should work. Sometimes variables and fixed values interact in ways that produce unexpected results, and I need to reconsider my assumptions."

"So you enter the problem from different angles and see how everything plays out."

Vala shrugged. "Well, yes. Sort of."

"Well, that's it. When you have several scientists together, and we link into the patterns so that all our visions come together in a unified moment, we create the theory from the perspective of many dimensions. We become part of the solution, along with all the other matter that surrounds us. Thus, what couldn't be utilized or manipulated, becomes accessible. In essence, it's about understanding the patterns of ... everything."

"Wait—what do you mean you *link?*"

"You know—like you and Serein communicate. Like Eric knows what you're thinking and feeling. You're linked."

Vala was stunned. Cassidy had mentioned *entering* the problem, even *seeing* the problem and the solution. However, she'd thought it was more metaphor than fact. She could readily lose herself in her work, but that wasn't the same, was it? She thought about all the testing, all the terms, all the analysis she'd undergone to understand how she accomplished the work she did. Savant was the term used at times. Crazy was the other word. Was this related to being gentem or simply being crazy? Was this something that was instinctive, genetic, to gentem in the way that the human instincts for acquisitiveness and rivalry existed? Gentem didn't seem to have the more combative instincts; was this—what to call it? *intuition?*—instinctive? And this linking? That wasn't going to fly with human scientists anywhere.

"Oh, my God, Cassidy, this is something that *can't* be done by humans. Right? This is similar to the healing, to Eric's empathy! This is a gentem thing! The thing humans call witchcraft or magic or – or just plain impossible."

Cassidy shrugged. "Humans do respond that way sometimes, but it isn't such an alien thing, and human children on this side have gone into the sciences, learning how to think in these terms. They can do it. I think what's missing is awareness and acceptance of the LifeForce. Think about Arthur C. Clarke's third law—"

"—Any sufficiently advanced technology is equivalent to magic," they said together, laughing.

Cassidy continued. "The natural forces aren't magic. Gravity isn't magic. They're not inaccessible to humans, either. Even human scientists recognize that we experience the world in many ways beyond the five senses. Vala, you can't see, physically, an atom. You can't even see the chemical composition of your own blood. That doesn't make either the atom or your blood magical. We transform concepts, ideas, into reality we can use to function. If humans understand that, then what more do they need?"

Vala held up her hand. "Just a minute. I need quiet."

Obediently, Cassidy sat quietly, and Vala tried to think about what he'd said and relate it to the unusual in her life. She looked at Serein who immediately opened his eyes and looked back. Why was she able to communicate with him? He was a thinking creature. She was a thinking creature. They were close. And they were predictable. In essence, they were utilizing natural abilities and predictability along with common sense. But *how?* She paced, stopped at the door and looked out at the inviting green forest, the paths on which one could run and run.

She looked back at Serein again. He yawned, closed his eyes again. He knew her thoughts didn't indicate they would take a real run.

Vala laughed. Serein had a way of cutting through the confusion to the crux; there was a gap between wishing to run and *going* running. So they should cut through the confusion to action itself. "Let's try it," Vala said. "The two of us. Let's just utilize it to do a little mini-Membrane, just within a limited area here, say for this stool. Can we make another stool like you did another Earth? I just want to get a sense of what you're discussing."

"Fine," Cassidy said. "But it's not *another* stool. It's the same stool but earlier." He held out his hand.

Vala stared at it.

"It couldn't hurt to have our physical presences linked."

"If that's not a line on GILS, it should be," Vala said. She took his hand but had a sense of dread. If this worked in the way she was beginning to suspect, contemporary humans wouldn't be able to grasp this concept without decades of training and shared lab work.

"Holding my hand isn't all that unpleasant," Cassidy said.

"What?"

"The expression on your face isn't difficult to read, Vala."

She laughed. "I'm sorry. I was just thinking about the implications of what you're saying as far as our goal is concerned. If this works, I'm afraid it could well mean that we can't explain it through science to humans. And sure as hell not with a unifying field called LifeForce. That sounds too dégagé." She shrugged. "Here goes nothing?"

"That's negative. I think we'll have something."

Vala laughed again. "That's just a phrase. It doesn't mean—anything," she finished lamely thinking that it must mean *something*.

Cassidy shook his head and sighed, then looked down at Vala's hand and smiled. "Now, let's just take the material you've been studying and condensing on our board from the beginning. Let's look at what we have and think about what it *means* in the world. Think about what the stool looks like on different levels, including its purpose. See how that is related to the next concept, one building on the other and affecting both what came before and where the next step will be; allow the future to change the past. Each step creates…"

Vala had no trouble with Cassidy's directions but any sense of how this would *create* anything eluded her. She'd been using a version of this, on her own, since she was a child. She thought of it as intuitive physics although the cognitive studies were incomplete to her way of thinking. She didn't discuss it with anyone.

Now, as she and Cassidy worked through the process together, her pictures were brighter, more solid. She could feel Cassidy's presence guiding her, not just verbally but almost like a beam of light. She did feel linked to...*something*. For the first time, she *felt* the presence of the computer, as well.

The entire room wavered, even undulated as though it were morphing or warping or... She began to realize that she wasn't working from the data but that each step, as Cassidy said, simply lead to the next and each indicated a relationship with the goal and with the starting point. The next step seemed to predict–no, *alter*–the past steps.

Next to the stool, the air itself changed, brightened–no darkened–or both. As though it were tearing. Vala thought of a slow-motion lightning strike. Then it was pulling together and shaping... something...a stool! Somehow it was the reverse of the stool at the same time and then–it was gone!

Vala gasped, jerked her hand away from Cassidy's and waved it around where the new stool should have been–had been moments before. "What happened?"

"We created a Membrane then placed the stool there, which became its own space, or time. That's what we wanted to do. It's a temporal isolation."

"How do we bring it back?"

"I don't know."

"What? What do you mean you don't know? Then how would you reintegrate the Earths without destroying them? How can you *not* know?"

"Vala, with Beta Earth, we've kept a reference point. Unfortunately, we don't have a reference point for the stool. I don't know how to find it. Marina may know. That's why I needed the reference point of the partial implants to find you and Eric. Obviously, we have the needed reference point for this Earth...we're here."

"So you kept coming to us based on a partial link?"

"I wasn't there, exactly. I worked with Obeah. He prepared a formula that put my body so deeply into a sleep, beyond any meditative state, that I was able to utilize the natural LifeForce wave patterns to find you and Eric. We were already linked, if incompletely. Think of us as twined particles, so although we weren't sharing physical space, we were still able to affect one another. In essence, the four of us can no longer be completely understood without understanding our joint relationships."

"Cassidy, this is going to add a layer of spooky to anything we try to convey scientifically. Do gentem create this sort of connection often?" Vala asked, thinking she wasn't sure she liked finding out she was in some sort of involuntary relationship. *Twined* in current pop culture meant a couple since marriage had become less popular.

"No," said Cassidy. "As far as I know, it had never been done. We've done various types of digital tattoos such as that on your palm, but not with the idea of linking individuals. The concept was all part of the overall set-up back when the Membrane was created. It was all woven together. We had to have a way to communicate through both time and space. My expectation is that we'll all continue to interact more closely and more powerfully over time, but I don't know."

Vala studied him. "And why were you chosen?"

Cassidy smiled. "In part because I was Marina's assistant–apprentice really. In part, because I begged and pleaded and nagged and offered up my eternal gratitude. I felt compelled to be a part of this project."

Vala dropped onto a stool that was still present. "So what you're telling me is that gentem have taken quantum mechanics and used it to affect your daily world."

"Sure. Isn't that what physics is for?"

"Cassidy, I'm going to have to think and study what you've told me a long while, but I fear none of this is something we can share immediately with humans. Not now. First, I don't think they can do this without entirely altering their thought patterns; what we're talking about is going to sound crackbrained. Second, if they accept the idea and think we're different enough to do something this powerful, something beyond their abilities, they'll hate and fear us. Remember what Obeah was saying about Professor Ellen Dissanayake and how humans isolate themselves into recognizable groups, then denigrate other groups?"

Cassidy was shaking his head and frowning. "I don't understand why anyone would hate someone else just because they had different skills."

"That's because," said a voice from the door, "you've not spent more time in the human culture, Cassidy. You can't understand what you haven't experienced. Just like the humans won't understand this science because they haven't experienced it. Vala is right."

"Marina!" said Cassidy. "We've been looking at the all the original work done on the Membrane, so Vala could better understand it."

"Do you understand it?" Marina asked.

"I understand the connections and the process, but not the full import," Vala said. She shook her head. "The complexity is immense, and it's founded on a firmer quantum understanding than any science I've researched. I need more time to think."

Marina nodded. "A wise answer. This is the compilation of our knowledge of how Earth, how *everything,* functions. We've always come at scientific understanding from that basis, which is almost a polar opposite to the human's approach. Just as with any scientific discovery, we didn't understand how we were utilizing these scientific truths until we researched it, went beyond simple instinct. In the past, gentem accepted the idea that we were witches and wizards, or maybe demons. We've come a long way in understanding ourselves. But we had to do it in secret."

She came in and climbed onto the remaining stool before continuing. "Creating the Membrane was a desperate attempt to have a place where we could live, learn, and develop in peace." Between her thin build and short stature—well under five feet—and her wistful expression, Marina looked wispy as though she could stretch into a column of smoke and drift away.

"So did you expect this place to be the end of your problems? Did you expect to live happily ever after, human-free?" Vala asked.

"Well…no, I guess not, exactly," she said. "We'd hoped that someday maybe we *could* live with humans and reunite."

"Why?" Vala waited while Marina looked puzzled. When she said nothing, Vala rephrased her query. "Why would you ever want to live with humans again?"

Marina shrugged. "That's been the natural evolution of Earth. Many of us wanted the harmony of peaceful existence but within the world that was created with all of us. To change that process felt artificial."

"Was everyone in favor of the separation? Did everyone want to leave, abandon their lives, friends, and family?"

"No ... individuals could choose to come or not. But I guess that was part of the desire to create a contingency plan, a way out. It *was* difficult."

"How did you make the plans, communicate readily without creating red flags among the humans?"

"I assume you're familiar with online gaming," Marina said. "We created a game about marginal people who wanted to re-create Earth and escape their persecutors. The game was deliberately dull and inane to discourage interest in it except among gentem. In fact, it used the term gentem: Gentem Earth. Ever hear of it?"

Vala shook her head.

Marina smiled. "See–dull works. In fact, a fund was left behind for those gentem who didn't choose to join us here to stay in communication and allow us to find them should it become possible to do so."

"So your expectations were mixed. You weren't fully committed." A sudden thought occurred to Vala. "What did the gentem do about human battles, wars, and other violence?"

Marina sighed. "Killing for the reasons humans kill is not part of our culture. In fact, we always worried that we would lose our ability to be part of Earth if we changed our nature. Gentem tended to be conscientious objectors or they managed to be connected with medical services. Or they ran away, hid, something that became almost second nature. Human culture has no room in it for the nonviolent resisters. Most of the individuals who became leaders in peace movements– gentem and human alike–were imprisoned or assassinated."

"Then how can you even consider chemical warfare?" Vala studied Marina carefully and was startled to see tears form in the corners of her eyes.

"Whatever the answer may be to that question, Vala, terrifies me more than the idea of Earth finally dying. Have the gentem so long been a sub-culture to the violent primary culture that we've evolved to something else? We're too close. We've been trying to figure this out for too long. Anger and frustration have shadowed our thinking. I don't want to overwhelm you, but we're all anxious to hear what you and Eric have to say. Your objective view is desperately needed. That's why we wanted you to *be* human as much as possible."

Vala could think of no response. This woman had lived more complicated science longer than Vala could imagine, and yet was depending on Vala and Eric for answers in her fractured world.

Marina nodded, apparently understanding Vala's silence, and got down from the stool. "So, my dears, I'll leave you to continue your work. Meanwhile, Vala, if you get a chance, you should visit your grandmother. She can give you insights on what human wars have meant to gentem. Cassidy, you're doing well. Good luck." She turned and left.

Vala swallowed hard. Her emotions were becoming difficult to ignore. Feeling increased pressure, she looked at Cassidy. He looked more serious and concerned than she'd ever seen. Vala sat on the stool. "We need to go through the portal and contact some scientists. I want to try to get some tests from regional areas to see what's happening with ephedra in regional water supplies. That will be easy to start and then we can look more deeply into the why of leakage through the Membrane."

"Let's stop at Obeah's clinic and bring him up to date."

As she, Serein and Cassidy ran to Obeah's clinic, Vala was paying attention to her deep breaths of the clean air. As she looked around the village, with its scattered buildings—most of which housed specialty small shops such as metal and wood working, glass work, or pottery—she realized she hadn't seen a child. Not ever. She stopped. "Cassidy, are there no children here?"

"A few. I think the last time I taught, there were fifteen. I haven't taught for a while as I've become increasingly distracted by you and Eric."

"Taught what?"

"The last class was on Fibonacci numbers and how they correlate in nature and in the nature of time; the sequences are important to LifeForce patterns."

Vala shook her head. "I don't mean adults–college students. I mean little kids–you know…" she paused holding her hand out about waist high.

"That's what I thought you meant," Cassidy said. "The children in my class ranged from what you would think of as six to twelve years. They take the class according to their current interests and knowledge."

Vala stared at him. Most of her college students probably wouldn't know much about Fibonacci numbers. She made a mental note to ask him more about that later. "And they're all gentem?" She was beginning to wonder if high intelligence was another gentem trait.

"No. We have human children, too. No one is excluded."

For now, she decided to just let the subject drop. Every time she was here, her lack of understanding seemed to grow.

At Obeah's, Cassidy provided a brief run down on what they were doing and what they hoped to accomplish. Obeah looked concerned. "Be careful," he warned, "of revealing too much of your activities and knowledge to the humans too quickly. They frighten easily."

Vala laughed, then shook her head at Cassidy who, she was certain, was about to ask why she had laughed.

"That's what Vala said," Cassidy said. "I'm learning that the gap between humans and gentem is broader than I'd anticipated."

Vala, somewhat startled to hear Cassidy voice her own thoughts about how distant the two cultures were from one another, quickly told Obeah of their experiment in Cassidy's lab. As she talked, she found herself becoming excited over what they'd done. "When Cassidy and I linked hands and then brought the concepts alive, I felt as though I were a kid suddenly granted three wishes!"

Obeah smiled and then looked puzzled. "Linked hands?"

"Yes, you know, held hands to link in the gentem way." Vala could tell Obeah was slightly amused.

Obeah shook his head and looked at Cassidy. "Do you think that it's wise to mislead her in this important work? She needs to know how this all works."

Vala looked at Cassidy. Had she been tricked somehow? It was all a big joke? "So it didn't happen? We didn't create a second stool?" Vala felt her nerves tingling, felt the urge to run back to the portal–hah! that was probably fake, too!

"Vala, don't jump to conclusions," Obeah said. "This is a little thing, but Cassidy has something to tell you."

Cassidy flushed deeply, turning his naturally bronze skin into firey copper. "Vala, I'm sorry. We didn't have to hold hands. It just seemed ... nice."

Vala stared at him, then started to laugh. "You just wanted to hold my hand?" Relief flooded over her and she grabbed him and kissed him on the cheek. "Let's get back to work." She couldn't remember when she'd felt happier. This felt so delightfully normal–and silly, something that had been missing in her life.

Cassidy said nothing, but ran by her side, with Serein on the other side, to and through the portal.

Wyatt and Eric were sitting in the garden with Aunt Char enjoying the late afternoon sun, which was less hot than it had been the day before. The breeze felt almost cool. Aunt Char smiled as she always did when she saw Vala.

"Welcome back! What's happened?" Wyatt asked.

Eric was smiling. He didn't ask how Vala was feeling.

Cassidy and Vala got some iced apple juice, settled into some chairs, and Vala explained their efforts at the lab and why Vala believed it wouldn't be useful to try to explain to humans at the moment. "We need to figure out some other way to talk about it, rephrase it in a way that fits with human philosophy or that is at least contained within the scope of human knowledge."

Wyatt stood, sat back down, stood again and spread his hands. "But if you make it clear that it just takes *someone* with the right skills – just like someone who is good at math or someone who has a knack for training horses – wouldn't people accept it?"

Vala sighed. "Think about it, Wyatt. As a scientist, if you're told to set aside all your instruments and technology to mentally create a concept and then utilize fundamental forces to make it happen, are you going to say that's good science?"

"Well..." He sat back down and stared into space.

"Are you talking about will power?" Aunt Char asked. "People understand will power."

"No," Vala said. "It's not related to any of the mind-control powers–like telekinesis, telepathy, or kinesiosis–if that's what you mean. It doesn't go against what's possible. For instance, I don't think one could simply set aside gravity to make space travel easier. Gentem may harness the fundamental forces, but it's within the scope of what those forces are and how they interact."

Eric was shaking his head. "It's going to be dismissed as pop-science. Even psychology comes into question. Have you ever read Arthur C. Clarke's claim that advanced technology comes across as magic?"

Vala and Cassidy exchanged glances, smiled. Vala turned and noticed Eric looking at one, then the other. This time, she did stick her tongue out at him.

Wyatt shook his head. "But you have positive proof. Look, I've accepted a lot here. You've shown me things. I've accepted them. Of course, there are skeptics, but this is the reality: evolution took a path thousands of years ago that produced another branch on the homo sapiens level. Those on that branch, though still human, have slightly different skills and abilities that will benefit us all. That will be accepted."

"No, it won't," Char said. "I've watched Vala grow up in a world that isolated her because she was smart, because she was tall and physically strong, because she has features that could suggest a mixed heritage. *Difference* is never accepted by people. Eric has gone through the same thing, Wyatt. You've seen that. Sure, they've turned out okay, but I think it's because no one knows *how* different they are and because they both had the advantages of money and intelligence."

"What about all the diversity accepted today?" Wyatt asked. His hands were moving faster as he talked, his desperation making him look as though he were trying to fly as his arms flapped with each accented syllable. "All ethnicities, religions, neopaganism, Voodoo, Nature Spiritualists–all kinds of whacky ideas are accepted!"

"Did you hear yourself, Dear?" asked Aunt Char. "Whacky ideas–the minorities, either by visible differences or beliefs, may not be actively hunted and killed as in the witch hunts, but do *you* respect such *whacky* things? Aren't they all marginalized? We don't even readily accept people who don't want implants. If they don't live in a Box, they can't even vote."

Wyatt looked at her, opened and closed his mouth a couple times, then sagged back in his chair, his hands twitching slightly in his lap.

"Wyatt, let's talk about our paper," Eric said. Wyatt said nothing, and Eric began explaining that they'd finished a paper and had posted evidence about DNA on social media sites.

Wyatt finally joined in. "The idea of humans with different DNA, a type never identified before, should start the ball rolling." Wyatt paused, lost in thought for a moment, and then added, "I've entered the material as not significant at this point, but just something to study. I'll have to prove the research, of course, but I thought I could use both Vala's and Eric's DNA profiles as initial evidence. I can't use anyone else because none of the rest of you have any identification, and we don't want to get into that."

"Can't you use some other gentem on Alpha Earth?" Cassidy asked.

"Really?" Wyatt asked. "You left other gentem here?"

"Of course," Cassidy said. "Quite a number didn't want to leave family or lives. Some had significant careers in the sciences or entertainment or legal fields. They thought they could help put various cultures on track. From what you tell me, other countries have made more advances on living in harmony with nature; it could be that some of the gentem there have had an influence. Everyone had the choice. Individuals must determine their own futures."

"This is huge, Cassidy!" Wyatt said. "Who are they? This could be the added push, depending on who they are, that we need to make a point!"

Vala agreed. "If enough influential gentem exist over here, that could be the impetus we need. Or maybe we just need to get out of the United States to another country."

Cassidy shrugged. "Marina said we could contact them through a game. We can ask Obeah."

Eric slapped himself on the forehead. "That was what my patient meant, the one who said I was gentem. Then he just ran away." He shrugged. "I had no idea what he meant, and he didn't seem to want to share." He shook his head. "So many little details... such a huge gap between us. I don't know how we can expect humans to be able to grasp it all in hours."

After a few moments of silence, each individual pondering, perhaps, the great differences between the two cultures, Vala cleared her throat and asked, "Have you heard from Tandra and Julia?"

Everyone shook their heads and lapsed into silence again.

"Should we try to contact them?" Vala asked.

"How?" asked Eric.

"Why, their phones—oh, scheisse! Cassidy, I sent them out there without any identification or phones or anything! What if they are in trouble?"

"What kind of trouble?" Cassidy asked.

Vala thought. "I don't know. But why aren't they back?"

"I haven't gotten any sense that they're in danger," Cassidy said. "Tandra *is* my sister."

Vala was amused to think that, for Cassidy, that statement eliminated any doubt.

"How about if we all eat?" Aunt Char said. "Then we'll see what comes next."

In minutes, they were all in the kitchen to wash, chop, and mix various vegetables and fruit, something House couldn't quite manage with its computerized food processors without mutilating the food. Then they carried plates back into the garden. Wyatt brought up three times finding other gentem on Alpha Earth. Finally, Cassidy and Vala agreed to go see Obeah immediately to find out if he had contact information.

As it turned out, Obeah had little information. "We don't track individuals the way humans do. They're very focused on counting and tracking ancestry and figuring out who was from which country and what the mixes are. We've never been as tied to that, another by-product of being long-lived, I think. That's another reason we're so comfortable on this side. No nations. No borders. No passports."

"The gentem on the other side must be comfortable there," Vala said.

"More or less. Some had children there, of mixed heritage. Some had simply grown comfortable with easy lifestyles and even a materialistic focus. I know that Quetzal wanted to stay. He was a tennis pro, but Fredericka and all their friends were coming here. Quetzal wouldn't object to the Membrane coming down. Maybe others feel that way. Yet, keep in mind that they must always hide their identity. I wonder if anyone can ever feel happy or free if they must hide who they are. How about you, Vala? Were you happy?"

Vala thought about her life and decided the answer was no.

"Is there some way we could find some gentem?" Cassidy asked.

"Remember when we left, we set up a website and a game and left funds to keep it going. We had also agreed on a coded message that could be sent out if any of us needed to make contact. It was to be put out as ads or on computers wherever possible. It was based on the Six Degrees of Separation Theory and was meant to sound innocuous. I have it written down here somewhere."

As Obeah rummaged through his notebooks, Vala studied all the bottles on Obeah's shelves. The bottles appeared to be scavenged on this side and recycled; some looked like whiskey bottles or even milk bottles. All were glass: no plastic. Most had notes on them she couldn't read. He wasn't using the English alphabet. She'd have to ask him about that.

"Here it is!" he called. He handed Vala the paper.

> Humpty Dumpty built a great Wall
> 6 degrees separate from humans all.
> Should the Wall fall, Humpty Dumpty
> will call: Come one and come some
> dumptygoose.com

"You don't have any poets?" Vala asked.

Obeah chuckled. "It wasn't meant to be great literature. The site is members only with a password required. The password is simply homosophosgentem1. Once entered, messages can be read and posted. The goal was to keep it dull and nonspecific. One family was assigned to maintaining the site in perpetuity." Obeah thumped his forehead with the palm of his hand. "What was the name they were using for themselves online? It was a human name, a common one, just for the purpose of the site."

"Jane Doe?" Vala said to make a joke.

"That's it!" Obeah said. "How did you know?"

Vala sighed. "So what can we post?"

"Let's visit the site first and make sure it's working," Cassidy said. "If not, maybe we can create one. We'll have to go through the portal again. We can't connect to your GILS here."

Within thirty minutes, they were in Vala's house alone—everyone had gone, but only Aunt Char had left a note to say she was going home. Vala sat staring at her computer at a website that was, indeed, still live, but nothing had been posted in a year except one note:

> If you're a member of this group, visit our new page at http://www.gentem.civ/. Use standard password.

At the new site, they found a variety of posts, mostly from those looking for some sort of support after a civil rights violation or wondering if anything had been heard from the "other side." Most made the users sounded like people utilizing psychic references.

After some discussion, they decided to put out just a feeler.

> Visitors from other side. Discussions about future connections underway. If interested, please post.

Vala hit enter. "Well, if we get no response, we'll have a sense for how disinterested individuals are. If we do get responses, how do we proceed? Should we have a meeting?"

Cassidy shrugged. "I guess—"

He stopped as a post showed up on the page. Within twenty minutes, the number of posts had turned into so many responses that Vala didn't want to try to reply to each.

"Where can we have that meeting?" Cassidy asked.

"I can get a classroom auditorium at U-dub. Let me make a call."

Although it was night, Vala tracked down the appropriate people and when she had finished, she'd reserved a room for the next day at 7:00 p.m. in a space that would seat 250. Had it not been summer, she'd have had to wait weeks, maybe months.

She posted again.

> Thank you. Information meeting–this group only–
> tomorrow at 7:00 p.m., UW, Seattle, classroom
> auditorium 983, Jacob Nelson Hall. Private.

There was another burst of posting. Various postings raised questions about trustworthiness. Then came a burst of postings from international users who wanted the meeting live on GILS.

"Is there anything we can say to assure them that their gentem connections won't be compromised?" Vala asked.

"Not that I can think of. No, wait, for many a mention of Obeah and Alarick would be a sign that we are either legitimate or that the entire culture has been discovered."

Vala started typing.

> Alarick no longer Chair, Obeah working on
> continued communication.

"How about that?"

"Do it," Cassidy said.

She entered the note. "Now, I'd like to make some contacts with some colleagues who are doing water studies in Britain, Turkey, and the East Coast of the U.S. I can leave messages in the U-dub research Universe; that's accessible everywhere and is monitored by the Guardians–I'm allowed contact there."

"I don't understand why you can't freely communicate," Cassidy said.

"The U.S. has spent the last decade seriously antagonizing every nation and fearing every nation except China and Russia. People have been convinced that terrorist attacks are unavoidable without Guardian oversight. Anyway, I'm going to tell them that some of my research included a look into transgenerational epigenetics and, in the process, found that some drinking water is contaminated with a sudden increase of naturally-occurring ephedrine. I'll suggest they test for that immediately."

Cassidy nodded. "You have a lot of resources. That must be satisfying even if other connections are limited."

Vala felt a wave of surprise; it *was* satisfying. She'd overcome a lot in her lifetime. After she finished, she called Eric who was almost at her house with Wyatt. "We've had a good response to Wyatt's DNA research postings already," Eric said. "A half-dozen scientists have already suggested that such a branch could produce surprises in DNA chains that would have significant effects over time. That could be a step toward acceptance."

"Excellent!" Vala was surprised that people were already onboard.

"Wyatt wants to know if you've heard from Tandra or Julia."

"No, I haven't," Vala said. "I'm getting worried. We should have given them a cell phone."

"I believe if she were in serious trouble, I'd know," Cassidy said, "but I'll meditate in the garden to see if I connect."

Vala passed the information along to Eric just about the time they arrived at the house.

"What do we do about Tandra?" Wyatt asked immediately.

Eric shook his head at Vala. "He's pretty tense," he said.

Vala laughed. "Really? And when did this happen?" It was painfully obvious that Wyatt was worried, angry, and slightly depressed. He could even be smitten with Tandra.

Eric shrugged. "I think it's just a passing focus to help ease tension."

"What is?" Wyatt asked.

"Just something Vala wanted to know about," Eric said with a wave of his hand.

"Eric, Cassidy's in the garden meditating, trying to get a sense of Tandra's situation."

"We should have given them a phone," Wyatt said.

"Hindsight aside, let's see how he's doing," Vala said.

When the three of them entered the garden, Cassidy, sitting by the fountain, visibly stiffened. "Wyatt, you're going to have to leave. Go in the kitchen and get some coffee or something. You're sucking up all the energy."

Wyatt looked hurt but went inside.

"Phew! That's better already," Cassidy said. He closed his eyes. Vala and Eric sat quietly nearby. As they all relaxed, it was almost as if everything stilled. Even the AI pollinators seemed to fly more slowly.

Suddenly, Vala could plainly _hear_ Tandra say _police_ and _come_.

"Uh-oh," said Eric.

"You heard that?" Vala asked.

Eric and Cassidy nodded.

Okay," Vala said. "Let's start calling until we find them. Then we'll have to go get them. Who knows what happened, but neither of them has any form of identification on them. This could get ugly."

They soon located them at a Union Street holding station that had been set up during the 2023 protest during the water rights hearings. The station had been maintained to help with various protests and shootings. It was illegal to protest the Federal government now, which cut down on gatherings and, surprisingly, shootings. "Cassidy, you stay here. You have no ID either."

"I'm coming," Wyatt said.

"Fine. With the three of us, we ought to be able to overwhelm them with credentials," Vala said.

On the way, they came up with a cover story that Tandra and Julia were floaters visiting them from Corona, New Mexico. They had little identification and what they did have was left at home. After all the ID for Vala, Eric, and Wyatt had been verified, they finally were able to get the two women released. One officer said she would likely come by later to verify Vala's address.

"But what did they _do?_" Vala asked.

The officer spun the story about Julia angry in the museum at the pop art exhibit titled Deforestation. "She began tearing into the exhibit. Guards stopped her before she did much damage, but they had to Taser her. The exhibit artist says she's not going to press charges, that she wants her art to motivate people." The officer's expression said that she thought they were all crazy.

In the car on the way home, Julia ranted. "It was _nothing_ but paintings of lumber and piles of lumber in the middle of the room! It should all be thrown out to make room for _art!_"

"She's right. It lacked no resemblance to art I've ever seen," Tandra said. "Not that I'm an artist. But Julia became very agitated, particularly after they told her they didn't have any art from Russia anymore because of a ban on foreign art in government-supported facilities. The docent had never heard of Julia."

"Art is passion! It's fire and hurricane and tsunami. Not piles of lumber!"

"Well, you two are going to have to refrain from any more excursions," Vala said. "You have no identification, and should anything come up, you could wind up in a bad situation, especially now that you're already noted in the system."

"How dare you tell me–" Julia started but, surprisingly, Tandra interrupted.

"She's right, Julia. I think we'd better just avoid any contact with this culture. We're out of touch, and we need to keep a low profile. Remember the work that needs to be done."

Julia made some sort of huffing sound and hunched into a sulk.

Egos were alive and well among gentem no matter how pacifist they were. That made Cassidy even more special, Vala thought as she remembered his acceptance of her various suggestions.

At Vala's, they walked Julia back through the portal. As they returned, Eric told Vala that he had sensed Julia had her own agenda in joining them. "I think she wanted to determine the prominence of her own art work on Alpha Earth. She's done with humans now."

In the garden, Vala warned, "Tandra is going to have to be super careful. The police may come by to check her out."

Eric nodded, then wiggled his finger at Vala to pull her aside. "Vala, I called Steve Brillig today, gave him the particulars on Jasmine and asked him to try to find out what happened to her and to the human child I replaced. I think it's important to know–at least for me. And maybe for all of us."

Vala rubbed the top of his head. "Probably a good idea, Eric."

"I really hate that, Vala."

She smiled. She didn't have to ask what he hated…she knew the idea of a displaced child would tear him apart. The head-rubbing was minor. Each day she better liked having a little brother. She was no longer sure how she got along without him, but she would be there for him in the future.

He looked up at her. "Yes, I hate the idea of the displaced child, but I also hate having the top of my head rubbed."

She groaned–he'd obviously been reading her thoughts again. She frowned. Then she rubbed the top of his head.

He glared at her. "Anyway," he said, "I finally got into my safety deposit box. There was little there: the Trust papers, some pictures of babies–you and me, I think–and some information about Jasmine's job with the magazine. Whatever she intended to leave for me isn't there."

CHAPTER TWENTY-TWO

Sunday night & Monday, July 9, 2029

In the garden, Vala, Eric, Cassidy, Wyatt, and Tandra more or less collapsed. Cassidy considered all the talk, the problems, the solutions, and the additional problems and the fact that it was apparently the middle of the night–he'd lost track–and decided that exhaustion was excusable although he was anxious to continue the work.

"It's been an interesting day," Wyatt said. "We've gotten a lot of attention. Some better than others," he said, looking at Tandra.

Tandra glared at him. "Well, I saw nothing here–from art to traffic to people–that makes me want to be a part of this society. The noise and the smells could kill a person even if the toxins in the atmosphere don't. Why is everyone bald and covered with colored, moving designs?"

"Not everyone," Wyatt said, rubbing his full head of hair.

"Out there." Tandra waved her hand around over her head. "I've never seen so many bald people."

"It's currently fashionable," Vala said. "The discontinued use of live food has resulted in deficiencies that affect hair loss in many people. Fab-meals are popular in high-prestige groups, so people want to look as though they've lost hair, whether they have or not. In addition, medics use a modified version of chemo to body sculpt; some people claim think it's a cancer preventative, but hair falls out."

"But don't they know the causes of cancer?" Tandra asked.

"Yes, but for the most part, cures are more popular than avoiding causes. People don't want to give up all the chemicals and carcinogens used in contemporary society. People still smoke, for instance."

Tandra slapped her forehead and flopped back in the chair. "They're insane. And the colors?"

"Tats," Vala said. "Some are digital and others have some sort of nanobot technology. I haven't looked into it much."

Cassidy agreed with Tandra. Everything he learned made human society unappealing, but he said nothing. Instead, he brought up the meeting scheduled for the coming night. "We have to decide what we're going to say, how to present the situation. The tone of the posts we saw earlier were suspicious about who we are and what the meeting exposes about them."

Vala called up the site on her phone. "A lot more posts. We'll have a full house." After scanning for a few minutes, she said, "It looks like the biggest question is whether the Membrane is down. I think people want to reconnect with friends and family."

Eric spoke up. "The first thing to do is to tell them that nothing has changed with the Membrane, but communication has been established. Then, how about saying we'd like to have an honest dialogue based on science that would allow for a harmonious relationship among both homo sapiens and homo Sophos."

That sounded like a good start to everyone. Vala composed a post that would follow Eric's idea but not use terms that could attract unwanted attention. Wyatt said he'd go to the meeting room in the afternoon and make sure the sound system and GILS connection were working, then he left to get some sleep. Tandra wandered back through the portal, still muttering about crazy humans. Vala made three more posts to reassure individuals and to say more information would be posted later.

"I'm going to sit here in the garden for a while. It's how I rest," Vala said. "If you two want to join me, that's fine. But I don't want to talk."

"I'm going to just curl up on the sofa, if you don't mind," Eric said. "It's quite large enough for me to sleep comfortably."

"Go to the guest room if you'd like. Aunt Char went home, and you won't be disturbed there."

Eric nodded and went upstairs.

Cassidy and Vala sat in the dark for a few minutes, and then Vala stood. "I was wrong. I don't want to sit here. I want to go through the portal. It's quieter. It smells better. It's more peaceful."

Cassidy said nothing but simply got up and joined her. On the other side, Vala paused. "Someone is here."

Cassidy stopped. "Oh, that's just Gulo. He hangs around here sometimes, hoping to race."

"He's a wolverine!" she said. She looked down at Serein who was sitting by her side, evidently uninterested in the odor drifting from nearby trees.

She communicates with the one next to her.

Cassidy was always startled when Gulo revealed more about his skills and intelligence.

They are close companions, Cassidy affirmed.

Race?

Not now. We're going to rest a while.

Gulo simply wasn't there anymore.

"Cassidy, can we figure out how to know what will happen to this place if the Membrane comes down? I understand that we'll be aware of only the one Earth, but can this place continue?"

Cassidy started to speak, paused, rubbed his lip. "I don't see how, not if the Membrane is down. It may be possible to go back through the portal–all those who wish to do so–and leave the Membrane intact, somehow without leaks. Perhaps with full separation, it would be like the stool, gone from our ability to access it." He shrugged. "I don't know. I don't know how to find out except to do it. And if we're successful at that, we probably won't know."

"That's unacceptable, Cassidy. We have to figure it out. Let's go to your lab."

They spent the rest of the night brainstorming ideas. They didn't notice daylight arrive but Vala stopped in mid-sentence and said, "Eric is looking for me. What time is it?"

"Daylight," Cassidy said. Vala's senses were strengthening, especially her link with Eric. So was her confidence. He glanced around. Their notes were wall-to-wall, but they hadn't found an answer. The question would probably be asked by the Council and maybe even by those at the meeting this afternoon.

Vala was turning and leaving speaking over her shoulder as she did so. "We have that meeting this evening, and I need to find Eric. I can't reach him when we're on separate sides." She yanked open the door and almost collided with Eric.

"You need to look down when going through a door," he said.

She laughed, the same musical laugh that Cassidy loved. "I was just coming to find you," Vala said.

Eric looked around the room. "What have you been doing? Not sleeping obviously. Not eating. I know you can function quite a while on minimum requirements, but not forever. We can have a big breakfast back at the house."

"Okay. We've been trying to figure out what will happen here if the Membrane comes down," Vala said. "Or if it doesn't?"

Eric's eyebrows went up. "It won't just stay as it is?"

"We don't know," Cassidy said. "Remember, the entire thing has been experimental anyway. We know if we do nothing, things will continue to worsen here and perhaps the two worlds will collide. That could, eventually, just become another Earth, in a million or so years, but meanwhile, everything we know would be extinct."

"Well, extinction may happen anyway," Eric said. Last night, terrorists made three major strikes in Japan. The U.S. government said, in effect, *too bad.* Japan is threatening Korea and China with missiles."

"If something like that happens," Cassidy said, "we're all doomed. If water and toxic fumes can penetrate the Membrane, it can never withstand bombs of that number and magnitude—not as it exists now anyway."

"The Council's gift of time is beginning to look irrelevant," Vala said, "especially since major shifts such as ships and skyscrapers are occurring. Let's go get ready for the meeting. Then we're going to have to do more analysis on what actions to take."

Cassidy's phone rang. He looked worried, then relieved. When he ended the conversation, he smiled at Vala. "The Council has met and agreed to scrap the idea of adding chemicals to the water. Marina says that they've determined the action doesn't fit within the ethical standards of the gentem. She said one thing we can't afford is to lose who we are even if it means annihilation."

Vala sighed. "Well that takes away the Council deadline, but not human politics or the collapsing Membrane."

Breakfast was sober, but an undercurrent of excitement helped. They'd have to take action quickly—one way or the other, this would all be over soon.

Chatter on the site was increasing. Excitement. Joy. Depression. Every emotion. Wyatt, who was the last to show up from his lab where he'd spent the night also not resting, told them that scientists were contacting him for more information on the DNA he had showing unidentified genomes. He had sent them the profiles and the sketch showing the lineage, and they wanted to start looking for others with the same gene sequence.

Cassidy felt uncomfortable; the situation felt unpredictable and unstable. "Maybe we need to slow this down," he said. "We now have scientists all over the world looking into this. Humans we don't know and who don't know the real situation. Maybe we should try to keep this more focused on the gentem—what they want us to do. Where they want to live. How they want to live."

Wyatt shook his head. "Knowledge has to be shared in order to influence cultures and governments. People need to know about you and how you all can benefit us. If we can create worlds—imagine it! No more limited resources! No more illnesses from environmental issues. If we need to, we can just emigrate to new worlds!"

"That's not acceptable!" Cassidy said. He felt as though a giant hand had closed around his heart. "You can't just use life and throw it away. Not human, not gentem, not *anything*. Creating a world was risky. We can't abuse power. What's wrong with you?"

Wyatt pushed up against Cassidy. "What would you do? Just save your own kind and abandon billions of people?"

Cassidy felt ill. He put his hand to his head, tried to think.

"Wyatt!" Vala yelled.

Eric shoved his way between the two men, put his hands out on Wyatt's midriff and pushed. "Stop it! This is counter-productive. You have to allow us to finish the research!"

"But we have to *tell* people!" Wyatt yelled as he regained his balance. "It's the only thing that can stop this political posturing and possible war. You have the abilities to make things better."

"Wait!" Eric said. "Wyatt, slow down a little. Please. We can't afford to disagree at this point. We have to be unified. Let's have this meeting tonight and then move forward with a clear sense for what's right for everyone. No one is saying *no,* but just relax. If we rattle too many cages, we could attract attention we don't want, like Julia did."

Wyatt's eyes narrowed. Cassidy could feel the anger from him, so he knew Eric had to recognize it. Vala leaned over and whispered in Cassidy's ear, "Get Tandra."

"Okay," Wyatt said to Eric. "But just till after the meeting. Then we need to take serious action." His jaw was tightly clamped.

Aunt Char returned, and they had coffee in silence. Within ten minutes, Cassidy was back with Tandra. The minute she walked in the room, Wyatt brightened. Tandra walked over to Wyatt, sat down and started talking in urgent, hushed tones.

Later, Tandra and Wyatt left for the lecture room to set things up; Tandra promised to keep a low profile. Cassidy reminded Tandra, three times, that she was without papers, but then Vala gave her an extra cell phone, a university ID badge, and a credit card with Vala's name on it. "If anything comes up, you're me," Vala told her.

Tandra nodded and left.

"Eric," Cassidy said, "would you monitor the gentem site and respond if it seems necessary? Vala and I are going back to the lab for a few hours."

Vala kissed her Aunt Char on the cheek. "You've been a blessing, keeping us all fed and taken care of. I promise to make it up to you soon."

She laughed. "I haven't had this much fun in years. However, I do want you to arrange a trip for me through that door you keep talking about."

"You've got it! Maybe even tonight."

Back on the gentem side of the wall, Vala turned to Cassidy. "I very much want to meet my grandmother. I think that's important–more important than obsessing over the lab work. I know time is short but…"

Cassidy nodded. "If you think it is important, then it is."

Vala studied him closely for a moment. Then she reached out and took his hand. "Thank you," she said.

Cassidy almost took a step back, but he kept her hand as they walked toward the scooters. "Why are you thanking me?"

Vala smiled. "The fact that you don't know makes the thanks doubled. Tripled. Googol squared. Shall we run?"

Cassidy shook his head and reluctantly dropped her hand. "Let's take scooters, just because it's quite a distance, and we're short on time. Once you see where it is, you may be fine with running there next time."

They walked over to the scooters parked nearby. "Are all these yours?" Vala asked.

"Mine? Do you mean only I can use them?"

Vala nodded.

"What a silly idea," he said. "They are here for whoever needs them." He shook his head. "You have reminded me of my early days with humans. I remember now: everything was personal property. Children used to fight over toys." He felt something tighten inside with the memory; then he felt a wash of gratitude that he hadn't been immersed in that culture.

They rode along sections of roadways that were passable but often had to veer from broken and cluttered pavement to dirt trails beside the roadways. Paved roads were one of the infrastructures that were unimportant here–in fact, they were environmentally detrimental–and they hadn't been maintained in these thirty years since the separation. Serein easily ran with them, his tongue lolling and his mouth open; he looked as though he were laughing.

Cassidy was proud of the trees and shrubs that had grown up around and through a lot of the pavement and concrete. "This area is freer of flooding because of better drainage now that there are fewer impervious materials around," he told Vala when they paused to move some branches off the path. He hoped she was enjoying the trip as much as he was.

They turned off on a dirt path that led to the nearby reaches of the Elwha River, then stopped on a rise overlooking the river and its final meanderings to the Strait of Juan de Fuca. They were in front of a log house that blended into the wooded background. A large garden dominated the south side and on the west side, four cows grazed in a large pasture. Chickens and ducks ambled around the pasture, clucking and quacking, and a coop sat a short distance from the house on the north, next to a small barn.

As they parked and climbed off their scooters, a statuesque woman came out of the small barn and toward them. Vala stood in one place, just staring at the woman, which Cassidy thought a little rude, but Vala could be unusual.

Cassidy walked briskly forward, nodded his head. "Greetings, Shereen. You look well."

She smiled, rested her hand on his arm. He felt almost instantly calm and assured.

"And this—" he began

"No need to introduce Vala to me, Cassidy." She strode toward Vala and held out both hands. Vala stood rooted, her face unreadable to Cassidy. She showed nothing.

She could be frozen, Cassidy thought.

Nonetheless, Shereen took Vala's hands from where they were hanging limply by her sides. As soon as she did so, Vala's head lowered and she began sobbing.

Shereen, almost a foot taller than Vala's 6'6", took Vala into her arms, embracing her tightly while her ample, loose shirt draped around Vala like a blanket. They stood like that for several moments, with Vala softly sobbing into Shereen's shoulder and then they stepped apart. Serein was standing a few feet away and didn't show any concern.

"You both must come into the house and have tea," Shereen said. "The water is hot, so we'll make a new batch."

"We don't have—" Cassidy started but stopped as Shereen's hand swept through the air in dismissal of whatever he had been about to say. He was still startled by the complete changes in emotion from Vala. Silence was probably strength.

Inside, the room was light around the rough-hewn table where Shereen placed a pot in a cozy and three hand-thrown mugs the color of an autumn sunset. No light source was evident for the bright room. Cassidy made a mental note to ask Shereen about that at another time. Vala was studying a photograph on a side table. "Where did you get my picture?" Vala asked in a soft and hesitant voice, the first words she'd spoken.

"That's your mother, Dear. Vala Shereen. I was surprised when we learned you'd taken her name."

Vala continued to study the photo as she spoke. "I legally changed it as soon I was of age. The name *Sarah* meant nothing to me."

Shereen smiled. "We have ways of knowing who we are." She turned toward Cassidy. "Sit down, Cassidy. You are just fine."

Cassidy, who had been wishing he'd stayed outside so these two could be alone sat down, feeling fine, and watched Shereen pour tea into the three mugs.

"You've warmed my joy and graced my spirit by coming to see me, dear Granddaughter. You've never been far from my thoughts. Now, drink tea and ask your questions. We have all the time you need," Shereen said softly while looking meaningfully at Cassidy.

He sipped tea and decided that they were, indeed, in no hurry.

Vala left the photo and sat down across from Cassidy. "I don't even know where to begin, but maybe you could give me a little family history? I don't know who anyone is."

Shereen nodded. "Unfortunately, your history has a lot of tragedy within it. We often seem to be in the right place at the right time to find the very worst of circumstances. Much of our family came from various Asian countries where we were very noticeable for our height. Misfortune of geography. Immigration was difficult because many of us, obviously Asian, weren't welcome elsewhere. On the other hand, witchcraft, as humans call any deviation from their own norm, wasn't treated as badly in Japan as elsewhere. Healers were always welcome."

Cassidy's thoughts drifted away briefly as he noticed a fox nosing its way through the front door. The fox slipped along the wall and disappeared behind some furniture. Cassidy caught a brief glance from Shereen and, thinking the fox was just fine, went back to sipping tea. Serein glanced at the fox, then ignored it, staying close to Vala.

As Cassidy checked back into the conversation, Shereen was saying "–grandfather was not only an empath but also a wonderful artist. In the next room, I have many of his paintings. Your mother adored my father and spent a lot of time with him in Japan while growing up. He and my mother, originally from Ireland, lived happily nestled into the foothills of Mt. Nabekanmuri. Unfortunately, once WWII began, your mother was not able to visit any more. We were living here in Washington at the time.

"Neither of us was obviously Japanese, and we weren't included in the round-up of Japanese citizens who were herded into camps. Humans all too often commit such travesties on their own kind, which is one reason gentem stay closeted. Anyway, with the dropping of the atomic bombs, much of our history ended along with many cherished Japanese traditions."

Shereen paused, poured more tea. Cassidy was uncertain what kind of tea it was, but he knew that he was much more mellow than when he'd arrived. Vala, too, was obviously more relaxed. Absorbed in the story, her face relaxed, softened, and her shoulders lowered. Cassidy realized, surprisingly, that he'd rarely felt that Vala was at peace, at least not consciously, but now it was palpable.

"Your mother's love of Japan and of your grandfather inspired her to get there and try to help those in need as soon as possible after the bombs dropped. Vala was a powerful healer, and she did a lot of good. She was strong enough to keep the effects of radiation poisoning at bay for a long time. It was a battle she knew she was losing when she decided to have you."

"I don't understand why she would decide to have a baby when she was dying," Vala said.

Shereen smiled. "That was when talk about the Membrane and about having special contacts on the other side were being discussed. No one, of course, wants to part from a child, and that included your mother—and your grandmother. Your mother, however, felt certain that you had a role to play in this situation, and I came to agree with her."

"But I have no idea what I can do. What I *should* do," Vala protested. "People keep telling me I'm supposed to be a hero, but I'm ignorant."

Vala slumped back in her chair, and Cassidy resisted the urge to jump up and comfort her.

"Sometimes, knowing you don't have the answer is the answer. You're not a super-hero, Dear; you simply have your own abilities, perspectives, and tasks. Since this all started, *letting go* has been part of the lesson—for all of us. In letting go, we often find we have a more certain understanding. I think you need to focus on that."

"Letting go of what? Who? How? I have no answers."

"You'll have answers when you need them. The first *letting go* is to let go of the need for answers. And don't forget to listen."

Vala shook her head, her lips thinned. Cassidy expected that she would erupt in frustration. She was good at that. Instead, she quietly asked, "Listen to what?"

"Why, yourself and your intuition, of course."

Vala sighed. "What about my father? No one talks about him."

"No one knows him," Shereen said then looked thoughtful. "Well, your mother did, I suppose, but we never discussed it. That was her business, and she didn't care to share it. Your mother never had a vow partner and no one came forth. He may not know of your existence."

"What's a *vow partner?*" Vala asked.

"Sometimes, not always, when individuals want children, they bond as vow partners to make sure the child is raised with full support. When children are grown, the partners may stay together, or not."

Vala stood. "I have a lot to learn about this culture. I'd like to stay in touch with you, no matter what happens next."

"Of course, Dear. I've been waiting for you to be here. You are as strong as your mother expected. We'll have time to talk."

They lapsed into some talk about the farm and the gentem hope for peace, then they hugged. As Cassidy and Vala climbed back on their scooters, Cassidy noticed that the sun and shadows were exactly as they'd been when they'd arrived. "How—" he began and then stopped as he caught a look from Shereen. Maybe later.

As they headed back to the obelisk. Cassidy didn't know if Vala had satisfied her need to connect, but he decided it wasn't his place to ask. Instead, as they were walking toward the portal, he asked, "Did you like her?"

Vala looked at him and smiled. "I loved her. I wish I'd known her all my life, but I'll be happy with what we have now. I feel like I belong now."

"You've lost only a short time."

Vala stopped walking and stared at him. "You know, I don't think I'm ever going to get used to the idea that you think in terms of centuries instead of decades for your life. That changes so many views that I'm not at all sure humans can ever accept it. The difference puts them at an extreme disadvantage. Limitations frustrate us…them. Longer life isn't something that can be taught. Something else to *let go,* I suppose. But Cassidy, I'm losing faith in any kind of peaceful relationship between humans and gentem."

Cassidy shrugged. Apparently, the things humans couldn't accept about differences was a very large number. "Wyatt may be right that genetic research could help modify human lifespan."

She said nothing.

He had a lot of questions he wanted to ask about her human interactions, but this wasn't the time or place. Since they didn't quite know what they were going to do or how or when they were going to do it, when they'd have time for that sort of talk was vague.

Chapter Twenty-Three

Monday evening, July 9, 2029

Back at the house, Eric greeted them with, "We have problems."

"Now what?" Vala asked.

Eric looked up at Vala and a tsunami of emotion made him take a step back. Something had happened with the two of them. He looked at Vala carefully and then relaxed. Something good.

He set that aside and answered her question. "Our gentem group website was hacked. Somebody's listening in. Also, some men were here–you know: communication implants, arrogant attitudes, and too much authority."

"Did they say which agency?"

Eric shook his head. "They didn't say, but they were Guardians. They didn't want us to know that because they were afraid we'd shut things down."

"They were asking about Tandra and Julia," Wyatt added.

"What did you tell them?" Vala asked, going over to stand by Wyatt who had the computer screen on.

"I told them that they'd left to take a road trip back home," Eric said. "I also told them I didn't know how to reach the two of them since they don't have implants. I said I'd call them if we heard. The agents didn't believe me. They think I'm a minor annoyance, probably because I'm short. They're monitoring House. They were aware of the fact that neither I nor you have implants. They have ears and eyes on us."

"I've dampened the house down," Wyatt said. "They shouldn't be able to hear us anyway, unless House itself is transmitting. I don't think it is. Later, I'll fortify the area with an electric field."

"I have no idea what you're talking about!" Cassidy said. "Are we in danger?"

Vala touched his arm. "Not at the moment, Cassidy, but we're going to have to be careful. It sounds as if our activities have generated interest on a government level. Is there any chance that the portal is generating energy in some way that could be picked up by others?"

Cassidy shrugged. "I don't know how it may appear on human technology, in part because I don't know anything about human technology. Certainly, the power fluctuates briefly when we use it."

"And we don't know that much about your technology," Wyatt said. "But we do have to be careful."

"How do you know the site has been hacked?" Vala asked.

"The site is protected by a number of systems that have been in place for quite a while," Wyatt said. "Most of them aren't much good, but one of those maintaining the site has set up a code that triggers any new visitor that hasn't quite matched the protocols. That was triggered today. I'm thinking that perhaps the setting up of the meeting, combined with Tandra and Julia's lack of ID, may be zeroing in on you and Eric as well as, of course, me."

He turned from the computer and scratched his neck. "Vala, your identity keeps repeating in new ways in the system. Apparently, your request that scientists look for chemicals in water supplies has also triggered a lot of attention. I don't know if my DNA material has caught their attention or not. Also, I'm close to the limit on my technology skills. If they pull any other tricks, I probably won't notice or, if I do, be able to combat them."

"It's a good thing we're on a deadline," Vala said.

Wyatt leaned on the counter and stretched out his back. "We have an idea for the meeting," He said.

As they all sat down to eat a meal, at Aunt Char's insistence, Wyatt outlined a plan he and Eric had come up with to make the meeting about the idea of extending the original online game,

Gentem Earth, into one focusing on how a subculture of marginalized individuals would create their own world and run away from the main culture.

"The idea is that this would leave the main culture without the benefit of their training and diversity, but that it would give them each a way to develop or evolve as they were intended and would avoid war," Eric said.

"Along with that is the question of *should that be done*," Wyatt added. "We can throw in some battles or something to make it look like a real game."

"Why don't you just name them as elves and dwarves?" Tandra said. "That has worked in the past to completely lose respect from the humans, so they quit paying attention to us."

"That may help us snoop-bomb," Vala said.

Eric looked at Cassidy. "Go unnoticed," he said, automatically translating.

"You know that game *Last Cabal*?" Wyatt asked.

All of them shook their heads.

"Of course not," Wyatt said. "Anyway, it's the most popular online game in the world right now. The idea is about individual heroes who have been beaten down in our various cultures and are fighting to assert themselves as individuals again. It makes each player one of the cabal. How about if we call this *First Revolt* within the game *Gentem Earth*?"

Vala laughed.

"That's terrible!" Eric said.

"Why don't we ask people at the meeting to select names? That would give the meeting another sense of purpose," Cassidy said.

From there, they set up a list of proposals to discuss, most of which were thinly veiled camouflage for issues surrounding the Membrane, including leakage and general decay; taking the wall down; trying to maintain the Membrane and allowing more individuals to go through it.

"We've got to go," Wyatt said. "People will be arriving. Tandra, you can't go. You're supposed to be on the road somewhere."

Tandra nodded. "I know. I have a proposal. Char has said she'd like to visit through the portal—"

Vala slapped her forehead. "I forgot. I promised her–"

"Well, let's walk her through, and then I can show her around while you're all gone."

Char did a little dance as they escorted her through the portal.

When they returned, Vala tried to talk Cassidy out of going to the meeting because he had no identification.

"Let's just give him some," Eric said.

Wyatt quickly set up some online profiles for Cassidy as a computer geek with a personal page on a couple online gaming sites and a background that looked a lot like his own, including foster care and education at Western Washington University. "Your name is the same, but you're 28 years old, which is more what you look like–"

"Again, this hang up on age," Cassidy said.

"Don't say things like that in public," Eric said.

"–you don't drive," Wyatt continued, "and you don't travel. You don't socialize. You play with computers. Got it? I've manipulated a birth certificate for you. It won't stand up under careful scrutiny, but it's okay to pass a quick look."

Cassidy nodded. "Are people here really this involved with computers?"

"It's a major addiction problem," Eric said. "Many of my clients have lost all sense of who they are and what they want in life because they're so involved with computer games. The issue has been growing since the beginning of this century. For a time, Wyatt, Steve, and I lived to play Game of Thrones, then we discovered our individuality by refusing to be immersed in games."

Cassidy shook his head.

"Didn't you play computer games, Vala?" Wyatt asked.

Vala shook her head.

"What were you doing?" Wyatt said.

"Going to college," she said curtly.

Wyatt dropped the subject.

After they'd parked at the university, they walked over to the classroom auditorium. There was thirty minutes until the meeting started, but the crowd already gathered out front would probably push the capacity of the room.

"SRO with some in the hall," said Eric.

Cassidy stopped and stared at the crowd.

"Yes," said Eric. "All gentem or connected somehow." Eric shook his head. "I wish I'd known about them when I was growing up. How sad that they all feel that they have to hide their identity."

The group was silent, which was almost eerie for a crowd these days, Eric thought. In spite of the silence, the tension was almost visible, a gray shroud, over the standing crowd, some very short, some very tall, and many just average human height. Every human-identified race and ethnic group was represented. Eric thought it the most representative group of diversity he'd ever seen.

Wyatt pushed into the group saying, "Welcome, welcome. We'll get started shortly. It's great to see you all. We'll just open things up and you can come in and find a seat." Wyatt sounded enthusiastic and natural, utilizing his classroom teaching skills.

As everyone filed in behind Wyatt, Eric became aware of low whispers and intense stares directed at him and at Vala. Of course, he thought. Most of them would have known of the plan to leave two children who were destined to have access to Beta Earth. They wouldn't have known exactly who they were, but stories probably abounded.

"Why are so many people staring at just the two of us?" Vala said, bending over to whisper in his ear.

"I think they know who we are–not specifically but the story of us and eventual communication through the Membrane. Remember: we're super-heroes."

Vala's expression soured as she moaned slightly. With Serein at her side, she marched stiffly up to the front of the room.

The room filled quickly. Wyatt, Cassidy, Eric, and Vala stood at the front of the room and looked around. All the seats were filled. People looked at one another and around the room nervously. They felt at risk just being here, which clearly communicated how important it was to them.

Eric slapped on the mic chips on his cheek, and Wyatt activated the live online feed.

"Welcome, everyone. I know this is a difficult meeting for many of us. We know that aliens may be listening, may even be in this room." He chuckled. "But, I promise you, we're safe here together, and we're here to have fun, of course. We want your input to help create a game about the reality of aliens; we may as well since the governments won't admit to their presence, right? Imagine a group, a subculture of aliens, among normal humans. They are quite different but managing to hide within daily life although they must always be careful and are always marginalized."

Wyatt picked up on Eric's reassurances quickly. "Right," he said. "And, to be honest, we hope that in the process of creating this new GILS game, we'll come up with new ideas about protecting individuals from government oppression in the real world."

Vala joined in. "For instance," she said, "we all know that implants can be dangerous. It's too easy to be tracked, so most people in our game won't have implants for all the activities the masses use. We'll make sure our game can still be utilized using external devices. We, ourselves, don't have implants, except for Wyatt here, who has gotten one primarily to use for lectures and meetings such as this. As you know, the governments and companies are making it increasingly difficult to function without an implant. We want to change that–at least for our game."

A murmur rippled through the crowd. Many were nodding their heads.

Eric hoped their ideas for the *game* would get them dismissed as a bunch of whack jobs or at the very least a new group of conspiracy theorists. He suspected, however, that Vala and Wyatt's jobs at the University would be imperiled. Unfortunately, the story they were unfolding was reality for gentem.

Wyatt said, "Yes, I have an implant in order to succeed at work. You know how limiting it can be to not have one. How many of you out there have gotten implants for that same reason?"

A scattering of hands raised.

Eric noticed two men, looking like movie stars dressed like *common people:* their clothes were too new, too carefully casual; their eyes were frank and confrontational, unlike those who didn't want to be noticed. They were edging toward the doorway. Eric smiled. Those two had already decided that this was trivial.

"So let me give you a basic set up of this game," Wyatt said. He called up a huge screen across the white wall behind him.

From there, they stuck to reality as they knew it for the gentem, only they presented it as humans falling victim to government spies and big business. They proposed a quiet rebellion of these victims to withdraw from the world. How would they make it work? What if it failed and those they were fleeing began to invade that space?

They passed around pads and pencils–no technology for this crowd–and they asked people to answer specific questions including whether it would be feasible for these fictional game characters to function in society, both if it meant *passing* as *normal* and also if it meant changing the primary culture to make it healthier and peaceful. Then they asked if the separation should be permanent or temporary.

"We don't need any information about you," Eric assured them. "This can be anonymous. We just need a sense for what you'd like to see in this game. Do our characters leave or stay? Change the world or abandon it?"

Eric didn't see any of the agents left by this point, but he realized there were a number of humans in the audience. He paused. How did he know they were human? When he looked at them, it wasn't just height or anything physical. He just knew. He hoped he'd have time in the near future to further explore this awareness.

When he told Vala about the humans, she said, "They're probably friends or family, like Wyatt and Aunt Char."

Eric felt some surprise that Vala accepted the information calmly. She was changing, too. Realizing she wasn't crazy was giving her confidence.

After individuals had been assured of their anonymity, they rapidly filled up pages of notebook paper. Eric winced at the volume of hand-written material their group would have to struggle through. No other choice existed; these individuals wouldn't give out any digital information. Many individuals didn't trust GILS. At some point, Eric made direct eye contact with Dakota who beamed a huge smile at him. Eric smiled back and was happy to think Dakota was getting his wish. Maybe.

The bulk of the meeting was spent in people writing and then turning in the papers. When that was finished, the crowd dispersed quickly; individuals didn't stand around and chat as they often did at events. The four were back at Vala's by 10:30.

"I didn't see any of those agents as we came home," Vala said.

"A car was following us though, and I saw one parked just down the street," Eric said. "We haven't escaped supervision."

"I think I'll go through the portal and see how Aunt Char is doing," Vala said.

"I'll go along. Maybe we can grab some food over there," Cassidy said.

"I'm going to have a sandwich," Wyatt said.

Eric shrugged. "I think I'll have a sandwich with Wyatt. If you need me to help bring Char through the portal, I'll be here in the garden. I'm anxious to start reading some of these papers."

After Cassidy and Vala had left, Eric settled down with a cold glass of ale, which Vala had started keeping for him, to start reading. Wyatt brought him a sandwich. "I stepped out the front door to look around. That car is still parked down the street."

"I don't think we need to worry about it now," Eric said. "I'm not sensing any danger, and they wouldn't have to follow us. You, Vala, and I are all fairly high-profile people, and you have an implant. I suspect they're just watching to see who comes and goes that may not be on their list. And you still have the blocks up for sound monitoring. Let's just sit tight, eat, drink ale, and read."

Wyatt laughed. "You were always calmer about most things— except the obsession about finding your sister, which turned out to be reality rather than obsession. Even if Vala isn't really your sister, you seem to have adopted each other." Wyatt sat down next to Eric. "Eric, I'm only now coming to an understanding of what this DNA variation means. The extent of it is huge. If you don't cooperate, you could be in danger."

Eric set the papers down to focus on Wyatt. "You're... envious? Really?"

Wyatt nodded. "Of course. See? Just like that, you know my feelings. That's one of your skills that's beyond human reach. Each of the gentem have different skills, all of which humans will envy and fear. And the idea of living for centuries? That alone is enough to get humans to chop you up and analyze your cells, brain to hallux. For instance, humans will wonder if blood transfusions or cell injections could give them that ability. And, look how Vala and Cassidy run, like cheetahs. Nothing in our medicine, science, or technology is coming close to that except maybe AI. After the fiasco in 2023 with the genetically modified pets, people have scaled way back on that. But the gentem present a whole new concept. I think the only way to protect you is to bring it all out in the open, be honest and clear to the general public. Just be open and cooperate."

Eric chuckled. "Remember that GMO guinea pig we bought, the one that grew pointed ears and a long tail?"

Wyatt nodded. "And then its wings grew odd little legs and the thing could only walk in circles." He smiled briefly, like the Wyatt of old, then sobered. "I also remember how big the organ harvesting from prisoners became in 2021. That became a science fiction nightmare for a while. I'm not sure where that would have gone if the 3-D imaging of organs hadn't had a major breakthrough." He paused and looked thoughtful. "Vala told me that human children on the other side are learning right alongside the gentem children, on the same level. I suspect that a lot of this may be something humans can train themselves into. If we bring it all out in the open, people will adapt."

"It's solipsistic, isn't it? You know, thinking the behavior of other people will change in light of your behavior? Being open terrifies the gentem for a reason, Wyatt. Think about history. We've had some incredible leaders, including some humans, who have had little long-lasting impact. Gandhi, Thoreau, Kakahi, Paul, King, Havel, Mandela. All over the world, we've had great examples and cultures have chosen not to follow them. In fact, we've jailed or murdered many of them. Being open involves risk."

Wyatt chewed his sandwich with the same enthusiasm a kid chewed on Brussels sprouts, not that many people ate Brussels sprouts anymore. Eric realized that the conversation was no longer foremost in Wyatt's mind. "There's more to your push for unification than cultural significance, Wyatt. Is it Tandra?"

Wyatt looked at Eric. "See? See how you do that?"

Eric laughed. "Anyone who looked at your face when Tandra comes in the room could read you, Wyatt."

Wyatt dropped his sandwich on the plate and slumped back in his chair. "The first time I saw her, it was if I'd finally found what mattered in the world. But what kind of life is that, Eric? When I'm dying of old age, she'll just look the same."

"Well," Eric said. "First of all, the gentem, with all we know about DNA these days, may well come up with ways for humans to live longer. Lifestyle alone would help. Second of all, as far as I can tell, gentem don't have the same attitudes toward relationships that we've been taught to have. Think about it. Most humans have trouble maintaining a relationship for seven years. Marriage has been becoming increasingly passé. People stay with those they enjoy until they don't enjoy it anymore. Imagine trying to stay together for life if you live hundreds of years. Sounds depressing."

Wyatt laughed. "That's true. My marriage to Nona was one of the last marriages I know of among our friends. Even then, in 2024, it felt a little odd, and Nona always wanted a closeness I couldn't give. The marriage itself always felt like we were playing roles in a 1950s television show. Remember those?"

Eric nodded. "Like 'Leave it to Beaver'?"

Wyatt nodded. "Nona loved those shows."

Eric smiled. It had been a long time since he and Wyatt had enjoyed this sort of conversation. "All that matters now, Wyatt, is that we're trying to do what we can to help everyone, gentem and human. I don't know what will happen. But I do know that you're a valuable person. I think Tandra knows that, too. She's definitely noticed you, but I'm not sure what that means to her."

"Really? Are you just saying that to make me feel better or is that your weird mind reading thing?"

"I've just noticed her noticing you." Eric laughed. "You'll have time to get to know her, I'm sure, no matter how human you are. However, you can't expect the same sort of monogamy humans expected in 1950s television."

Wyatt laughed. "Thanks, Eric. You're right. I have to remind myself that we're working on something important. All the other stuff, that endless biogentic engineering, has felt like playing God to no purpose. We simply don't know enough. In my opinion, we're using people's greed and dissatisfaction to make them willing guinea pigs. Now that some huge breakthroughs that could really help humans have come along, I'm going to be shut down."

Eric could sense Wyatt's resentment building again, so he shifted the subject a little. He thought about telling Wyatt he wouldn't be shut down on Beta Earth. But Wyatt still wanted to share information. He skipped to something less controversial. "One thing that puzzles me in particular is the height thing. The only way it makes sense to me is if the two height groups evolved separately, in different environments that affected height needs."

"Well, we don't know anything about that Homo Uzgenia-Krygyzstian the gentem claim. We only know we're missing some links still."

Eric was about to comment, but the garden quiet was interrupted.

"Eric! Wyatt! Hello!" called Char, suddenly beside them in the garden with a smiling Vala and Cassidy.

"You had a grand time!" Eric said, noticing Wyatt's beaming smile as Tandra followed them into the garden.

"Oh, Eric, what a magnificent experience. That's life as it's meant to be lived. I'm going to gather some things and go back. Tandra has said I can stay at her place, and Obeah—what a *gorgeous* person—is going to let me work with him, learning more about herbs and techniques to promote a more harmonious lifestyle. They have a huge selection of live food, growing vegetables everywhere, so I can do some of that, too!"

"What about your home and your cat?" Wyatt asked.

"Snaffles is going with me, of course. Vala can do whatever with the house. I'd already put it in her name anyway."

"You what?" Vala said.

"Well, what else would I do? You're the closest person to me. No children and a dead husband."

"Let's get some sleep, and then I'll run Char to her home to gather whatever she wants," Wyatt said.

Everyone agreed, although Char was disappointed that she couldn't go right back. They scattered to various places for some sleep, followed by an early breakfast on Tuesday morning. Then Wyatt ordered a two-seater driverless with storage capacity.

"Wonderful! Let's go!" Aunt Char said.

Eric laughed, delighted with her enthusiasm but not surprised.

For anyone not addicted to technology or money or other focuses of the U.S. culture, the other side would be a welcome haven.

"Vala," Eric said, "Wyatt spotted a large car parked down the block. According to House, it's still there. We were probably followed here from the meeting, and we'll probably be under surveillance for some time."

Vala nodded. "I expected that from the time the gentem site was hacked."

"Humans have kept their paranoia about anything different, obviously," Tandra said with a sigh. "Here we are, once again connected, and Cassidy and I don't dare go out into the world. What does that tell you about the odds for our success for living harmoniously with them?"

"Be patient, Dear," Aunt Char said. "You know that for all the officials and bigots, there are humans like Wyatt, like me. We want to be inclusive."

"She's right," Vala said. "On the other hand, it's true that bigotry cycles through all the cultures pretty regularly. Sometimes, it's nationalities–immigrants, for instance–or religions–at one time the Catholics and then the Muslims and for thousands of years, the Jews–and sometimes it's skin color. It's rooted in emotions, the primitive rather than rational parts of the brain."

"Neanderthal." Tandra said.

Vala laughed. "You have your own bias, yes?"

Tandra flushed fiery copper on her cheeks, contrasting nicely with the usual sandy-gold skin tones. Eric understood Wyatt's interest in her, but Eric doubted it was more than a crush.

"The simple truth is that if this is going to work, gentem have to accept that they have to live in a world where bigotry exists, on both sides. That doesn't mean it can't be resolved," Eric said.

"It hasn't always been resolved well," said Char. "The Kurds, the Maori, the Tutsi, the Native Americans, and the Armenians were all but wiped out, with some groups completely gone in recent history."

Vala shook her head. "The gentem aren't large in number. I think it would be unwise for them to distinguish themselves except as humans with a slight DNA variation. Then we can add more information as we go. Gentem are going to have to be willing to be human, homo sapiens."

Eric felt a flash of anger from Wyatt, anger he quickly suppressed. His opposition to keeping gentem differences minimized could create problems.

"Sure, that's an option," Wyatt said with his eyes focused on the floor.

Was he just waffling? No, Eric decided, he was convinced that the truth had to be public. He was avoiding confrontation.

"Well," Vala said, "the immediate step is to continue seeing how those at our meeting last night felt."

After Wyatt and Char left, Eric considered talking with Vala about Wyatt and his building resentment. Perhaps it would be better to wait. They all had enough to think about.

The four of them went into the dining room and sat at the table, bent to the task of sorting through the hundreds of pages of comments gathered. Eric had already started, trying to sort the comments into categories. "Some of them," he said, "are concerned with how to connect with family. Others address the issue of keeping the separation. Most, want information about emigrating to the other side. I thought if we had categories, and then fed them into the House computer, perhaps we could get statistics faster."

Cassidy nodded. "Sounds like a good plan to me. I'm perhaps more used to working with paper than you are, and I scan quickly. How about if I start sorting with Eric and Tandra and, Vala, you start entering them into the computer."

As they began working, Eric quickly realized Cassidy hadn't been exaggerating his abilities. Vala was entering the information as quickly as Cassidy sorted it. Eric and Tandra eventually left the two of them to the work. "We'll get drinks," he told Vala.

In the kitchen, Eric climbed onto a stool at the counter. "Tandra, sit a minute?"

After she nodded and joined him at the counter, Eric said, "You're still angry, more so than makes sense from your conversation with Wyatt."

She shrugged, then nodded. "Vala is right. I have a lot of anger toward humans, not individuals like Wyatt and Char but the human culture. Char behaved beautifully today. Everyone she met fell in love with her. She'll be a wonderful addition to the community. But when humans form their groups, or tribes, they quickly become insider and outsider oriented; it's like they're always frightened that a difference signals their inferiority or a possible loss to them. You know what it's like, being an outsider. When I was a child, I grew used to hiding my abilities. I couldn't hide my height. The only place I was welcome was on a basketball court. I hate basketball."

Eric chuckled. "No one ever asked me to play."

Tandra smiled, then chuckled. She was, he thought, incredibly beautiful when she smiled. "I don't imagine you were," she said.

"You know, Wyatt is smitten with you," Eric said.

"I know."

"Wyatt has been my friend since we were kids. In foster care. In fact, he has been the only consistently loyal, close friend I knew while growing up, although Steve Brillig was there part-time." Eric hesitated, then added, "I happened to learn that at one time you were in love with a human, a woman."

Tandra cocked her head to one side. Her lips thinned, and Eric could tell she was battling with her temper, then it subsided. "I was. It didn't work out. That has nothing to do with Wyatt."

"So you're not interested only in women?"

Tandra drew back slightly and her brows pulled together. "Huh?"

Eric mentally slapped himself. He'd made an assumption that human sexuality mores he'd grown up with were true for gentem. He opened his mouth, shut it again. "What I mean," he started, paused, tried to finish, "...that is, if you aren't interested in having relationships with Wyatt because you don't care for men, you should tell him. He's ... sensitive."

Tandra laughed, and, again, Eric was struck with her beauty.

"I'll be honest with him, Eric. I know that humans are overly-emotional. As it happens, I'm *not* smitten with him. His recent emphasis on helping humans by giving up our freedom and becoming donors for genetic experiments has made certain I never will be. I don't trust him. But, it's not that I'm biased toward men or women. I'm attracted by personality, not person. Wyatt, although terribly focused on one thing at a time, is intelligent and funny, but…I don't trust him, Eric."

Eric, instead of saying he also had some concerns about trust, settled for "Thank you."

Just then, Wyatt and Char returned. Wyatt was pulling a small trunk and Char was carrying a small bag that held only a cat.

"The car is still there," was the first thing Wyatt said, then, "Where are Vala and Cassidy?"

"They're in the dining room working," Eric said. "They were being so efficient that we took a break. That doesn't look like much for a move," Eric added, gesturing toward the small trunk.

"Most of it is for the cat," Char said. "And some books published since the separation–books on natural foods and medicines that I thought may be useful. I don't have stuff that I want except some pictures. They're in there."

Eric nodded. He admired her more all the time. People rarely were able to pick up and move that simply without feelings of loss; letting go could be very liberating or, for some, terrifying. "Well, you'll have Vala," he said.

"And that's the world," Char said, grinning.

Wyatt came back from the dining room. "I guess I'm the only person concerned about the car," he said.

Tandra smiled. "There's nothing we can do about it except be careful. Why become alarmed over something that isn't trying to eat you at the moment?"

Wyatt looked at Tandra and visibly relaxed.

"Well, when and how do I get back through that portal?" asked Char.

"No time like the present," said Tandra. "Let's go get you settled. I'm not doing anything right now anyway."

Tandra went to the dining room, yelling, "Vala, Cassidy, take a break. Let's take Char through the portal!"

"Why don't we just link her?" Cassidy said. "Then she can come and go as she likes."

"I didn't know you could do that," Eric said.

Cassidy shrugged. "Well, that was an impulsive suggestion. But why wouldn't it work? It's really just a digital implant, but it's self-replicating if it's joined to a complete implant. I think, if we just harvest a bit of the spiral off my palm—a scraping should do—and place that on Char's palm, then unite it with a complete implant, a precise copy will form and activate. With Eric and Vala, it was almost instantaneous. Starting this way, it may take a few minutes."

Vala shook her head. "Cassidy, when that happened with Eric and me, we were both quite ill. It was disorienting. Like suddenly in free fall."

"I have a suggestion. I think if all four of us hold hands, that reaction could be mitigated. You and Eric were linking up with each other with incomplete implants, so that link had to be boosted through the obelisk to connect with Tandra and me on the other side. If we're all here and in contact, perhaps the effect will be mild."

"*Perhaps?*" Vala said. "Cassidy, this isn't a good idea."

"Quit being such a mother hen," Char said. "Let's go for it!"

"Try it on me first to be sure," said Wyatt.

Cassidy looked from one to the other. "I'm sure it's safe. It may not work, but I can't imagine how it would hurt either of you. I've been thinking about this since I realized Serein simply went through the portal as soon as Vala was keyed to it. Char and Vala are already linked emotionally, so let's start with her."

"What do I do?" Char asked.

Cassidy looked up and into the distance, rubbed his lip and said, "Okay, I think I've got a method in place. First, I need something sharp and smooth. Vala, do you have a scalpel?"

"Not here. I have some in my lab."

"I have one," Eric said. "I've used this one very little." He pulled a scalpel out of his pocket. It was in a leather sheath.

"Why do you have a scalpel?" Vala asked.

"I use it to carve. Sometimes it helps me think." He pulled out a half walnut shell that had Serein's profile etched into it.

"That's beautiful!" Char said.

"You're full of surprises, Eric," Vala said while turning and admiring the walnut.

After *ooohs* and *ahhhs* over the carving, Cassidy sterilized the scalpel then slipped it barely under the skin and removed the last

322

eighth inch of his spiral. "Okay, Char, I'm going to make a very tiny incision and slip this into it."

"What about infection? Or rejection? Or–" Vala started.

"Stop it!" Char said. "Go ahead, Cassidy."

Serein was pressing against Vala, and Eric reached out and patted her arm.

"Okay!" Cassidy said. "Now Char, hold hands with Vala, the right hand with the spiral. Eric, you hold Char's other hand, Tandra, hold Eric's hand. I'll hold Vala's other hand and Tandra's hand."

They all reached out and formed a small circle holding hands.

"I feel like a child about to play a game," Char said. "How do we know–oh! My!"

At first, Eric had no idea why Char had exclaimed. Nothing felt any different. He shut out external thoughts, including awareness of the range of emotions and thoughts around him, particularly Vala's tension. Then, surprisingly, he felt that tension release. Then Eric gradually became aware of deep currents of emotions for all of them as a whole, not individuals.

It was as though he had stepped into a pulsating egg-shaped space that was brilliant light and golden parallel lines while, at the same time, harmonic resonance vibrated, hummed, around them. Each end of the egg was an orange-yellow, but the center was intense, bright yellow. Within that field, were four tightly compacted– what?–entities?–packed with intense colors. Suddenly the colors shot through the yellow, then the orange, and he was surrounded in the egg of color that was flowing, circulating up, in, down and out, as though the two ends were poles.

He felt larger, more expansive, then realized the egg was like a magnet, bringing in another tightly compacted point. When it hit the center of the egg, it erupted, joining the energy flow in a flash of intense magenta and then, suddenly, it was all gone.

He was still standing in the same place. Wyatt was still seated on the chair looking skeptical. But Char was standing wide-eyed like a child who'd just seen a rainbow for the first time.

"What the hell was that?" she whispered.

Vala laughed. "I've never heard you swear before, Aunt Char. Are *you* all right?"

"I'm wonderful! I'm astounded! Look at my hand, Vala!" She held out a palm with a faintly glowing spiral. "We match!"

"The colors!" Eric said. "And shapes. What was that, Cassidy?"

Cassidy shook his head. "Didn't see any colors. Or shapes." He smiled. "Perhaps you were aware of our linking more as feeling. Did you see color, Vala?"

Vala shook her head. "More like geometric patterns, like things aligning when magnetic poles are set up."

Cassidy nodded. "Tandra?"

"Mmmmmm. Just...comfort...like dipping into hot springs at midnight when the stars are all singing."

"It's my turn," said Wyatt, standing.

Eric laughed. "First, let's see what happens when Char tries the portal."

Char glanced over in the area where people had been coming and going and gasped. "*That's* it?" she said. "That's been here all along, and I couldn't see it?"

Before anyone could say more, she dashed over and into the portal. Within seconds, she was back. "What freedom. Oh, thank you so very much. All of you." Tears were gathering in her eyes. "I'm very grateful you've included me."

"My turn!" Wyatt yelled.

For Eric, the experience with Wyatt was very like the first one but less startling. It went quickly. Just as it was subsiding, Wyatt screamed.

Eric sensed his deep pain immediately. "Where does it hurt?" he asked.

Wyatt was holding his forearm, shining with new blisters.

"It's his implant," Vala said. "We've got to get it out. The thing is burning out or something."

Eric whipped out his scalpel, deftly created an incision and popped out the implant. "Vala," he said, "get your first aid kit."

She looked at him surprised. "I don't have one."

"Yes, you do," Char said. She went upstairs, then returned with a small box. "I set it up when you moved in," she explained.

Eric found various items he needed and applied them, including a pain medication. "How's that?" he asked Wyatt.

Wyatt nodded. "Much better. Just an aching burn."

Cassidy looked horrified. "I'm sorry, Wyatt. It never occurred to me that we could have an issue with the other implant."

Wyatt shook his head. "It's not your fault, Cassidy. Now we do know. Unintended consequences: we all know about that." He grinned. "It's not bad, and I don't think it will even leave a scar."

The two of them went in and out of the portal a few times, laughing.

"Aunt Char," Vala called. "Wyatt! Could you come here a moment?"

When they came over, she continued, "I hate to spoil your fun, but Cassidy has pointed out to me that each time the portal is used, House power fluctuates. That could be monitored. I think we're going to have to use the portal sparingly."

"Do you realize what this means?" Wyatt said. "The portal can be easily adapted to work for humans. It could mean that the other side could become a point where we could all unite. If people see how the world can be, we could possibly achieve what we want–a cessation of the disastrous behavior that is causing Earth's issues. After all, this removes limitations on resources. People could earn portal rights, maybe to multiple worlds! Infinite worlds that–"

"Whoa!" said Vala. "We can't be indiscriminate about humans coming and going. That could destroy what the gentem are creating there. Politics. Business. Like the pilgrims going to the East Coast and killing off the natives. Name a country, Wyatt, that hasn't been wasted by the inclusion of big business raping the environment for resources."

"It's also," said Cassidy, "our escape hatch. We can't expose ourselves or the portal too soon, Wyatt. Let's see what's going to happen."

"Does this mean I can't move tonight?" Char asked.

"No," said Vala. "Go ahead. Do you want someone with you?"

"I'll go with her," Tandra said, "and help her get settled. We're going to make sure your cat can't get outside. We have a lot more predators than you're used to and, although some of them are willing to give domestic animals space, others aren't quite so obliging." Tandra grabbed the case and, without any more comment, they were gone.

Eric went back to the dining room table and glanced over the papers, which had all been input into the computer. "Vala," he called. He continued when she came over. "If I'm reading these papers correctly, almost all of these individuals don't want different options. They want out. They want to leave this side and shut down access so no more changes can occur over there. I find five notes from those who think we should try to establish open relationships with humans. All five say they're half human."

Vala nodded. "You're right. I noticed the emphasis as we input the data. Overwhelmingly, the answers indicate a strong desire to escape and make it permanent. They say they're living here in hiding, trying to pass as human. Many say they've been physically abused. And, of course, they have no civil rights because humans don't grant those to individuals who can't be classified."

"Humans just don't understand," said Wyatt. "The key is to make public the science that shows that the homo sapiens and homo Sophos are off the same evolutionary tree and that we can work together to make the planet whole and healthy again."

No one spoke. Eric could sense Wyatt's tension and frustration increasing. "Look, Wyatt, we just need to slow down–" Eric started.

"No! We need to hurry. Otherwise, information will leak out in bits and be misleading, even dangerous."

"Wyatt, we need to continue working on this as a group," Vala said.

"Sure, sure, after all I'm the only human here, so my ideas are inferior, right? You're no different in the desire to marginalize the minority."

Eric felt the emotional withdrawal from both Cassidy and Vala. "Wyatt!" Eric said sharply. "You're creating a rift here. Come on! Let's talk."

He took Wyatt into the other room, got him to sit down, and started trying to talk him down. Wyatt had his wall up, a wall built out of his conviction that he was right. This was probably similar to the Dunning-Kruger effect, illusive superiority, and that was a bitch to counter-act.

Eric lowered his voice and slowed his speech while trying to explain that no one was saying *no* but rather saying they had to take everyone's need into account. Nothing was final.

"Okay. You're right. Look, Eric, just let me be for a while, and I'll calm down. I was just excited by what has happened."

Eric shook his head. "Wyatt, you're saying what you think I want to hear. Stop. Think. You're a part of this entire process and have been from the beginning. You've met most of the primary players. No one has excluded you on any level, but we must have a sense of security. Remember, humans are not those who have been discriminated against by the gentem; it's the other way around."

"Well, what about all the marginalized humans out there?"

"Wyatt, those marginalized humans have been excluded by other humans, not gentem. And that only proves the point that this behavior seems to be a character trait of homo sapiens, eusocial... ethnocentric. The genetic inclination is there."

"That's another point, Eric. If the gentem are genetically different, this gives us a way to alter that aspect of human behavior. We need to make this public, open up the research, and..."

"And what, Wyatt? Achieve world peace? Is that what you're thinking? Don't you suppose that drive toward tribalism is intrinsically woven into the culture? Remember all those who have tried peaceful lives?"

Silence. Then Wyatt nodded slightly. "Just give me a few minutes, Eric."

Eric could tell that Wyatt was retreating deeper into himself. He was calmer and that was the best Eric could hope for. He went into the kitchen where Vala was talking on her phone. When she ended the conversation, she gave the phone a sharp slap and tossed it on the counter. "Here we go," she said. "That was the University President. He's been contacted by the Guardians about my *information* regarding the water testing with colleagues in different countries."

"What about it?" Eric asked.

"That was all he told me. Except he wants me at a meeting in the morning in his office to discuss the matter." She was drumming her fingers on the counter. Serein stood and whined.

Vala clucked her tongue and shrugged. "Of course, I don't *have* to go because I'm on sabbatical, but if I don't, problems could arise for the university as well as for me–for us. Damn guardians. If they call this terrorism, I could lose all my rights, even go to jail."

"Don't we want people to start engaging with these issues?" Cassidy asked.

"The problem is the Guardians. The organization was created to attack first, and they have no oversight. They regard everything as suspicious if it doesn't conform to their laws and restrictions. If they pick you up, all your individual rights go away. Any information they learn can be kept from the public. If that organization gains control of our information, of the portal, it all becomes the become property of the U.S. government."

"No one can own science!" Cassidy said.

Eric and Vala both sighed. "Slapping *Top Secret* on scientific discoveries is common and proves you wrong," she said.

"What will you do?" Cassidy asked Vala.

"I'll meet with the President at 8:00 a.m.," she said.

"I'll go with you," he said.

"Oh, no!" she said. "You can't go anywhere near the Guardians. You're illegally in this country–this *world*–with no identification."

"I have my birth certificate and old passport," he said.

"Really?" Eric and Vala asked at the same time.

"Of course," he said. "You keep forgetting that I lived on Alpha Earth throughout my early school years, including college. Of course, it wasn't in this country. And I was born in Ireland."

She laughed. "I keep forgetting because you look more my age. But I'm afraid a birth certificate from Ireland and an out of date passport from Australia will do you no good at all."

"How about me? Or Wyatt?" Eric asked.

"No, I need to go alone, Eric. Let's not draw any more attention to ourselves. Meanwhile, I'd like to talk to Wyatt and see if anything else has come up with the paper that he has out on DNA."

"Hey, Wyatt," Eric called, walking into the front room. "Wyatt?" he called again. He checked upstairs and then silently cursed himself for not being more alert.

He returned to the kitchen and shook his head at Vala and Cassidy. "He's gone."

CHAPTER TWENTY-FOUR

Vala felt almost dizzy at what appeared to be a breaking of trust. What was Wyatt thinking?

Eric had his hand on her forearm, and she looked down at him.

"Remember, Vala, your horror when you found out that the goal of some of the Council was genocide. That their only sure solution was to eliminate the problem by eliminating the source? Wyatt hasn't gotten beyond that. He's still thinking in terms of working this out with the humans, and I think he sees us right now as *other*."

"But that idea has been abandoned!" Vala suddenly put her hands over her ears. She didn't want to ask the next question, but she had no choice. "Eric, did you *know* this was happening?" Vala felt a fear that Eric was slipping away.

Eric shook his head. "No, Vala. I'm not defending Wyatt because I'm turning away from you. I knew he was struggling, but when I left him to think a bit ago, I thought he was just working through his feelings."

"But Eric, you and he have been friends for decades. We've included him in everything. Oh, *scheisse*! He can come and go at will through the portal now!"

"He can't take anyone else without help, Vala," Cassidy said.

"He knows how we gave an implant to him. That was a major mistake." Vala felt like screaming.

"We can find him. Stop him. He's probably gone to the lab," Eric said.

"Eric, you're closest to him. Concentrate on making a connection with him. House, computer," Vala said. When the screen was pulled up, she said, "Too bad we burned out his implant."

Using Eric's knowledge of Wyatt, combined with a little logic, they tracked Wyatt. "The U, of course," Vala said. "We'll have to go get him."

Eric left the room, his head bowed thoughtfully, and headed for the garden.

"We have to keep Eric in this," Vala told Cassidy. Could they lose Eric? Was he strong enough to handle this? If Eric and Wyatt couldn't cooperate, they needed to forget everything except escape. "Cassidy, you stay here and try to see what Wyatt is posting or who he's contacting." She went out to the garden and found Eric. "I'm sorry, Eric, truly, and I know you're hurting right now, but I need you to come with me. I think Wyatt needs that, too. I can't do this without you."

Eric nodded.

Serein jumped up and walked next to Vala to the garage, and the three of them clambered into Vala's pod.

As they sped to the university, a black car following them, Vala asked, "So what do you think he'll do, Eric?"

"My guess is that he'll get in touch with people about his DNA research, give more evidence, and suggest that this separate branch is significant and that it could be significant to human progress."

"In effect, he'll turn gentem over for research."

"Wyatt doesn't intend it in an intrusive way," Eric said. "He's thinking in terms of a blood sample, a cheek swab. He can't see beyond that to what other humans would do. Wyatt believes openness will bring about cooperation."

"What else?"

Eric shrugged. "I don't know if he'd tell anyone about the portal. After all, he has no proof of any of that. I just don't know. He's in an emotional condition I've never seen before. Keep in mind that his wife recently left him, too. He's feeling totally alone."

At the university, they went directly to Wyatt's lab. He was there, talking via GILS with three colleagues at once on projected screens. He was explaining the ramifications of different abilities of homo Sophos. When he heard Eric and Vala, he turned. "And here are those whose DNA samples you have. Come on in, Vala and Eric, and join the conversation. These are scientists who've read our paper and are very interested."

Eric winced at Wyatt's tone, reminiscent of a carnival booth operator.

Vala strode up to the center of the room, where she could be seen as well as heard, and smiled. "Good afternoon," she said. "I'm sure we'll meet more formally later on. As Dr. Roberts has explained, we've been looking into these DNA connections and that split off the timeline of evolution for homo sapiens. However, as he also knows, it's too early to publicize findings. It's been only a week since we first found this, and only one DNA test has been completed. No other tests have been made."

"Is that true, Dr. Roberts?" asked one of the scientists.

"Well, yes, but–" began Wyatt, but he was cut off by one of the other scientists.

"It's irresponsible to jump to such conclusions at this stage!" said one of the other scientists. "If you get significant data, let me know."

One by one, the projections shut off as scientists logged out of the conversation.

"What the hell do you think you're doing?" Wyatt screamed. "We don't have time for the usual time-consuming reports and publications and endless protocol. We've got to convince these people of the truth before it's too late!"

Eric put his hand up. "Wyatt, please listen. You're endangering lives here. We have to ease information out for people. The gentem trust us. We have to respect them. You *know* that."

"What else have you done?" Vala asked.

Just then, the lab door slammed open. Two men strode in and flashed badges too quickly to identify.

"I'm Agent Bradshaw and this is Agent Wilson. Which one of you posted information about alien DNA?" asked the taller of the two, Bradshaw. Although tall, he was still about two inches shorter than Vala although his shoulders were double the size of hers.

Aliens? Had Wyatt dipped into dark space? Vala wondered.

"I'm Dr. Roberts," Wyatt said. "I'm trying to get the word out that people need to stop damaging the environment immediately. If they don't, protestors are going to start poisoning water supplies."

Had they forgotten to tell Wyatt that the Council had scrapped any plans for the water contamination? Was Wyatt really turning them in as terrorists?

"How do you know this?" Agent Bradshaw asked. His voice, though low, seemed to fill the room with a low bass that lingered after he quit speaking.

"Well," Wyatt began and then stopped. He looked at Vala, then Eric. "Look, recent DNA evidence has come to light that indicates that another branch of humans, that is homo erectus, developed. Those individuals have differences. They live longer and they seem very sensitive to environmental conditions. Some of them are very tall and some tend to be short. They are determined that pollution be controlled. They're eco-terrorists."

"He thinks," said Eric, smiling, "that the world is being sabotaged by elves and dwarves, gentlemen. He thinks that Dr. Glen is an elf and that I'm a dwarf. Well, I *am* short." Eric pulled out a couple of his business cards and gave one to each.

Vala, speechless, felt as though she'd slipped into a bad movie. Eric looked composed, confidant.

Agent Wilson laughed, then stopped when Agent Bradshaw glared at him.

"This is a false call?" Bradshaw asked.

"No!" yelled Wyatt. "It's not that they're elves and dwarves. Well, sometimes they've been called that. But they wrote the folklore. Even for witches. They're just homo Sophos…" Wyatt eased into silence. Vala suspected he knew he wouldn't be able to get beyond that claim. Then he held his hand up, palm out. "Look!" he said. "This mark allows me to go through their portal–" He stopped again.

Vala felt like crying as she looked at Wyatt's face, slowly draining of color and animation. Eric's face darkened and his eyes looked flat, almost colorless.

"Can I see some ID from you two?" he asked.

Vala handed him her University identification, and Eric handed them his medical ID.

"No implant?" Bradshaw asked them both.

They both shook their heads. So far, it wasn't a law that all individuals utilize implants, but Vala suspected that would soon be changing. "I work with too many types of machinery in my research," Vala said. "An implant could interact with the various frequencies and cause distortions. I can't even carry an old cell phone into my lab," she lied.

"And many of my patients are leery of implant technology," Eric said. "I find it easier to talk with them if I don't have one myself."

"Is Dr. Roberts one of your patients?" Bradshaw asked.

"Only informally, Agent. We're friends."

"What the hell are you saying, Eric? How can you say these things about me? You *know* I'm telling the truth!" His face changed, and he held out his right arm. "Look, if you don't believe me! They hacked my implant out!"

Bradshaw looked at Eric. "What happened there?"

Vala shook her head, trying to think. "He had his arm in the electron-spectrometer when doing spatial saturation pulses—it shorted out his implant and caused a burn." She was hoping Bradshaw didn't know enough to question her story.

The agents nodded. "Sorry for the interruption," Bradshaw said. "Be careful about contacting us in the future." They turned and left without another word.

Eric shook his head. "They weren't saying everything. They know we were also connected with Tandra and Judith. They don't believe any of us."

Wyatt's facial muscles were rigid. He covered his face with his hands.

"I'm very sorry, Wyatt," Vala said. "What you were doing was betraying our trust in you. I know you're scared about what is happening, but this isn't the way to help. This is partly my fault. I forgot to tell you that the gentem Council has scrapped all plans to use chemical warfare. That's no longer a possibility."

"Really?" Wyatt asked, looking up at her.

"Yes. Really. Ask Cassidy. Now, will you go with Eric?"

Eric, resting a hand on Wyatt's shoulder, stood silently behind Wyatt's chair.

Wyatt shrugged. "Sure. Why not? I've been discredited in every way possible."

"Eric, take him to the house…maybe to Obeah. Wyatt, you need some rest. I'm going to stay at the University for a bit and see what's been posted where." She gave Eric her identity card for the pod. Just tell the pod to adjust your seat. I'll get a driverless later."

As soon as they'd left, Vala went to work trying to find everything Wyatt had just been posting. Hacking his system wasn't difficult with the information she had on him and her knowledge of University protocols. She quickly found out that her efforts to discredit Wyatt had been very successful. However, even some of his older work was being called into question. She deleted his new information and sent out a memo saying he was going on sick leave along with a note to the Department Dean saying he'd be in touch shortly to discuss a sabbatical. She hoped he would be able to recover his standing should he wish to continue at the University.

With that thought, Vala realized that she had no intentions of coming back. Then what? Was she making plans or just skimming the horizon of a black hole? What if they couldn't stop the Membrane decay?

As she started to look into some of her own material and responses from colleagues looking into the drinking water tests, she was distracted by recent news. The US had issued statements that they were ready to deploy nuclear weapons if any more were used by *anyone*. Contamination of water supplies was probably the least of this world's problems. The reference to weapons would, of course, be taken as a threat against Free Europe.

Vala shook her head. Vala couldn't think of a time in history when peace dominated the globe. Bombs had killed her mother. All Vala's work to figure out ways to clean up toxic waste and radioactive materials seemed futile. She'd never be able to keep up.

A part of her wanted to put her head down and cry. Instead, she went back to reading responses, but was interrupted by a voice. "Cassidy?" she said and turned around.

No one.

Vala!

The voice was in her head! *What the hell?*

I did it! I've figured out the connections for us to communicate by tying into our links. We should all be able to do this, at least with the obelisk operating. With a little training, all four of us can do this. It's like your global network. But smaller.

Vala laughed. *Much smaller. Have Eric and Wyatt arrived?*

Yes. They went to see Obeah. I went along. Obeah gave Wyatt something to help him sleep, then we'll all try to talk to him.

Okay. I have just a little more to do here, then I'll be back at House.

No goodbyes, no closure. He was just gone. That will take some getting used to, she thought.

As it turned out, every scientist had found increased levels of ephedrine but not in great quantities. Alarick had been very thorough, but he'd not saturated waterways. Most of the scientists had alerted authorities to possible terrorism. Oops. Had she opened the same door to chaos that she had just closed with Wyatt? She posted some random questions about naturally-occurring ephedra to try to ward off the terrorism angle. Worried and uncertain about her next step, she shut things down, locked up, and called a driverless to go home. Serein was restless. They hadn't been running much and he sensed her discomfort, especially when, as she entered the driverless, she spotted the black car. It followed her home.

Eric arrived back at the house at the same time that Vala did. She'd never seen him seem dark, the light in his eyes gone and his cheeks sunken. "Wyatt?" Vala asked.

"He's dropped. I didn't expect him to wig out, Vala. Obeah says he'll sleep now, and maybe all tomorrow." Eric shrugged. "'Tis what 'tis."

"Well, he may have done nothing that we didn't inadvertently do ourselves. All those scientists I contacted found increased ephedrine levels and each reported possible terrorism to authorities who, in turn, notified their agencies for investigating terrorism."

"Do you think that's why they want to see you tomorrow morning?" Eric asked.

"I'm almost certain of it."

"Vala, don't go."

She laughed. "What alternative do I have?"

"Let's just all go through the portal and end this. Everywhere we turn, we run into suspicion and fear. It's not safe for you to go there."

"Eric, you're allowing your emotions to block your good sense. We have to follow this road. If I don't go, everything could be shut down. What about all those gentem we've contacted? They want out, Eric, not abandoned. We can't do to them what was done to us."

Eric sat down on a garden swing even though it was wet from the light rain. "Sometimes I wish I didn't know about any of this. Except for finding you, this is an opioid nightmare."

Vala sat down next to him and Serein sat in from of him and offered a paw. "Our lives have changed, that's true. But I'm glad I met my little brother."

Eric smiled suddenly. "Yeah. Well, it's not all bad, is it?"

Vala rested her hand on his arm. "Do you know where the others are?"

"Well, Wyatt's asleep. Tandra is talking with the Council. Probably about Wyatt. Char is settling in and spatter-chatting nonstop. Cassidy is ... actually, I have no idea where Cassidy is."

"Maybe he's resting. I think we all could use some rest. Maybe some food. House, we need stew."

She heard beeping in the kitchen. "Let's eat and rest. Morning is going to come early."

Morning came even earlier than Vala had expected. Cassidy and Tandra showed up at one a.m.

"Sorry to wake you, Vala. The Council had a long meeting; we've just come from there."

"You both must be exhausted. Do you need sleep?"

"No," Tandra said. "We must talk."

Vala didn't like the sound of that. "Well, then, frobotein?"

Cassidy's nose wrinkled. "Just green tea, please."

Tandra and Vala had House make frobotein and Cassidy sipped his green tea as they sat in the kitchen out of the drizzle.

"So, flare."

"What?" Tandra said.

"Tell me the bad news," Vala explained. She would have to purge her language of slang.

Cassidy set down his tea. "It's about that recent nuclear explosion test in the Sea of Japan; it sent a wave of radioactive particles through to Beta Earth. Gentem have evacuated to at least 100 miles, but the animals, of course, are in serious jeopardy. As are various plants. The Council is desperate. Some of them even brought up the idea of just rejoining Alpha Earth and doing massive protests and urgent demands. The frustration level is immense. No one knows what to do."

"They gave us time!" Vala protested.

"Now we've got two days. They feel the crisis has arrived."

"That plan to stage such protests is suicide," Eric said from the doorway where he stood looking as though the crawl from sleep had been difficult.

Vala stood and paced. "I've got a meeting this morning that I think is related to ephedra in the water, so people are already alerted to that, Tandra. However, if the Council members try a direct appeal and are identified with what could be perceived as terrorism, or even as aliens, they'll be wiped out. They don't have papers, and they're not up to speed on this culture. Please try to get the Council to give us just a little longer. And if they insist, a better approach may be to send a diplomatic group to the UN Security Council, UNESCO, the International Atomic Energy Agency, and The Preparatory Commission for the Comprehensive Nuclear-Test-Ban Treaty Organization."

Vala stopped pacing and looked directly at Tandra. "Make them understand that any kind of protest event in one country, especially the United States where it's illegal anyway, isn't going to get much attention. If they decide to do that, we'll have to go global in one day."

"We need to mobilize the gentem on this side," Eric said. "They don't want reintegration. They all want to leave here and go over there. The best thing any of them say about life here is that it's tolerable. That's not just in the U.S.; it's global. We've had responses online from every country."

"But what good will that *do*?" Tandra said. "We'll be right back where we were before Eric and Vala created the portal. We'll just have more of a mess if, after a huge migration, we try to merge the cultures. We don't know *how* to make the Membrane work!"

"Wait!" Vala said. She was feeling her way into a new way of thinking. "I think maybe our perspective could use a slight shift. We've been trying to figure out what's wrong with the Membrane. Maybe we need to think about why it's working; if we could seal it, make the split permanent with everyone on the side of choice, then we wouldn't have to worry about Alpha Earth. It has to do with Marina's *expectations*. Remember what she said, Cassidy?"

"What she said? Beyond the concept?"

"Yes. Cassidy, we need to go see Marina."

"Let's go," said Eric and Tandra in tandem.

They found Marina in her lab surrounded by her work, illuminated on walls, counters, and in the air. "You know," she started as they entered, "we could make teleportation simpler if we established linking spots, plasma enhancers, for individuals in strategic places around the globe. Although we're still in a position of having to manipulate about 4.5×10^{42} bits, that wouldn't be as much of a problem if we had more links and maybe more of the plasma generators set up."

"Simpler?" said Vala, stopped in her thinking about their primary problem by that idea.

"Yes. It's fairly simple between my lab and Cassidy's lab, for instance, but that's movement from inside one quantum computer to another. Those are more complex to set up than the links and obelisk used for you four. Improving our understanding of teleportation would be one more way to avoid travel time and pollution."

Cassidy rubbed his lower lip with his thumb. "That should work. Judging by what I see here, you—"

"Not now, Cassidy," Vala said, shaking herself out of the impending immersion into teleportation issues. "Marina, do you remember what you told me about your expectations for the Membrane when you implemented the science for its construction?"

Marina nodded, but her eyes were unfocused and she was chewing the inside of her cheek.

Vala knew the signs of a preoccupied scientist, but she persisted. "Will you look over the science with me now?"

"Is this something that's immediately useful?" Marina asked while looking longingly at the work she had spread out.

Vala nodded and Cassidy shrugged.

Marina had the material available on her computer, so, within her heavy sighs, they pulled it up. Vala skimmed through the material, then said, "Here! Look at this transition in the power sequence to initialize the creation of the Membrane!"

Marina obediently looked. "Yes, what about it? That allows the portal to be created. It's also an allowance for the entanglement within the photons included in the spirals—wait! Vala, that's it! The reason for the leaks, isn't it?"

Vala nodded. "I think so. You've created a two-faced membrane, one that is allowing the natural inclination for balance between the two sides."

Cassidy pushed closer to the computer image. "What? Where?"

Vala pointed and said, "The Membrane was designed and constructed to fail, to allow for passage through it, Cassidy. That was its purpose, so you could someday reestablish contact. You were trying to hang on instead of letting go! The obelisk, which you think of as only boosting communication for linked individuals, also enhances the built-in failure."

Cassidy frowned, drew back, rubbed his lip. "So looking for why it wasn't working was taking us in the wrong direction? Yes! Why did we not see this?"

"Because of our expectations, Cassidy," Marina said. "We worked not on what the science required but rather what we wanted—possible reconciliation—and that's what we got. We didn't think about the fact that the structure would be weakened by trying to hold it in an incomplete phase."

Cassidy shook his head but said nothing; he stared upward and rubbed his lip—he was going over the science in his head.

"I don't get it," Eric said. "What does that tell you?"

Cassidy jumped up and started pointing at various points in the data. "We designed the Membrane to have leaks for communication.

It's not failing; it's working just the way we wanted. It's like building a dam with thin plates in it that will sooner or later leak to release pressure. We built in design failure."

"If we seal those points, we have no more leakage?" Tandra asked.

Vala and Cassidy both nodded, but then she shook her head. Then she sat down abruptly. "It's a little more complicated than that—in effect, the entire concept will be fortified. But it means a complete and final break. It means eliminating any future communication or movement between Alpha Earth and Beta Earth. The two places will truly be separate worlds."

"It means abandoning Earth," Eric said.

Cassidy shrugged. "In a sense, this is the new vision we were hoping you'd provide, Vala, but it's extreme."

"No," said Tandra. "It means saving our Earth and leaving the other side to the humans to manage. Or not. But isn't it still one Earth, Vala? I mean, it's just a copy, right?"

Vala sighed. "Yes—and no. Remember what Cassidy said? Once they're no longer linked, it's like taking a picture of something and then taking the picture far away. The picture represents the original, but things can happen to the picture or to the original with no effect on the other. They become parallel. They'll develop their own histories. In a hundred years, the two could be radically different. I think. Some scientists argue that parallel universes do affect one another. Cassidy?"

He shrugged, lifted one eyebrow. "We're in new territory. I suppose the idea of somehow keeping both was naïve. Like being sort of pregnant. With a total split…"

As his voice faded, Vala remained silent. The solution was elegant and simple, but it was the polar opposite of what she'd hoped to do. It was saving Earth, at least this one, but not in the sense she and Eric had expected. Expectations. Letting go. "Since this all started, *letting go* has been part of the lesson—for all of us. In letting go, we often find we have a clearer journey."

"What?" Eric said.

"That's what my grandmother said when I went to visit her. We all have to learn to let go. Did you see how Aunt Char left everything except her cat?"

"If only we'd known," said Marina.

"We did what we could," Tandra said, "but we allowed our hopes that humans would change to set us up for failure. Vala, the humans *did* know, too, about what they were doing to Earth. You've read history."

Tandra was right. Humans knew the science about how they were mistreating their environment, but they were always convinced Earth was too big to be destroyed and that somehow, at the eleventh hour, technology would waltz in with solutions. And gentem knew, with long experience, that they weren't going to adapt to human culture or environmental destruction. But no one wanted to change worlds, to let go of what was considered home. That choice had faced every person who had ever emigrated.

"It's not a clear fix," Vala said. "We're still doing something that, to my knowledge, has never been done."

Cassidy nodded. "And it will be permanent...probably."

Vala nodded. "The fix could fail. It could destroy the Membrane and, maybe, everyone on one side or the other of it. Or both sides. "We could create the biggest bomb of all: colliding worlds. But considering where we are at this moment, and how things have been working, I don't think that will happen."

"On the other hand, every time we make a choice, we're creating a parallel path for what a different choice would represent," Marina said. "This is very like the debate we had thirty years ago." She sat on a stool. "You remember, Cassidy? That huge question of *what if* plagues the choice. Perhaps the best answer is to eliminate the worst case. If we can do that, whatever ensues is bound to be better. No?"

"Maybe. But this is a huge group decision, and it's changing both places in huge ways," Vala said. "We can't foresee the effects."

Cassidy sat near Marina. "As Marina says, we can't eliminate unintended consequences. But we can avoid the pitfalls of poorly thought out intended consequences. The effect of a mass emigration will be significant in the human culture," Cassidy said. "They'll lose many of their strongest environmental and peace advocates. The lack of balance could spin their culture off into worse situations."

"Yet those groups aren't having the effect they'd like," Vala said. "I know because I've been a part of that. Of course, the effect may be greater than we know simply because we don't know what it would be like without that influence."

"Individuals have often fled in large groups when they've been discriminated against or been systematically destroyed," Tandra said. "The mainstream culture went on."

"They weren't, of course, just gone. They could continue being an influence from another place," Vala said.

"Choice," Eric said, "is a huge responsibility. I'm reminded of Robert Frost's poem, 'The Road Not Taken,' which ends with

Two roads diverged in a wood, and I—
I took the one less traveled by,
And that has made all the difference.

"Well, that's the crux, isn't it," Vala said. "We don't know what that *difference* will be."

"We'll do what we should have done the first time," Marina said, her voice strong. "We'll include those on Alpha Earth who want to join us."

"I agree," Cassidy said.

"It's the best solution, I think," said Eric.

"Great! I'm going to go tell the Council what we're planning," said Tandra. "I'll let you know what they say, but I think I know. We'll do a poll of those living on this side of the Wall. You've done that poll on the other side, right?"

Eric nodded. "The results indicated almost unanimously that gentem want to emigrate."

"Okay," said Tandra. "I'll tell you when the Council will meet, Marina."

Their clarity and enthusiasm strengthened Vala's resolve. "Eric, alert the gentem on the other side. We'll need to act quickly because we've caught the attention of the Guardians—and others, undoubtedly. Get the word out, surreptitiously, that everyone who wants to go to the other side must be ready in 24 hours, say midnight Wednesday. They can take only what they can carry. The most important thing to have is books or downloads of books and research. How are we going to get them through the Membrane? And the animals? We have to bring as many as possible."

"You're going to have to somehow key them into portals," Marina said. "It's going to be a huge task. And risk. The Membrane could fail with that many portals open."

Cassidy was pacing. "Well, part of this fix will require going back to that initial point where the portal and links were established. At that point, animals and gentem were able to enter. Maybe they can again?" Cassidy paused, then he said. "I have to run."

Vala nodded and with Serein they were out the door of Marina's lab and off on the trails leading west toward Port Angeles. Without speaking, they ran the round trip of thirty miles in one hour. Vala's thoughts were running with her, trying to think of ways to move thousands–millions?–of biological creatures, gentem and animal alike, into another world.

When they plunged back through the portal, they looked at each other and immediately went into the dining room to try to formulate their ideas.

"Look," said Vala, "it's impossible to bring gentem or animals from all over the world to this portal. We've got to set up a way for us to tag them and open temporary portals without crashing the entire Membrane. Leaks all over?"

"That'll take too long," Cassidy said, shaking his head. "We can't do it individually, keying a portal to an individual. We'd be frenzied trying to keep everything intact. Individuals have to be able to simply see the membrane and walk through it–leak through it–on their own as happened on the day it was first created. Same with animals. We'll have to make the Membrane fluid for everyone we want to allow in."

"DNA!" Vala said.

"Of course," Cassidy said. "That's what we did before. We'll use your global net to create a net capture of the Uzgenia-Krygyzstian DNA Wyatt identified. Then we can identify all other DNA–"

"Egads, Cassidy, you're talking about creating a positive connection. Why not just filter *out* what we don't want? Make the Membrane fluid again to everything *except* Neanderthal DNA?"

Cassidy grinned. "That simplifies it, doesn't it? What about humans without Neanderthal DNA? They'll be able to see the Membrane."

With that thought in mind, they did a search to try to figure out what percentage of the population that would include. At that point, Eric walked in. "I've notified gentem through the site that this is going to happen. I've put some details in as a suppositional idea for a game...questions are flying."

"Okay, Eric, we'll need to have you continue fielding that arena. We're going to have more details shortly," Vala said. "We're going to try to make the Membrane visible to everything that lacks Neanderthal DNA, so individuals, including animals, should be able to pass through wherever they are. They'll have to be careful. In some cases, for instance, their homes on Beta Earth may have collapsed. They will be better off to go to a place that has always been open and on high ground. Avoid fire areas."

"Some humans, most likely of African descent, may not have the Neanderthal gene," Eric said. "Most humans will, however, even if it's minute."

"Even minute should exclude them. Tell the gentem that they need to encourage animals to step through as well. Any who communicate with animals should do so."

"Also," Cassidy added, "will you get word to Tandra and Marina that we'll need gentem to be alert to any humans who happen to come through. They'll need to know what is happening and that they have only a short time to decide to go or to stay. Also, if gentem have connections to humans who want to come through, they'll have to surround them and walk them through. Or carry them."

"Oh," Vala added, "tell everyone that their implants must be removed, just in case. I don't know if it will be an issue since it's not a link, but we don't want people injured."

"What about those who don't want to emigrate?" Eric asked.

"They just don't go through. But when we disconnect, access will be gone," Cassidy said, then added, "forever."

Vala thought about that forever. She'd never have a chance to change things with her adopted family. She'd be done with her career. Nothing would ever be the same.

Eric turned to leave.

"Eric!" Vala said. "Make sure they're clear on the *forever*. Their lives will never be the same. They can't come back."

Eric nodded.

"And also…"

Eric waited patiently.

"Let them know," Vala said slowly and deliberately, "that this could all go horribly wrong. They should be prepared."

Eric nodded then said, "Vala, I heard from Steve today. Some Guardians stopped by his office and asked why he'd been looking into your past. He told them that he had a client who thought that he could be related to you. He had to give them my name. He was warned to stay away from us. Vala, I'm very sorry I started all that."

She reached over and rubbed the top of his head. "Hey, kid, if you hadn't, none of this would have a resolution. You did good. Just tell Steve to back away and protect himself."

"I already did." Eric nodded soberly and left without complaining about the head rub.

Vala wanted to grab Eric, tell him it was okay. He was losing one life, but they'd make another. They had to make this work. They *must*, Vala thought, make this as precise as they could. "We're going to be playing with huge forces, Cassidy, both natural and political. I'm hoping it will work, but I'm not sure. Are you?"

He shrugged. "Let's keep working and see what we've got."

For the next five hours, they worked. Tandra came in at one point and said that all gentem on Beta Earth had been alerted and expressed support for the permanent split. Eric had also gotten the message to her and she'd spread the word that gentem should be prepared for implant problems and the arrival of some confused humans.

Finally, as both Vala and Cassidy finished visualizing the end result they expected and making sure they were both comfortable with the complexity and logic behind their work, they looked at each other and smiled. This was it. They had the full plan for closing the portal and sealing the Membrane. They also had confirmation that those they'd need to help were ready. Cassidy was ecstatic, literally quivering with renewed energy.

"Well, you're going to have to work on details while I go to my meeting at the University," Vala said.

"Why go?" Cassidy asked. "If this all works, you won't be going back to work there."

"I've got to try to ward off the Guardians. They're still watching the house. And it sounds as if they're investigating me. If I don't cooperate, we'll have them in here before we can put our plan into action. It's all a chess game, and it's my move."

Tensions were high when Vala left for the Wednesday morning meeting. Eric asked her again not to go. "I have a bad feeling about this."

"It's just like playing chess, Eric. Or Kriegspiel." She smiled. "I'll be fine." She noted Eric's expression; he knew she was worried.

Vala expected that Cassidy would quickly become absorbed in double-checking their work. She'd suggested he involve Eric, keep him busy. She even, reluctantly, left Serein with orders to obey Cassidy, then took a driverless.

She skipped going to her lab but went, instead, directly to the President's office. Because of the many government grants she'd received, she knew the President and his office well. He'd always been very supportive, but Vala knew that support could fade quickly if the Guardians put pressure on the University. Money and power were synonymous.

The door opened automatically for her, so she'd already been recognized and announced. When she stepped through the inner door, she stopped abruptly. In addition to President Musa Kamau, she was faced with Daman Devi, the Dean of Sciences, which, these days, had a huge and secret department as well as the usual departments, and five other people, two of which were the agents she'd met with Wyatt the day before. Agent Bradshaw looked smug. Everyone looked formal in their suits and shiny shoes. Vala wore her usual running attire.

She nodded and strode forward to stand across the desk from the President. She worked at presenting a confidence she didn't feel. "Good to see you, Musa. Although a surprise, especially since I'm on sabbatical. What's this about?"

"Thank you for coming," Kamau said. "Won't you please have a seat," he said, gesturing at a chair where one of the women, who was probably another agent, sat.

Her lips pursed and then slid to the left. If she was as irritated as she looked, she kept it to herself. She stood and walked stiffly over to the windows and stood with her back to the room, a silhouette against the distant Mount Rainier.

Vala said, "Thank you," to no one in particular and sat down, leaning back and crossing her legs casually.

"Vala, I know you're always busy," President Kamau began, "so I'll get right to the marrow. Apparently, you contacted a number of scientists in various countries and asked them to check water sources. They found chemical contamination, which most of them quickly reported to the authorities. These people," he gestured around the room, "represent the Freedom Guard. Their primary concern, of course, is where this substance came from and how you knew about it and why you didn't report it."

"Well, in reverse order, I didn't report it because I didn't know if there was contamination. That's why I asked. Scientists," she said, looking at Bradshaw, "confirm facts rather than spread rumors."

She looked back at Kamau. "As I'm sure you know, plant growth has modified over the past few decades in response to changing climate and other factors whether people—or governments—believe it or not. One of consequences is that we need to watch for contamination from previously unlikely sources. I found traces of ephedrine in some water samples I recently tested. That's never happened before. In larger amounts, this could be a serious problem. I wanted to find out if anyone else had found ephedrine and if they, as do I, suspect that the source is a result of increased ephedra growth. I haven't even learned yet if that's possible. However, another possibility is that some people are using it illegally, and that could be a source." She paused, uncrossed and re-crossed her legs.

No one said anything, so she continued. "In short, I don't know where this contamination came from, I don't know how wide spread it is, and I don't know how much of it is out there. So I asked."

She looked back at Bradshaw. "I should think all that is open and clear, Agent Bradshaw. So what is the purpose of this meeting? Surely you don't want me to report to tell you what I *don't* know."

"You know each other?" asked a gray-haired and dark skinned gentleman who had been sitting quietly on a couch near the door. Vala rarely met anyone who made her feel petite. He had to be at least seven feet and 250 pounds. Judging by Bradshaw's sudden stiffening, Vala suspected this quiet giant was the senior of those present.

Vala nodded before Bradshaw could speak. "We met yesterday, when a colleague of ours had a melt-down. Remember, Masu?" she said turning back to Kamau. "I linked you about the events with Dr. Wyatt Roberts."

Kamau winced. Vala knew he didn't always read his links. "Of course. Certainly. Wyatt is a good scientist, but he overworks."

"I'm Lead Agent for this particular investigation," said the gray-haired man quietly. "Shaun Patrick. The reason we're all here is that this sudden increase in chemicals in drinking sources in such diverse areas is highly suspicious. We need to consider terrorism."

"But," Vala said, turning to look at Patrick, "doesn't terrorism focus attacks? If this is global, isn't it more likely to be something more general, maybe random? And I understand the amounts are small. Certainly, you can consider terrorism, but I'd have to wonder what target you'd think terrorists would have."

The man shrugged. "That's what we're investigating." He stood. "Thank you for your time and openness. In the future, please inform our department of any discoveries of this sort."

He seemed friendly and relaxed, but Vala braced herself. He was after something else.

"Also," Patrick continued, "we're interested in a couple other things that have come up. They seem to connect back to you."

"What are they?" Vala asked. "I'll be happy to help if I can."

"You suddenly went on sabbatical. Why? And, if you're on sabbatical, why are you still working?"

Vala laughed. "I took sabbatical because I have a number of personal interests right now that I want to research and evaluate. Since they're not directly related to the work I've been doing with grants, I wanted to do them on my own time. I can't imagine *not* working, Agent Patrick. Can you?"

He smiled, his brilliant white teeth not at all sharp. He could be someone's grandfather. His attitude had probably been carefully shaped and polished over decades. "Also, we've detected power fluctuations at your box. Any explanation?"

Vala shrugged. "I've been utilizing a lot of computer and House equipment since I've been on sabbatical. I suppose that could be it. Since I've not seen your documentation, I can't be more specific. If you'd like to give it to me, I'd be happy to research it. I'd also like to know *why* you're monitoring my electrical use."

Patrick smiled again but said nothing.

"What about that gathering you had here at the university the other night with that bunch of crazies?" Bradshaw said abruptly.

"*That's* where I'd seen you before," said Vala. "I thought I recognized you when we met yesterday. Why were you there?"

Patrick had given Bradshaw a dirty look and spoke in his place. "He was there because the conversation about *creating a perfect world* and other similar phrases had triggered our system. Since that has come up, what was that about?"

"One of my personal interests is determining how people perceive our world and what they would change if they could create something different. As you may know, many scientists think humans are bent on destroying the environment. Is it self-destruction? Is it stupidity?" Vala paused and looked directly at Patrick as though expecting an answer.

After a few moments of silence, she smiled. "Tough questions, aren't they? So the people in that group don't trust technology, don't trust government agencies. I'm wondering why. How are they falling through the cracks? What possible contributions could they be making to improve our culture and societies in general? I'm working with a friend, Dr. Eric Kine, who is a psychiatrist, on that project. We're creating an online game that would involve these people. I told you that my interests weren't correlated with my grant projects. Anything else?" As she spoke, she was grateful for the script she'd practiced in her head. She wasn't lying. Not really. She stood without waiting for a response.

"As a matter of fact," said Patrick as he sat down again, "I was wondering if it's true you've considered emigration to Mexico."

The only way he could know about that is if they'd investigated all her old GILS searches and emails or had been eavesdropping on House for longer than she'd realized. There was no point in lying. "I've considered it. I find the scientific restrictions here difficult. Scientists need to be able to communicate, share information freely."

"I'd drop that idea for now," said Patrick. "With your background, emigration could present a security risk. Maybe in the future. I think that covers it," Patrick said to Kamau.

Vala said, "Okay. I think I'll go to my lab, gather some material, and then go home."

"That won't be possible," said Patrick.

Vala walked over and stood directly in front of Patrick. She took advantage of the opportunity to look down at him as he slowly stood. "Going to my lab? Or going home?" She asked quietly.

He just smiled, now looking down slightly at her. "Going to your lab, I'm afraid. We have people there."

"People there? In my lab?" She turned and looked at Kamau. He seemed smaller than usual.

"I saw no harm since you're on sabbatical," Kamau said. "And they have the authority, you know."

Vala shrugged. Her mind was racing about what she may have on her server, but she knew she didn't dare give her nervousness away. "Fine," she said. "So later on, if I need some of my notes, do you have a problem with my linking?"

"No, not at all," said Patrick, although Vala had been looking at Kamau.

"Thank you," she said to no one as she turned and walked to the door. She felt a wave of relief as it opened, then she heard Patrick again.

"By the way, Professor Glen, you bailed out two people recently and got their charges dropped. Those people had no identification, and they haven't been seen since. Do you know where they are?"

Vala inhaled deeply and turned slowly around. "No, Agent Patrick, I do not. They are members of that group of *crazies,* as Agent Bradshaw calls them, but they are more extreme. They were traveling, but you won't find them linked to much of anything. They do *not* trust the complexities of Freedom Guard roles and powers in average people's lives–you know, to do things such as keep them out of their own work areas." She gave him her best smile.

He nodded. "That's all right. We'll find them. What about this Eric Kine? He's another one that seems to prefer not being linked, and he's been spending a great deal of time at your box. Are you two twined?"

"Eric explained to Agent Bradshaw yesterday why he doesn't have an implant. I don't know how his box is set up. As to our relationship, it's none of your business, but I did tell you a bit ago that he is a friend. Also, House is my personal and *private* property, not a government box." Vala turned and left. She desperately wanted to run home, but the last thing she needed was to be followed while running at thirty miles an hour. She called a driverless.

Back at House, Serein plastered himself next to Vala as he sensed her tension. Eric gave a half-hearted wave and "Hi" from where he sat in the kitchen working in the gentem chat room. In the living room, Vala found that Cassidy had explored, after a battle with House, on the computer, gathering information about current human science, particularly in relationship to quantum field theory. His lower lip glowed red, almost blistered from his reflex action of rubbing his lip with his thumb. When Vala was able to get his attention, he was shaking his head at her.

"Vala, not only is there nothing on unifying quantum field theory for LifeForce or anything like it, human scientists *can't* seem to even see the concept when I provide equations such as those we looked at in Marina's lab."

Vala's scalp prickled. "How do you know, Cassidy?"

"I've been contacting them and discussing the idea of an imperative to create life. I've presented clear data. They can't—"

"You've been contacting them? Who? Where?"

"All over, mostly Europe, but my point—"

"Cassidy, you can't *do* that. I'm not allowed to talk with other scientists without going through an approved channel. *Why* are you doing that?"

Eric walked in. "Problem?"

Cassidy frowned. "Damn! I remember you saying that before. It slipped my mind. I was just looking for current information to take back with me to Beta Earth, and I entered a discussion forum. Vala they were *ignoring* any possibility of the unifying field, the very thing that affects how all quantum fields work together. Without perceiving that, we couldn't have Beta Earth, we couldn't function with, well, *everything!* I'm beginning to think that even our ability to run fast may have more to do with creating localized shifts in the zero-point energies of various quantum fields than with our physical development."

She was shaking her head. "Human scientists just haven't progressed that far–"

"No, Vala. Think! When you saw the equations, you understood, no?"

Vala nodded.

"These scientists didn't. It was as if they couldn't even *see* the equation. The concept itself is beyond their ken. I think this may explain part of the huge gap between the gentem and human approaches to life."

"I don't understand your equations, or most of what you're talking about either, Cassidy," Eric said. "So how come I can utilize this force?"

"Because you can *feel* it, Eric. You just *know.* But these are scientists that–"

"Opening gate," House said.

"That's new. House is set to warn. Let me check that."

Agents were coming through the gate toward the front door. One was Agent Bradshaw. Vala opened the door. "This is an unwelcome surprise," she said.

"Somebody here has been using your computer while you were at our meeting to interact with foreign agents."

"They weren't *agents,* Agent Bradshaw, they were scientists. My friend was doing research for details for our game, and he didn't realize accessing scientific chatrooms was a no-no. I've told him."

"We need to talk to him," said Bradshaw, trying to push past her. The block he was hitting was Serein. "I'd hate to see your dog get hurt, Lady."

Vala backed up and waved Serein over. "There's no one here except my friend Eric," she said loudly.

Eric came walking into the hallway. "You call me?" he asked, smiling.

"You were accessing foreign scientific chatrooms?" Agent Bradshaw asked.

Eric nodded. "Vala says I shouldn't have. I didn't realize it. I'm trying to understand quantum stuff to help work with our game. I thought maybe I could get help. What I was trying to suggest to them didn't seem to make sense. We'll have to come up with something else, Vala," Eric said, shrugging convincingly.

"Search," Bradshaw said to the other two agents.

"I'm going to file a formal complaint," Vala said.

"You'll find the forms to do so on our Web page," said Bradshaw as he smiled.

Vala didn't bother to follow the agents as they prowled her house, which was scantily furnished at best, so the search didn't take long. She and Bradshaw locked eye contact and neither spoke or shifted their stance. After a short time, the agents came back, shaking their heads.

"Make sure that this doesn't happen again," Bradshaw said.

"Well, he was disappointed," Eric said as Vala slammed the door. "He wanted to drag you out in restraints, I believe."

Vala took a deep breath. "Where the hell is Cassidy?"

"I was on the roof," Cassidy said as he came toward them. "I couldn't get to the portal; they were watching. The roof was easy to access from the bedroom window. Vala, I'm really sorry. I got caught up–"

"It's okay, Cassidy. I'm screwed anyway. If I were planning on staying here, I'd probably be headed for confinement. The government figures they own me. They're playing the game faster now."

"We're going to have to speed up our timeline, too," Eric said. "Those guys have your scent, and they're not going to make their next move. They're going to set up heat sensors to detect people."

"There's not much we can do to speed this up," Cassidy said. "We've got too many individuals involved."

"I get the sense that both of you have reservations about this working. Is that right?" Eric asked.

Vala shrugged. "I'm in new waters here, Eric. I don't know how deep, how fast, or how cold they are. Diving in seems the only way to find out."

Cassidy nodded. "Eric, we know the science works. It worked last time. We've identified the likely reasons, flaws, that have caused issues. The only thing that worries me is getting everyone to cross over in the right time frame so that people aren't separated, left behind, or transported to Beta Earth without even realizing it."

"Well, I've spread the word as much as possible. Individuals are making sure all those who should know do know. I've also told them to watch for those who may cross unintentionally and don't want to remain on Beta Earth. Everyone is anxious that individuals be where they want to be, so they'll be helping each other."

Eric gave them a weak smile. "I'll get back to it." He left.

"At least the basics of both places are the same. I mean, it's the same Earth," Vala said.

"But with decades of differences," Cassidy said. "Keep in mind that Alpha and Beta have both been undergoing changes. They aren't mirror images anymore. That's what makes collision frightening."

"Well, the mood here is gloomy," Tandra said, coming into the room. "This is almost as buoyant as being with the Council."

"Hi, Tandra," Cassidy said. Then he explained to her his recent discovery about human's total inability to create localized shifts in the zero-point energies of quantum fields.

Tandra shook her head. "What?"

"That's what you do when, for instance, you spark flames around your finger tips or even when you're healing someone with Reiki. I think it's instinctual to work within LifeForce."

"I'm aware of the presence, almost a vibration, and ... Cassidy, I'm not a scientist. Do humans analyze how they talk or think or digest food? What we do is an automatic process."

"We need to study this," Cassidy said. "How about if we–"

"Not *now*, Cassidy!" Vala said, raising her hand in a stop gesture. She understood how he'd become wrapped up in the topic and splattered on GILS. "Whatever fields or dimensions or forces or magic we're working with, the Guardians are working out of a perspective immersed in paranoia, suspicion, and intimidation. And if what you're saying is true, I can understand why humans would fear us. So how are things with the Council, Tandra?"

"They're nervous. Marina grasps what you're talking about and the others are nervously agreeing. Most wish humans didn't exist, but they do. The biggest worry is that somehow this world will vanish, that we'll be back where we were in human society again, trying to hide our abilities and culture."

Eric returned, looked around with his eyes narrowed as though he were in pain.

"Eric, you look awful!" Tandra said. "What happened?"

"Thanks, Tandra. You never fail to say what you think." Eric shook his head. "Just having trouble over the situation with Wyatt. But the gentem are ready. I've set the time for midnight, midway between dusk and dawn. That's only seven and a half hours from now, so whatever we need to do before then, we'd better start."

"We'll need all our data we've accumulated, so we need to move it to Beta Earth. Let's download all we can. If there's any stuff you want over there, get it now. We need to make sure we're set."

Eric and Cassidy got busy downloading. Tandra went back to alert the Council and help with communications to gentem around Beta Earth. Vala made some phone calls, made a quick trip to see her lawyer to leave her funds and property to help with gentem and environmental causes and needs, which he said he could arrange. Eric left at one point, too.

By 9:30, they had gathered again at House. They had fruit and veggie plates set out. Vala was downloading more research and books to take with her. Char had gone over to visit Vala's mother and other family members. "I'm going to see about having them come with us," Char had said when leaving. "Vala, don't you want to come along and at least say good-bye?"

Vala shook her head. "I called Mother yesterday, and she asked me not to bother her any more. She said, 'Really, dear, you're all grown up and, well, you're not exactly a part of this family's social set. Look, I'll call you about our Christmas party, okay?'" Vala shrugged. "To be honest, it didn't bother me much at this point."

Char shook her head and left.

"How can humans disregard family that way?" Cassidy asked.

"They just can't develop room for including much beyond themselves," Tandra said. "From what I've learned, that's changing a bit with nanotechnology, but they have kids like rabbits. I guess they just don't mean that much."

Vala repressed her anger. "Your culture abandoned two of your children to a human culture you couldn't tolerate. Neither of you talks about your family. Bonds seem thin and very flexible to me. How can you two talk about human interpersonal actions?"

Cassidy's eyebrows were up. "I'm sorry, Vala. I can see your point. Keep in mind that we didn't want to abandon you. As to the other, we are casual with our family connections, I guess. But I love my parents deeply. We move around and pursue our interests, but I always know where my parents are. Tandra and I are closer than many brothers and sisters, but that's because we've both been absorbed by this Membrane situation. I think that, perhaps, we don't worry about running out of time to contact each other. I know if I ever need anything at any time, I can always count on my family. Actually, I can count on *all* gentem. I consider them all family."

Vala shrugged and went back to work. She knew her life with humans was over. Even if she stayed, she'd never be allowed to work on anything not approved by the government, she was sure. She'd never be an agent for change.

Cassidy prowled GILS, looking for material he wanted to take with him. It was nearly eleven o'clock when House announced strangers approaching the gate. Vala called up the view screen. "It's those agents from earlier today, Cassidy. At least they haven't shut House down. Quick, grab Eric and Tandra and your materials—get through the portal. I'll handle them. You've got to make sure everything is ready to go. Take Serein with you."

"You come, too!" Cassidy said.

"Char isn't home yet. We've got to keep things smooth for a while longer. Go! We don't have time to argue."

"Open the gate!" Vala told House as the group scrambled to get through the portal.

Vala went to the door, opened it, and greeted Agent Bradshaw with, "Really? Again?"

"You've created electric blocks around your house. Why?"

"To keep out prowlers and spies," Vala said.

"Stand aside. We're coming in."

"Not without proper authorization."

"We don't *need* authorization, Glen. You and your friends are security threats." He handed her a Federal document. "We're taking over the premises. You need to answer questions."

They pushed past her.

"Do what you will," she said.

She walked through the midst of them to the patio door.

"Where are you going?" Bradshaw asked.

"I don't want to watch you violate my privacy. Frankly, you're making this the worst sabbatical anyone ever had. I'm going to sit in the garden," she said.

"Bradshaw, go with her," said a husky voice.

Vala looked back surprised. She hadn't seen Agent Patrick come in. Bradshaw looked irritated at being given babysitting duty but went with her to sit in the garden.

"Isn't this peaceful?" Vala said. Serein whined softly from the other side, and she sent him a message to lie down and wait.

"Where are all your traitor friends and your vicious dog?" Bradshaw asked.

Vala said nothing.

After about forty minutes, Agent Patrick came outside and demanded to know where her friends were.

"Excuse me?" she said.

"Your friends were here. Where did they go?"

"Well, Aunt Char is visiting family."

"We know about her. What about Eric Kine and those others who were here?"

"I assume Eric's at home, but he could be somewhere else. I thought you were following everyone."

"You can try jerking me around all you want, but you'll be getting no more special privileges. We know there were others here just before you opened the door because we picked up their heat signatures. Now even the dog is gone, so you've got some sort of safety hole in here. Where is it?" Patrick spoke calmly. Time was on his side.

"I've never bothered with a safety hole," Vala said. "I'm a

scientist, and I know if we come to the point of needing safety holes, we're all dead anyway."

"Bradshaw," Patrick said, "take her to the car." He continued speaking via a communication implant. "Wilson and Edwards, stay in the garden and keep a watch. Jenkins and Michaels, you watch out front. We're going to headquarters. I'll have some investigators over with special equipment to find the others."

Vala picked up on Cassidy's thoughts and tension. *No!* Her thoughts were emphatic. *We can't risk them discovering the portal! I'll be back! Keep Serein calm.*

She said nothing aloud as they left but sent a silent message to Serein to obey Cassidy.

What would the agents do to Aunt Char?

Vala had to figure out how to get a release or to escape and get back here shortly before midnight. How she would do that was anyone's guess.

CHAPTER TWENTY-FIVE

Wednesday night, July 11, 2029

Cassidy tried to keep his thoughts calm to convince Serein to stay with him. "Follow Vala's orders," he kept telling the dog both silently and aloud. Then he, Eric, and Tandra took Serein to Obeah's where they filled Obeah in on the latest news.

Obeah shook his head. "Abandon those who surrender sense to fear—to misquote Shakespeare. Human nature often fights back before a threat emerges."

Cassidy shook his head. "Vala has told me they've changed. They've become more accepting of others. She said new laws were passed in 2021, after all the Christian attacks on other churches, that have generated change."

"Cassidy, laws of equality and diversity have been routinely passed and then routinely circumvented, or outright broken, by humans for hundreds—thousands—of years. You know, many herd animals fear anything not like the mix of the herd." Obeah shrugged. "We have our own fears, mostly of humans, no? Besides, this fear is political. From what you've told me, the United States has become extremely isolationist, an attitude that's rooted in paranoia and acquisitiveness."

"It must be the genetic code," Eric said. "Even when I thought of myself as human, I was often horrified at cruelty to those of us with differences. I've just always thought I was odd."

"What will they do with Vala?" Cassidy asked Eric.

Before Eric could speak, a groggy voice came from the cot

against the wall. "They'll interrogate her. In a secret location. She won't get away." Wyatt was struggling to sit up, and Eric went over to help him.

Breath stopped, Cassidy winced at the sharp pinpricks of fear throughout his body. He found his breath, closed his eyes for a moment, then said, "Obeah, we've got less than one hour before we're going to open up immigration to all gentem and then seal the Membrane. We've got to bring Vala here. We need her! We're not going to abandon her again!"

Obeah was shaking his head. "Cassidy, you're thinking about teleportation, something I've heard of being used eons ago, but the knowledge has escaped. I know of no gentem who has that particular talent now."

"Marina is working on it, but she has a long way to go. I've done experiments on a less ambitious scale," Cassidy said, "and I've written up ways for it to work. Yesterday on Vala's computer, I found research to support my ideas: a 1993 paper *Teleporting an Unknown Quantum State Via Dual Classical and Einstein-Podolsky-Rosen Channels*. Even humans are thinking about it. I can use that idea, with the linking Vala and I have, to make it work. She and I together can bring her here."

"What keeps you from going there?" Obeah asked. "Or both of you ultimately occupying the same space at the same time? Or Vala winding up somewhere that is nowhere?"

Cassidy rubbed his lip. "My intention," he said, firmly. "As Marina says, we must apply what we understand, our theories, in order to prove them."

Eric spoke from the cot where he still sat with Wyatt. "Cassidy, if we lose you, too, our project fails. We need you to make our plan work to migrate people and seal the Membrane. Millions are dependent on you. Vala wouldn't want you to risk it."

"Of course, she wouldn't," Cassidy said, "and that's all the more reason why I should. I wouldn't want her to risk it for me, either. But she would. Besides, I'm concerned that she is essential to our efforts. She's powerful. More powerful than I."

"Let me try it," Wyatt said. "I have a lot to make up for."

Cassidy shook his head. "First of all, you don't have to *make up* for this. Besides, humans haven't done anything like this. You don't understand LifeForce at all. Or the math. She and I are linked."

"Are you sure you're linked any more than she and I are?" asked Eric.

"I've communicated with her through thought while she was at the university," Cassidy said. He could see the surprise on their faces. "Besides, Eric, you don't understand the math either. I don't have time to teach anyone." Was he being foolish? Could this be done? Would he somehow hurt Vala? As his mind riffled the possibilities, he became aware that Eric was speaking again.

"...don't see how..." Eric paused, shrugging. "So you're not that sure, are you?" He sighed. "She won't be alone, Cassidy. She'll be distracted. And you need to know that if she doesn't immigrate, I won't either."

"Then we'd better do it now," Cassidy said. "I'll go to my lab and pull together my notes and thoughts. Obeah, if you have anything to help, send it over with Eric. When I have the material pulled together, I'll go to the obelisk, next to the portal."

"How can I have something to help when I have no idea what's needed?" Obeah shook his head. "I'll offer prayer, Cassidy, for all of us."

Cassidy and Serein ran to the lab, arriving in five minutes. Cassidy found all his files and material on teleportation. He refused to dwell on the unknowns because he could see no alternative; he had to stay positive. He tried to organize his notes and memorize the math while he ran to obelisk. He focused on communication as he had last time.

Establishing contact was easier this time, but communication was more difficult. Apparently, she was seriously distracted by whatever was going on around her; in addition, sending through the portal created interference, but he could see men in her garden, so he didn't dare go through. Trying to communicate was like trying to be heard in the middle of a high wind.

Vala, you have to try to shut out your surroundings, everything. What you're hearing, what you're seeing. Distance yourself. Focus on me, what I'm saying—

Her reply cut in and out, fuzzy and unfocused. Serein whined.

Vala! Focus! His urgency blasted through his own mind.

Almost immediately, the clarity increased, then he heard precisely, *I'm listening.*

I'm going to bring you home. We'll use our link we share through the palm implants. I'm going to link my implant more directly with the obelisk, which should strengthen your connection to it, too. You could feel a vibration, and it's possible we may both feel nauseated. But you should wind up here at the obelisk.

That can't be done, Cassidy.

Vala, focus on the math. Build forward. Start with what we looked at in my lab and Marina's lab. We're going to shift the zero point energy for all matter between us. We're going to simply bring us together by eliminating the space between us...

Cassidy entered a world without words, and he felt Vala joining him.

It was like being detached from the physical universe, sharing some new space with her—

Suddenly she left the process, and he could feel her alarm.

Just as quickly, she returned, but she wasn't as strong. Nonetheless, they quickly connected again. He made small adjustments, changes, and then he realized she was doing the same. They were creating this world of teleportation together, two linked particles, drawing on the energy of everything surrounding that spot where they needed to meet—

He paused as he was applying a final bit of shifting:

$$\sum z, x \in \{0,1\} |\beta zx\rangle \otimes XxZz|\psi\rangle = z, x$$
no, not right...Vala, wait!
$$\tfrac{1}{2} \, |\psi\rangle \otimes |\beta 00\rangle$$

—then, it was broken.

Cassidy fell out of the flow, looked around him and realized he was still at the obelisk. But he was alone.

Then he saw Serein dashing past him, into the portal, and there, through the portal, he could see Vala, on her hands and knees, retching. Cassidy dashed forward into the portal and then could hear her yelling, "Run, Char! Into the portal! Now!"

Then, "No, Serein! No!"

And the dog was leaping toward a man who looked terrified. He was raising his hand, in which he held...what? A phone?

Then Vala was up and leaping between the man and the dog just as the thing in the man's hand emitted a blast of light that hit Vala. She fell while both Serein and Char were entering the portal, and they both turned back.

Cassidy dashed past them while yelling "Go!" to Char. He sent the same urgent command to Serein. Then he was grabbing Vala's hand and, as the man's hand was swerving first toward where Char had disappeared and then at them, they were both running, or was he running alone? Carrying Vala? The blast of light started--then, simply never reached them. Cassidy half-dragged Vala to the obelisk where both Serein and Char were.

"What the hell happened?" Char was asking.

"Not now. We have to contact the others," he said, pulling out his phone.

Even as he was calling, Eric, Wyatt, Tandra, and Obeah were arriving.

"Only a few minutes!" Eric yelled.

Others began arriving, and Cassidy recognized them as some of the strongest scientists they had, including Marina. "Is everyone familiar with the plan?" Cassidy yelled.

Some were nodding, others were simply moving forward. They were forming a huge semi-circle around the obelisk. Vala was doubled over and her breathing was heavy. "Are you okay? Can you do this?" he asked.

She nodded, and Char was supporting her efforts to rise. "Should Wyatt be here?" Vala asked while pointing at him standing on the edge of the activity.

Cassidy shrugged. "There's really nothing to be done about it now." He went over and whispered in Tandra's ear. "Keep an eye on Wyatt?"

She nodded.

"Time!" Eric called.

Cassidy quickly joined the semi-circle. Each individual worked on creating a part of the whole. To Cassidy, it was like being part of an orchestra, only he could hear each individual as well as the entire harmony. First the Membrane itself, the space in which Beta Earth rested, was reopened and then held in place as quantum particles were split, spins reversed...this time, it wasn't necessary to rebuild. Just hold. All over the world individuals were crossing–

Cassidy suddenly realized they weren't going to be able to hold the opening for as long as they intended. The gravity of Beta Earth was too great to start with. Space was distorting too fast. "It's going to close off!" he yelled. "Tell everyone they have to hurry to get through–only moments! Focus on slowing the gravitational wave!"

Cassidy was aware of the influx of voices and beings–some were almost singing aloud while others were silent but Cassidy's body tingled almost as if he was standing near lightning strikes. Then one in particular, powerful, radiating strength: Vala!

Everything held! Just a few more moments–

Then a thundering boom and wave power, knocking Cassidy to his knees.

All was silence.

Nothing.

Cassidy looked around him. A crowd had gathered, more than could be accounted for in their former population. Children, adults, and animals–was that an elephant? How the hell? And humans. Were they here on purpose?

He spotted Eric, rooted in place, staring at someone... Jasmine! They almost touched hands, then she was gone. Cassidy started toward Eric, and then he spotted Vala. She was on the ground and Obeah knelt beside her.

When Cassidy joined them, Obeah said, "She was wounded."

Cassidy nodded. "Light—laser, I think. Or some sort of electrical energy. Where is she hit?"

"The upper right shoulder, then angled across her chest to her left rib cage. She must have been moving quickly. I don't believe it's too deep, but help me take her back to the clinic."

"I'll go with–"

"Cassidy!" Tandra grabbed his arm. "Just before it all ended, just as the portal was closing, Wyatt ran through. He–I don't know if he made it, but he's not here."

"Obeah, take Vala." They got her into a scooter. "I'll be there shortly."

Cassidy found Eric standing near the obelisk, staring toward the area where the portal had been and where, now, there was only more pitch-dark night. Eric looked up at Cassidy, and the tears on his cheeks reflected starlight.

"I'm so very sorry, Eric. I know he was your brother."

Eric nodded. "He did all he could have done. He couldn't give up the hope that something can be done to salvage the human culture there. He's tied to that world and couldn't let go."

Cassidy nodded, put his hand on Eric's shoulder. He decided not to say that it was uncertain whether Wyatt could have survived that mad dash into a collapsing portal, particularly since there would never be any way of finding out.

"Eric, I saw you with Jasmine."

Eric almost brightened. "Then it wasn't my imagination. She *was* here, as if this completion was essential to her continuing."

Cassidy nodded, then said quietly, "Vala was hit by some sort of laser. Obeah has taken her to the clinic."

"What? We must go there! Now! I need to focus. I didn't even know."

"Take a scooter, Eric. I have a few things to take care of here, and then I'll run down."

Eric ran for the scooters.

Cassidy turned his attention to the milling crowd, then quickly realized it wasn't as disorganized as it looked.

Local residents were each gathering up groups of people, explaining that quarters had been set up for them until further arrangements could be made. Friends and families were reuniting. Cassidy chastised himself; he'd never once thought of what individuals would do or need once they were here, but the Council had obviously covered his omission. He hoped new residents were receiving the same welcome everywhere.

He saw Murell talking to the elephant. She already had a group of animals gathered peacefully to one side, predators and prey alike standing calmly. He hadn't thought about that issue, either.

Delara walked over. "Will this hold, Cassidy?"

She had never been one for easing into a conversation. "It should," Cassidy said. "We haven't built in a contingency for future contact. We've severed all connections. This one has no built-in doubts."

"Except, I understand, for the human Wyatt?"

Cassidy shrugged. "We have no connection with him, however. There's no portal and even though he has the palm implant and is, therefore, linked, I'll be disassembling the obelisk, so there'll be no power boost. He'll be alone."

"But, still," Marina said softly from behind Cassidy, "the resonance is there. Linked particles can be galaxies apart and still be entangled. However, I agree that it's highly unlikely we'll ever be aware of him. Unlikely but not impossible. Eric will be the most sensitive to it."

Delara nodded. "We'll be very busy in the coming weeks helping newcomers adjust. I'll expect your help. Some are in distress. The transition was quicker than expected, and some families have been separated. Some humans didn't get back through in time." She turned and walked away.

Everything here was under control. Cassidy ran to Obeah's clinic. "How is she?" he asked as he went through the door although he knew the answer as he took in the calm expressions on the faces of the group sitting around the table drinking tea: Char, Eric, Tandra, Obeah–he paused in his scan. Alarick? Why?

"She's okay, Cassidy," Tandra said. "Whatever that weapon was, it wasn't a direct hit, didn't you say, Obeah?"

Obeah nodded. "The burns are mostly superficial although deeper would have been bad. Some of her ribs were laid bare and one was partially slashed. She must have been moving at a high rate of speed, which helped. She's been treated and is resting. Leave her alone until she wakes naturally. She should be up and around in a day or two and fairly well healed in a couple weeks. Why was she injured?"

"One of the Guardians," said Char. "I came home to find four of those agents in the house. They wouldn't let me leave again, but I finally talked them into letting me sit in the garden. One was with me all the time, so I couldn't use the portal, but I was only a few feet away."

Char paused, started to speak, stopped, then shrugged. "Suddenly, Vala just appeared in front of me, on her knees, retching, obviously disoriented. Then she looked around, saw the agent and yelled at me to run to the portal. I tried to help her up, but she pushed me away and told me to go. Then, Serein came charging out of the portal just as I was entering, and Vala was yelling *No* and leaping toward the agent…I don't know…it was chaos. Cassidy came through and pushed me again, all the way through the portal." She gave Cassidy a look like his own mother would have given him had he not done his chores.

Cassidy squatted down by Obeah's chair. "About that sudden appearance, Obeah. I don't know how that worked. I had it wrong. I stopped, fell out of the process…I think, maybe, Vala did that on her own. I don't know how." He didn't know what else to say.

Nodding, Obeah said, "Vala is going to have many surprises for us. Both she and Eric are tapping more deeply into ancient connections than we've done in a long time. Perhaps we'll learn more about how that's possible over time."

Cassidy stood, pulled out a stool by the kitchen counter and sat on it. "Anyway, Vala's command got Serein to go to the portal," Cassidy said, "but the fire was originally intended for him–where is he?"

"Beside Vala," Char said.

Of course, thought Cassidy. "Vala got between the agent and Serein. She saved him, too."

"How did you and Vala get to the portal?" Eric asked.

"I think the agent was disoriented by that time. Certainly, my appearance was a surprise. People and animals were popping in and out of the air from his perspective. I grabbed her arm, and we ran or I pulled her. I'm not sure. I saw a flare of light, but it couldn't penetrate the threshold of the portal." Cassidy shook his head. "I had expected Vala to arrive at the obelisk, but I guess I didn't figure that concept into the equation correctly. I should have compensated for distortion. On the other hand, I didn't have anything to do with her ultimate arrival."

"You mean you somehow transported her from wherever the agents had her to the garden? Like *Beam me up, Scotty?*" asked Char.

Cassidy looked at Char and wondered why the reference

seemed familiar, and then he remembered all the *Star Trek* he had watched as a child, before the Membrane. He smiled. "I guess so. I need to see all those films again. But I didn't do it. Vala did."

"I worry about Wyatt," Tandra said. "He knows all about us and Beta Earth and he's linked to the four of us."

"We'll take down the obelisk," Cassidy said. "He'll have no channel for communication. He doesn't have any of the exact knowledge. Besides, there's no portal and nothing built into Beta Earth to have one. I suspect we're already more distant in time from Alpha Earth than we ever were before."

"But he knows how to find any gentem who stayed on the other side, isn't that right?" Eric asked.

"He probably didn't even make it back. The portal was collapsing when he ran into it," Tandra said.

Even Cassidy could feel the blast of emotion from Eric. He blanched. He stood abruptly and went out the door.

"Leave him for a bit," Obeah said as Tandra stood. She sat back down.

"I'm sorry. I didn't think," she said.

"Why would anyone have stayed?" Alarick suddenly asked.

"Because they had family who didn't want to give up everything or because they, themselves, had found a good life. Or because they didn't make it in time. We had less time than I'd expected. Some have found ways to fit in—like Eric and Vala had, for instance," said Cassidy. He thought about their childhood, the way they'd been treated, and added, "I guess."

"They'll have to entrench deeply," said Tandra. "The website will probably be dangerous now."

Obeah shook his head. "We never know another's path completely. For that matter, we don't even know where our own path leads. None of us know where the actions of the past couple weeks, or even decades, will eventually lead."

"Speaking of what we don't know, do we have any idea what or who all arrived here?" Char asked.

"Well, if our calculations were correct," Cassidy said, "about twelve million globally. Several hundred thousand humans probably. And a huge number of animals," Cassidy said and then shrugged.

"It was optional, of course. Individuals had to walk through. But they'll be scattered everywhere. Some could be in trouble, depending on where they came through and what animals came with them. I saw Murell with a large group of animals, including an elephant. Maybe from a zoo? And we could have some humans who wandered through in ignorance if they didn't have Neanderthal DNA. They won't be happy."

"How did you arrange for the animals?" Char asked.

"The Membrane would have been visible for all of them, but they would have to go through it. We put out the word for individuals who could communicate with non-gentem beings to call them, but most of them won't be familiar with that sort of communication, so who knows. We also communicated with animals on this side to call others. We'll be collecting data."

Tandra laughed. "I suspect there will be a lot of confusion in some of the animal prisons around the world when their inmates are gone today."

"Tandra, they're called zoos and Wildlife Parks," said Obeah.

"With bars," said Tandra, shrugging and then stretching.

The group talked for a while and then dispersed, each attending to different chores. Cassidy pulled Tandra aside. "So did you have feelings for Wyatt? Are you okay?"

Tandra shook her head. "There was something–a spark. But he is obsessed with changing the world. The human world. He couldn't let go of it. He would have been very unhappy here, Cassidy. I don't know what happened to him, but I hope he's happy somewhere. He told me before he left, 'I have to try. Somehow I'll be in touch.' I'm going to go find Eric and talk with him."

Cassidy decided it would be better to not pass those words around to others.

The next evening, Vala was already up and moving around. Serein, Eric, Aunt Char, Tandra and Cassidy gathered around her like a support structure. "Look," she finally said. "I'm sore and stiff, but moving is my best hope for recovery. Everyone go do something, and Cassidy and I will go for a walk."

"Excellent idea," Obeah said. "But no running."

Vala smiled. "I don't want to run."

She and Cassidy went out to amble aimlessly, but automatically wound up at the spot where the obelisk had stood.

"They'll never stop trying to track us down, trying to track down any gentem left there," Vala said. "It will make the witch hunts look like a party game in comparison. Humans know too much about us."

"But why?" Cassidy asked. "The connection is gone. We're no threat."

"It's the fountain of youth and power, including, thanks to you, teleportation," Vala said. She smiled at him. "The prediction was that by this time, mortals would be almost immortal because of technology: implants, AI, or super foods. Instead, it's been one debacle after another with rejections of implants or parts of the body lasting while other parts diminish. Serious illness risks have doubled because of pollution and chemicals. Insect-born diseases are on the rise, particularly from mosquitoes." She shook her head.

"Vala, you were who was responsible for the teleportation. I lost the flow, lost the connection. You utilized a far deeper connection than I was providing."

She looked at him intently. "That's intriguing. We'll have to look into that. For now, I'm looking forward to some peace, to opportunities to enjoy the harmony here on Beta Earth. I know I have time." She smiled. "Last year, I figured I was one-third of the way through my life. This year, I'm almost a child, and I have no known limits. Humans would dissect me to discover how to utilize that."

"What do you want to do with time—or freedom from time?"

Vala shook her head. "I have no idea. My work now is mostly irrelevant. In a world that isn't creating pollution and toxic radioactivity daily, I don't need to worry about cleaning it up. I'm thinking I may travel. See how this world is faring now. See if my work can't find me. I'd like to see how gentem and animals are settling in to their new world. And I'd like to see more of this world, clean and fresh." She gestured around her and inhaled deeply. "What about you, Cassidy? What are you working on?"

He shrugged. "Cleaning up the aftermath of introducing millions, maybe billions counting non-gentem species, into society.

Then? I don't know. I've spent years working out ways to contact you and Eric, to open the portal, to bring enlightenment to the human world. The Council and even Obeah kept warning me that humans were not receptive to such differences as the gentem possess. I wouldn't listen. So I need to think about our success and our failure."

She laughed again, making Cassidy smile. "You don't listen 'cause you're a teenager." She looked thoughtful. "Cassidy, join me. Let's travel together. Find out what the world needs now, how we can enrich it." She reached out and took his hand. "Let's help settle individuals and animals here and then travel and find out where we can help them adjust, where we can explore, what we can learn. We'll find our work and our place. Let's help to make this a good world."

The idea surged through him, and he felt an impulse to begin immediately. "Yes. And let's ask Eric to go, too. He needs some friendship support now."

Race?

Cassidy laughed. *Not now, Gulo. We have to go.*

Later, Cassidy heard Vala say.

Without more discussion, they turned their backs on where the portal had been, where the obelisk and stood, and went to find Vala's little brother. He was at Obeah's, talking to Char about what it meant to suddenly find themselves in a new world. "Have you seen Murell's animals?" He asked Vala as she walked in. "She's working to try to get them to their natural environments. She's amazing!"

Cassidy grinned. Even he could read Eric when it came to Murell.

"I wish we had ways to help those on Alpha Earth," Vala said. Before I left, I saw the lawyer and had everything I possessed put into Trust for gentem use. The lawyer said he could do that. I'm not sure how."

Eric laughed. "I did that, too. At least they'll have some resources. He was gentem, you know."

Vala thought about all the clues, especially his height, acceptance of their situation, and his long tenure at the law firm. "I'm not surprised."

When Vala and Cassidy talked about their travel, Eric agreed immediately to travel with them.

"And Murell?" Vala asked, smiling.

Eric grinned back. "There's time," he said. "And she might show up here and there. She's traveling, too, trying to help place all the animals where they'll be happiest."

As they sat around the table, drinking tea, and relaxing, Cassidy was feeling more peaceful than he could ever remember. Then Tandra came in.

"We have a problem—actually a *lot* of problems."

Cassidy groaned and Vala tightened her lips.

"Hi, Tandra," Cassidy muttered.

"We have more unintended arrivals than anticipated," Tandra continued. "For instance, a plane came through with the pilot and six-hundred passengers. The pilot is gentem and, apparently, he was effectively carrying the others. Some boats. Some other incidents… we already have gentem and humans at odds."

"Those poor people," Eric said. "They've lost everything."

"Where are they?" Char asked.

Tandra sighed. "A center has been set up in Australia for displaced humans. The idea is that they can be educated there and then disperse as they please."

"We'll have to leave immediately," Vala said. "They mustn't be marginalized."

Cassidy looked at her carefully. She was fearful. Why?

Vala stood and walked to the door, stood looking out.

A light wind shushed through the fir, many over one-hundred feet tall. Cedar limbs quivered and scented the air. A wolf call echoed through the trees. This was a primitive and healthy Earth.

Then Vala bent over, coughing from dense smoke. Fire-blackened stumps surrounded her. There was no village, no one nearby. Hot, smothering air was hanging suspended over rising, dark waters.

Earth was dying.

She closed her eyes. They'd failed. The same future, unstopped, swallowed all hope.

"That's not real, Vala! Open your eyes." Eric spoke sharply. Cassidy looked at them and wondered what they were seeing.

Vala opened her eyes. "What was that, Eric?"

"A fear. A negative possibility. But not the truth. Nothing you can't overcome. Nothing you and your brother can't overcome."

Cassidy joined them at the door and put his hand on Vala's shoulder. "He's right, Vala. We can carve out the future, and it will be a good one for gentem and human alike."

"Your ship will be ready in the morning," Tandra said. "The Council hoped you'd volunteer to go. You'll have twenty human volunteers joining you along with Misha to encourage sailing weather onboard. Gentem are already gathering in Australia to help out."

Cassidy turned and looked at Tandra. "Are you coming?"

She shook her head. "I've found what I need to do with the Council. We're juggling issues globally. We're going to make space for a human representative on our Council. You can help the Australia Center residents set up their own group."

"Char?" Cassidy asked.

She, too, shook her head. "Obeah and I will be working together." She looked at Obeah, and he smiled back. Even Cassidy could read that look.

Cassidy turned back around as he heard a gasp from Vala. A firefly flew in circles for a few moments then lifted into the trees and away, leaving a small trail of sparking light leading toward the harbor.

"Here we go, little brother," Vala said. "Earth is calling."

Her laughter, like flute notes, drifted away on the breeze following the firefly trail.

AUTHOR BIO

Marian Blue began working as a journalist in 1972 for San Miguel Basin Forum in western Colorado. After that, she worked as freelance and staff for a variety of newspapers and magazines, both print and online; her work has been collected into anthologies. She began editing work in the 1980s for newspapers, magazines and books. Books she has written and edited include nonfiction and poetry. Along the way, she taught writing and communication classes for Writers Digest Schools and various community schools and colleges, retiring from 20-years teaching at Skagit Valley College in Washington. Today she writes and edits from her small farm on Whidbey Island.